Dedicated to the five hundred brave, compassionate, and pioneering young women who served as flight nurses in World War II. I pray their stories will inspire a new generation.

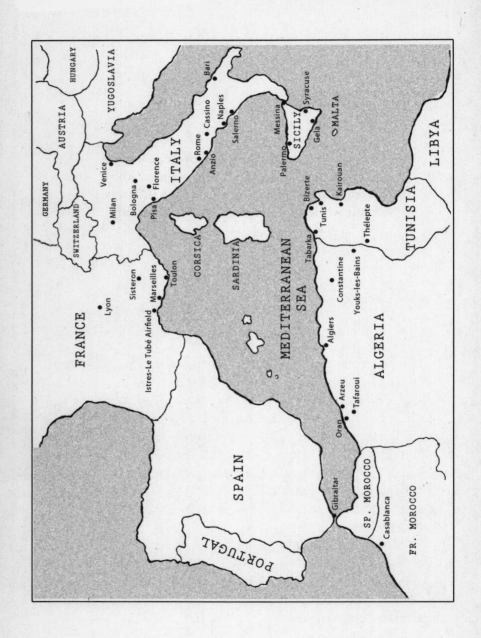

"I love the nostalgia and drama of the WWII era. No one takes me back there better than Sarah Sundin. *With Every Letter* is a beautiful love story and has everything you want in a novel: romance, suspense, and characters you care about from the very first page. A marvelous beginning for her new series. I can't wait to read the next book."

—**Dan Walsh**, award-winning and bestselling author
of *The Unfinished Gift*, *Remembering Christmas*,
and *The Discovery*

Praise for Sarah Sundin

"Sarah Sundin is an extraordinarily gifted storyteller who puts the reader in the cockpit of B-17 bombers as easily as she crafts an achingly emotional World War II romance."

—**Cheryl Bolen**, Holt Medallion Winner, Best Historical

"Sarah Sundin is a master at lyrical writing, and she has that rare talent of being able to combine humor with heart-pounding action."

—**Melanie Dobson**, author of *Love Finds You in Liberty,
Indiana* and *Refuge on Crescent Hill*

"Sarah takes us on a captivating romantic ride through the fascinating and horrifying days of World War II. A must-read."

—**Bonnie Leon**, author, the Sydney Cove series
and Alaskan Skies series

"A great read for those who love romance, WWII-era settings, or just satisfying stories."

—*RT Book Reviews* on *Blue Skies Tomorrow*

"A riveting tale based on the real-life adventures of her great-uncle, Sundin's novel features characters living large under emotional and physical stress, while the setting provides invaluable details and insights into the wartime mind-set."

—*Booklist*, starred review on *A Memory Between Us*

"A captivating story that offers an unflinching look at the 'good old days' that weren't always so good—and assurance that even when times are hard, God is faithful."

—*Crosswalk* on *Blue Skies Tomorrow*

Books by Sarah Sundin

WINGS OF GLORY

A Distant Melody
A Memory Between Us
Blue Skies Tomorrow

WINGS OF THE NIGHTINGALE

With Every Letter

WITH *Every* LETTER

A Novel

SARAH SUNDIN

R
Revell
a division of Baker Publishing Group
Grand Rapids, Michigan

© 2012 by Sarah Sundin

Published by Revell
a division of Baker Publishing Group
P.O. Box 6287, Grand Rapids, MI 49516-6287
www.revellbooks.com

Printed in the United States of America

Library of Congress Cataloging-in-Publication Data
Sundin, Sarah.
    With every letter : a novel / Sarah Sundin.
        p.   cm. — (Wings of the nightingale ; 1)
    ISBN 978-0-8007-2081-0 (pbk.)
    1. Letter writing—Fiction. 2. Friendship—Fiction. 3. World War, 1939–1945—Fiction. I. Title.
PS3619.U5626W58 2012
813'.6—dc23   2012012960

This book is a work of fiction. Names, characters, places, and incidents are the product of the author's imagination or are used fictitiously.

Published in association with Books & Such Literary Agency, 52 Mission Circle, Suite 122, PMB 170, Santa Rosa, CA 95409-7953

Map design: Stuart and Tiffany Stockton, Eagle Designs

12 13 14 15 16 17 18   7 6 5 4 3 2 1

1

Walter Reed General Hospital
Army Medical Center
Washington DC
October 2, 1942

Lt. Philomela Blake believed mornings should start gently, with the nighttime melting into golden sunshine and birdsong luring to wakefulness.

Most nurses on the morning shift assaulted the patients with electric light and harsh voices, but not Mellie.

She pulled the cord of the blackout curtain and sang "At Last," and the volume of her tune built with the intensity of light. Hurting and healing men deserved a soft hand.

On the nearest bed, Corporal Sloan shifted under the blankets. He'd undergone an appendectomy late last night. "Any dame . . ." He cleared his throat, his voice raspy from the ether. "Any dame with the voice of an angel must have a face to match."

Mellie's song and her hands stilled. How many soldiers dreamed of a beautiful nurse who might fall in love with them?

He rubbed his eyes, looked at her, and his smile flickered.

Papa called Mellie his exotic orchid, but American men seemed to prefer roses.

Mellie opened the blackout curtains all the way. "How do you feel this morning, Corporal?"

"Um, fine. Fine, ma'am."

"I'll be back with your morning meds." She patted his shoulder and headed down the aisle to the nurses' station. Her cap felt loose, so she adjusted a bobby pin that clamped it to the helmet of thick black braids coiled around her head. Her crowning glory, Papa called it.

Poor Papa. Acid ate at her stomach, and Mellie dove into song to neutralize it. The Filipino folk song "Bahay Kubo" reminded her of traipsing through the jungle with Papa on his botanical excursions. It reminded her of his love, as warm as the Filipino sun. It reminded her to pray for him. If only he hadn't sent her stateside a year ago. If only he'd come with her. No news had arrived since the Japanese conquered the Philippines a few months before, and the State Department and Red Cross hadn't found out Papa's fate. How could she go on without him?

Work kept her busy, but worry pricked up and made her restless.

She opened another blackout curtain and gazed out onto Walter Reed's manicured grounds. A year in Washington DC was enough. So much more of the world waited to be explored. The war thrust barriers between her and adventure, but it offered new paths as well.

The door to the ward opened, and Lieutenant Newman, the chief nurse, leaned in. "Lieutenant Blake? Please come to my office on your lunch break."

"Yes, ma'am." The meeting had to be about her upcoming transfer to the Air Evacuation Group forming at Bowman Field in Kentucky. A smile climbed too high on Mellie's face, and she covered her mouth.

When the Army Air Force announced plans to train nurses

to assist in air evacuation, Mellie had begged the chief for a recommendation. Flight nurses would fly into combat areas, load the wounded, and care for them in the air. They would be stationed all over the world. Perhaps even in the Pacific, close to Papa.

Next month, Mellie would begin training. That thought put an extra trill into her song.

"Must you?" At the nurses' station, Lieutenant Ingham scrunched her heart-shaped face into a frown. "That infernal singing. Honestly, Philomela, we're all sick of it."

"Sorry." Mellie's cheeks warmed, and she picked up the tray of meds she'd prepared earlier. How could she stop doing what she was born to do, something that provided relief to her patients? When she sang, pain-wrinkled brows smoothed. She returned to the ward and her song, but in a softer voice.

Philomela meant "nightingale," and her first storybook was *The Nightingale* by Hans Christian Andersen. The emperor of China treasured a pet nightingale and its song. But when he received a mechanical singing bird, he forgot the nightingale, which retreated to the lonely forest. While the little bird in the story longed to return to court, Mellie felt most at home in the forest, bringing musical comfort to passersby.

Next month, she'd enter a new forest.

"I can't believe you missed last night's meeting, Philomela." Lieutenant Newman's big blue eyes stretched even wider.

"I thought it was optional. For a morale program." Mellie shifted in her seat in the chief nurse's office.

"It is, but I want everyone to participate. You do want to participate, don't you?"

"Well, I . . ." She lowered her gaze and straightened the skirt of her white ward dress. "I didn't really consider it."

The chief walked to the window and heaved a sigh. "Oh, Philomela, I don't understand you. You're an excellent nurse, but I simply don't understand you."

"It's a letter-writing campaign, isn't it? To men we've never met?"

Her lovely face lit up. "Yes. To the officers in my husband's unit. It's an Engineer Aviation Battalion based in England. It will all be anonymous. Isn't that fun?"

England sounded like fun. Writing to a strange man did not. "I wouldn't know what to say to someone I've never met."

"Say anything you like. I imagine you write a nice letter. You speak excellent English for a foreigner."

Mellie restrained her sigh. Always with one foot in one land, one foot in the other, never belonging in either. "Actually, ma'am, I'm an American. I was born in the Philippines, yes, but my father's American and my mother was half-American, half-Filipino."

"Yes. Well then." The chief fingered the window casement. "Well then, I'm sure you write a lovely letter."

Mellie rolled the hem of her skirt in her fingers. "But I've never . . . I've never written to a stranger before."

"He's hardly a stranger. He's an American officer. All the other nurses are excited about it. I need one more volunteer, or one poor gentleman won't receive a letter."

She stretched her skirt back down over her knees. "That would be horrible, but maybe . . . maybe someone would be willing to write two letters."

"Come now." Lieutenant Newman sat on the edge of her desk, right in front of Mellie, and she leaned close. "Please, Philomela? I would be so disappointed if you didn't participate. Especially after I recommended you for the Air Evacuation Group. I didn't mention how you don't have any friends here. Perhaps I should have." She glanced down to the desk and traced her finger back and forth, as if erasing her recommendation.

Mellie's throat swelled shut. "But—but why would any man want to hear from me?"

The chief flashed a bright smile. "Remember, it's anonymous. No names, no pictures. Just a nice letter to encourage our boys overseas."

Mellie dropped her chin and squeezed her eyes shut. She felt so awkward in social situations.

"Oh please, Philomela? Please? It's only one letter."

Mellie lifted her head. Outside the window, the horizon beckoned. "One letter," she whispered.

―――――

"One letter." Mellie groaned. The blank sheet of airmail stationery taunted her. "Lord, what can I say?"

In the hallway, a group of nurses squealed and giggled. Mellie peeked around the post of her bunk. The ladies hooked arms and strolled away, laughing and chatting, off to some fun activity.

Longing tugged at her chest. She set aside the stationery and stroked the worn burgundy cover of the scrapbook she used as a writing surface. On the black pages inside lay her childhood friends, who had kept her company on countless lonely days at home and abroad. She flipped through, and her friends offered paper smiles just for her, paper ears to listen, and paper eyes that accepted her.

Children from magazines, catalogs, and newspaper articles. They'd never played hopscotch with her or whispered their secrets to her.

A thin substitute for friendship, but it was all she'd ever had. Overseas, she'd been the only child on Papa's expeditions. Stateside, the boys and girls found her odd and foreign.

Halfway through the scrapbook, the faces shifted from children she had needed to children who needed her.

The first, a little fair-haired boy, had started her mission of mercy. His mother stood behind him, one arm clutched around his shoulders, her face angled to the side, chin high and brave and fearsome. The boy wore short pants and a little jacket. One foot toed in. One hand grasped his mother's forearm around him, the other hung limp by his side. With his chin dipped, he looked at the newspaper photographer as if his life had been stripped from him.

It had. His father had just been sentenced to death for murder.

The nation cheered. No one cared about the boy. So Mellie cut his picture out of the newspaper, pasted it in her scrapbook, and prayed for him.

Others followed. A hollow-eyed little girl with stringy blonde hair, riding an overloaded jalopy from the Oklahoma dust bowl to points unknown. A colored boy blinded by a fire, his eyes swathed in bandages. A Filipino girl, her face disfigured by a tropical disease.

Mellie prayed for them every day. While the other children had provided a sense of companionship, these children provided her with purpose. What if she was the only person praying for them? Even in her isolation, she could still extend mercy.

She glanced at the empty sheet of stationery on her bed.

Across the ocean, perhaps another young man needed her. What if a letter could ease his fears or worries or loneliness? What if her prayers could strengthen him?

What if he wrote back?

Mellie's breath caught. On paper it wouldn't matter if she were a rose or an orchid. Perhaps a friendship could develop, still a paper friendship, but more than she'd ever had before.

"Lord, give me the right words." She set the stationery on top of her scrapbook and put pen to paper.

2

HMS *Derbyshire*
Liverpool, England
October 24, 1942

Lt. Thomas MacGilliver Jr. prepared to walk the plank.

"Ahoy there, mateys." Tom stood on the superstructure of the British transport ship and grinned. Below him on the deck, the men in his platoon gaped and laughed. He turned to Privates Earl Butler and Conrad Davis behind him. "Got it?"

"Sure thing, Gill." Butler clamped the four-inch pipe under his beefy arm and gripped it in his hands. The length of pipe crossed the metal railing for the superstructure and stretched over the deck ten feet below.

"Hey, boss!" Private Bill Rinaldi stood beside Butler. "You're going swimming with the sharks."

"Yeah. Watch out for those English sharks. On a ship." Tom climbed the railing, held on to it, and arranged his bare feet on the pipe. The rough texture from corrosion in the salty air would help him keep his footing. He stretched his arms wide and slowly rose to standing.

Mumbled praise built into a low chorus, and Tom smiled. The men needed a diversion. Any day now the U.S. 908th Engineer Aviation Battalion would sail to North Africa for

Operation Torch, although only the officers knew the destination. In a few weeks, the men would know the taste of battle.

"This, boys, is what a cantilever bridge is like." He stepped forward like a tightrope walker, curling his feet around the rusty pipe. Another step and the murmurs grew. His construction work on Pittsburgh's bridges to put himself through engineering school had paid off. "The bridge can handle my load because Butler and Davis provide a counterweight. Imagine another segment coming from the other direction toward me, also balanced by a counterweight. Where the two segments meet, you only need a pin to join them."

He stepped to within a foot of the end, his arms outstretched, and gazed down at the laughing crowd. Everywhere, always a laughing crowd. But never a friend.

Tom cleared his throat and flung a smile back on his face. "As long as you do your calculations and get the right counterweight—and Butler's got plenty of that . . ."

Hoots and hollers rewarded him.

"Hey, Gill!" Rinaldi called from behind him. "Did you calculate that Butler's ticklish as a little girl?" He wiggled his fingers near Butler's thick midsection.

"Don't!" Tom squatted and grabbed the pipe. "No, Rinaldi. Don't!"

The pipe wobbled as Butler edged away from his friend. "Don't, or I'll—"

"Should have thought of that before you dumped salt in my coffee." Rinaldi jabbed Butler in the ribs.

The pipe lurched to the side and broke Tom's grip. He grasped for it, but it bounced away. He dropped to the deck, banging his hip and his shoulder.

The men howled with laughter. Tom hoisted himself to his feet and rubbed his sore hip. He'd get a bruise, but it was worth it.

Someone pulled the plug in the basin of laughter, and it all drained away. Tom turned to face Capt. Dick Newman, commander of Company B of the 908th. Tom saluted. "Captain."

"Lieutenant." Newman's dark eyes took in the scene. "Another engineering lesson?"

"Yes, sir. Someone's got to educate these lumps."

"A little less education, a little more discipline." But the corner of the captain's mouth flicked up. He stepped to the side and motioned to the man behind him. "Just assigned a new man to your platoon, Staff Sergeant Larry Fong."

"Hey! What's a Jap doing here?" That voice—Tom's platoon sergeant, Hal Weiser.

Tom settled a smile on Weiser. "Fong's a Chinese name, not Japanese. The Chinese are our Allies, remember? And the sergeant's an American."

"Three generations, sir." Sergeant Fong wore a bright smile. He had some height to him, matching Tom's five foot ten.

Tom extended his hand. "Nice to meet you, Sergeant. Welcome to the platoon."

Fong shook his hand. "Thank you, Lieutenant . . . ?"

The moment suspended in air, the always-too-brief moment when Tom could be one of the guys. Before they knew his name. Mom was right when she discouraged him from changing his name—lying would be wrong—but he still wished he were someone else.

He set his face in the proper cheerful expression. "Lt. Tom MacGilliver."

The sergeant's eyebrows popped up in recognition.

Captain Newman set his hand on Fong's shoulder. "The sergeant will take Weiser's place as platoon sergeant, and Weiser will take Duke's squad, since Duke's in the hospital and won't join our excursion. Fong had a couple years of engineering school at the University of California before he got called up. That's why I put him with you, Gill."

Tom's grin widened. "Cal, huh? I went to the University of Pittsburgh. We can pick each other's brains."

"Sorry, sir. I didn't get past my lower division work. But after the war—can't wait to get back. In the meantime, on-the-job training."

"Great. Glad you're in my platoon." He motioned for the sergeant to come with him and set a path down the starboard side of the ship. He could think of several reasons for the captain's decision, the least of which was to put the engineering student with the graduate engineer. Chinese or not, the sergeant wouldn't be accepted in authority over a squad. And Tom's platoon served as the dumping place for men the other two platoon commanders in the company didn't want. The misfit platoon.

A brisk breeze snaked by, and Sergeant Fong held on to his garrison cap. "Say, Lieutenant, that's a bum rap of a name. Just like MacGilliver the Killiver."

Thank goodness Tom had years of experience smiling over the pain. "He was my father."

"Your . . . I'm sorry, sir."

"He left when I was five and was gone when I was seven. Barely knew him. And I take after my mother. Completely harmless."

"Of course. I never—I didn't mean—"

"So what field of engineering are you interested in? I'm in civil."

Fong's face relaxed a bit. "Electrical, sir."

"Good." Tom nodded and leaned on the ship's railing. He gazed around the estuary of the Mersey River, where dozens of British and American transports anchored, holding the Eastern and Center forces for the invasion of Algeria. The

Western force would sail straight from the U.S. to French Morocco.

"That would be a good place for a bridge." He pointed northwest to where the Mersey narrowed between Liverpool and Wallasey. "A suspension bridge. The towers and cables would resemble sails, honor Liverpool's nautical history."

The sergeant frowned. "Isn't there a tunnel under the river?"

Tom rearranged his arms on the ship's railing. "Tunnels are so . . . impersonal, hiding underground as if the two sides were ashamed to associate with each other. Bridges are visible, personal, proud to make the connection."

Larry squinted at the empty space over the river. "Yeah. Yeah, I see what you mean."

The design flew together in Tom's head. "I want to build bridges all over the world, connect people and places."

"Great goal, sir."

"Mm-hmm." If only he could build a bridge between himself and one other human being.

———

Gray and white images flickered on the screen in the ward room as Jimmy Stewart and Margaret Sullavan bantered in *The Shop Around the Corner*.

No one displayed rage and anguish and depression like Jimmy Stewart. Through his acting, Tom could feel those emotions without risk, the tightened muscles, the quickened pulse, the drooping face. Mom said movies were a safe outlet. Movies and prayer. Tom never missed a chance for either.

And Jimmy Stewart displayed plenty of emotion in this film. An underpaid store manager, unappreciated by his boss, found love in an anonymous letter exchange, only to find that the woman he'd grown to love was actually the obnoxious clerk he parried with every day. Only in Hollywood could that come to a happy ending, but it did, with a kiss and a crescendo of music and a fade to black.

The tail end of the film whap-whap-whapped in the projector, and Tom jumped up to still the reel.

The thirty officers of the battalion shifted in their seats, ready to leave, but Captain Newman stood and held up a hand. "Excuse me, gentlemen. That's not all. Please be seated."

Tom settled back into his chair.

"With Lieutenant Colonel Black's permission . . ." Newman nodded to the commanding officer of the 908th. "I have an invitation for you."

He put one foot on a chair and raised a sheepish smile. With his square face and dark good looks, he could be in a movie himself. "This is my wife's idea. Personally, I think it's corny, but my wife's a beautiful woman, so what can I say?"

Tom joined in the men's laughter.

"This movie inspired her. She charmed the nurses in her charge to write letters to you oafs. Anonymous letters, like in the movie."

He held up a stack of envelopes. "You each get one letter. You can reply or not, your choice. If you do, play by my wife's rules, or she'll make my life miserable. No names, no pictures, and no personal details—hometown, people's names, anything like that."

Tom sat up taller, and his mouth drifted open. If he were in an actual movie, a shaft of light would have pierced the deck of the ship and landed on him.

Anonymity.

Free from the prison of his name, he could be himself. He hadn't had that with another soul since he was seven. Even with his mother, he kept tight control to reassure her.

He squeezed his eyes shut. *Lord, please. Let the letter be from the right sort of woman.*

Lieutenant Newman passed out the envelopes, and Tom ripped his open.

A snapshot tumbled out. A pretty brunette in a cheesecake pose.

He sighed. Even though she'd broken the rules, he read the letter. The young woman gushed over movie stars and big bands and dancing with her friends, and said she sent the photo so he'd write back. So he'd know she wasn't an ugly hag.

Tom looked up. All around him, men smiled and pointed to their letters. Once again, alone in a crowd. He'd pass the letter on to a man who would appreciate her froth and bubbles.

A few rows ahead, three officers broke out in raucous laughter, centered around Lt. Martin Quincy, one of three platoon commanders in Company B.

Quincy stood. "You fellows want a laugh? Listen to this dame—'Before I start this letter, I must be clear that I'm searching for friendship, not romance. I don't want to mislead you or toy with your affections. I do apologize if you hoped for a romantic letter from a perky beauty.'

"You know what that means?" Quincy shook the letter. "She's a cross between a monkey and a cow."

"You lucky dog." Lieutenant Reed, the third platoon leader, broke down in laughter. "Imagine your children. Your ugly mug and hers."

Quincy cussed. "Just my luck. Who wants to trade?"

"I do," Tom whispered, but his voice didn't carry over the crowd's jeers.

Quincy crumpled the letter and lobbed it into the trash can by the door.

The men rose to leave, but Tom stayed in his seat, gaze

fixed on the trash can. No one deserved to be thrown away. Abandoned.

After the officers left, a private arranged the movie reels for rewinding, and Tom retrieved the letter from the trash. He worked it open. Thin old-fashioned handwriting crossed the page, and a flowering vine had been penned up the left side of the paper, with a little bird perched in the top corner. She might not be perky, but she was creative, and Tom smiled.

He skimmed the part Quincy had mocked and read on.

An anonymous correspondence appeals to me. In the real world shyness bars me from friendship, but letters remove that barrier. I must warn you, I have little experience with friendship, but I can offer you encouragement and prayer and a listening ear. If this sort of correspondence appeals to you—and I realize it seems strange—please read on. If not, please know you will still be in my prayers.

If you've continued, you probably wonder what kind of woman I am, but anonymity restricts what I can share. I am an only child. My mother died when I was two, but my father is the dearest, most wonderful man, who loves me deeply. I spent half my life stateside and half abroad, accompanying him on botanical excursions. In the jungle I was isolated from other children, and at home I didn't fit in with the American boys and girls. As a result, I didn't learn how to make friends. Most people consider my upbringing lonely and odd, but it was a delightful adventure in many ways.

In the wilderness, I took care of my father and his helpers when they were sick or injured. This is how I found my calling to be a nurse. Nothing gives me greater joy than comforting the sick and wounded and nursing them back to health.

I'm afraid you'll find my stories odd. As you may have guessed, I'm not like most young women, and I'll understand if you don't wish to correspond.

Whether or not you choose to reply, I'd like to fulfill this program's purpose of improving morale. I appreciate your willingness to sacrifice and the hard work you perform in the service of our country. My prayers are with you.

Sincerely,
an anonymous nurse

Tom lay the letter down and smoothed it in his lap. This was his kind of woman.

3

Bowman Field
Louisville, Kentucky
November 2, 1942

In the dark, Mellie lugged her gear from the bus stop toward the administration building at Bowman Field. She was supposed to meet the chief nurse, Lt. Cora Lambert, in her office before six o'clock. Would she still be there two hours later? If not, how would Mellie know where to go?

Since no one was around to see, Mellie let herself smile. She wanted adventure but hardly expected it on an air base in Kentucky.

Following the instructions she'd received in the mail, Mellie located the administration building. The doorknob turned in her hand—unlocked, thank goodness. She stepped into the dim entryway. At least she could camp inside if Lieutenant Lambert had retired to quarters.

"Hello?" Mellie called.

A door creaked open, and yellow light washed down the hall. "Lieutenant Blake?"

"Yes, ma'am."

"Come in. Mercy, you're late."

"The bus was delayed at the Louisville depot." Mellie

entered the office and set down her gear. "I'm glad you're still here."

Lieutenant Lambert took Mellie's hand in both of hers. "How nice to meet you."

"It's nice to meet you too." As long as she told herself this was a professional encounter, not a social one, she'd be fine.

The chief's gaze circled Mellie's head. Her brown eyes widened, her smile flattened, but then she blinked and gave a genuine smile. "Lieutenant Newman spoke highly of you, and I think the world of her. We went to nursing school together."

"Thank you, ma'am." Mellie unfastened her blue cape.

"Oh, keep that on. I'll show you to quarters. You must be exhausted. Are you hungry? Poor dear. The mess is closed, of course."

Mellie followed the chief's tall, trim figure outside. "I bought a sandwich at the train station."

"Smart thinking. We'll need that here." Her voice lowered into a growl.

Was that an invitation for a question or just complaining? Mellie winced. She never knew how to respond. "Oh?" she said.

"You poor thing, coming at such a time."

For once, Mellie had chosen the right path. "Oh?"

The chief flung up one graceful hand. "Just two weeks ago—two weeks—the Army Air Force called for an air evacuation group with both heavy and light transports, but now—now some Director of Military Requirements says he won't approve puddle jumpers."

"Puddle jumpers?"

"Heavy transports are the large cargo planes, the C-47s. Light transports are smaller puddle jumpers meant for short flights. That was the idea. Light transports can go into combat areas, because they don't need a long airstrip, and the heavies for the longer hauls. But now? Well, Directors of Military Requirements should keep their noses out of medical care."

Mellie adjusted the strap for her barracks bag over her shoulder. "Isn't that our purpose? To fly close to combat areas?"

"Exactly." Lieutenant Lambert's eyes glowed in the moonlight. "Whisk the patients out of danger, speed them to hospitals, and care for them en route. And some desk jockey can't see the vision. Granted, it's revolutionary putting women close to combat. But we can handle it."

"Yes, ma'am. That's why I came."

"Good. You girls are wonderful. So brave and passionate. Some of the nurses did mock air evacuation for the big Army maneuvers in Texas. They just got back. We split them among the three squadrons. You'll be with Vera, Alice, and Kay. Lively girls and very qualified. They were stewardesses with Pan Am. Perfect for flight nursing. Not only are stewardesses required to be registered nurses, but they're trained in how to deal with emergencies in the air."

Stewardesses. Pretty and perky. "Wonderful."

"Here we are." Lieutenant Lambert opened the door to a wood-frame building. "They had to scramble to build nurses' quarters. Nothing for women, of course."

Mellie stepped into a hallway filled with the scent of fresh-cut pine.

"Six to a room. Each squadron will be divided into four flights with six nurses each. Rooming together will let you make friends."

Mellie sighed. If only it were that easy to make friends.

Lieutenant Lambert knocked on the second door on the left and led Mellie into cramped military quarters. Two bunk beds stood along one wall, and on the facing wall stood another bunk bed, a sink and mirror, and two wooden chairs. Yellow ruffled curtains hung on the window at the end of the room, an addition by one of the women, no doubt.

Two nurses on the bottom bunk closest to the window scrambled to their feet.

"Hi, ladies," Lieutenant Lambert said. "Are Vera, Alice, and Kay still out?"

"Nine o'clock curfew, ma'am," the taller of the girls said in a Southern accent. "They still have time."

"They'll be back soon," the shorter girl said in a matching accent. "Is this—are you . . . ?"

"This is Lieutenant . . ."

"Philomela Blake. *Fill*-o-*mell*-a."

"Well, isn't that the sweetest old-fashioned name?" The shorter girl clasped Mellie's hand in hers, warmth in her blue eyes and an expectant smile on her face—the smile of someone always well liked and never disappointed. "I'm Georgie Taylor and this is Rose Danilovich. We've been friends forever. Inseparable. But we're not exclusive." She leaned closer, brown curls as bouncy as her voice. "We simply love making new friends."

In Mellie's experience, friendliness never lasted long, but she'd enjoy it while she could. "Nice to meet you."

"I'm leaving now, ladies," Lieutenant Lambert said. "Have fun getting acquainted."

"We will," Georgie and Rose called as the chief left.

Mellie scanned the room. All the bunks had been claimed except the top bunk on the left. "Is this mine?"

"Sure is." Rose wore her sleek dark blonde hair fashionably curled above her shoulders. "Little rack there for you to hang your things, shelf above, barracks bag on the floor. You know the drill."

"Mm-hmm." Mellie unfastened her cape and hung it up, then added her dark blue service jacket.

"Philomela," Rose said. "Don't think I've heard that name before."

"It comes from a Greek myth. It means 'lover of music' or 'nightingale.'"

"Oh!" Georgie sat on her bunk and leaned forward, her hands on the edge of the mattress. "Nightingale. And you're a nurse. Isn't that the sweetest thing? Like Florence Nightingale herself."

"Mm-hmm." Mellie fumbled with bobby pins, removed her garrison cap, and set it on the shelf. How could she escape before she said something stupid? Would it look rude if she claimed fatigue and went to bed?

"That's a mouthful though." Rose leaned against the post for the bunk. "What do we call you?"

Only Papa could call her Mellie. Nicknames were reserved for intimates, he always said. "Just call me Philomela."

"All right then." Rose sat next to Georgie. "Where are you from?"

"California mostly."

"Mostly?"

Mellie clasped her hands together. She couldn't go to bed yet, but where to sit? The lower bunks belonged to other girls, and the two chairs were draped with drying stockings. She perched on the edge of a chair, away from the laundry.

"Mostly?" Rose repeated.

Mellie drew a deep breath and gazed at the ceiling. "Papa was a botany professor at Stanford. We spent half our time in California, half on excursions. The Philippines mostly, but also the Dutch East Indies, Burma, French Indochina."

"How exciting," Georgie said. "To think Rose and I never left Virginia before this old war started."

"Mm." Mellie wrestled with a smile, wanting to be polite without unleashing its startling fullness.

Laughter rang in the hallway, the door flew open, and three women walked in, a brunette, a blonde, and a redhead, like a poster for Pan American Airways.

They stopped inside the door and took in Mellie. Identical little twists appeared on their lips.

"You must be the new girl." The redhead lost the twist. She walked over, and Mellie stood to shake her hand. "I'm Kay Jobson. Welcome to the squadron."

"Thank you. I'm Philomela Blake."

"My, that's quite a name. I'm Vera Viviani." The brunette shook Mellie's hand without looking her in the eye, a little smirk on her full lips—as full as Mellie's, but her mouth didn't have the breadth Mellie's did.

"Alice Olson." The blonde had a wide-eyed, innocent beauty, but her eyes glinted as she exchanged a glance with Vera.

"You'll be my bunk mate." Kay patted the bedpost. "Sorry to stick you on top, but I'm usually out late. I'd hate to wake you when I climb up there."

"I don't mind." Any bunk seemed luxurious compared to a bedroll on the jungle floor.

"Sneaking out for a date tonight, Kay?" Vera pulled off her black Army Nurse Corps pumps and tossed them in the corner.

"Nope. Mondays are still open." Kay stretched out on her bunk, her strawberry blonde hair fanned on her pillow. "Give me time. I've only been here a few weeks. Bob on Tuesdays, George on Wednesdays, Harv on Thursdays, Bill on Fridays, Clark on Saturdays—he's special, and I take Sundays off. It's the Lord's Day, after all."

Vera and Alice laughed. Georgie and Rose didn't. Neither did Mellie.

"Shocked?" Kay looked up at Mellie with a spark in her green eyes. A spark of challenge and something else, something Mellie identified with—the expectation of rejection.

Mellie's fingers felt numb. How could she have anything in common with a girl like Kay? She lifted her chin and shook her head. "I'm not shocked."

"Give me time." Kay closed her eyes. "I'll shock you."

The ladies got ready for bed, and Mellie's shoulders relaxed. She wiggled out of her blue uniform skirt, took off the black tie and light blue blouse, and put on her nightgown. From her bag, she pulled out her mahogany hairpin box. Aurelio, her father's favorite guide, had carved it for Mellie's tenth birthday. Mellie traced the orchid painted on the lid, and her throat squeezed shut. *Lord, please keep Papa and Aurelio and all the others safe under the Japanese.*

Starting at the crown of her head, she pulled out dozens of hairpins until two long, thick braids flopped down her back, almost to her knees. She undid the plaits, then brushed it out, a long process.

The room fell silent. All watching her.

"My goodness," Georgie said. "What gorgeous hair."

"Thank you." Like Jo March in *Little Women*, Mellie had her "one beauty," her long thick hair. She gathered it over her shoulder and into her lap to braid it for sleep.

Vera let out a little laugh. "When was the last time you cut it?"

"I never have." She could still see Papa's sweet face marred by haunting pain as he warned her over and over. "A lady never shortens her hair or her name."

Silence spoke louder than any words could have, and Mellie's chest tightened. Why on earth had she said that out loud?

"A lady never shortens her hair?" Vera fluffed her glamorous dark hair. "What's that make me?"

"Obviously not a lady," Alice said with a snort. "But neither am I."

"What about me?" Kay rolled over on her bunk. "I've got a nickname too."

Vera gasped. "Shameless hussy."

"I never claimed to be anything else."

Mellie lowered her head and gripped her mass of hair down by her waist. Why couldn't she keep her mouth shut? No one understood how important this was to her and Papa. How could they when she didn't tell them, and how could she tell them without exposing the family shame?

Georgie was a nickname too, and both she and Rose wore their hair above the shoulder, as did all young ladies nowadays. All but Mellie.

Remorse flooded through her. She stole a glance at Georgie and Rose, who had been so nice to her. Georgie dropped her gaze, and Rose picked up a book.

"I . . . I'm sorry." Her fingers tangled in her hair, and pain zinged through the roots. If only her pain could erase the pain she'd inflicted. "I didn't mean to hurt anyone."

"You're living in the wrong century, sister," Vera said.

Mellie shut her eyes against the damp heat welling inside. Why did she have to be so odd?

4

HMS *Derbyshire*
Atlantic Ocean
November 6, 1942

Tom sat on his bunk, as close to privacy as he could get at
sea. Mom encouraged him to keep a journal, but he never
bothered. Seemed so impersonal. But writing Annie, his
anonymous nurse, provided the personal touch he craved.

Only one letter had been mailed before they sailed, but
on board, he'd written a pile of them. Poor girl had no idea
what she'd started.

The rocking of the transport ship made writing difficult,
but it also gave him inspiration.

> Beneath these surging waves is a vast world I
> can only imagine. Do the starfish look up at
> our convoy and wonder about our school of loud,
> gigantic fish? Do the sea anemones jive to the
> tunes the boys play on their harmonicas? Do the
> octopi watch the U-boats slither by, and could
> they send an ink cloud to warn us?
>
> You thought your stories were odd. Welcome

to the little world inside my head. I'd love to hear your stories, the odder the better, and I pray you choose to send them. We both need friends.

"Lieutenant MacGilliver?" a deep voice called out.

Tom craned his neck to look to the doorway, where Corporal Reilly, Captain Newman's clerk, stood. "Yes?"

"Sir, the captain would like to see you in his cabin."

"Thanks, Reilly." Tom extracted himself from the tight confines of the bunk and grabbed his overcoat. After seeing Newman, he'd take a nighttime stroll on deck in the fresh air. The men were restricted to soap-free saltwater showers every three days, and the cabin had grown rank.

Twelve days at sea made Tom feel like a true sailor, stepping over raised thresholds while ducking his head, and scampering up and down the ladder-like stairways.

He entered Newman's cabin and saluted. "You wanted to see me, sir?"

"Have a seat, Gill." The captain sat at a miniature desk next to his bunk and motioned to a chair. He held up a bottle of scotch. "Drink?"

"No, thank you, sir." Booze had turned his father into a bum and then a murderer. He never wanted to find out what it would do to him.

Captain Newman shrugged and poured himself a shot. "You'll change your mind in a few days."

"We'll see." Tom managed a grin.

"Tonight we'll pass through the Straits of Gibraltar under cover of darkness. Another day at sea, then after midnight we'll land at Oran, Algeria—if the U-boats don't spot us first."

"Yes, sir." So far the convoy had traveled all the way from England without a U-boat encounter. A miracle.

Newman sipped his liquor and peered over the rim at Tom. "Can you handle it?"

"Absolutely, sir." Fear had never found a home in his soul.

"More important, can you handle your men?"

Tom rubbed his hand over his forearm, making the little blond hairs stand at attention. "Of course. They like me and trust me."

"They like you as a man. But will they follow you as a leader?"

"Don't see why not."

Newman sighed and picked up a stack of papers. "Three companies in this battalion. Three platoons in my company. You know which of the nine platoons has the most discipline problems? Yours. By far."

Because he got all the misfits. "Yes, sir. They're spirited."

"Spirited." The captain ran his hand through his dark hair flecked by gray over the ears.

"They'll settle down. They're cooped up on board with nothing to do."

"It's more than that. They see you as a pal, one of the boys."

Tom nodded. That's what he wanted.

Newman took another sip of scotch. "It doesn't work. Look at Quincy's platoon. He's got those men under tight control. They're scared of him, and he uses that."

Fear as a means of control? "That's not the kind of man I am, sir."

"But you've got your name. Your name alone sparks fear. Use it."

Tom sat back in the chair. His eyes stung. "I can't. I won't."

Newman leaned forward. "You're a good man, Gill. But they don't have to know that."

"I can't be anything else."

The captain lowered his head and let out a deep sigh. "I took a big chance when I chose you. Sure, you're an actual engineer, and we need engineers like crazy. But for the other commanders, that faded away when they saw your name."

"I understand, sir." When he and his mom moved to Pittsburgh after his father's execution, none of the teachers wanted Tom in their classrooms. Too dangerous. And if not too dangerous, too disruptive. Seven years old, and no one wanted him. That hadn't changed.

Newman raised his head and looked Tom in the eye. "I saw something in you I liked. I saw goodness. I saw intelligence. I saw ingenuity. That's why I took you. But now I need to see something more. I need to see you lead these men with authority. This is life and death, Gill."

"I won't let you down, sir."

"For heaven's sake, if you won't use your name, at least use your rank. That's why you have it, so the men will obey your orders instantly."

"They will, sir. I guarantee it." They'd obey because they liked him and wanted to please him, not because they feared him.

Captain Newman grunted. "I'll hold you to that. Now go get some sleep. You won't get much, if any, tomorrow, and from then on, who knows?"

"Thank you, sir." Tom left the cabin. He climbed stairway after stairway until he reached the deck, and he drew in a bracing breath of cold sea mist. Deep breaths. Deep breaths.

He pulled on his overcoat and turned up the collar. The cold gave him an excuse to hide his face until his smile returned.

His men would follow him. They had to. After the war, he'd need a solid recommendation from Newman to get a job. The name MacGilliver rubbed the luster right off his engineering degree.

His chest filled with unbearable, unallowable heat. Dad hadn't thought about what his actions would do to his family. Tom had to bear the burden of his name for the rest of his life.

His breath steamed in front of him, and he blew it off, blew it all off. He had to. *Lord, help me keep control. Help me lead my men. Help me prove myself.*

He headed toward the bow of the ship. Despite Newman's advice, Tom wouldn't get much sleep tonight.

A sharp burst of laughter ahead of him. Two men pushed a third man, jeering him.

Tom paused, and his hands clenched in his coat pockets.

"You heard me, chopsticks. Whatcha doing out at night? Signaling your buddy Adolf? Telling him our plans?" Hal Weiser, the lunkhead.

Larry Fong held up one hand and walked away at a brisk pace. He laughed too. "I'm one of you. American through and through."

"That's what all spies say." Who was that with Weiser? Sergeant Lehman? He shoved Larry, made him stumble.

Tom dashed forward, a grin on his face. "Hey, guys! Sergeant Fong, there you are. I've been looking for you. Weiser, Lehman, get some sleep while you can."

Weiser's fingers worked by his side. "We're just having fun."

"Yeah, but it's late. Good night, boys. Fong, I need to go over something with you." He put his hand on Larry's shoulder and led him toward the bow.

Weiser and Lehman grumbled, but they didn't follow.

Larry's muscles remained tense.

Tom jiggled his shoulder. "Never mind them. They flunked geography."

A harsh laugh. "Great. Put that on my tombstone."

"When they see they can't rattle you, they'll leave you alone and find other prey." Tom stepped up to the bow and leaned his elbows on the railing. "Looked like you smiled the whole time. Do you ever stop smiling?"

Larry cocked one eyebrow. "Do you?"

"No," Tom said with a laugh.

"Me neither. I don't dare."

Tom gripped his elbows. He had to be cheerful to show people he wasn't a killer. Larry had to prove he wasn't the enemy. "Has it always been like this for you?"

"Not much in San Francisco. A bit at Cal. But when the war started, it got bad. That's why I joined up. It didn't help."

"Give them time. When they see what you're made of, you'll win them over."

"Maybe. Maybe not. In the meantime, I'll serve my country as best I can. At least I'm not locked in a relocation camp like my Japanese friends. Just as American as I am, not that I can say that out loud."

Tom nudged his arm. "You just did."

"You're different. You understand."

"Yeah." Tom understood more than Larry knew.

In the darkness, the other ships of the convoy showed as a hint of shape, as too much black against the shimmering sea, as a disturbance of the waves. More black lay ahead on the port side, a giant triangle cut out from the starry fabric of the night sky.

"Gibraltar," Larry whispered, as if his voice might carry to the enemy.

"Wow." The British territory stood guard at the entrance of the Mediterranean, between Spain to the north and Spanish Morocco to the south. Officially neutral, Spain was one of many unknown variables in Operation Torch. Only a few years earlier, Hitler had helped Franco rise to power in the Spanish Revolution. Would Hitler call him on his debt?

"What do you think the French will do?" Larry asked.

"Who knows?" The French were the biggest variable. French Morocco, Algeria, and Tunisia were occupied by Vichy France, the government set up in southern France after the Nazi victory in June 1940. A few weeks later, the British sank French ships to prevent them from falling into German hands. Over a thousand French sailors had died. The Vichy hadn't forgotten.

Tom drummed his fingers on the railing. "The top brass thinks the French will drop their guns when they see Americans wade ashore. But if they don't fight us, what will the Nazis do to Vichy France? It could go either way."

"What about the Germans? Sure, the British just routed them at El Alamein, and Monty's got Rommel on the run. But do you think Rommel will send troops into Algeria?"

"Who knows? Lot of unknowns. Our army's one of them. None of us have seen combat yet."

"Yeah, well, it's been almost a year since Pearl Harbor. About time we got in the fight."

"Yep." Gibraltar grew more massive in Tom's sight. Only one thing he could count on—the Rock of Ages, far stronger than Gibraltar.

5

Bowman Field
November 7, 1942

Bits of cloud flecked the sky as if angels had indulged in a pillow fight. Mellie crossed the tarmac toward a C-47 cargo plane and lifted her voice to stir up the feathery clouds, singing "All the Things You Are."

She rounded the plane's tail and stopped short, her song suspended on a low note. Three nurses already stood by the cargo door, wearing their dress blues. Mellie had planned to arrive first.

Vera Viviani snickered and whispered to Alice Olson, "All the things he is will never be hers."

Although her cheeks flamed, she gazed around with a neutral expression as if she hadn't heard. How embarrassing that they thought she pined for love. She just liked the song. At least her dark complexion hid her blush.

Mellie glanced at her watch. Today they were supposed to do something productive for a change. So far they'd done nothing but calisthenics and marching drills as the brass argued about whether or not to use the nurses and in what capacity.

A tune drifted to Mellie—"Keep 'Em Flying." Rose Danilovich and Georgie Taylor marched to the plane, arm in arm, belting out their own lyrics. "Get us flying. Get us in the air. Get us flying. Grounding us ain't fair."

Mellie smiled and pressed her fingers to her mouth. Georgie had a rich, strong alto, which would blend nicely with her own soprano. Rose sang off-key but with courage and spirit.

"Come on, ladies," Rose called. "Sing along. We've got a squadron theme song."

"A song?" Kay Jobson stepped back and crossed her arms. "Then I need to transfer."

"We're nurses," Alice said in a condescending tone. "If you want to sing for the troops, join the USO."

Mellie edged forward. Her heart thumped, but the conversation had crossed into the professional domain. "As nurses, our job is to comfort our patients. What could be more comforting than music?"

"That's right, Philomela." Georgie grinned and extended her free arm. "You'll join us in our song, won't you?"

Mellie froze. The image of her singing arm in arm with two other girls was such a foreign image. Appealing, but so strange.

"But Philomela's a lady." Vera pressed a hand to her chest. "That would be beneath her."

Georgie's hand settled back to her side, the invitation fluttered away, and Mellie ducked her chin. She'd never make friends. How could she when she didn't know how? And how on earth could she learn? Mellie felt like she was learning to walk at the age of twenty-three.

Mellie blinked hard and studied the plane. The Douglas C-47 was the military version of the DC-3 passenger plane used by civilian airlines. Painted a muted medium green, the plane had a cute snub nose and a large square cargo door. Between the cargo door and the tail, the U.S. Army Air Forces' white star on a blue disc was painted at eye level.

"Good afternoon, ladies." Lieutenant Lambert strode up, followed by four enlisted men, and she beckoned to about three dozen nurses scattered nearby. "Today these gentlemen will instruct you in the proper use of the litter."

A tall blonde nurse raised her hand. "Won't medics carry the patients?"

"Ideally, yes." Lieutenant Lambert motioned for the ladies to stand in a circle around the enlisted men. "This is experimental, as you know. No one's performed medical air evacuation in an organized manner. Our plan is to gather patients at airfield holding units. We'll fly in, and medics will load the patients under our guidance. However, this is war, and war doesn't follow plans. If there aren't any trained personnel on the ground, you'll recruit and train. If you're under fire or ditching a plane, you'll carry patients yourselves."

"Oh my," Georgie whispered to Rose.

"You're little but strong," Rose whispered back. "You can do it."

Mellie studied Georgie's pale face. Did she really lack confidence in her abilities or was she scared?

Lieutenant Lambert pointed to one of the men, blond and strapping. "Sergeant Kowalski will take over from here."

"Ground litter!" Sergeant Kowalski called out.

A private lowered a folded litter to the ground and unfastened the straps.

"Open litter."

The private did so. A canvas litter with aluminum poles stood on stirrup-shaped feet.

"Private Gibson."

One of the men lay on the litter, and the other men strapped him in position as the sergeant barked more orders. They assumed rigid positions at the foot and head of the litter.

"Prepare to lift."

The men squatted and grasped the handles.

"Lift. Forward march. Understand, ladies?"

Mellie nodded. Simple enough, but she couldn't imagine such a regimented process under fire.

"Break into groups of three and practice. One as patient, two as litter carriers, and rotate."

Every one of Mellie's muscles tightened. Why couldn't they assign groups instead of letting the women form their own? All around her, women coalesced into trios, with a bit of negotiation when friends had to be separated, but no one was left out. Except her.

She edged backward and twisted her hands together. If only she could turn invisible.

Someone tapped her on the shoulder. "Trying to get out of work?"

Mellie spun around and faced Capt. Frank Maxwell, the surgeon assigned to her flight of six nurses—tall, well built, and movie-star handsome. Half the girls swooned over him and bemoaned the fact that he was married and the father of two. "No, of course not. I was . . ."

He studied her through narrowed green eyes. "Miss Burke, isn't it? I've heard about you."

"Blake. Lieutenant Blake." And what had he heard?

His eyes narrowed more.

Mellie winced. So he didn't like being corrected by a woman. She'd worked with doctors like him before.

"Well, Lieutenant, so you think you already know how to do everything and don't need training like everyone else?"

"That wasn't . . . I just . . ." How could she admit she was too shy to barge in where she wasn't wanted? "I don't have a group."

Captain Maxwell gave her a flat smile. "So, find one."

Mellie surveyed the crowd, all practicing and laughing and neatly divided.

"Think you're too good to work with others, huh? That's what they're saying."

Her mouth dropped open. Why did people couple shyness with conceit? "I never . . . I don't think that."

"Good. Find a group or we'll find a nurse who fits in."

"Yes, sir." As Mellie walked away, the physician's gaze burned a hole between her shoulder blades and straight to her heart. Shouldn't her nursing skills matter more than her social skills? They said they wanted women who could work independently. When had that changed?

She wound her way through the groups. Three. Three. Three. No one looked at her.

Off to the side, Georgie and Rose carried a litter holding Private Gibson. Georgie caught Mellie's eye. "Philomela! Don't you have a group?"

Mellie's fingers hurt from all the twisting she'd given them. She shook her head.

"Come join us and give the private a break."

He scrambled out of the litter. "You've already given me plenty of breaks. A broken arm, a broken noggin . . ."

Rose laughed. "Don't worry, Philomela. It's Georgie's turn to be dropped."

Gratefulness turned up Mellie's smile before she could cover her mouth. "I won't drop you."

"Why not?" Georgie lay on the litter, hands tucked under her head. "That's the fun part."

Mellie fumbled with straps and handles, and she and Rose lifted the litter.

"Do you think they'll send us back to Alaska?" Georgie asked Rose. "It was beautiful there but so cold."

"Maybe." Rose led them on a zigzag course around the other groups.

"Where do you think we'll go, Philomela?"

Mellie glanced at Georgie's smiling face below her, surrounded by a puff of brown curls. People rarely asked her
opinion. "The Pacific, I hope. We could support the Guadalcanal campaign or bring patients home from Hawaii."

"Ooh, I like that idea. Eating pineapple on the beach and
learning the hula." Georgie wiggled her hips, which set the
litter swaying.

Mellie grasped the litter poles and almost laughed.

"Careful there, hula girl," Rose said. "I'm hoping for England. Those handsome wounded airmen need a lift home."

Georgie clucked her tongue. "You sound like Vera, Alice,
and Kay. Look at them now. And he's a married man."

The threesome stood by their litter, chatting with Captain
Maxwell. Vera leaned close, said something, and patted the
doctor's arm. He tilted back his head of shiny black hair and
laughed. He didn't seem to mind that they weren't working.

"Left turn," Rose called. "You don't have to search. You've
got a fine boyfriend."

"I do," Georgie said with a sigh. "Ward is fine indeed.
Don't worry, Rose. We'll find you someone. How about you,
Philomela? Do you have a boyfriend?"

No one had ever asked her that question before. "Me?
No. No, I don't."

"We'll look for you too. Won't that be fun?"

Oh dear. Mellie shifted her gaze up to the back of Rose's
head. That would be a long, painful, and fruitless search.

"All right, ladies," Sergeant Kowalski said. "That's enough
for today. Tomorrow we'll learn how to transport the litters
into the plane."

Mellie and Rose set down the litter and unbuckled the
straps.

Georgie got to her feet. "We have free time before dinner.
What should we do, gals?"

Mellie blinked. Georgie actually looked at her. But Rose's smile stiffened, and Georgie's head tilted a bit too much.

Her heart sank. She'd drag down any activity, Georgie wouldn't be as happy as she thought, and Rose would be annoyed at her for ruining their fun. Mellie would feel more awkward and out of place than if she were alone. Best to stay in the forest.

"Thank you, but I need to . . ." She gestured toward the buildings. "I need to run errands."

She strode toward the Post Exchange, her stomach churning, and she poked loose bobby pins back into her coil of braids. What was wrong with her? First she wanted to make friends, then she turned down an invitation. No wonder she didn't have any friends. That would be the last time Georgie reached out to her.

The PX radiated warmth from a furnace, the smell of coffee, and the laughter of people who actually had social capabilities. The mail usually arrived by this time, although Mellie hadn't received any yet. But every day she checked. What if she heard word about Papa today?

"Do you have any mail for me?" she asked the clerk. "Lt. Philomela Blake."

He reached into a cubby, flipped through a stack of envelopes, and pulled one out. "Yes, ma'am."

Her heart flew into her throat and blocked her voice. Papa! Finally she'd know if he was alive and well. She mouthed a thank-you to the clerk and took the letter in trembling hands. A thick letter. How was that possible? The Japanese placed strict limits on the length of letters from prisoners, and the State Department or Red Cross would only send one thin sheet.

The return address read, "Lt. Edna Newman, Walter Reed General Hospital."

Mellie's heart landed with a thud in her stomach. Still no word about Papa. *Oh, Lord, you're the only one who knows how he's doing. Please keep him safe.*

"Anything else, ma'am?" the clerk asked.

"A—a coffee please." Why did she ask for coffee? She was already shaky, and now she'd have to stay in the PX until she finished the beverage.

She took the cup and saucer from the clerk and surveyed the PX. Booths ran down one side of the building, where nurses and pilots sipped Cokes and coffee. One empty booth stood in the far corner, and Mellie slipped in, her back to the crowd.

Why had Lieutenant Newman written her? Perhaps she'd sent paperwork from Walter Reed.

Mellie opened the envelope. Another envelope lay inside, sealed and unaddressed. A short note from Lieutenant New-man accompanied it.

> Dear Lieutenant Blake,
>
> I hope all is well with you. Please give my best to Cora Lambert.
>
> Thank you for participating in the letter-writing campaign. Here is your response. Since you are no longer at Walter Reed, it would be more efficient to mail your response directly to my husband. I've let him know to expect your reply. To maintain anonymity, please put your letter to the gentleman in an unaddressed envelope inside an envelope addressed to my husband: Capt. Richard Newman, O-111897; Co. "B" 908th Engr. Bn. (Avn.); APO 528, c/o Postmaster, New York, N.Y.

Your pen pal will give his letters to my
husband, who will mail them directly to you.

Mellie stared at the note and read it again. Who on earth
would respond to her letter?

It had to be a mix-up. The letter must be meant for another
woman. She'd scan the letter to make sure, then send it back
and let Lieutenant Newman sort it out.

She opened the envelope. Square, manly handwriting covered a piece of paper, and a suspension bridge was penciled
across the top with a firm, practiced hand.

Dear Annie the Anonymous Nurse,
Pardon the nickname, but I couldn't address
a letter to "blank."
You're probably surprised to get a reply. As
you thought, most of the men are looking for
romance. I'm not, but I _am_ looking for a friend.
If we met, you'd think we had nothing in
common. You'd find me sociable, cheerful, and
surrounded by a crowd. But in that crowd, I
have no true friends.
You say anonymity appeals to you. Well,
it sets me free. For reasons too numerous to
mention—and forbidden by anonymity—I can't
be myself in public. I always have to be sunny.
But in anonymity, perhaps I can be myself.
You offered encouragement, prayer, and a
listening ear. If that offer still stands by the
time you get to the end of this letter, I'll take it.
I offer the same to you.

Who am I? I'm a nameless civil engineer.
I serve in an Engineer Aviation Battalion,
the Army Air Forces' version of the Seabees
but without the catchy name. Someday soon,
we'll land with the first or second wave of
an invasion force and build airfields from
rubble or wilderness under fire. The odds of our
meeting in a professional manner are high.

Like you, I have no brothers or sisters. My
father is gone, and my dear mother raised me
alone. We have more in common than you'd
think.

To me, your background sounds intriguing,
and I'd like to hear your stories. I don't mind
odd. In fact, I enjoy it. However, if you're
apprehensive and don't want to write back, I'll
understand.

No matter what, I'll pray for you. You nurses
put yourselves in danger and deal with the
messes we men make. I hope we never meet
professionally, and if we did we'd never know
it, but I'm sure I'd be in good hands.

Sincerely,
(make up a nickname
for me if you have the
guts to write back.)

The letter rippled in Mellie's shaking hands. It was for
her. It was genuine. One lonely soul reaching out to another.

Now what? Her mind spun, and she stuffed the letter back in the envelope. She strode out of the PX, her coffee untouched, her head down, her eyes misty.

A chance for a real friendship? Just what she'd wanted. Yet her stomach filled with acid. She didn't know how to be a friend. She only knew how to be a daughter, a nurse.

"No. I can't do it." She belonged in the forest. The forest was safe. If she stepped into the clearing, something horrible could happen.

A bird twittered on the roof of a building she passed.

"My little nightingale," Papa always said when Mellie sang to him, when she tended him when he was sick. "My angel of mercy."

Papa said mercy was the Lord's gift to her, the gift she gave back to others. Mercy came easily on the hospital ward, but in the outside world?

Mellie stepped between buildings, out of sight of passersby, and leaned back against the wall. She pulled out the engineer's letter and scanned it until her vision blurred.

Something barred him from friendship just as her unconventional looks and shyness barred her. She needed someone who didn't see. He needed someone who didn't know.

Most of all, he needed mercy.

Her legs sagged. She glanced up to the rectangle of purpling sky between the buildings. "Lord, you want me to do this, don't you? Please help me. Please don't let me fail him."

6

Tom surveyed his platoon on the ship's deck—three squads of thirteen men each, gathered in the darkness. The men masked fear with stoicism or wisecracks or grumbles about it being two o'clock in the morning.

"Sure could use a smoke," Hal Weiser said.

Nobody offered him one. On this moonless night, even light from a cigarette could tip off the enemy to the ship's position.

Today the Vichy French were the enemy. After almost two centuries of friendship and support, French soldiers were firing on Americans. Bright orange flashes onshore, crackling gunfire, and booming mortars confirmed it.

While the Western Task Force landed in Morocco and the Eastern Force landed at Algiers, the Center Force was landing on three beaches surrounding the port of Oran. Beach Z at Arzeu lay farthest to the east. After the beachhead was secured, tanks would sweep southwest to airfields at Tafaroui and Le Sénia, and Tom's battalion would patch up damage.

"Okay, men, you can do this," Tom said, grin fixed. "Make sure your helmet's unfastened and your shoes untied."

"Ain't that cheerful?" Bill Rinaldi squatted to unlace his shoes. "If the Frenchies shoot up our boat, our helmets won't drag us down. Ain't it nice to know it'll take us longer to drown?"

Tom adjusted his carbine strap over his shoulder. "No one will drown or get shot. The French are putting on a show before they surrender to prove to Hitler they tried."

A sailor tapped Tom on the shoulder. "Your landing craft is ready, sir."

"Thanks." Tom peered over the side to the craft in the dark water below. "Okay, men, let's go. Africa is waiting."

"Belly dancers," Earl Butler said. "Better be some luscious little belly dancers waiting for me."

Rinaldi poked him with his elbow. "For you, they'd better be desperate little belly dancers."

"Watch out, or you'll end up with a luscious, desperate little case of syphilis." Tom clambered over the side of the ship and anchored his feet in the landing net. "Remember what the sailors said. Hold on to the vertical ropes, not the horizontal ones, so the man above you doesn't smash your fingers."

"Smashed fingers would get me out of this racket," Sergeant Lehman said.

Swell. Just what Tom needed—a squad leader with a bad attitude. "This is the best racket in the world. By the end of the day, we'll control two airfields. The French will give up by sunset. Then we can push east into Tunisia while the Brits push west. Rommel will beg for mercy."

"Sure he will, Lieutenant Sunshine," Weiser said, but humor warmed his voice.

Tom made his way down the net, feeling with his feet for the rope rungs. "Okay, Weiser-guy, you and your squad are next."

The men eased their way down the net, grumbling and

cussing, gear and gas masks and rifles slung across their backs so they wouldn't get tangled in the ropes.

"You're almost there, sir," a British voice said from below, and a hand brushed his knee. "Place your foot here, sir. Now ease yourself down."

Tom held on to the net by his waist. With his left foot on the rim of the boat, he stretched his right foot down until it hit the deck.

The sailor braced Tom's shoulders. "Jolly good, sir."

"Thanks." Tom faced a tall, gangly sailor. "Let's take care of the rest of this gang."

"Gang, sir?"

Tom laughed. Americans did have a gangster reputation abroad. "Figure of speech. My platoon. Half of it, anyway."

"Yes, sir. We'll take care of your 'gang' right well."

Tom and the sailor helped the men into the boat. No one fell overboard, although several tumbled to the deck. Two of his squads boarded the Landing Craft, Assault while Larry Fong and the other squad boarded another LCA.

The coxswain wheeled the landing craft away from the transport and across the bay, covered by gray clouds from the Allies' smoke screen. The craft's wake glowed grassy green from phosphorescence. Tom stared, transfixed. Even in times of war, God created beauty.

A whistling sound, a great splash about a hundred yards to starboard, a giant plume of water in the air.

Tom ducked. Men swore. One man retched overboard. After two weeks on the open ocean, he wasn't seasick.

One of the British machine gunners in the back of the boat cursed the French. "See if we ever defend your country again. How many of our fathers died in the trenches in the last war? How many of our lads died when the Nazis blitzed through? Too many, I say."

"Easy now," the other gunner said. "Soon we'll all be friendly-like again. Then we can take on the Nasties together."

Tom swiveled his attention to the bow, where the coxswain conferred over charts with the fourth crewman and pointed at various spots on the shore. Were they lost?

The coxswain swerved the boat farther east. Another LCA burst out of the smoke screen and headed right at them. The sailors yelled at each other and pulled parallel, while Tom gripped the side of the boat for support. After a shouted conference, they agreed on a course.

Tom puffed up his cheeks with air, then blew it out. In this war, Operation Torch was the first joint operation between the British and the Americans, the first big landing for the U.S. Army, and the first American land action outside of the Pacific.

If they failed today, it would set back the effort against Germany for a long time.

And the American troops were as green as the wake behind the landing craft.

"We'd better not prove to be yellow too," Tom muttered.

In a few minutes, the LCA neared the shore. Orange flashes of tracer fire illuminated the scene. Landing craft swarmed. Some had grounded offshore, probably on sandbars.

The LCA pulled up to the beach. A scraping sound on the hull, and the boat stopped fifteen feet from the shore. Tom scanned the beach. No gunfire greeted him.

The bow ramp creaked open and splashed cold seawater on Tom.

He'd get wet anyway. "Come on, boys." Holding his carbine over his head, he headed down the ramp. He dropped into the chilly ocean, up to his waist, and sucked in a breath. "Come on in. The water's fine."

He sloshed to shore. His men followed, directing less-than-fine words at the water.

Once his feet touched African soil, he tried to sprint, but his legs wobbled and the ground pitched around him. His untied shoes didn't help. Too much time at sea. How long before he redeveloped land legs?

He staggered to a sand dune and ducked into its shelter, his carbine clutched to his chest. *Please, Lord, don't make me fire it. Don't let me kill someone.*

In basic training, his first shot on the rifle range had hit the center of the bull's-eye. Dead center. "MacGilliver really is a Killiver," someone had quipped. Tom had directed the rest of his shots to the outer rim of the target. He made sure his score was high enough to pass but low enough to silence the comments. If only he could silence the school-yard rhyme that never left his head.

> MacGilliver the Killiver
> Needed gold and silliver,
> Begged from the DeVillivers.
> Old bum MacGilliver.
>
> MacGilliver the Killiver
> Shot them through with skilliver.
> Our tears will never spilliver
> For old Tom MacGilliver.

"Gill! Gill!" Weiser prodded him in the arm. "What now?"

Tom shook out the memory and glanced around. Two dozen shivering dark shapes hunkered by the sand dune, the passengers from his LCA. Now he had to find the rest of his platoon, the rest of his company, and the road to Tafaroui. Easy as Mom's blackberry pie.

After he tied his shoes, he peeked above the sand dune. All looked clear. He motioned to Weiser, and the signal went down the line. Tom swept his arm overhead, leaped to his feet, and scrambled over the dune. Sounds to his rear assured him the men were following. Just as he thought they would.

No sign of other people. No sounds of gunfire. No roads or paths. He ran for a stand of scrub pines where he could get his bearings. His legs cooperated better, but the land still heaved from side to side.

"Hi yo, Silver!" a panicky voice shouted from the pines.

Tom dropped to the ground and shouted back the campaign's countersign, "Awa-a-a-ay!" He didn't want his men shot up by a trigger-happy GI.

"Howdy, Lone Ranger." Relief tinged the voice now.

Tom got to his feet and led his men to the pines. Sand clung to his wet uniform and made it even heavier. He squatted below the branches and shook hands with a sergeant with a broad face. A dozen men hid in the brush with him. "Which outfit?" Tom asked.

"Sixteenth Regimental Combat Team. Can't find the rest of my platoon. This whole thing's a stinking mess."

"We're with the 908th Engineer Aviation Battalion. Don't suppose you know where the road to Tafaroui is."

"Don't know where *I* am."

"We're in Algeria. That's all I can say."

"Sure about that?"

Tom chuckled and looked around. The beach curved around the bay, and gunfire rang out to the northwest. "Suppose we should go where the action is."

"Go ahead. I'll wait for the action to come to me."

Tom stared into the sergeant's eyes. Although the man wasn't in his unit, Tom could order him as an officer. "Come on. We need every hand, every gun."

"Nah. I should wait here for the rest of my platoon. They landed thataway." He pointed southeast, away from the town of Arzeu, away from danger.

Tom hesitated. The man was lying, but Tom didn't want to make any enemies.

He turned to Bernie Fitzgerald, Weiser's assistant foreman, who carried the map and compass. "Fitz, any idea where we are? How far the road is?"

"Don't know. Can't find any landmarks. I think we're about a mile east of where we were supposed to land."

"All right. We'll head toward town, see what we find." Tom led his men away from the shelter of the trees.

Keeping low, he hugged the side of a bluff and made his way west. Soon he spotted a large landing craft unloading a tank. He motioned for the men to get down, and they dropped to the sand.

"Hi yo, Silver!" Tom shouted.

The armored troops glanced around, rifles at the ready. "Awa-a-a-ay!"

Tom rose and lifted one hand in greeting. When the other men lowered their rifles, Tom led his platoon to the landing craft. "You boys with Combat Command B, by any chance?"

"Sure thing, Lieutenant."

"Great." The 908th was supposed to follow them to Tafaroui. The day looked a lot brighter.

———

A GMC truck rumbled down the rough Algerian road. Tom kept a smile on his men, crammed in the back of the truck open to the pale gray sky. The infantry had secured Arzeu not long after sunrise, and the tanks dashed for Tafaroui.

Tom had found truck rides for his platoon. Thank goodness he'd located Larry and the other squad, but he'd heard nothing of the other two platoons in his company.

For lunch, Tom spread canned cheese from his K ration onto a cracker as the truck bounced along. They passed through a vineyard, the foliage snipped off to expose bare, twisted vines, then through an orange grove, bright with fruit.

He had plenty to tell Annie in his next letter. Although he couldn't mention where he was, he could tell colorful stories. Now he could mail his stack of letters. But would they push her away? Possibly, but they'd served a good purpose, and he wouldn't change a word.

The soldier in the passenger seat leaned out the truck window and faced Tom's men. "Village coming up."

"Get your weapons ready." Tom gobbled his cracker and made sure his carbine was ready to go. The French weren't succumbing as quickly as the brass had hoped.

Little stone houses with tile roofs lined the road. Stone walls fenced off each home.

The men fell silent. Tom studied the roofs and trees and walls, and he erased his smile. Couldn't have the men think he was eager to kill.

A high-pitched zing. A bullet pinged off the roof of the truck.

"Take cover!" Tom vaulted over the side of the truck. The shock of landing reverberated up his legs.

Another shot rang out. His men shouted and scrambled out of the truck. Tom hurdled a low stone wall in front of a house and flattened himself behind it. Half his men joined him. The others hunched behind the truck.

Tom scanned the rooftops and windows across the road. He didn't want his boys hurt.

A muzzle flash from a rooftop, and another shot rocked the truck.

Tom's stomach tightened. He had a great line of sight on the sniper. But how could he shoot a man? Then he'd be a killer. How could he live with himself?

He braced his carbine on the wall and leveled it several feet below the French army cap across the way.

Another bullet skittered across the rocky road.

"There he is!" Weiser yelled. "Get him, boys."

A barrage peppered the rooftop, a French rifle dropped to the ground, and Tom sighed from relief and from grief. He didn't fire a shot, but the man died anyway.

A shadow fell over him, a human-shaped purple shadow. Tom held his breath, flipped onto his back, and pointed his carbine at the shadow.

An elderly gentleman leaned over him, his skin a deep olive. He wore a long, curly white beard, a brilliant green turban around his head, long grayish robes, and a curious expression. Not fearful. Just curious.

Tom eased his weapon down, pointed to the American flag patch on his left shoulder, and lifted a shaky smile. *"Bon jour."*

"Bon jour." The man grinned and patted his lips with two fingers as if smoking a cigarette.

"You want a cigarette? Cig-a-rette?" Tom said, as if slow speech would cross the language barrier. Keeping his eyes on the native Algerian, he fumbled open the pocket where he'd stuffed his ration and pulled out the pack of four smokes that came with each meal.

The man grabbed the pack, grinned broadly, and hurried back to the house. *"Vive l'Amérique! Vive l'Amérique!"*

A nervous laugh escaped Tom's lips, and his men joined him. "Hey, fellows, why didn't General Eisenhower think of that? We should have dropped cigs instead of paratroopers."

To his left, Rinaldi elbowed him. "Say, Gill, that was a real Lucky Strike."

Tom chuckled. "They do like Camels around here."

"Come on," the truck driver called out. "Let's load 'er up."

Still laughing, Tom got up and climbed back in the truck. But his hands shook.

Within an hour, they reached the airfield at Tafaroui, on a flat expanse of dirt with rocky hills in the distance.

Tom hopped out of the truck. "Okay, boys, camp under that palm tree over there while I find out what's going on."

He waved at Sergeant Fong in the truck behind and motioned for him to follow. First he had to find someone in charge.

A captain approached, wearing the golden tank insignia of the armored forces on his lapels. Tom's lapels bore the Engineers' two-turreted castle.

He saluted. "Lieutenant MacGilliver with the 908th Engineers."

The captain returned the salute. "Your captain's looking for you. Your battalion got split up."

"Like everyone else today. Airfield's secure?"

"Yep. No thanks to the Army Air Forces. Most of the C-47s got lost on the way from England. They got the signal mixed up, decided to land at the field instead of dropping the troops. The French fired at the planes. They're scattered all over. A lot of them landed on the Sebkra d'Oran, that dry lake west of here."

"Too bad." Only about a dozen cargo planes parked on the field.

"Of course, they tipped off the Frenchies that we were invading, so they gave our tanks a good stiff fight. We blasted them out, took three hundred prisoners." He pointed across the airfield. "There's your captain."

"Thanks." Tom headed over to Captain Newman. Footsteps thumped behind him, and he turned around. "Hey there, Larry. Having a fun day?"

"More fun than a day at Playland." Larry fell in step beside Tom. "Any snipers fire at you?"

"One. The boys took care of him. You guys?"

"A fellow in an orange grove. I don't understand. I'd think the French would welcome our help throwing the Nazis off their backs."

"Guess not." He stepped onto pavement. From what he could see, Tafaroui had a paved runway and taxiway but no paved hardstands for the planes to park on. One good rainstorm and they'd be yanking planes out of the mud.

A whistle overhead, and Tom and Larry flung themselves to the pavement. An artillery shell whammed into the ground a couple hundred feet to their left, throwing up a fountain of dirt.

Tom got up, brushed gravel from his cheek, and straightened his helmet. "Looks like we've got friends on that hill over there."

"Swell. Let's send them a present."

"Too bad I'm out of cigarettes."

Captain Newman stood by a C-47 cargo plane with Lt. Martin Quincy. While Tom was built like a baseball player, Quincy had a linebacker's physique, complete with a face that looked like it had taken too many tackles.

Newman smiled at Tom. "Glad you decided to join us. How's your platoon? Any news from Lieutenant Reed's platoon?"

"Platoon intact. No word on Reed. Our equipment here?"

"Unloading at Arzeu. Quincy has his platoon and squad tool sets."

Tom avoided Quincy's gaze. "Lehman's squad lost their set on the beach, but we've got the rest." More like they decided it was too heavy to carry and they ditched it.

Quincy snorted. "Lehman needs a good whipping."

Newman's face had a pinched look. "We need those tools."

"I know, sir. Maybe someone will find the kit and send it to us."

Quincy fluttered his hands by his shoulders. "Maybe the tool fairy will put it under your pillow at night."

Tom laughed as if the joke didn't have a mean, sarcastic edge. "Maybe she'll bring a pillow too while she's at it."

"We'll have to make do." Newman crossed his arms over his field jacket. "Here's the story—Quincy and his men did a quick survey. The runway's got some shell damage, not too much. The buildings are intact, but we need to do a thorough sweep for mines and sabotage. I'll put Quincy to work on the runway, and Gill, your men will check out the buildings."

"Yes, sir." He and Larry returned to where the platoon lounged under a palm tree. "Okay, boys, airfield's secure and we've got a job."

Rinaldi rolled onto his back. "Ah, Gill. We've been at it since midnight. We need a rest."

"You got one. Come on, this is why we're here."

"I'm finishing this orange first." Butler held up a glossy beauty. "I need my nutrients. I'm a growing boy."

The men didn't budge. They chatted and joked and tried to steal Butler's orange.

Tom fingered the strap for his musette bag, the small haversack that held his necessities. He glanced behind him, where Quincy's men lined up. With a single barked command, Quincy's platoon was ready for action.

Tom's smile felt stiff and useless. He needed to get his men to work, but how?

Rinaldi grabbed Butler's orange, held it to his cheek, and danced around, singing "Tangerine."

"Hey, fellows," Tom called out. "First squad to finish their job—I'll buy them oranges."

Thirty-nine heads swiveled to him. Thirty-nine pairs of eyes lit up. Thirty-nine men got to their feet.

Tom outlined their tasks, divided up the buildings, and

reminded them to watch for booby traps. A squadron of Spitfires was scheduled to arrive from Gibraltar late in the afternoon, and the base needed to be ready.

The squads headed for the buildings, and Tom smiled at Larry. "Now I just have to find thirteen oranges."

"Hank and Bob and I will take care of that." The platoon's jeep and truck drivers had nothing to do until the vehicles arrived.

"Thanks, Larry. I appreciate it." Tom pulled some crisp new francs from his wallet.

"I hope it'll always be this easy to bribe the men."

"Yeah." A frown threatened Tom's face. He wouldn't always be able to bribe them. Then what? How could he convince them to do a job they didn't want to do?

7

Bowman Field
November 16, 1942

"Voila!" Kay Jobson struck a model's pose, gesturing to the litter bracket she and Alice Olson had assembled in the C-47.

Mellie joined the other nurses in applause. Assembling the aluminum brackets required many steps and plenty of practice. Since the planes carried cargo and troops to the front, litter supports had to be assembled after they landed and unloaded. C-47 crewmen grumbled about how the 218 pounds of equipment reduced the amount of cargo they could transport. There had to be a better way.

"Excuse me, ladies. I'm looking for Lieutenant Blake," a corporal called through the open cargo door.

"That's me."

"Lieutenant Lambert and Captain Maxwell want to speak with you, ma'am."

"Right now?" She couldn't afford to miss the drill.

"Yes, ma'am."

Alice and Vera exchanged a knowing look.

"I'm coming." Mellie eased her way down the ladder, straightened her skirt, and followed the corporal to the headquarters buildings. If only they'd issue trousers to the women.

Why did Lambert and Maxwell insist on meeting her now, when she was about to learn something useful? With such haphazard training, would they ever be ready to do some good? The wounded deserved air evacuation. The Marines continued to take heavy casualties on Guadalcanal. In North Africa the French had capitulated after three days of battle, and now the Army could drive east and fight the Germans, who were pouring into Tunisia.

Had the engineer gone to North Africa? His battalion was stationed in England, and he said he'd head to combat soon. In her reply she'd nicknamed him Ernest. He seemed like an earnest man, and she liked the allusion to the play *The Importance of Being Earnest*, with its mistaken identities and name mix-ups.

She'd added Ernest to her daily prayers.

The corporal held the door open for Mellie.

"Thank you." She went down the hallway to the chief nurse's office.

"Please have a seat, Philomela." Lieutenant Lambert pointed to a chair across from her desk. Captain Maxwell stood by the window.

"Thank you, ma'am."

The chief fingered a pen on her desk. "As you know, we're on shaky ground. On Wednesday we activated three squadrons, but on Thursday General Arnold declared there would be no light air evacuation. So today I have to make some decisions."

"Oh dear." The commanding general of the Army Air Forces had restricted them? Would he allow any air evacuation at all?

Lieutenant Lambert raised her head, a hesitant look in her brown eyes. "They doubt us. They believe women are prone to cattiness and gossip and can't be trusted with important matters. Many men would love to see us fail."

"I understand, ma'am." But why was she only talking to Mellie?

"Each squadron must run as a team. In the field, we'll need to rely on each other. If you girls don't get along, the brass will see it as a sign of feminine weakness and undependability."

Mellie's lips tingled.

Lieutenant Lambert frowned at her pen. "I don't know how to say this, Philomela. You've been here two weeks. Your flight of six nurses is the least cohesive here at Bowman. And every time I look, you're alone."

A band of pain constricted around Mellie's chest. "I tend to keep to myself."

Captain Maxwell crossed his arms and huffed. "That's the problem."

Lambert tapped her pen on the desk. "I indulged in a phone call to Edna Newman at Walter Reed. Now, she wanted me to know what a competent and caring nurse you are. The patients sing your praises. But the girls—well, she said you didn't have a single friend there."

Mellie blinked hard. "It's never interfered with my work, ma'am."

The chief grimaced. "I understand, but this isn't a ward. We have to work together, and we can't let one person drag us down. This is too important for the future of nursing, for all the wounded men who need our care. We cannot fail."

"I won't drag you down. I'll make an excellent flight nurse."

"I'm sure you would—if you could work independently. When I looked at your application, I was impressed by your time in the wilderness. You have skills that would be useful to us in the field, but only if you share them. This must be a team effort or we'll fail. You need to get along with the other nurses."

Captain Maxwell paced to the other side of the room.

"No room for hermits here. Plenty of other nurses—friendly, pretty girls—would love to take your place."

Mellie gripped her hands together hard in her lap. She mustn't succumb to tears. "I want to be a flight nurse. More than anything. What do I need to do?"

Lieutenant Lambert shot the surgeon a quick glance, then back to Mellie. "You need to show improvement. You need to make some effort. I'll give you one more week, but no longer."

Mellie had failed to make a friend in twenty-three years of life, and now she had one week. Impossible. "One week?"

The chief leaned over the desk, her eyes filled with compassion. "I do want you to succeed, Philomela."

"Thank you, ma'am." She tried to smile but couldn't.

The chief dismissed her, and Mellie escaped out into the hallway. Her vision blurred over, and she couldn't see where she was going. She leaned against the wall, out of sight of the office.

What now? Competent and caring wasn't enough? She had to have friends too?

She'd found a job she was passionate about, a job that used all her skills for great good, where she knew she could succeed and excel. Suddenly a wall loomed before her, a wall she couldn't climb.

All her life, always rejected. In the Philippines, the girls didn't like her because she was too American, and in America, the girls didn't like her because she dressed funny and wore her hair funny and her smile split her face in half—like a monkey, they said.

Mellie's eyes stung and she swiped tears away. Ernest knew how to make friends. Perhaps she could ask him for advice. Yes, she'd write another letter and ask him.

But it would be too late. She had a week, only a week. A sob gurgled in her throat.

"Better look for her replacement." That was Captain Maxwell's voice.

Mellie sucked in her breath. Eavesdropping was rude. She should leave, but her feet wouldn't budge.

"I am." Irritation tinged Lieutenant Lambert's voice. "Please remember, you are in charge of your flight, but I make the personnel decisions for the nurses."

"Can you at least find someone who doesn't look like she's wearing a beehive on her head?"

Mellie clapped her hands over her ears and dashed out of the building. A beehive? Her fingers explored the braids that wound from her hairline up to her crown.

All her life people had made fun of her hair. Was that the problem? If she cut her hair and looked more like the other women, would she be able to make friends?

Through her hazy vision, she made out the nursing quarters. She strode inside and into her empty room.

Georgie's sewing scissors sat on her bunk on top of folded blue fabric. Mellie grabbed them and wheeled to the little mirror over the sink. She couldn't change her darker skin tone or her wide slash of a mouth.

But she could change her hair.

Mellie held the scissors between her and her image. Her long hair was part of her identity. Who would she be without it?

She gazed deep into her own dark eyes, which looked so much like her mother's eyes in the single photograph she owned.

Her mother. The haircut started it, her father said. If she hadn't bobbed her beautiful long hair, she wouldn't have plummeted into decadence and neglected Papa and Mellie. And she wouldn't be dead.

Mellie's head slumped, and she braced her hands on the edge of the sink. The scissors clattered inside. She couldn't do that to Papa. He lived. He had to live. And when he returned, she wanted him to find his little Mellie just as he left her.

She raised her head and studied her face, so different from every other woman she knew. Would a haircut have made a difference anyway? Would women flock to her because of a haircut? Would she trust their friendship if they did?

"No," she whispered.

She swayed, and she gripped the sink for support. Now what? She had a week to make friends or she'd lose the chance to become a flight nurse.

If she couldn't or wouldn't change her appearance, that left her behavior. How could she learn in one week what other women had learned over a lifetime?

Sounds outside drew her attention, and she peeked out the window around the yellow ruffled curtains Georgie had sewn. Men and women walked in small groups and passed each other with bright greetings. They made it look so easy.

In the distance, Georgie and Rose came into view. The C-47 drill must have been dismissed. Rose's sleek dark blonde head dipped closer to Georgie's brown curls. Their faces looked serious as they talked.

Mellie had overheard dozens of their conversations. They shared everything, from the mundane to the intimate. Openness seemed to be the foundation of their friendship.

A shiver ran through her. As a girl, whenever she'd shared anything about herself, the other girls were baffled or derisive. If she opened up here, she ran the high risk of rejection.

She retrieved the scissors from the sink and returned them to Georgie's bunk. Georgie and Rose had sat there when Mellie said ladies didn't shorten their hair. If she shared, she ran the risk of hurting others.

Mellie straightened her service jacket. For the sake of her dream, for the sake of becoming a true nightingale who brought comfort and mercy to others, not just on the ward but in the outside world, she had to take both risks. "Lord, I don't want to be rejected, and I certainly don't want to hurt others. Please help me."

She charged outside, to the wide blue sky, onto the open green lawn, away from the shelter of her forest.

Georgie and Rose strolled in her direction. They'd made friendly overtures in the past, and they were her only hope.

Mellie marched up and stopped right in front of them. "I want to make friends."

Rose's head tipped to one side, and Georgie's eyebrows elevated.

Mellie pressed her hands over her mouth. "That was awkward, wasn't it?"

"A bit." Georgie gave her half a smile, which melted into concern. "Have you—have you been crying?"

Mellie jerked her head toward the administration building. She nodded. "Lieutenant Lambert gave me one week. If I don't learn to get along with others, I'll be replaced."

Rose cleared her throat. "So you want to be friends with us to keep your job."

"No." She turned back. Alarm pulsed in her ears. How could she be open without hurting them? "All right, the deadline drove me, but I do want to make friends with you. I didn't fit in anywhere growing up, and I've never had friends. I'm tired of being alone. And I—I like the two of you. You're kind to each other, to me, to others. And you sing."

"We sing?" Georgie said.

"I like that."

Georgie cracked a smile. "You have a beautiful voice. We could use a soprano."

Mellie's shoulders relaxed. "I'm a soprano."

"We know." Rose winked at her.

A smile crept up Mellie's face, but she stopped before it scared them away. "To be honest, I don't know what to do next."

Georgie took Mellie's arm and tucked it under hers. "How about you join us at the mess for dinner? We'll get to know each other better and take it from there. Do you like that idea, Philomela?"

Mellie nodded. Her throat clamped shut, but she swallowed hard so she could speak. She wanted to give them something special, something she'd never given anyone but Papa. "Please. Please call me Mellie."

8

Oran, Algeria
November 21, 1942

"Best part of this leave—no mud," Larry Fong said. "Far cry from Tafaroui."

Tom chuckled. "Where the mud is deep and gooey." Rains had hit a few days after they secured the field, and as he'd predicted, created a mess. They needed pierced steel planking for quick runways and hardstands, but PSP was deemed a low shipping priority by someone in Washington who'd never winched a Spitfire out of ankle-deep red clay mud.

He and Larry gazed over Oran's harbor, where a break-water protected three wharves in the blue-green bay. Crews labored to clear wreckage. During the Torch landings the French had demolished most of the port facilities, and two Allied ships had been shot to pieces in a deadly, failed attempt at a frontal assault.

Tom turned and faced Oran's collection of sand-colored and whitewashed buildings. Rocky, scrub-covered hills cupped the city, and an old Spanish fort perched high on the west-ernmost hill.

The fighting had shifted to Tunisia, where the Allies made slow progress. Their goal was to meet up with Montgomery's

British Eighth Army approaching from Egypt and surround Rommel in Libya.

Tom inhaled briny air. "We've got a few hours. What do you want to do?"

"I want to buy something for my parents and sister. And I'm hungry."

"Me too. Let's hope we don't get dysentery."

"If so, we'll join the line at the dispensary when we get back."

Tom grunted. His whole platoon had come to town on leave today. Most had scattered to sample the red wine the Algerians produced in abundance—or to search for syphilis. They'd keep the battalion medical detachment busy.

Tom and Larry headed down a narrow street lined by four-storied buildings with wrought iron balconies and shuttered windows. Other than the garbage in the street, it looked like a postcard of Paris.

The leave motivated his men to work. The B-17 Flying Fortresses of the 97th Bombardment Group were transferring the next day from Maison Blanche Airfield near Algiers to escape constant attack from German planes based in Sicily. They needed more facilities at Tafaroui. Captain Newman had offered the company leave if they met the deadline. He'd looked at Tom when he said this, not at Quincy or Reed.

Bribery only went so far, but he refused to scream and threaten like Quincy or leave cold, imperious orders like Reed. In time, Tom's friendly persuasion would work. It had to.

A group of Arab boys in short dirty robes scampered past. They gave the Americans the "V for Victory" sign. "Okay! Okay!" they shouted.

Larry pulled a blue booklet from his pocket. "If only we learned Arabic as fast as they learned English."

The street opened up to a plaza lined with open-air stalls. "A bazaar," Tom said.

"A *souk*," Larry read from *Instructions for American Servicemen in North Africa*. "That's what it's called in Algeria."

"*Souk*." Thank goodness Newman had assigned Larry as his platoon sergeant. The man spoke French and was fascinated by the local culture. He made a good surface-level friend, but Tom couldn't afford to let him or anyone in deeper. Emotions acceptable for other men churned behind his smile, too dangerous to reveal.

Strong, exotic smells wafted in the air, and hundreds of people milled about—French men and women in European dress, Berbers and Arabs in turbans and robes, and American servicemen in uniform. After the French surrendered on November 11, everyone acted as if the three days of fighting had never happened.

"Great rugs," Larry said. The first stall held carpets fashioned in colorful diamond patterns. "Need one for your tent?"

"They'd go well with my crystal chandelier." Tom fingered the short wool loops on one of the rugs. "Wish I could send one to my mom. Kind of big."

"Smaller ones over here." Larry lifted a rug about two feet long. "My dad would like this."

The stall owner engaged in intense bargaining with a Frenchwoman, but he sent Tom a predatory salesman's glance.

"Let's keep looking," Tom said. "We can come back."

The next stall held baskets full of grains, and the one after that displayed citrus and figs and dates. Tom marked its location. At the end of the day, he'd buy a load of fruit to supplement the tinned rations and motivate the boys.

A salty sea breeze set items in the next stall jingling. Tom strolled over. Jewelry—that's what he'd get Mom.

Bangles and necklaces and earrings, much bolder than Mom wore, with bright stones set in copper or brass or silver, and lots of doohickeys dangling down. A bracelet caught his eye, formed of delicate links set with stones of cobalt blue, turquoise, olive, and amber. With her fair coloring and blue eyes, Mom would like that.

Tom turned to find the trader—and he saw the brooch. Concentric circles of the same stones as the bracelet surrounded a star of brilliant blue. Mom wouldn't wear it, but he saw Annie in his mind. At least Annie as he pictured her, unusual and exotic, with dark eyes and hair, the kind of girl who traipsed through jungles and drew birds.

Would she like a pin? Sure, she wore a uniform on the job and she probably didn't go out much, but why shouldn't she have something pretty, something unusual and exotic?

The trader sidled up, wearing a creamy turban and robe, speaking a long string of Algerian Arabic, and gesturing to the jewelry.

Tom racked his brain for the word for yes. *"Naam."*

"Naam? Mleh. Mleh." He smiled and stroked his curly black beard. More Arabic, maybe some French mixed in.

"Larry?" Tom said. "Need some help bargaining."

"How much you willing to pay? I'll start lower and work my way up."

Tom paused. Fifty francs to the dollar. "Hundred fifty each."

Larry spoke with the trader in French. He turned back to Tom, eyes big. "He only wants fifty."

"Wow." Tom pulled out some of the large French money. Seemed like stealing, but the trader grinned as if he were the thief.

Larry bought a necklace with red stones for his mother and a similar one in green for his sister.

At the next stall, the merchant held a bowl under their noses. "Couscous? Couscous?"

Tom stared into the bowl—little beady things, kind of like

Malt-O-Meal, with chunks of meat and vegetables on top. "Larry, any idea what *couscous* means?"

"Looks like a grain, but tastes like noodles. They cook it with gravy and lamb and vegetables." Larry waved the booklet in front of Tom. "You ought to read this thing."

"The same booklet that says, 'Little rainfall is experienced on the coast'?" Tom pointed to the bowl. "Want to try couscous?"

The merchant closed his eyes, smiled, and rubbed his stomach. "*Mleh. Mleh.*"

"*Mleh* means *good*," Larry said in a slow, high voice as if talking to a small child. "And yeah, I'd love something with flavor. I don't know how you white boys eat that bland stuff you call food every day. Must be why you're so pasty."

"Careful. You'll end up round eyed and pasty yourself."

Larry let out a low growl. "Make my life a lot easier."

"Nah. That's the coward's way out." That's what Mom told him every time he grumbled about changing his name. Cowardly and deceptive. It would be a lie, and lies were always exposed by the light. The truth might be difficult, painful, and alienating, but how could he lie every time he wrote his name?

The merchant seated them at a table that backed up to a low whitewashed wall, set bowls of couscous before them, and poured cups of minty-smelling green tea.

Tom dipped his spoon into the bowl. "Here goes." Strange spices hit his tongue, like nothing he'd ever tasted before. Not hot-spicy, just strange.

Larry mumbled in contentment. "Cumin, coriander, garlic, mint. There's more to seasoning than salt and pepper."

"Maybe one new seasoning at a time." Tom swallowed. This would take some getting used to. He scooped another spoonful.

Something brushed his leg.

He startled, and a chunk of meat dropped to the ground.

A little dog darted out and grabbed it.

Tom laughed. As a boy, he'd always had a dog. He picked out a chunk of meat—lamb wasn't his favorite anyway—and held it out, clucking his tongue.

The dog's pointed ears pricked up. His brown eyes honed in on Tom and sized him up with an intelligent look.

"Come here, little guy. You hungry?"

"Don't encourage him, Gill."

"He looks hungry. Come here, boy." Every one of the dog's ribs showed under his short-haired coat. Beautiful coloring—golden brown with white paws and chest. His tail curled in a complete circle, the underside white like a deer's.

He took a step toward Tom, then another, and snatched up the meat.

A shout rang out. The merchant dashed from the stall, waved his arms at the dog, and kicked at him. The dog ran off with impressive speed.

Tom sighed. Dogs listened and understood and didn't care about your name.

"You like dogs, huh?" Larry said. "Never had one."

"Never? They're the best. I had a beagle named Rufus when I was little. Best friend ever." Tom shoveled couscous into his mouth. Rufus had absorbed buckets of tears when his father was arrested, tried, and executed. He had to stay in California with an uncle when Tom and his mother moved back to Pennsylvania. Couldn't take him on the train, Mom said. He got a new dog in Pittsburgh, a spaniel named Molly. He loved Molly, but she could never replace Rufus.

Love didn't work that way.

"My sister wanted a cat," Larry said. "She'd sneak them into the apartment, and Mom would shoo them out. Mom keeps canaries."

Tom laughed. "That would be a disaster."

Larry's dark eyes glittered. "It was. Cat knocked over a cage once. The bird swooped around, the cat jumped at it. Mom chased the cat with her kitchen knife. I never laughed so hard in my life."

Tom grinned and took another spoonful. He had a strange sensation of someone standing behind him. Breath on his neck.

He tensed and turned, his spoon in front of him.

The little dog stood on the wall behind him, cocked his head to one side, and snatched the food from Tom's spoon.

"Why, you little thief." Tom laughed and extended his hand slowly. The dog consented, and Tom scratched him behind the ears. "Should expect that on the Barbary Coast—Ali Baba and the Forty Thieves."

"Barbary Coast was pirates," Larry said. "Ali Baba was in Arabia. You need to read more."

"I read plenty." The fur felt great to Tom's fingers, and the dog leaned into Tom's hand. The mutt needed a friend, a provider. And a bath. Tom offered him another chunk of lamb. "Here, boy. Open, sesame."

The dog gobbled the meat and made a funny chortling sound.

Tom laughed. "Is that your name? Is Sesame your name?"

"Come on, Gill. Don't name it."

Tom rubbed Sesame behind the ears. If he could give his platoon something to rally around, something to instill identity and pride, the men would work because they wanted to.

"He needs a name. He needs a home." Tom flashed Larry a grin. "And our platoon needs a mascot."

9

Bowman Field
November 23, 1942

Mellie shivered. If she could move around, the damp, chill wind blowing over the airfield would be more bearable, but she stood at attention with all the nurses assigned to the 349th Air Evacuation Group. For the last time.

Her week of grace concluded today, but whenever Lieutenant Lambert came around, Mellie seemed to be alone. Would her efforts be in vain? She shivered again.

Standing next to her, Rose nudged her. "What's the matter, California girl? Too cold for you?"

"So much colder in Virginia, huh?" Mellie whispered, although the visiting brass were still inside the C-47, watching a demonstration.

"We get snow. We're hardy folk." Georgie had a smile in her voice.

"You?" Rose laughed. "You're ride-a-horse hardy, not camp-in-the-Yukon hardy."

"Six months in Alaska," Georgie said. "I'm hardy."

"Six months huddled by the stove, you mean."

"No, you're mean."

Mellie chuckled. She felt more like a referee than a participant in this friendship. Rose and Georgie's relationship dated to early childhood, complete with the teasing, squabbles, and love of a lifetime together. Mellie would never share what they did, but she was grateful to be included.

She'd written more letters to Ernest the engineer, describing her blossoming friendship. Too many letters, perhaps. Would he see her as desperate and run away? Or would he be pleased at her efforts, pleased that he'd encouraged her? And would he help her learn how to make friends?

Rose and Georgie had helped. They'd gently told her the other girls thought she was conceited because she never smiled. So Mellie experimented with a partial smile and prayed it would be enough. Every day, she reminded herself to greet people and make small talk, same as she would with patients on the ward. Overcoming shyness was hard work.

And Lieutenant Lambert hadn't even noticed. Mellie's dream of serving as an adventurous pioneer flying mercy to the battlefield evaporated, leaving her emptier than before the dream came. The Bible was true: "Hope deferred maketh the heart sick."

"Ssh!" The hiss started with the women closest to the cargo door and worked its way down the line. The nurses stood taller and straighter.

A man descended the ladder and pulled his service jacket down over his paunch—Colonel Casey of Troop Carrier Command. He offered a hand to help Lieutenant Lambert, Vera, and Kay down the ladder. Lieutenant Lambert had chosen Vera and Kay to conduct the demonstration as the most experienced of the nurses.

Vera flashed Colonel Casey her winning smile, with a touch of a flirtatious chin dip.

Mellie wrinkled her nose. The purpose of this demonstration was to convince the brass of the importance of medical air evacuation and of the nurses' capability. Flirting could help their cause—or shatter it.

Casey grinned and sucked in his stomach. Flirting worked with him.

Colonel Alberts of the Medical Corps emerged from the plane and then General Schmidt from Army Air Force Headquarters in Washington. Tall and dashing, Schmidt fit the role of an aviator.

Vera and Kay returned to the ranks of nurses, and the three visitors approached a podium. The chief nurses and flight surgeons stood to the side.

General Schmidt tapped the microphone. "Thank you, ladies, for an informative demonstration. We will take it into consideration when we make our decision."

Mellie frowned. That didn't sound promising.

The general launched into a speech about the demands on the Army Air Forces and the many commands vying for scarce personnel and supplies.

While the general spoke, Colonel Casey smiled at the ranks with his gut cinched in. The Air Evacuation Group needed his planes, facilities, and personnel. Did he smile because he was on their side or because dozens of curvy figures stood before him?

Colonel Alberts glanced at his watch. The Medical Corps controlled health care in the Army, but physicians ran the Corps, and some held nurses in low regard. Would they cede decision-making power to a nurse, even for the length of a flight?

General Schmidt, for all his dash, fixated on supplies and manpower. When he reminded the women of the dangers of flight and combat, Mellie's breath drained out of her. The Army would return the nurses to the safe little hospitals where they belonged. The dream would die for all these women.

He wrapped up his speech and stepped down from the podium. No one replied.

Everyone shook hands, the visit over, the cause lost.

Why didn't anyone speak up? Sick and wounded soldiers deserved the best possible care. Wasn't that worth the sacrifice of resources? This was the time for bold speech.

Mellie glanced around. No one stepped forward. No one was willing to risk a reputation or career.

Her breathing stopped. What about her?

Her favorite Bible verse, Micah 6:8, said, "What doth the Lord require of thee, but to do justly, and to love mercy, and to walk humbly with thy God?" Was she willing to sacrifice for the sake of justice and mercy?

Why not her? After years as the only female on Papa's expeditions, she knew how to stand up to men. And public speaking bothered her less than personal conversation.

Of all the women, she had the least to lose since she'd be leaving anyway. She'd formed the flimsiest of friendships with Georgie and Rose, but Vera, Alice, and Kay hadn't warmed in the slightest.

Speaking up would assure her dismissal, but the hope of air evacuation for all those wounded soldiers meant more to her than her job.

If she had to leave, she might as well leave with a bang.

Mellie stepped out of rank and marched forward several paces.

"What are you doing?" Rose said in a harsh whisper.

"Excuse me, sirs!" She stood tall, her hands relaxed at her sides, although her heart flopped around in her chest.

Colonel Casey turned to her, eyebrows raised. Colonel Alberts and General Schmidt remained in conversation.

A buzz of whispers ran through the nurses, and the other members of the brass faced her.

"Excuse me, General Schmidt, sir. May I have permission to speak?" Her training in military etiquette was inadequate, and she'd probably broken countless rules.

The general gave her a quizzical look, then turned to the chief nurses and flight surgeons. Lieutenant Lambert whispered something then gave Mellie an incredulous look. Captain Maxwell glowered across the tarmac at her.

She drew a deep breath and focused on General Schmidt.

He crossed his arms over his chest. "Permission granted, Lieutenant . . . ?"

"Lt. Philomela Blake, sir, and I have something to say."

"So I see." One corner of his mouth tipped. "Proceed."

"Thank you, sir." Mellie swallowed hard. "We're so glad you came today. As you can see, air evacuation would be an efficient use of scarce resources. Since cargo planes carry supplies or troops in only one direction, it makes sense to carry the wounded on the return flight, relieving pressure on ambulance services."

The general cocked an eyebrow at her.

Second thoughts trembled inside, but she pressed on and offered a small smile. "Since manpower is short, it also makes sense to give the wounded prompt medical care so they can return to service as quickly as possible. What could be speedier than air evacuation?"

"Exactly, sir."

Mellie whipped her gaze to her right. Kay Jobson stood beside her, smiling at the general.

"Lieutenant Blake is right," Kay said. "In a few hours, a plane can cross a mountain range while an ambulance would take days. Swamps, jungles? Not a problem in the air. And a plane can cross oceans without worrying about U-boats."

Mellie shook off the shock of Kay helping her. She had more points to make. "Won't the men on the front feel better if their wounded buddies are whisked to safety under the care of a trained, professional nurse?"

"Absolutely," Kay said. "Knowing the same care awaits them if they need it. High morale . . ." Her lovely eyes scanned the cluster of men. "High morale is a scarce commodity indeed."

General Schmidt nodded, his forehead knit together under his service cap.

Mellie chomped back a chuckle. The ladies spoke his language. One more serious point to make. "Thank you, sir, for your concern about our safety. But remember, the women of Britain have courageously endured months of bombings. Surely we'll be just as brave as our British sisters. Wouldn't you agree, sir?"

How could he disagree with such a statement? "Well, of course. Of course, young lady."

Kay took another step forward. "We're eager to serve, sir. Not one of us is scared of flying or combat. Many of us are trained stewardesses. We're here because we love to fly, we care about our servicemen, and we love our country."

If only they had a flag to wave.

The general surveyed the rows of nurses. "Ladies, do you agree with your colleagues?"

A warm murmur built behind Mellie. "Yes, sir."

Mellie met Kay's gaze. Kay gave her the quickest wink and faced the brass. Perhaps Kay had warmed to her after all. The thought turned up the corners of Mellie's mouth.

General Schmidt lifted a salute. "Thank you, ladies. If nothing else, you're courageous—and persuasive. I'll take this into consideration."

Mellie saluted back. "One more thing, sir."

"One more thing?"

"We want to wear trousers."

Someone gasped behind Mellie.

"Trousers?" the general said. "Isn't that rather unladylike?"

"It's practical, sir. You watched the demonstration. We squat and climb and lean over to perform our duties. If we wore trousers, we could concentrate on our work, not our modesty."

"I agree, sir," Kay said. "If one more soldier looks up my skirt—I don't care how sick he is—I'll smack him." She lifted a sweet smile. "Sir."

Stifled giggles swept the ranks.

The general turned to the chief nurses. "Trousers? Do you endorse this?"

Lieutenant Lambert clasped her hands in front of her. "Well, sir, trousers would be warmer than skirts. And it would be easier for the women to put on a parachute harness in case of emergency."

"We'll take that into consideration as well."

More salutes, more handshakes, and the brass departed.

Mellie turned to Kay. "You said you'd shock me someday. You just did. Thank you for standing up for me."

"Standing up for my *job*. Besides, I didn't want you to have all the fun." Half a smile, and she left to join Vera and Alice, who hugged her.

"Goodness sake, Mellie." Georgie grabbed her hand and gave it a tight squeeze. "You were so brave, so bold."

"Someone had to say it. Why not me?"

Rose shook her head and grinned. "We didn't know you had it in you. My, oh my."

Lieutenant Lambert strode toward Mellie. "Lieutenant Blake, may I have a word with you?"

"Pray for me," Mellie whispered.

"We will," Rose and Georgie said.

The chief nurse motioned to Mellie, and they fell in step. "You surprised me today, Lieutenant."

"Sorry, ma'am. I feel strongly about the benefits of air evacuation."

"I noticed. I meant I was surprised to hear you speak up at all."

"I grew up with men. I can handle men—in a professional setting, at least. Women, on the other hand . . . well, I don't always understand them."

The chief nurse laughed. "Do we understand ourselves most of the time?"

Mellie let herself smile. "Perhaps not."

"Your week is up."

"I know." A soft sigh escaped and blended into the wind.

The chief gave her a compassionate look. "You've made changes, and I see you've made some friends."

So she'd noticed after all. "I'm trying, ma'am."

Lieutenant Lambert gazed across the tarmac and held back her brown hair against the wind. "Captain Maxwell is not happy. He says you could have endangered our cause today. A lot of men don't like outspoken women."

Mellie crossed her arms across the dark blue wool of her service jacket. "I'm sorry. I tried to be polite and diplomatic, but—"

"You were. You did a great job. That little speech helped." Lieutenant Lambert stopped and flipped up a smile. "And I like outspoken women."

Words slipped around Mellie's mouth but couldn't gain their footing. Did that mean she'd get a second chance?

Lieutenant Lambert patted Mellie's arm. "Don't worry about Maxwell. I'll take care of him. You just keep up the effort with the other women, okay?"

The adventure of friendship and air evacuation outshone the forest. "I will."

10

Constantine, Algeria
December 6, 1942

"Come on, boy. Not much farther." Tom led Sesame through the crowded depot and outside, where the dog bolted for the first bush. Though he weighed only twenty pounds, he was strong and fast, and Tom gripped the leash he'd fashioned from leather belts from the *souk*.

He breathed in air untainted by cigarette smoke, body odor, and the other strong smells of the train. In front of him stood a statue of the Roman emperor Constantine, whom the city was named after. Beyond that lay Tom's objective.

"Hey, Sesame. Want a walk?" While the men of the battalion disembarked from the train, Tom used his pup as an excuse to explore what caught his eye at the end of the four-hundred-mile train ride. He crossed the road in front of the station to a low stone wall.

"Wow." A gorge plunged beneath him, all rugged red rock, with scrubby bushes and palm trees at the bottom. On the far side of the gorge, the city's buildings grew, their walls extending straight up from the face of the canyon.

And a bridge. His pulse quickened. A good, old-fashioned stone arch bridge stood to his right, and a beautiful one.

Larry had told him there were Roman ruins in Constantine, even an old viaduct. Unlikely Tom would have a chance to see that. He was here to build an airfield, not to sightsee. He etched the bridge's massive curves into his memory and turned back to the station, a yellow building with a tile roof and arched windows.

"Come here, Ses." The dog trotted back from the end of his leash, and Tom petted the smooth ridge of his back, unfurling the tail. It sprang back into its coiled position. "Okay, boy. Back to work."

At the tracks, the men of the 908th unloaded heavy equipment and vehicles from flatbed train cars. Tom hooked Sesame's leash to his belt loop, gathered his platoon, and assigned his men to trucks and jeeps for the ride to the construction site, about thirty miles southwest of Constantine, near a village called Telergma.

A week before, the Allied advance in Tunisia had stalled at Djedeïda, only fifteen miles from Tunis. The Germans held the coastal plains with great airfields, while the Allies were stuck in the mountains and had only three muddy airfields within two hundred miles of the front.

The Luftwaffe's air superiority made the Allies stop to regroup, and now the Germans had launched a counteroffensive.

The Allies needed more airfields, drier and closer to the front.

Tom headed to his jeep. He was building a bridge of a different sort, to connect bombers to their targets and fighter planes to the troops and ships they needed to protect. For now, it would do.

Captain Newman joined Tom's jeep driver, Hank Carter, in the front seat, while Tom sat in the back with Sesame and the men's musette bags. The larger barracks bags would follow in the trucks.

As the convoy lumbered out of Constantine, Hank studied the sky as much as the road. German Stuka dive-bombers menaced the front, but the Luftwaffe wouldn't venture toward Telergma until they realized an airfield was being built.

Sesame poked his head over the side of the jeep, and the wind buffeted his ears. Soon he lay down with his head in Tom's lap, and Tom pulled out the latest letter from his mother to read again. To pray over again. The last section made his stomach squirm.

> Thank you for telling me of your anonymous correspondence. However, I do feel you'd be better off with a journal. A few things cause me concern. What if you get accustomed to being open with this woman and forget to maintain the cheerfulness that serves you so well? What if you become attached to her—or she to you—and reveal your identities? What if she rejects you? I'm afraid you'll set yourself up for a broken heart, and perhaps her as well.
>
> You're a wonderful young man, Tom, and someday a godly young woman will see that. In the meantime, please don't settle for what looks like the easy road but could be the road to heartbreak.

Yep, his stomach still squirmed. He didn't worry about himself, but he'd never thought about breaking Annie's heart. She said she wasn't looking for romance, but what if they did fall for each other? He could handle unrequited love. He'd done it before. But what about her? What if she insisted on revealing their identities? He couldn't risk linking his name and his true self. It would be over.

Who was he kidding? It hadn't even started. Most of the men had received responses. Maybe his first letter had been too secretive and raised alarms for her. Or maybe the deluge of shipboard letters made her think he was deranged.

He smiled and stroked his dog's sleeping head. Oh well. It was fun while it lasted.

Up in the front seat, Captain Newman let out a loud groan. "I don't know why on earth I let my wife talk me into this."

"Into what, sir?"

"This stupid *Shop Around the Corner* thing. These blasted letters." He held up a handful of envelopes. "Sort them out. Figure out which letters go to which man. Then package up the letters for the girls. I feel like I'm running a matchmaking service, not a battalion."

Tom sent him a grin. "Sorry, sir."

"Yeah, you and your pile of letters. At least she doesn't write as much as you do. Only two here."

Tom's heart turned over. "Two?"

"Yeah." He flipped through his map case and handed back two envelopes with "Gill" scrawled on them in masculine script. "Last time I let my wife have her way."

"Yeah." His voice felt stiff, his fingers like chunks of wood. Annie had written him back. Two letters. That meant she wanted to correspond. With him.

He jammed a finger under the lip of the first envelope and worked it open, then the second. One was written November 7, the other November 16. She wouldn't have received his shipboard letters yet. He unfolded the first letter. In the top right corner, she had drawn a cardinal sitting on a maple branch.

Dear Ernest,

Since you didn't suggest a nickname for yourself, this is what I chose. If you've read *The Importance of Being Earnest*, you know it's about a man who takes a name that isn't his own, and a comedy of mistaken identities follows. I also think Ernest is a fine, solid name. If you prefer something else, let me know. I'm fine with Annie.

I was surprised to receive a reply, but pleased. I can't imagine why you were intrigued by my letter, unless it was truly one lonely soul responding to another. That's why I replied as well.

Each of us has a barrier to friendship. Despite your barrier, you've managed to attract friends on at least a superficial level. This interests me. I hope our correspondence will help me learn to make friends too. Is that selfish of me? Perhaps our letters will also help you deepen your friendships. We can certainly pray about it.

So what shall I talk about? My odd upbringing? My social inadequacies? My meditations on Scripture? Sweet stories of my father? Friendship is unfamiliar to me, and I don't know how to proceed. But I have to start somewhere.

Last week I transferred to a new unit, which offers wonderful opportunities and challenges.

However, a new base always means a few weeks of settling in. The nicest girls try to include me, I respond in an awkward manner, they give up, and then I retreat to my usual solitude. In the meantime, whenever possible, I stroll in the forested hills and enjoy the soft fall of rain and the song of the cardinal in the maples.

As for you, please tell me anything you'd like within the constraints of anonymity and military censorship.

Not knowing what else to say, I'll sign "my" name.

Annie

Tom's throat felt thick, like it did when he had a cold. "Thank you, Lord," he whispered.

She was hesitant and warm and vulnerable and honest. And she needed him as he needed her.

He wanted to shout over the ocean so she'd get his answer immediately. Yes, write about anything at all, but write and write and write.

He proceeded to the second letter. No drawing this time.

Dear Ernest,

I hesitate to write you again. My reply couldn't have reached you yet, and I haven't received any further letters from you. Since you're overseas, the process could take a month or more.

I need advice, and you're the only one I can think to ask.

Even if you have only superficial friends, you present yourself in such a way that others accept your company, even seek it. I need to learn this. My job depends on it. My new chief nurse told me if I don't make friends with the nurses, I won't be able to stay. This job fulfills my dreams to travel and be independent and blaze new paths, and I'm heartbroken.

Two of the nurses reached out to me at the beginning, until my awkwardness pushed them away. Today, after the chief nurse gave me a one-week deadline, I reached out to them. I've never done anything like this before in my life. It was extremely uncomfortable, but they're kind souls and sat with me at dinner. I think it went well, although I have nothing to compare it to.

I know I need to trust in the Lord, but honestly, Ernest, this terrifies me. Whenever I've opened up to others in the past, it's always ended in rejection.

If you have any advice, I'll take it.

Here I've gone on for a page about myself and not asked you a single question. Do you see why I need advice about making friends?

Please forgive me. How are you? I don't know if you've joined the most recent large invasion, and I know you can't tell me, but I'm praying extra hard in case you have. I hope you'll reply. I'd love to hear your stories and dreams and thoughts.

My prayers are with you.

Annie

Tom's chest felt lighter, as if all the air over Africa had entered and lifted him up, filling him with enticing strangeness. A true friendship lay before him in all its uncertainty and promise. For the first time since his father's death, he could be genuine with another person. Best of all, this friendship wouldn't be one-sided. She'd asked for his advice, and that made him feel bigger and stronger.

Mom had made her point. He'd be careful with Annie's heart and make sure she knew their friendship could never grow beyond anonymity. But this was too good a gift, and all good gifts came from the Lord. How could he turn away God's graciousness?

He returned the letters to their envelopes, settled back in his seat, and rubbed Sesame's ears. *Sesame and Annie—thank you, Lord.*

The convoy wound its way through a village and turned south to a raised plain. Tom leaned forward in his seat. "Is this it?"

"Yep," Captain Newman said. "Telergma."

When the jeep stopped, Tom climbed out and unleashed Sesame. The dog was a good little hunter and always returned.

A cool wind brushed his cheeks. He squatted down and crumbled soil in his fingers. More sand content than clay, not unexpected so close to the Sahara Desert. The Twelfth Air Force had done well selecting the site. The high ground and sandy soil would drain well. The open land had good approaches for aircraft.

Tom strolled along as trucks and jeeps parked and men unloaded. Few trees or bushes to remove. Of course that meant less lumber for building and fuel for campfires. He kicked at a boulder. That would have to go, but he didn't see too many obstacles.

The runway would run east to west, aligned with the prevailing wind. Buildings and control tower to the north. He could see it in his mind. Tonight he'd set down plans with the other officers.

Tom turned his face to the pale sun. "Then I've got a letter to write."

11

Bowman Field
December 11, 1942

Captain Maxwell distributed cardboard boxes to the eight tables in the classroom, ending with Mellie's flight of six nurses. He set a box in front of Vera Viviani and flashed her a grin. "This is the only one you get, ladies. Plasma is a precious resource. Treat it with care."

"Of course, sir." Vera glanced through her long lashes. "I treat everything with care."

"I'm sure you do. You ladies are fine examples of—" His gaze landed on Mellie. His smile twitched.

Although her heart folded in two, Mellie turned to the box and patted it. "Let's get started."

"This is exciting, isn't it?" Georgie gave her shoulders a cute little lift. "Someday we'll get to administer plasma in flight."

Maxwell returned to the front of the classroom. The nurses would keep the handsome surgeon busy with questions they really didn't need to ask.

Vera pulled the box to her end of the table, Alice tore off the tape, and Kay lifted the lid.

Mellie frowned. They only had one box and needed to share. Should she speak up? "I think that box is for all six of us."

Alice looked up with wide innocent eyes. "Oh . . . well, of course. But there's only enough work for two or three."

Mellie chewed on her lip. "Perhaps we could put it in the center of the table so everyone could see, then we could take turns performing the steps."

A corner of Vera's mouth flicked up. "Who put you in charge?"

Mellie dropped her gaze to the table. She thought she'd been polite, but she'd failed again.

"Come on, Vera." Rose held up her hands, palms outstretched. "Mellie has a point. We'll fly alone, so each of us needs to know how to do it. This may be our only training."

Mellie glanced around the room. The other flights of nurses cooperated, laughing and helping each other. "In the field, we'll need to work together."

Kay reached in the box and used a drawstring to pull out two tall tin cans. She set them smack in the middle of the table. "I don't want to do all the work around here."

Alice's face reddened, and Vera pursed her lips.

Kay flipped her strawberry blonde hair off her shoulders. "Rose, Georgie, open the cans. We'll go clockwise. Is that fair, Philomela-Mellie?"

She nodded. "Thank you. And please call me Mellie." She couldn't tell if Kay's teasing was friendly or mean-spirited, but at least they'd all get to train. They needed it.

Something had shifted in Washington. Generals called for air evacuation in the Pacific and North Africa, and everyone rushed to get the nurses off the ground. On November 30, Gen. David Grant, the Air Surgeon, made a public call to recruit flight nurses. Bowman Field buzzed with activity. The day before, two squadrons were officially activated and named the 801st and 802nd Medical Squadrons, Air Evacuation, Transport. Mellie was in the 802nd.

Rose and Georgie pried keys off the tops of the tin cans and opened the lids. A little whoosh signaled the breaking of the vacuum. They laid out the contents of the cans—a 300-cc glass bottle of sterile water, a bottle containing translucent white flakes of dried plasma, rubber IV tubing, and needles.

Mellie scanned the instructions that came in the box, then passed them on to the others. "First we need to transfer the water to the plasma bottle." After she wiped both stoppers with rubbing alcohol, she poked a double-ended needle through the rubber stopper in the water bottle. Tilting both bottles sideways, she inserted the other end of the needle into the plasma bottle. Water gurgled through and wet the flakes.

Vera took the bottle assembly and swirled it to dissolve the plasma. "It's losing the vacuum. Must not have been done right."

Mellie winced. She'd been very careful.

Georgie patted Mellie's forearm and smiled at Vera. "Sometimes that happens. That's why they include an airway needle."

Vera inserted the needle into the rubber stopper of the water bottle. Air rushed in, and the water resumed its flow. "What are your plans tonight, gals?"

Georgie pushed the rubber IV tubing to Alice. "Rose and Mellie and I are going to see *The Road to Morocco* at the Palace Theater downtown—Bob Hope, Bing Crosby, and Dorothy Lamour. Doesn't that sound fun? We'd love it if y'all joined us."

Vera, Alice, and Kay gave Georgie a blank look. The question hadn't been directed to her.

"Isn't that sweet of you?" Alice inclined her blonde head. "I'm going out with my boyfriend."

"I have a date," Vera said.

"Friday's Bill's night." Kay arched one eyebrow. "He ships out soon. Gotta give him something to fight for."

Mellie studied Kay's face. Why did she delight in shocking people? Why did she need so many men to feel complete? And what kind of hurt produced such behavior?

Alice giggled. "Gordon should give *me* something to fight for. I'm shipping out soon. He's staying here." Then her face stretched long. "I sure will miss him."

"I understand," Georgie said. "I'm going to miss Ward. At least here he can visit every once in a while. He's just a hopeless little boy when I'm away. Goodness, he was beside himself when I was in Alaska. But now I'll be overseas. Poor thing."

"Yes. Well." Alice pulled the water bottle and needle from the plasma bottle. "Why is it if a man goes overseas, his woman is supposed to wait for him, but if a woman goes overseas . . . ?" Her mouth crimped.

"Oh, honey." Georgie stretched one hand along the table toward Alice. "I know he'll wait."

Alice jerked up her head. "I didn't say he wouldn't."

Georgie's hand retracted.

Mellie stared at Alice. How could someone so beautiful have insecurities? And how could she snap at Georgie, who only wanted to give the whole world a hug?

She wanted to pat Georgie's arm or hand or something, whatever girls did. But would that comfort her or embarrass her?

Rose and Georgie exchanged a soft look, a twitch of a smile, a humorous lift of the eyebrows. How did they do that? Friendship took practice.

Mellie shouldn't have stopped at the PX on the way to the theater. If she'd known Ernest had written eight letters and they'd all arrive today, she would have waited. But now she sat on the bus, trying to read and absorb, while Rose and Georgie sat in the seat in front of her, watching with expectant grins.

> I'll never understand man's inhumanity to man. Just because his ancestors came from China, not Europe, my platoon sergeant gets teased, excluded, and worse. He's a good man—smart, funny, bighearted, but all they see is the color of his skin.
>
> Isn't that why we're fighting this war in the first place? Because the Germans hate the non-Germans? Because the Japanese hate the non-Japanese? How are we any better?
>
> Poor Annie, saddled with my rant. But that's one of the reasons I crave your friendship. I can't rant to anyone else. And this kind of nonsense makes my blood boil.

"Well?" Georgie's Southern drawl slung the word up the musical staff. "What's he have to say?"

Mellie wanted to soak in Ernest's words. He cared deeply about his men. He hated how people judged others. And he'd chosen her to confide in. Yet she lifted her head to engage with her friends. "He says all sorts of wonderful things."

"It's so romantic," Georgie said. "The meeting of two hearts, two minds."

"It's not romantic, it's—"

"I wish Lambert would set up something like that." Rose crossed her arms on the seat back and leaned her chin on her forearms. "About the only way I could meet a fellow."

Georgie nudged her with her shoulder. "Nonsense. A lovely girl like you? Give it time."

"You're the one talking nonsense." Rose wrinkled her freckled nose. "You're the sweet flower the boys buzz around. I'm the blunt-talking sidekick. In the movies the sidekick never gets the boy, or if she does, it's the hero's loudmouth best friend, and the sidekicks insult each other and exchange weird smacking kisses. That's not for me."

Mellie smiled although Ernest's open letter called to her. "The insults or the kisses?"

"Neither," Rose said with a laugh. "I want a fellow who says nice things to me and kisses me like I'm precious. Georgie has that with Ward. I want it too."

"Well, you can't have Ward." Georgie winked. "But we'll find you someone, right, Mellie?"

"Me?" She laughed. "I can't be much help. Men don't look at me unless I'm changing their bandages or giving them morphine."

"You did something right to get engineer-man to write eight letters," Rose said.

Mellie shook her head and stared at the letter in Ernest's square handwriting. She couldn't imagine what she'd done to deserve pages full of funny shipboard stories, deep musings on God, and insights on friendship and loneliness.

Her fingers itched for pen and stationery, but she tucked the envelopes into her Army Nurse Corps shoulder bag.

Rose looked out the bus window. "We're here, ladies. Louisville's finest theater."

"I love the Palace," Georgie said. "The theater alone is worth the ticket price."

"I can't wait to see it." Mellie stood and followed the girls off the bus.

"Ta-da!" Georgie swept her arm up to the marquee. "Isn't it grand?"

"Yes, it is." The façade of the Palace featured intricate carved masonry and a colorful marquee, which must have been even more impressive before wartime dimout regulations.

The women purchased their tickets and entered the lobby.

"Oh my." Mellie had never seen anything like it. An ornate carpet of red and blue and gold, a high vaulted ceiling, and walls and alcoves covered with frescoes and tiles and carvings in the Spanish baroque style, all in those riveting reds and blues and golds.

"Don't you feel like doing the flamenco?" Georgie struck a pose, one arm curved overhead, the other flung around her waist.

"Not now, Señorita Tayloroso." Rose linked her arm with Georgie, then extended an arm to Mellie. "Coming, Señorita Blakerado?"

With a slight hitch, Mellie lifted her arm. "Sí, sí, Rosita."

"Rosita. I like that. Better than Señorita Danilovez—can't even say that—goodness! Maybe the fellows would like me better with a name like Rosita."

Georgie led them up the carpeted stairs. "If you stopped fussing about the fellows, they would like you better. Now smile sweet at those flyboys."

Three men in leather flight jackets and pilot's "crush" caps trotted down the stairs toward them. "Be still, my heart," the shortest of the men said with a lopsided grin. "Do I see three lovely ladies in need of escort?"

"Nope." Rose pushed ahead, right through the threesome, Georgie and Mellie in her wake. "You see three lovely ladies about to ship out, perfectly capable of entertaining themselves, thank you."

Masculine laughter billowed up, and the tallest of the men trotted after them. "A spunky one. The blonde's mine."

Rose spun to face them. "The blonde is her own woman, and if she belonged to anyone, it wouldn't be to a cocky flyboy with more nerve than brains."

Georgie shot a funny look at Mellie behind Rose's back, and Mellie covered her mouth so she wouldn't laugh.

The flyboy took off his cap to reveal wavy blond hair, and he bowed. "I've got brains enough to know when I've met my match. Lt. Clint Peters, and I'm in awe."

"That makes one of us."

The third officer laughed. He had a square jaw and auburn hair peeking from under his cap. "Clint, you're outmatched. Ladies, I'll get him out of your hair."

"Uh-uh, Coop." Clint grabbed his buddy's arm. "This is Lt. Roger Cooper and this is Lt. Bert Marino, both single and available."

"But not looking," Roger said. "Now be a nice boy and leave the girls alone."

"I'm looking." Bert grinned at Georgie. "How 'bout you, curly-top?"

"That's sweet of you." She flushed and smiled. "But I have a boyfriend."

"Ah, they always do. You too, toots?" His gaze turned to Mellie and swept from her shoulders to her toes. A slow smile enveloped his round face. "Tell me you're single. Please."

Mellie's face and fingers tingled. Her jaw drifted down. Never had anyone looked at her or spoken to her like that. "Uh . . . I'm . . . not looking. Not looking." It worked for his buddy, why not her?

"Even if we were looking, we're not looking for the likes of you." Rose spun on her heels and marched up the steps. "Come on, ladies."

Mellie's feet felt like an elephant's, heavy and clumsy and too big. She almost tripped on a step but managed to catch up to the others.

Georgie laughed. "You sure told him, Rosita. But did you really want to? Didn't you just say you wanted the fellows to like you better? He sure likes you, and he's cute too."

"And full of himself."

"Maybe. But Mellie would be wise to stay away from that Bert."

She stopped at the top of the stairs and stared at Georgie. "No one's ever looked at me like that."

"Never? With a cute figure like yours? Oh, I doubt that. And you have the prettiest eyes, very exotic. Why, you'll get gobbled up if you're not careful."

Mellie's thoughts tumbled like a kaleidoscope. Papa always said she had an exotic beauty, but he was biased. She'd never heard that from anyone else. Mellie ventured a smile. "Rose knows how to beat them off."

"Stick with me, sister." Rose strode into the theater and led them to seats in the middle.

Mellie sat down and gaped at her surroundings. The theater resembled an open-air Spanish courtyard. Building façades lined the walls, and a brilliant blue ceiling arched overhead, pierced by starry white lights. "It's magnificent."

Rose nodded. "Gorgeous."

"Yes, you are," a gruff voice said from behind.

Mellie whipped around. The three airmen occupied the seats behind them.

Clint leaned forward on his knees, his eyes sparkling at Rose like the little lights above. "I've never believed in love at first sight—until now."

Rose lowered her chin. "See yourself in the mirror?"

Clint laughed. "Didn't I tell you, boys? She's the one for me."

"He does this all the time, doesn't he?" she said to Roger.

He frowned. "No. Actually, he doesn't. He's never done this before."

"I haven't." Clint's face lost the playful look. "First time ever. Because it's the first time I've seen you."

Rose spun back to face the screen and crossed her arms.

Mellie searched her face—the drawn mouth, the tented eyebrows, the wide eyes. Was Rose scared?

"What's your name?" Clint asked, his voice soft as a pillow.

Rose shook her head. Her eyes glistened.

Clint turned to Mellie. "Please. I need to know her name."

Mellie glanced back and forth between them. What if he'd told the truth and this was love at first sight and they were meant to be together? But no, Rose looked like she was about to cry. "Sorry," Mellie said.

"All right." Clint leaned close to the back of Rose's head. "I know the Lord brought us together tonight, and I know he'll bring us together again. Forever."

Rose's head jerked at the mention of the Lord's name.

The theater lights dimmed, and in the darkness, Rose wiped her eyes.

Mellie settled back in her seat. Was that what love was like? A sudden revelation? Or did it grow over a lifetime as it had for Georgie and Ward? Papa never related how he and her mother had fallen in love.

How much depended on looks? How much on personality? How much on hearts and minds?

She folded her hands over her shoulder bag, and Ernest's letters crinkled inside. A pureness about the relationship appealed to her, free of looks, free of the crass form of attraction that Bert fellow demonstrated.

It could never be love, but it could be wonderful.

12

Telergma, Algeria
December 12, 1942

"This is how my squad got the dozer, Gill. Honest." Sgt. Lou Moskovitz squatted by the M1 heavy tractor and picked dried mud from the track rollers. "When was the last time Kendrick cleaned this thing?"

"Don't know." Tom stood behind the wheel and peered at the two air pre-cleaners that stuck up from the hood like stumpy antennae. The dirt level rose to the top of the glass windows in the pre-cleaners. How much dirt had been allowed into the engine?

"Wow," Larry said from behind the dozer. "You should see the gunk in the sediment sump drains."

Tom squeezed his eyes shut, tipped back his helmet, and massaged his throbbing forehead. Dirt and water had accumulated in the fuel tank. Not good.

Kendrick came from a construction background, had experience with heavy equipment. Why had he neglected basic maintenance? The 908th couldn't afford to lose what little equipment it had.

Tom settled his helmet back in place and hopped to the ground. After several days of heavy rain, the battalion had a chance to finish the airfield in the next day or two, but only if the equipment worked. "Moskovitz, Fong—see if you can siphon off the fuel, then drain out the sediment. Let's hope no damage was done. I've gotta find Kendrick."

"Listen for the sound of rolling dice," Moskovitz said. "Then you'll find him."

Tom forced a laugh. "Sounds right."

He headed across the field past clumps of French and Arab locals the battalion had hired. They weren't much help. Neither was his platoon. Moskovitz's squad lounged near the dozer, unable to work until the equipment was serviced. Lehman's squad dug a trench to expand the sanitary facilities at a leisurely pace. Where was Weiser's squad? They were supposed to finish the headquarters building, but that sector was quiet. And where was Kendrick?

Tom entered HQ. In the room to his left, laughter rang—and the funny chortling sound Sesame made when he was happy.

He passed through the doorway, still missing its door. Kendrick, Weiser, and Weiser's men sprawled on the floor among lumber scraps, hand tools, and sawdust. Steam flowed to Tom's aching head, and he smiled as he'd trained himself to do.

"Hey, Gill! Watch this." Bill Rinaldi held out a chunk of Spam from his ration tin. "Sesame, shake."

Sesame lifted his paw and swatted Rinaldi's hand.

"Good boy." Rinaldi fed him the Spam.

"Yeah," Tom said. "Too bad he's the smartest one in the room."

The men groaned. Someone chucked a lumber scrap near Tom's feet.

He resisted the urge to kick it back hard. "Why are you goofing off? Got a job to do and we finally have decent weather."

Earl Butler traced patterns in the sawdust with his finger. "Aw, Gill. We can't. The wood's soaked from the rain. Better let it dry out."

"That's what I told the boys." Hal Weiser let out a puff of cigarette smoke. "Besides, it's Saturday. We need our beauty rest."

"Too late for the lot of you," Tom said with a grin. "Might as well work."

"Come on, Gill. Have some fun." Bernie Fitzgerald gathered a pile of scrap. "Build a bridge. You know you want to."

Kendrick's face lit up. "Betcha a dollar you can't do it in under five minutes."

Tom studied the scraps, and a design formed in his head. He could do it in three minutes, tops. "Forget the money. I finish in under five minutes, you guys go work your tails off."

"I don't know." Rinaldi leaned back against the wall. "I smell a con."

Tom's back and his smile stiffened. He had to get these men to work. "Four minutes."

"Three and we have a deal."

A nasty taste filled his mouth. He had to make a bet to get a job done. But what choice did he have? "Deal."

"Gill! Gill, you in here?" A gruff voice called from outside.

Swell. Lt. Martin Quincy. Fresh pain jolted Tom's skull.

"There you are. Newman wants to—" Quincy stopped in the doorway. His jaw lowered. "What's going on here? Don't you nitwits have a job?"

Tom pulled himself tall. "They're getting back to work right now."

"Back to work? Looks like they never started. Who's in charge here? You? Weiser, isn't it? Get these men off their sorry behinds on the double."

Weiser took a drag on his cigarette. "When we're done with our break."

Curse words flew out of Quincy's mouth like bees from a hive, stinging all in their path. "Break? I'll break something if you clods aren't out of here by the count of three."

The men jumped to their feet and scrambled out of the room. Sesame too.

But not Weiser. He fixed a sullen gaze on Quincy and blew out a slow puff of smoke. "Whatcha think you're gonna break?"

Quincy's hand shifted to the pistol on his hip. "Move. Or I'll put a bullet where it'll do some good, cut off your lazy line of dunderheads forever."

Weiser eased himself up, cussed under his breath, and sauntered out of the room.

The fire in Tom's head threatened to melt his eyeballs. He turned to Quincy. "You didn't have to yell at my men. I—"

"Someone had to."

Tom's hand tightened around the web strapping of his pistol belt. "It wasn't necessary. I had it under control."

"Control?" He barked a laugh, his fleshy face contorted. "You have none. That's why my men have to do our work and yours. I'm tired of it."

"I'm sorry, Quince. We'll do better."

"No, you won't. You don't have to." He flung a hand toward the doorway. "Newman won't touch you. He's scared of you. Everyone's scared of you. Think you're a bomb about to explode, think you'll go on a murder spree like your old man."

"I'm not like that." Tom's voice came out low.

"'Course not. You're a pansy." He shook a finger in Tom's face. "Look at you, smiling like a fool. I'm chewing you out and you're smiling. Someday I'll smash in that smile of yours."

Tom knew his cue to leave. He marched out the door. "I need to get to work."

"Yeah, run away, pansy. Least your old man didn't run away from a fight."

The pain in Tom's forehead dripped liquid fire behind his eyes, and he braced himself against the raw wood of the wall.

One dark, drunken night on the streets of Hollywood, Thomas MacGilliver had begged Max and Lucille DeVille for money. The famous director pulled a gun to protect his wife, the sweetheart of silent movies. The men tussled over the gun. It fired. Lucille DeVille dropped dead. Heartbroken, her husband collapsed over her. Another shot, and he joined his wife in death.

Tom's dad went to the electric chair.

If only he'd run from that fight.

"What's going on? I heard you outside." Captain Newman strode in, glaring over Tom's shoulder at Quincy. "I'll have no threats in this company. You're officers. Act like it."

Quincy's face twitched, but he lowered his gaze. "Yes, sir."

"Settle your differences like gentlemen. And not in front of the men."

"Yes, sir," Tom said.

Newman crossed his arms. "Now, about today's work. A squadron of B-26 Marauder medium bombers is due tomorrow. Quincy, how's the runway?"

"Got the loam and caliche down. Almost done with the gravel."

"How are the hardstands?"

Tom rubbed his temple. "We have a problem with the dozer. Once it's fixed, we'll get going."

"I see HQ has a long way to go." Newman glanced around the building.

"They'll finish today."

Quincy let out a harsh laugh. "If by today you mean February."

Tom's head ached from the pulsing heat. "I mean today." He'd enlist Moskovitz's squad while Kendrick fixed the dozer, and Tom would work until midnight if necessary.

"Thanks, men. Quincy, you're dismissed." Newman tilted his head to the door.

Quincy broke out in a smug smile and left.

Yep, Tom was in trouble. Not Quincy. The bones in his head just might snap from the pressure.

Newman waited until Quincy left and he studied Tom. "Don't let him talk to you that way. Be tough with him."

"I'm fine." Tom made himself chuckle. "You catch more flies with honey than vinegar, my mom always said."

"Yeah? What if honey makes a man sick to his stomach? Quincy needs vinegar. He respects vinegar."

Tom shrugged. "I know how to deal with bullies."

Newman frowned. "Quincy's no bully. He's angry with good cause. Your men don't do their share, and he and Reed pick up the slack."

Shame compressed his chest. It was his job to motivate the men. "I'm working on it."

"Really? I don't see improvement. You've got the expertise, you work harder than almost any man here, but it's not enough. You've got to get your men to shoulder their responsibility."

"I'll talk to them."

Doubt tugged the corners of Newman's eyes. "If you don't . . . well, I'll have to figure out something else."

Fiery hands squeezed his temples, but he kept his face calm. Something else? Was that an ultimatum? Could Tom be demoted or transferred? "May I get to work, sir?"

Newman nodded. "Dismissed."

Tom headed for the medical detachment tent. Would aspirin help? This was more than a headache. This was anger with nowhere to go. At home, he'd climb a tree and rant to the skies. No trees at Telergma, no privacy, no place to rant. Tonight he'd write a long letter to Annie. Poor woman got all his rants nowadays. Why on earth did she keep writing?

He wouldn't have to worry about her falling in love. A smart girl like Annie wouldn't fall for a man with no future.

He tore off his helmet and pressed his hand against his forehead, as if he could crack it open. Then the heat and pain would drain away.

If he failed at this job, what would he do after the war? He might find construction work, but his education would be wasted. The bridges in his head would never find their way out, never span divides, never link the divided.

"Lord, help me." His father had destroyed. Tom needed to build.

13

Nashville, Tennessee
December 25, 1942

A passing locomotive rocked Mellie's train, which was parked on a siding in Nashville. Mellie sat propped up on her pillow in her sleeping compartment.

What a strange Christmas. Last-minute orders packed the 802nd onto a train bound for Morrison Army Airfield in Florida. Training was cut short. They were going overseas.

Their destination had to be North Africa, the only active combat theater to the east. The 801st would head west to the Pacific. If only the squadrons had reversed. Mellie wanted to be closer to Papa.

Instead she'd be closer to Ernest. She spread out his last letter, where he described his new dog and included a darling sketch. Did Sesame's tail really curl like that? The kindness of Ernest's heart made hers feel soft as Christmas fudge.

And the brooch he'd sent was stunning. She fingered the delicate workmanship. The stones sang of azure skies and turquoise waters, amber sands and olive trees. She didn't know when or where she'd wear it, but she knew one thing—she was glad she'd never mentioned the flight nursing program.

He worked on airfields. Only twenty-five flight nurses

belonged to her squadron. If they flew into his airfield, he'd identify Mellie. That could never happen. They both needed anonymity.

But dozens of hospitals and hundreds of nurses had gone to North Africa. If she described her nursing duties in a general manner, he'd think she worked on the wards.

"'O come, all ye faithful, joyful and triumphant.'" Georgie's smooth alto and Rose's rough voice bounced into the railroad car.

The curtains on Mellie's compartment flew open, and the two nurses peeked in.

"Come on, Mellie-bird." Georgie tugged one of Mellie's braids. "We need your voice. We're caroling up and down the aisles."

Mellie laughed. "In our nightgowns?"

Rose flipped a bright red scarf over her shoulder. "Christmas ain't over till we say so."

"Let's straighten up, and out we go." Georgie picked up the letters strewn over Mellie's blanket. "Mm, more letters from Ernest. That boy sure thinks a lot of you. And look at you, memorizing his every word. Why, I think you're sweet on him."

Blood rose to Mellie's cheeks, and she stacked the letters in her stationery box. "It's not like that. I just enjoy his correspondence."

"Mm-hmm." Georgie winked at Rose, then pulled Mellie's arm. "Come on. Let's spread holiday cheer."

"You have enough for the entire train." Mellie kicked off her blanket, and her scrapbook tumbled to the floor. She'd forgotten she had it out.

"Ooh, a scrapbook." Georgie picked it up. "May I?"

All the blood that had risen to her cheeks drained right out. In second grade, she'd shown the scrapbook to Louise

Fairchild from her class. Louise made fun of her. The next day in school, the teasing was worse than ever. How could she blame them? Who wouldn't laugh at someone who only had paper friends?

Her flesh-and-blood friends frowned at her, confused. Friendship required openness and trust and the risk of rejection. If she shut them out, the curtain would drop and separate them once again.

Mellie gazed at the well-worn scrapbook. If she wanted to move beyond paper, she had to take that risk, over and over again. "I don't show it to anyone but Papa. It's embarrassing."

"Embarrassing?" Rose said.

"It's rather odd." Mellie tucked in her feet to sit cross-legged. "Please sit down. I'll show you."

Georgie's eyes widened, and she and Rose climbed onto Mellie's bed. The curtain fell in place, a false promise of privacy. But no other nurses were in the car.

Mellie set the book in her lap and traced the lines of the word *Memories*, which had once been gold. "These are pictures of my childhood friends."

"Doesn't sound odd to me." Rose tugged her nightgown over her knees.

Mellie drew a long breath. "My father and I were in the Philippines when I was little. My grandma was concerned because I didn't have anyone to play with, so she started this scrapbook for me."

She opened the book. "She cut out pictures of little girls from magazines and wrote stories beneath each one. 'Caroline and Philomela play jacks together.' 'Mary and Philomela go to the cinema and share a bag of popcorn.' 'Edna and Philomela play jump rope and hopscotch on a sunny day.'"

"That's very sweet," Georgie said.

Rose lifted one eyebrow. "What's embarrassing about that?"

Mellie turned another page. "Papa and I came back to California when I was six. I was so excited to make real friends. On the first day of school, Papa braided my hair, and I wore my prettiest dress from the Philippines. It was bright red with a long skirt and wide sleeves and a little capelet and lots of embroidery. I loved it. But the American girls all wore short drop-waist dresses and had their hair bobbed below their ears. They called me monkey girl." She squeezed her eyes shut.

"Oh dear," Georgie said. "Children can be cruel."

Mellie nodded, her neck stiff. "Once again, I had no one to play with. So I added to the scrapbook and wrote my own stories."

"You must have had *some* friends," Rose said.

"Nope." She raised a limp smile. "I was too American in Asia, too Asian in America. So I stopped trying and kept to myself. I read and drew. I had imaginary adventures with my paper friends. But I never had someone to play jacks or hopscotch or jump rope with."

Georgie's eyes misted over. "You poor thing. That's so sad."

Mellie rolled her eyes. "It's just plain odd."

"Not everyone's like those girls," Rose said in a soft voice. "You just needed to reach out to the right sort of girls."

"That's what—that's what I'm doing now." Mellie blinked and passed the scrapbook.

Georgie lay the scrapbook on the bed between her and Rose, and sent Mellie a tiny smile filled with compassion and gratitude.

Mellie's throat tightened—not a lump but a rock—and her eyes watered. "Please. I want you to look at it."

Rose and Georgie turned the pages carefully. They smiled

and commented and asked questions. With kindness. Toward the middle of the book, they shared laughter with Mellie about childish misspellings and her more outlandish tales.

Warmth filled Mellie's soul. So this was friendship—the pain of ripping open one's heart rewarded with intimacy and understanding. This was what she'd longed for all her life and never known.

Rose paused and inclined her head. "This one's different."

"A boy," Georgie said. "No name, no story. He looks so sad. Heartbreaking."

Mellie sucked in her breath. Oh dear. The children she prayed for. Louise Fairchild said the pictures were disgusting. Mellie's hand stretched toward the album to protect the vulnerable.

Georgie and Rose looked at Mellie expectantly. They could be trusted to feel compassion for these poor children. They were the right sort.

Her breath returned in a soft stream. "Do you remember that horrible story of MacGilliver the Killiver?"

"Of course," Rose said. "Jump-rope rhyme."

"That's his son."

"He had a son?" Georgie said.

"I felt sorry for him, how everyone hated his father. I cut out the picture because I thought he needed a friend. Someone to pray for him."

"I wonder what happened to him," Georgie said.

Rose shook her head. "With that background, he's probably in jail or aiming for it."

"I don't think so." Mellie gazed at the picture. "Look at that sweet face. And his mother—see how she protects him? With the Lord, anything's possible."

West Palm Beach, Florida
January 1, 1943

"It's impossible, Mellie." Rose pointed to a crowd of soldiers in bathing trunks heaving coconuts at palm trees. "If they can't do it, neither can you."

"Coconuts take skill, not force." Mellie shook the hairy fruit, and the milk sloshed inside. Nice and ripe. She crossed the warm sand to the group of soldiers. "Excuse me, gentlemen. Do any of you have a pocketknife?"

One of the men sized her up. "Honey, you think you can open that with a pocketknife?"

Something squirmed inside her. Dealing with men was easier wearing a nurse's uniform than a bathing suit. She'd pretend she wore the white dress and cap. "This is just the first step. Do you have a knife?"

"Sure do. I was a Boy Scout. I'm always prepared." He squared his scrawny shoulders and grinned at her.

She gave him her new partial smile. "Well . . . ?"

"Yeah." He leaned over a jumble of clothing on the sand, pulled out a Swiss army knife, and handed it to her. "Can I have something sweet in exchange?"

Mellie tucked the coconut under her arm and concentrated on the knife. Was he making a pass at her? He must have been trapped on base for months without a female in sight.

"Coconut's sweet," Rose said. "And that's all you'll get."

"Ah, you're killing me. Three cute little things and I can't even get a kiss."

More men gathered around the nurses.

Mellie found the three "eyes" in one end of the coconut. Cute? What would Ernest think if he saw her?

How could she let herself think that way? Ernest would never see her. And if he did, he'd be nice to her but nothing more.

Mellie plunged the knife into an eye, three times, then pried out the triangular wedge. She tipped up the coconut, and the milk dripped into her mouth. Oh, she hadn't tasted the rich sweetness for over a year.

"You can drink it?" Georgie said.

"Mm-hmm. It's wonderful. And it's good for sore throats too." Mellie handed her the coconut.

Georgie lifted the fruit. Some of the milk splashed into her mouth, some onto her chin. She made a funny face and wiped her chin. "That's . . . different."

The men laughed.

"My turn." Rose took a swig and wrinkled her nose. "At least I can say I tried it."

"Can I? It's my knife." The soldier tried some and squinted at the sky. "Sweet. Not as sweet as a kiss though."

No doubt about it—wartime made men act strangely. Mellie glanced at Georgie and Rose and gave them a quick shrug.

They giggled. Mellie had managed to communicate in their language, and she smiled.

"All gone." A stocky soldier tossed the coconut up and down like a baseball. "You didn't get it open, dolly."

"That's next." She took it back and walked to a picket fence separating the beach from the road. She turned the coconut so the hole faced down, raised it high, and impaled it on a picket. A firm twist, and the fruit split into neat halves.

"Well, I'll be," the skinny soldier said. "Cute and clever too."

Mellie handed him a coconut half. "Use your knife to carve out the fruit. It's tasty." Most of them had probably never eaten fresh coconut before.

The men produced more knives and cut the coconut into bite-sized chunks. Others followed Mellie's example and split coconuts on pickets, the milk spurting out. The laughing crowd pressed in on Mellie. She took a handful of chunks and retreated to her beach towel, where she lay down on her stomach.

The warm, humid air caressed her bare legs and arms, the sound of breaking waves soothed her ears, and the crisp, moist fruit filled her mind with memories. If she closed her eyes, she could imagine Papa's voice.

Feminine laughter approached, and a fine spray of sand landed on her calf. Mellie lifted her foot and shook off the sand.

"Oops. Sorry." Rose stretched out on her towel. "That was quite a demonstration."

Sweat dribbled down the back of Mellie's neck. If only she could free her hair, but that would lead to a tangled, sandy mess. "The benefit of an odd upbringing is knowing odd things."

"That odd thing almost got you a date," Georgie said from her towel next to Rose. "You just needed to smile more."

Mellie knew better than to let her full smile loose. Her smile earned her the nickname Monkey Girl. "I'm not looking for a date."

"Of course not. Your heart belongs to Ernest." Rose batted her eyelashes.

Mellie laughed and swatted her gently on the arm. The teasing felt even warmer than the sun. "And yours belongs to that Louisville flyboy."

Georgie rested her chin on her folded arms. "Speaking of hearts, who's got Vera's? She talks about dates, but I never see her with a man."

"I think it's some withered old man with gobs of dough." Rose tilted back her head, and the breeze lifted her hair.

Mellie ran her fingers under her braids along her damp skull. Long hair had drawbacks. "Perhaps she's just private."

"Well, *she's* not private." Georgie pointed her chin toward Kay, who strolled down the beach in a two-piece swimsuit. Three handsome men scrambled for position at her side. "I think she's holding auditions. We've only been here a week."

The gossip twisted Mellie's insides. She had to change the subject. "We won't be here long. Once we get our personnel and equipment, we'll ship out."

"In the meantime, Kay's got them lined up." Rose rested her chin in her hands. "The boys get what they want from her."

Kay turned and laughed at something one of the men said, her shoulders back, her chest lifted, and she swiveled her hip just so. She didn't have the shapeliest figure, but she knew how to use it.

"I don't think so," Mellie said. "I think she's filling some need bigger than one man can fill."

"So she needs seven."

"She needs the Lord," Georgie said. "But she runs like a thoroughbred when you mention Jesus."

Mellie studied the redhead, who stopped and gazed out at the ocean, oblivious to the men at her side. Despite her social skills, Kay was less open than Mellie.

Was that how Ernest came across? Friendly but superficial? Yet inside he was so deep and fascinating.

Warmth drew her eyelids shut and turned up the corners of her mouth. She was the only person who knew that part of him.

14

Thélepte Airfield
Tunisia
January 15, 1943

Tom could go deaf at Thélepte. The first airstrip had been completed in December, and the P-40 fighter planes and A-20 Havoc light bombers made a constant low-grade roar. But the construction work on the second airstrip rattled his eardrums.

In the distance, Arab workers gathered rocky soil in baskets and carried it to dump trucks. At the field, a gravel crusher ground the rocks, a dozer spread the gravel, and men from the 908th laid interlocking pierced steel planks on top. A single runway required two thousand tons of PSP, the entire daily capacity of the flimsy North African rail system. But what a difference PSP made—easy to lay and repair, and it didn't sink into the mud.

"Good job," Tom shouted up to Conrad Davis, who drove the dump truck. "You guys might beat Moskovitz's squad this week."

"Nah." Davis flapped his hand. "We don't stand a chance."

"Sure you do. Just keep up the hard work."

"Sure, Gill." The truck lumbered back to the excavation site.

Competition served as Tom's best disciplinary tool, but coming up with weekly rewards for the winning platoon challenged him. Thélepte lay on a semidesert Tunisian plateau within ninety miles of the front, where the Axis and the Allies jabbed at each other from defensive positions. Frequent Luftwaffe bombing raids had driven away most of the villagers—and their produce.

Tom leaned down and scratched Sesame behind the ears. "What should I offer this week? First choice on sleeping positions in the ravine? First in line for chow? The driest slit trench in the next air raid?"

Sesame cocked his head to one side and chortled.

"Thanks, but I don't think the men want the next rat you catch." Tom straightened the dog's harness, a cut-down cartridge belt. He was training Sesame to deliver messages. Maybe it was his imagination, but Sesame stood taller when he wore his working-dog belt.

Tom checked his watch—1449. At 1500 he had his Friday meeting with Newman and the platoon leaders to review the past week's work and prepare for the following week. For once, Tom could hold up his head. His platoon had completed most of their work. Quincy and Reed would have little to complain about.

"Come on, Sesame." Tom led the dog away from the work site and toward the headquarters dugout. He pulled Annie's latest letter from inside his Parsons field jacket to read again while he walked.

My new friendships have made me think
more about my mother, and I feel compelled
to tell her story for the first time, even though
it's shameful. The Lord has shown me I need
to forgive her, and writing it down should

help. Thanks to anonymity—and your kind heart—I feel comfortable telling you.

My mother was only seventeen when she married my father, and I came a year later. The pressures of motherhood convinced her she'd never lived. She bobbed her hair and neglected my father and me in favor of speakeasies, wild living, and—I'm ashamed to say—other men. When I was two, she was killed in a drunken car accident.

I believe I've forgiven her for that, but the Lord is showing me a new dimension to forgiveness. My mother's abandonment and death deprived me of an important relationship. So many things can only be passed from mother to daughter. My father tried, bless him, but how could he teach me to dress and style my hair and interact with little girls?

You probably have a similar situation. For both of us, death severed a crucial relationship, and the remaining parent tried to fill that hole. Your father's death deprived you of having a man to work alongside and learn manly things from.

In addition, our parents' deaths gave us more difficult lives. I'll never understand or excuse what my mother did, but I must fully forgive her.

Tom folded the letter and stuck it back inside his jacket. The sun streamed down on the barren plateau, but a sun without heat and chill winds made the Westerners and Southerners grumble.

Tom was a Pennsylvania boy, not a California boy. Thanks to his father.

He grimaced. He'd never thought about forgiveness as Annie did. Keeping up a sunny front required shoving away anger and sadness, but resentment ran in a buried river in his soul.

Dad had abandoned him. He loved booze more than his wife and son. On the day his drinking cost him his job, he came home and smashed the kitchen chairs. In the middle of the night, Mom wakened Tom and hurried him to her sister's house.

Dad begged her to come back. Tom heard him at the door, pleading, his voice throaty, and Tom wanted to run to him, to his daddy, but Mom held him back. She loved her son and wanted to protect him.

Tom passed an A-20 and its flight crew in their sheepskin-lined leather jackets. He greeted them and continued on his way.

Another memory intruded, and he wrestled with it. Daddy coming home in the evening, dusted with the sharp smell of the explosives used in his demolitions work. "Where's my Tommy?" he'd call.

"Here I am!" Tom would run up, hop on one foot, and stretch his hands tall to the ceiling.

"Oh no! It's a burglar!" Daddy's face would fill with mock terror, then he'd tackle Tom and tickle him.

"It's me, Daddy. It's me," Tom would say between giggles.

"It's my Tommy? Why, I didn't recognize you, you grew so much today."

When Tom caught his breath, Daddy would swing him up onto his back, gallop into the kitchen, kiss Mom—which made Tom break into more giggles—then gallop around the house.

That's what he stole from Tom when he chose liquor.

He stopped and closed his eyes. "Lord, I haven't fully forgiven him, have I? He took so much from me. Help me. Help me forgive him."

Sesame leaned against Tom's leg, his brown eyes warm and penetrating.

"God sent you into my life, didn't he?" Tom's voice came out husky, and he rubbed Sesame's ears. The dog saw what he hid and loved him anyway.

A man let out a shrill whistle behind him, by the A-20.

An air raid.

More whistles broke out. Pilots scrambled to their planes, fastening parachute harnesses and yanking on leather flight helmets.

Tom shielded his eyes and gazed west. Sure enough, black dots appeared beneath the afternoon sun.

"Here we go again." He gathered Sesame into his arms and raced away from the airfield, the Luftwaffe's target. He dropped into a slit trench and sheltered the quivering dog between his body and the earthen wall.

Sesame didn't mind construction noise, but he hated the explosions during an air raid.

More men jumped into the trench, a whole line of them, helmets like stones in a stream, rifles like reeds along the banks.

After Tom attached the leash to his pistol belt, he readied his carbine. He had to look ready to shoot even if he didn't intend to do so.

One P-40 sped along the runway and lifted into the sky, and another followed. The propwash raised a cloud of dust on the ground.

"Go, boys. Get 'em," the officer next to Tom said.

A mechanic to Tom's right adjusted his steel helmet. "We're the 33rd Fighter Group. We ain't gonna let Jerry get away with this."

Tom glanced at the faces around him, eyes lit up and focused, as if watching a college football game and not a struggle for life and death.

"Here they come, boys."

Tom hunched lower in the trench but peered over the edge. German Junkers Ju 88s, skinny twin-engine bombers with strange bubble-like cockpits, about ten of them.

Two more American P-40s took to the air, then a P-40 bearing the French Tricolor on its tail.

"Hey, the Lafayette Escadrille's joining in today," Tom said.

"'Bout time," someone grumbled.

"Be fair," another fellow said. "The French had never seen the P-40 before. Takes time to learn a new plane."

"What's the escort? Me 109s?" Tom asked. The German Messerschmitts were some of the best fighter planes in the world.

"Me 109s. Yeah."

"Wait." An officer flipped through a deck of aircraft identification cards, printed with silhouettes of different types of aircraft. "Might be Macchi 202s."

"Italians?" the mechanic said.

"Sure. We're fighting them too."

"I know that."

"Look at the engines when they come by. The 202s got a big old engine, not sleek like the 109."

"What do you think the quarterback will do?" Tom said. "Punt or go for the long pass?"

Men turned and stared at Tom.

He chuckled. "We sound like we're in the bleachers at a football game—not a battle."

"Same thing," the ground crewman said with a laugh. "Who wants a beer?"

A chorus of "I do, I do, I do" ran down the line.

But this was no game. The American antiaircraft guns opened up with booms that shook the ground and made Sesame tremble.

Tom pressed the dog's pointed ears shut.

The first Ju 88 passed over the field and dropped a string of bombs, kicking up dirt and steel from the runway. "I know what we'll be doing tomorrow," Tom muttered.

Some of the men in the trenches popped off shots at the bomber, and a P-40 buzzed around the larger plane. Bullets zipped through the air, and yellow tracer fire lit the path.

The Ju 88 climbed and turned to the east, but the P-40 stayed with it, bullets hitting the mark. One of the bomber's engines gave off clouds of black smoke. The wing snapped in half. The plane spiraled to the ground.

An explosion rocked the earth and took the lives of the bomber's crewmen.

A whoop rang out from the trench. Tom joined in because he had to, but cheering death made his stomach churn.

The tail of the bomber stuck out of the wreckage, and flames licked at the painted swastika. This was why the Americans had to fight, to kill. Because the Nazis were bent on destruction, and destruction was the only way to stop them.

Bomber after bomber plummeted from the sky, nine total. But no P-40s fell, and no Americans or French died, so it was considered a victory and a cause for celebration.

Tom soothed his little dog. "Someday, Sesame. Someday this will all be over. Then we can build."

15

USS *Lyon*
New York Harbor
February 7, 1943

Mellie leaned on the railing of the USS *Lyon* and belted out "Manhattan Serenade" over the rumble of the ship's engines. Hundreds of personnel from the 325th Fighter Group and the 802nd Medical Air Evacuation Transport Squadron crowded the deck. The Manhattan skyline passed by on Mellie's left, and the scenery shifted perspective moment by moment.

In two weeks she'd be in Africa. Not only would she get to explore a new continent, but Ernest's letters would arrive more quickly and the conversation would flow.

Her song swelled, filled with the joy of friendship and motion.

The last month and a half had been nothing but hurry and wait. Hurry to Florida. Wait for personnel and equipment. Hurry to Camp Kilmer. Wait for overseas processing. While in New Jersey, the 802nd worked at a civilian hospital during a measles epidemic. Alice Olson complained that they were flight nurses, not ward nurses, but Georgie reminded her they should help where needed.

Last night they were told to pack, destination unknown.

The news Mellie had longed for drained the color from Georgie's face.

She sighed. Perhaps Captain Maxwell should be more concerned about Georgie's fear than about Mellie fitting in. He still circled Mellie like a hawk and swooped down on infractions. She'd dared to question a medication order for one of the measles patients. Although Mellie was right, he still complained to Lambert. His hawkishness and Vera and Alice's cattiness seemed designed to drive Mellie into a mouse hole.

She launched into the final verse of the song, determined to be a mouse no more.

"There you are. Just had to follow that voice." Georgie wormed her way through the crowd to the railing, her face ruddy from the wind and cold.

"Where's Rose? Still not well?"

"Yeah. She's lying down. Once a month." Georgie lifted an apologetic smile, as if she'd revealed a deep secret.

"I hope she doesn't get seasick on top of it."

"Rose? This is the only thing in the world that gets her down." She pointed across the Upper Bay. "Look. There's Ellis Island and the Statue of Liberty just beyond."

Mellie shielded her eyes to view the red and cream brick buildings of Ellis Island. She could imagine a steamship pulled up to the berth forty years before and a crowd of immigrants in peasant caps and shawls swarming from steerage into sunshine. "So much history here."

"All those huddled masses desperate to come to America. We're headed the wrong way."

Mellie tugged her overcoat tighter and studied Georgie's atypically downcast face. "Why don't you want to go?"

Georgie snapped up her gaze. "What? I want to go. This is what we trained for."

"So why do you look like your mother just died?"

"Do I?" She rubbed her gloved hands over her cheeks. "Oh dear. It shows? Do you think Rose noticed?"

"No. She's too excited to notice anyone's misery."

"Misery. Is that what this is?"

Mellie smiled. "Has your life been so wonderful you've never felt miserable before?"

"Sure I have. My grandparents passed away. That was miserable. Though I was a tiny thing. And when I was ten, my favorite horse broke his leg and had to be put down."

"Mm." Mellie gave her a soft nod.

Georgie sighed. "All right, my life's idyllic. My mama and daddy and big sisters love me to pieces. I grew up on the most beautiful horse farm you can imagine. I always had Rose and Ward."

"But now you have to leave Ward."

A deeper sigh. "I know he'll miss me, but I can't abandon Rose. We've always done everything together. We need each other."

Papa's face flashed into her mind. Up until the past year, they had always been a team. Now he was alone. If he lived. Her eyes watered, and she blinked hard.

Georgie gazed up at the overcast sky. "Rose and I complement each other. She makes me try new things, and I soften her rough edges."

"You two are good for each other. And for me." If only she had something to give to them.

Georgie held back her curls on one side and fixed a firm gaze on Mellie. "Rose can't know how scared I am. If she knew, she'd slap me. With good reason. I'm scared of the U-boats. I'm scared of being caught in combat. I don't know if I can handle it."

Mellie hesitated, but she'd learned from four months of

friendship. She put her arm around Georgie's shoulders. "You'll do fine. The Lord will be with you. So will Rose, and so will I."

"Please don't tell Rose I came just for her. She thinks I'm as excited as she is, and it's best that way. Besides, when I pretend to be happy, I end up feeling happy."

Mellie smiled. She still had a lot to learn from these ladies.

"Promise me," Georgie said, eyes wide. "Promise not to tell Rose."

Her breath caught. She'd never been asked to keep a confidence before, a solemn responsibility. But she knew the sting of betrayal and could never inflict it on another. "I promise."

Georgie's expression overflowed with warmth. "I knew the minute we met we'd end up the best of friends."

"You did?" Mellie's nose stuffed up, and she sniffed. "If only I'd known when you did. Maybe I wouldn't have been so shy."

"All in God's time. Now, look. Lady Liberty herself."

Expressions of awe and wonder flooded the deck of the troop transport as hundreds of airmen and nurses craned their necks to see the immensity of the statue.

Mellie leaned back her head and braced it in one hand to support the weight of her hair.

Liberty faced east, one arm cradling law and justice, the other holding high her torch. She strode forward, out of the broken chains of bondage, her face determined and visionary. She offered hope and freedom to the world, and no adversity of this time or any time to come could restrain her.

"I can't believe we're leaving." Tears meandered down Georgie's cheeks.

"Don't you see? This is why we're leaving." Mellie pointed to the statue as the ship curved around the island. "Liberty Enlightening the World—that's her full name. She isn't facing

America. She faces the world, showing the enslaved nations what freedom looks like, a beacon in the darkness."

Georgie pulled a handkerchief from her coat pocket and patted her face. "We're not supposed to keep the light to ourselves, are we?"

"No. That's why we're going." For a disorienting moment, it seemed as if Liberty looked down at her, circled her, and imparted a blessing. A shiver started at her hairline and worked over her scalp. These hundreds of men and women were leaving with the blessing of the nation, to protect that nation and restore freedom abroad. "Lord, help us do your work."

"It's his work, isn't it?" The light returned to Georgie's eyes, as if Liberty's torch had passed on its fire.

Mellie nodded. "God gave us gifts of mercy and healing. We can't keep those gifts to ourselves. He wants us to use them for him."

***

USS *Lyon*
Atlantic Ocean
February 11, 1943

"Don't peek. Peeking is cheating." Rose tugged on the knot of the blindfold.

Mellie stubbed her toe on the metal threshold of a bulkhead. She wriggled her nose to scoot the blindfold up a bit. "I thought this was supposed to be a pleasant surprise."

"It is." Georgie tugged on Mellie's elbow and guided her down a corridor. "Just wait."

"Staircase. Up you go."

Mellie groped for the cold metal handrails, which were almost vertical. "If you want to kill me, why not throw me overboard and have done with it?"

"Nonsense." Rose patted her back. "It's more fun this way."

Mellie laughed and climbed up. A brisk whirl of air and the rush of waves against the steel hull told her she was almost to the deck. A rotation system allowed everyone a short amount of time topside each day and gave the sailors room to work. Only a storm would keep her in the cramped stateroom shared by twelve nurses.

Georgie's small hand cupped Mellie's elbow. "You're on deck."

Mellie drew a deep, damp, salty breath. Women were clean creatures, but limited water meant little bathing, and the stateroom stank.

After Rose untied the bandanna, Mellie blinked and looked around. She stood on the fore portion of the ship's deck under a mushroom-shaped platform for an antiaircraft gun. This was a surprise?

Georgie held up one finger, two, three, and she and Rose sang "Happy Birthday."

Mellie's knees felt loose. A birthday surprise? For her? Papa always gave her a nice gift, but he never made a big fuss.

Georgie beamed as if it were her birthday. "Rose, give her the—well, it's not a cake, but it'll have to do."

Rose reached into the musette bag she wore across her chest and pulled out a Hershey bar. "We couldn't think of a way to get a cake on board without squishing it, but with sugar rationing, a candy bar is just as nice."

Mellie took the chocolate. "It is. Thank you. We'll share, see how long we can make it last."

Georgie and Rose laughed. "Ten seconds?" Rose said.

"Five." Mellie worked her finger under the wrapper.

"Not yet." Rose took the chocolate bar and returned it to her bag. "We have to give you your present first."

"Present?" They'd already given her the best present ever— they'd thought of her.

Georgie stepped to the side. White squares had been chalked onto the wooden deck. "Hopscotch," she said. "And two playmates."

The chalk lines wiggled in Mellie's vision. Her throat felt thick.

Rose pulled a rope out of the musette bag. "Georgie sweet-talked some poor sailor into loaning us some line for a jump rope. Jacks were tough. Metal jacks, rubber ball—you can't buy either now."

"Shortages, of course," Georgie said. "Thank goodness Mama mailed me my old set before we sailed. I'm glad she didn't donate them to the scrap drive and the rubber drive."

"What do you want to play first, birthday girl?"

Mellie's lips undulated like the waves below. "You—you did this for me?"

"Oh, honey." Georgie whipped out her handkerchief and handed it to Mellie. "Of course we did."

"It was her idea," Rose said. "After we saw your scrapbook on Christmas."

Georgie took Mellie's hand. "I know this doesn't restore your childhood, but I hope it helps."

Mellie dabbed at her face. She hiccupped and covered her mouth so she wouldn't break out in a full-blown sob. "It does. It does help. Thank you so much."

"What's first?" Rose held up a little cloth drawstring bag and a rope. "Jacks, hopscotch, or jump rope?"

Georgie laughed. "To think you never wanted to play those games when we were little. You wanted to run around with Ward, climb trees, and play baseball."

"Mm-hmm." Rose lowered her gaze, and her mouth tightened. She poked around in the drawstring bag. "Hopscotch first. We'll use jacks as markers. Do you know how to play, Mellie?"

"I watched often enough." A sudden memory burst in—Lupe Rodriguez inviting her to play in second grade. Mellie shyly said no, tired of being hurt. But Lupe was new to school, the daughter of a maid, and she didn't fit in with the children of Palo Alto's academic elite. Protecting her own heart, Mellie hadn't shown mercy to someone who needed it. She sent up a quick prayer for forgiveness.

Georgie slipped a jack into Mellie's hand. "You go first."

Mellie swallowed hard through her swollen throat. She tossed the jack and hopped through the course.

"Georgie, you go next," Rose said. "This was your idea."

"A fine idea it was." Georgie fanned her face in her best Southern belle fashion and took her turn.

Rose's jack landed in the square next to Mellie's. With one athletic leap, she cleared the hurdle. "Speaking of Ward, any news in today's letter?"

"Wasn't that the sweetest thing?" Georgie handed Mellie another jack. "Sending me off with a packet of fourteen letters, one to open each day?"

"Mm-hmm. Any news?" Rose asked.

Mellie threw the jack, but she sneaked a glance at Rose. Her smile seemed flat, her voice high.

Georgie shrugged. "The usual farm news. Planning the spring planting and all."

"So nothing new." Rose's gaze darted to Georgie, hungry, then scooted away.

Mellie's mouth drifted open. Oh goodness. Rose and Georgie and Ward had been an inseparable trio. In fact, Ward had been closer to Rose than to Georgie until high school. Was Rose . . . ? Could she be . . . ? Mellie felt Rose's pain as a stab in her own heart.

Rose was in love with Ward.

And she was too good a friend to Georgie to interfere.

Rose complained that the fellows didn't look because the only fellow she wanted didn't want her. She snapped at that flyboy because her heart was already taken.

Fresh tears filled Mellie's eyes.

Georgie attempted to hop over three squares as the ship shifted course, always zigzagging to avoid U-boats, and she fell on her backside. "I should have worn my life jacket a bit lower for padding."

She and Rose broke out laughing, and Mellie attempted to join them.

Two friends. Two secrets. One person who knew both.

Mellie trembled from the responsibility.

"I lost, so I get to pick next." Georgie gathered the jacks into the bag. "Jump rope."

Mellie and Rose took the ends. After a few tries, they coordinated the rhythm.

"One, two, three." Georgie watched the arcing rope and nodded with the count. She inserted herself neatly and hopped away. "Ready, girls? 'MacGilliver the Killiver needed gold and silliver, begged from—'"

"No!" Mellie's hand dropped. The rope wiggled and flopped to the deck.

Georgie stumbled. "What?"

"Not that rhyme. I hate it."

"Oh." Georgie's mouth went as round as her word.

"That's right," Rose said. "The little boy in your scrapbook."

"He's real."

"I'm sorry. I didn't think." Georgie scrunched up her mouth. "Please forgive me."

"Of course." But Mellie drew back slightly. Georgie and Rose talked openness but kept secrets. They talked kindness but gossiped. They talked mercy but chanted a rhyme that trivialized three deaths and humiliated a child.

"Let's try again. We know plenty of rhymes." Rose circled the rope and laughed when it went nowhere. "Come on, Mellie. You need to join in."

Mellie stared at the rope, a symbol of how they'd overlooked her many faults, swept her into their circle, put up with her odd ways, and thought of her in a deeply touching way. How could she not offer them a fraction of the mercy they'd offered her?

She picked up the rope and smiled, brimming with gratitude. "Let's play."

16

Thélepte Airfield
Tunisia
February 17, 1943

Tom parked his jeep and squinted up through the haze. The last of the 81st Fighter Group's P-39 Airacobras took off and joined the formation over Thélepte.

"They won't have to go far to find a fight," Larry Fong said.

"Nope."

General Erwin Rommel's Afrika Korps raced north from Gafsa and west through Sbeïtla, converging on Kasserine Pass. Thélepte stood in the way. The U.S. II Corps tried to hold off the German panzers, but the Twelfth Air Force couldn't take any chances. Thélepte had orders to evacuate by noon and to destroy what they couldn't ship out.

Tom looped Sesame's leash through the steering wheel. "Stay here, Ses. Good boy."

He and Larry got out of the jeep. Sergeant Lehman's squad laid mines on the main road east of the airfield.

"Hey, Lehman. How's it going?"

"Swell. Leaving gifts for the Nazis." Lehman rubbed his jawline, gray with stubble and dust.

"Who's got the diagram?"

"Diagram?"

"The placement of the mines. So we can find them when we come back."

Lehman waved his square hand as if swatting a fly. "There won't be any left. Rommel will find 'em all. We'll blow the Desert Fox sky-high."

Tom glanced at Larry, who puffed his cheeks full of air and shook his head. Without a diagram, mine removal would be slow and dangerous work.

"I need that diagram," Tom said. "Where's your foreman? Put him on the job."

"You kidding, Gill? Those tanks will roll up that road any minute. You heard the scouts. The Jerries are bearing down hard on Fériana. That's only five miles away. I'm mining this road and getting my tail out of here."

Tom glanced south over the barren plateau toward Fériana. Artillery thumped in the distance, and the dust of combat marred the horizon. His chest felt tight. "A diagram is essential."

"Sure. I'll pull one of my men from blowing up tanks so he can draw a picture."

Tom's pulse throbbed in his temple. He looked his squad leader in the eye. Quincy would cuss and scream at the man. Reed would issue a cold command. Both officers would get a diagram.

But Tom—what could he do? He had to fight with both arms tied behind his back and his feet hobbled. Breaking those bonds and acting like a normal man would undo a lifetime's work.

"The Lord always provides a way," his mom used to say.

Tom gritted his teeth. Where was that way?

"Say, boss," Larry said. "You've got to check on Weiser and Moskovitz. I'll stay here, put together a diagram as best I can."

Tom released a sigh and all his tension. He clapped his platoon sergeant on the shoulder. "Thanks."

Larry gazed down the road. "How long?"

"It's 1040. The security inspection starts at 1100. Get to the rendezvous site at 1115. We need to be out of here before 1200."

Larry tipped him a salute. "See you then."

"Thanks again, buddy." He returned the salute. He didn't want to acknowledge Lehman, but years of training forced him to say good-bye with a smile.

Back in the jeep, he rubbed Sesame behind the ears. "At least you obey me."

Tom drove west parallel to the main runway. That morning, 124 fighter planes had flown off to strafe German troops and tanks. After their missions, they'd land at Tébessa, Le Kouif, and Youks-les-Bains safely behind the front lines. For now. What if Rommel broke free and pushed the Allies back out of North Africa?

Out on the runway, trucks towed eighteen unserviceable planes into place to be blown to smithereens.

"What a waste." Tom pulled up to the supply dump, where men loaded trucks to the limit. Nothing could be left behind for the Germans to use.

After he secured the dog's leash, Tom hopped out of the jeep to find Weiser. Like everyone at Thélepte, his squad had started work at one o'clock in the morning. The order to evacuate had come at midnight, and no time could be wasted.

Tom scanned the work crews—ground crewmen and head-quarters personnel from the fighter groups, members of the Twelfth Air Service Command, as well as the 908th Engineers. All worked at a frantic pace.

Where was his squad leader?

Tom weaved among the crates and burlap sacks and rushing

men, from one end of the supply dump to the other. No sign of Weiser's squad. He jogged down dirt steps to a dugout, where an officer tacked a map of Stalingrad to the door. The Germans might be momentarily victorious in Tunisia, but they'd just suffered a horrendous defeat to the Soviets in Stalingrad.

"Anyone in there?" Tom asked the officer.

"Just rats and booby traps."

"Looking for someone?" Martin Quincy stood at the top of the steps. "Like Weiser?"

"Yeah." Uneasiness crept up Tom's spine. "You seen him?"

"His squad truck took on half a load of supplies. Then Weiser and his men climbed in, and off they went." Quincy knifed a hand in the air to the west. "Won't be hard to find them. The snakes left a yellow trail from their slimy yellow bellies."

"Oh no." The engineers were supposed to be the last troops out.

Quincy cocked his head. "Whatcha gonna do? Give 'em lollipops?"

Tom didn't know what he'd do. He stomped up the steps and headed for his jeep.

"You won't do a thing," Quincy yelled after him.

Tom walked hard, swung his arms hard, stretched his fingers out hard. He had to do something. Weiser let down everyone at Thélepte. What kind of men abandoned their duty? What kind of officer let them get away with it?

A useless officer like Tom, that's who. He climbed into the jeep, untied Sesame's leash from the steering wheel, and drove away to find Moskovitz. He glanced at the little dog. "What can I do, boy?"

Smiles and bribes and competition weren't enough. The military had rules. Discipline needed to be doled out, and that was Tom's responsibility as an officer. As a man.

If he didn't learn how to discipline, his men would continue to let down the battalion and the Allied cause. But what tools remained?

Mom's tools worked on the playground, in the classroom, and on the job site when he wasn't in charge. But they failed him now. They weren't a man's tools. His father never passed on a man's knowledge, never equipped him to function in a man's world.

He raised his head and let out a growling roar. He thumped his hand on the steering wheel. "Lord, how can I lead men when I can't be a man myself?"

At the west end of the airfield, Tom pulled up to the rendezvous site by the road to Youks-les-Bains. He'd leave the jeep while he checked on Moskovitz, who was supposed to be blowing up planes. Best not to get the vehicle or the dog too close.

"Stay here, Sesame." Tom jogged toward the runway and checked his watch—1105. "Please, Lord. Please let Moskovitz be doing his job."

A ball of flame erupted and shook the earth. Black smoke roiled up into a flaming column. One of the planes. Seventeen to go. They planned to douse them with the sixty thousand gallons of aviation fuel they couldn't evacuate and take the planes out of German hands as well.

Efficient. Smart. But Tom hated to have a hand in destruction.

His ankle turned on a rock, but he kept running. His father loved to blow things up. That was his job—demolishing old buildings and bridges. He loved the explosions, loved seeing everything crumble into a pile of rubble, loved taking down the work of years in seconds.

"He destroyed everything, Lord. How can I forgive that?"

Another explosion, closer, and Tom stumbled. He had to

forgive. God commanded it. As Annie said, he didn't have to understand or excuse his father, but he did have to forgive. What right did Tom have to hold back his forgiveness?

"I don't, Lord. Help me forgive Dad."

Dozens of men lined up at the tankers, filled gas cans, and ran them out to the aircraft. Urgency filled the air, as pungent as the gas fumes.

Thank goodness Moskovitz worked hard. He called out orders and hustled his men. A string of petty teenage crimes had landed Moskovitz in Tom's misfit platoon, but the man rose above his reputation.

"Hiya, Gill." Moskovitz raised a hand in greeting. "How much longer we got?"

"Not much. You've blown up two—"

An explosion pounded Tom's ears, another, and another. "Five planes?" He shouted over the roar of flames and the pop of snapping metal.

A thunderous explosion. Tom leaned on the tanker for support.

"Six," Moskovitz said. "Ain't it fun?"

"Yeah. Fun." An inferno raged before him, a blaze of orange flame, black smoke, and gusts of heat.

"We may have a humiliating defeat, but at least we get to blow things up." Moskovitz hefted up a gas can. "Better get back to work."

"Yeah. Meet at the rendezvous as soon as you can. We've got to be out of here by noon."

"Sure thing, Gill." Moskovitz trotted off with the gas can toward a P-40 with a shot-up engine and a crumpled tail fin.

Tom stared at an empty gas can at his feet. He had a few minutes before he needed to return to the rendezvous. He should help. But how could he engage in destruction?

He knew the answer. They didn't have time to cart away

the fuel and planes. If they left them behind, the Germans would use that fuel in their own aircraft to strafe and bomb Allied troops. They'd repair the P-40s and use them to spy.

If Tom and his men didn't destroy, good men would die.

Tom lifted the gas can, filled it with amber fluid, and screwed on the cap. He ran out to the P-40 and poured the fuel over the nose of the plane, anointing it for its death.

He couldn't watch the funeral pyre. He ran back to the tanker. The explosion shoved him in the back, and heat curled around him.

Tom set his jaw, filled the can, ran out, and doused another victim. Burning carcasses littered the runway, and nausea swirled in Tom's stomach.

Nonsense. No one else on the field thought twice about it.

He returned to the tanker, determined to take out as many planes as possible. Why should he be different from the other men?

"Looks good." Moskovitz made check marks on a clipboard. "We've got teams on all the aircraft. Let's blow this tanker."

The men tossed the gas cans under the tanker and vacated the area.

Ed Giannini and Felipe Lopez from Moskovitz's squad set up a pole charge, blocks of TNT strapped to a long pole, which they leaned against the tanker. Lopez spooled out detonating cord to a safe distance, then lit it.

Tom ran with the rest of the men toward relative safety. The tanker blew. Several of the men fell to their knees and got up, embarrassed.

At the rendezvous area along the road to Youks-les-Bains, Captain Newman marched around, pointed at vehicles, and called out orders. The men piled into trucks.

Larry stood by Tom's jeep with Hank Carter, the driver.

"Hi, Larry. Got a diagram?"

"I'm sorry, Gill." Larry's eyes looked darker than usual. Furrows ran like railroad tracks up his forehead. "I tried to catch him, but he's too fast."

"The diagram?" How could a diagram be too fast? But Tom followed Larry's gaze to the jeep. Barracks bags filled the backseat. Where was Sesame?

"I got here when a bunch of planes blew. He took off. I tried to grab the leash, but you know how fast he runs."

Tom's face felt cold. The leash. He must have forgotten to tie the leash to the steering wheel. "Where'd he—which way did he go?"

"After you."

"Oh no." Tom spun and faced the runway, the burning planes, and the clouds of black smoke. His dog? In there?

"Okay, Gill, ready to go?" Newman strode over. "Let's head on out."

"No." Tom turned to his CO. "I've got to—I've got to take care of something."

"We've got to get out of here. The Germans are in Fériana."

"Five minutes." Tom couldn't wait for permission. He took off running.

"I'll come with you, Gill," Larry called out.

"Thanks." Tom ran hard. Smoky, dusty air burned his lungs. He had to find Sesame. What would the Germans do? Use him for target practice?

Sesame depended on him, trusted him, and Tom could not abandon him, could not let him down.

"Sesame! Sesame!" His voice competed with rumbling trucks and crackling explosions.

"Sesame!" Larry called. "I'll go down this side of the runway. You go down that side."

Tom nodded. What was the dog thinking? He hated explosions, turned into a quivering mass of fur during air raids.

That was when he had Tom by his side. He was looking for Tom.

Pain rent its way across his chest. "Sesame! Lord, help me find him." He peered around burning planes and inside dugouts. Where would Sesame look for him?

He stopped in his tracks. All these explosions. Like an air raid.

"The slit trench." Tom wheeled away from the field. "Sesame!"

He leaped into the earthen trench, whipped his head left, then right.

Sesame cowered down, his face burrowed against the wall. Relief tumbled around in Tom's chest. "Sesame," he said in a low voice. "Here, boy. I'm here."

He lifted one eyebrow.

Tom clucked his tongue and crawled forward. "Here, boy. It's okay now. Everything's okay." He reached out his hand. Sesame didn't draw back, so Tom stroked his warm head covered with short tawny fur. "Hey, boy. I'm here now. It's okay."

Sesame whimpered and raised his head, his brown eyes questioning but trusting.

Tom gathered the dog in his arms and buried his face in that soft fur. "I can't believe I almost lost you."

Sesame licked Tom's face, concentrating below his eyes. Tom scrunched his eyes shut—his wet eyes. He was crying? When was the last time he'd cried?

The day Dad died. Two decades without tears. Was he losing control? He couldn't afford to do that.

Tom drew a deep breath, climbed out of the trench with Sesame in his arms, and jogged back to the jeep.

Larry ran on the other side of the runway, waved at Tom,

and raised a fist of victory. For a fellow who had never owned a dog, he'd become awfully fond of Sesame.

Tom held that dog tight. In this life he had God, Mom, Annie, and Sesame. But Sesame was the only one he could hold.

17

Oran, Algeria
February 22, 1943

Mellie leaned against the wrought-iron railing on the grounds of the old French villa and absorbed the full rainbow of color around her. Purple-tinged clouds hovered over the gray-blue Mediterranean. Orange and red hibiscus and magenta bougainvillea spilled over the villa's yellow walls.

"So beautiful," she said to Georgie and Rose. "I haven't seen colors like this since I left the Philippines."

Georgie's cheeks glowed. "This is wonderful, isn't it? From Ernie Pyle's columns in the paper, you'd think North Africa's nothing but mud and gloom."

Rose laughed. "We're almost four hundred miles from the front."

That distance shortened every day. Mellie shuddered. In the past week, Rommel's tanks had rolled over Allied strongholds, stormed through Kasserine Pass, and driven the Allies back over fifty miles. The Germans took five American airfields and thousands of prisoners. Mellie prayed Ernest wasn't among them.

"Can you believe this place?" Alice Olson strolled across

the grounds with Kay and Vera. "K rations for dinner, sleeping on the cold, hard floor, and now it looks like rain."

Rose chuckled. "Thank goodness we came ashore yesterday. Alice has new and different things to complain about."

"I was worried she'd run out," Georgie said.

Mellie didn't join their laughter, but she did smile. Alice's whining had even gotten on Vera's nerves.

"Ladies!" Lieutenant Lambert called from the doorway. "Come inside please. Mail call and then we head to our bivouac area."

"Mail call." The phrase hopped rabbitlike over the grass. They hadn't had mail for over two weeks.

The twenty-four nurses of the 802nd MAETS sat on the floor of the villa's main room, void of furniture. The ladies wore their dark blue service jackets now paired with matching trousers. On board the *Lyon*, Georgie had helped the ladies refashion their jackets into the new waist-length style.

A sergeant passed out mail, and the ladies chattered like parakeets in the Filipino jungle.

Mellie received four letters from Ernest. She opened them and examined the dates—February 2, 6, 9, and 13. All before the German offensive. In Mellie's heart, the thick pool of worry for Papa expanded to cover Ernest.

Georgie waved a Victory Mail envelope in front of Rose's face. "Look at this. Mailed February 8. We didn't know where we were going, but the Army Post Office did."

"From one of your sisters?" Rose glanced at the envelope. "Your parents?"

"Ward. Now that he discovered V-Mail, I'll never get a full letter again." Georgie opened the square envelope and pulled out a single sheet, one-quarter the size of a normal letter. She squinted at the contents. "He'd better improve his handwriting. Look at this."

Rose obeyed too eagerly. "It's manly handwriting."

"Doesn't he know they photograph his letter, put it on microfilm, ship the film overseas, then print it here all itty-bitty?"

"At least he wrote."

Georgie sighed and gazed at Mellie's envelopes. "I wish he wrote like Mellie's man."

"He's not my man." A bubbly feeling in her chest contradicted her words. Over two weeks had passed without word from him, but now his warmth and insight and humor lay on four precious pieces of paper.

She smoothed out the earliest letter and smiled at Ernest's familiar square handwriting. Although she didn't know his name or face, she knew his heart and mind and soul, what mattered in a man.

The feelings that billowed inside her—were they nothing more than affection for a friend? She was so new to friendship it was hard to tell, but her feelings for Georgie and Rose didn't compare. Her feelings for Ernest flipped her organs around and frolicked on her lips and tingled over her skin.

Was it love? How silly to fall in love with a man she'd never met.

And futile. Anonymity was the foundation for their friendship. He needed anonymity to express his feelings, and she needed it too. If he met her . . .

A shiver disrupted the bubbles.

If he met her, he'd be disappointed. Her looks were simply too . . . unconventional, so she hid behind anonymity.

For the first time in her life, that bothered her.

She closed her eyes and prayed for forgiveness. The Lord gave her a good life—serving him by serving others. Not only could she support herself, but she enjoyed travel and adventure. To ask for love on top of all that would be greedy.

"Is Ernest all right?" Georgie asked.

Mellie's eyes popped open. "Ernest? Yes, I'm sure he's fine. I haven't read much."

"Admiring his handwriting?" Georgie's smile tipped to one side. "It's a lot better than Ward's."

"What's Ward have to say?" Rose looked over Georgie's shoulder.

"The price of feed, too much rain, the usual. You know us, like an old pair of shoes, comfy and boring. Oh, he said to say hello to Danny. Ah, his old childhood nickname for you."

Rose's eyes softened. "Tell him I said hello back."

A sigh flowed from deep inside Mellie. She wasn't alone in tumultuous feelings and unrequited love, if love was indeed what she felt.

She turned to the first letter.

Dear Annie,

Today's friendship tip—ask questions. Most people love to talk about themselves. Even shy people warm up when someone shows interest in them. Ask where they're from and what they do. Ask their opinion on the weather and the war. Ask about their family and friends. You can have a lot of conversation without revealing one thing about yourself. I'm an expert at that.

All's fine here except occasional unwanted visitors from above. Sesame doesn't like them, but they don't bother me. I like to think I'm courageous, but in reality, I'm not terribly concerned whether I live or die. Mom and

Sesame and you are the only reasons I hop in the slit trench. Do you think people have more fear when they have more to live for?

I apologize for the tone of this letter. You're the only one who knows I'm in a foul mood. Everyone else thinks I'm happy. But how can I be when my CO doubts my abilities, when I doubt my own abilities, when my men don't listen to me? I'm giving you friendship tips. Got any leadership tips for me? If I don't learn how to lead, my career's over.

Thank goodness for anonymity. I'd hate to lose your respect too.

Mellie looked up from the page. Some of the ladies were still reading and some had gotten up to get their gear ready for the truck ride and hike to the bivouac area.

Poor, sweet Ernest, trying to advise her when he needed advice himself. But his words did more than awaken her concern. They prodded the bubbles back to life.

She gave him a reason to live? Right up there with his mother and dog?

With effort, she reread the last paragraph. Anonymity. He needed anonymity. She couldn't let her feelings gallop out of control.

"Oops. Wrong Lieutenant Blake." Across the room, Wilma Blake from another flight stood up and waved a letter. "Mellie, got one of your letters again."

"Thanks, Wilma." Another letter from Ernest? Maybe he'd have news from after the offensive. Mellie stood and met Wilma halfway. However, the letter wasn't the usual envelope in an envelope from Captain Newman. The return address—the Red Cross.

"Oh my goodness." Her knees wobbled and her hands went cold. Papa was dead. No, Papa was alive. No, they still didn't have word.

"Mellie, are you all right?" Georgie called.

"The . . ." Her tongue stuck to the roof of her mouth. "The Red Cross."

"Heavens." Georgie scrambled to her feet and over to Mellie. "Sit down. Sit down and take a deep breath."

"Papa." The word tumbled out of her mouth, high-pitched and tight.

Georgie eased her to the ground, and Rose scooted to her other side.

"Are you okay?" Rose asked. "Do you want us to read it for you?"

Mellie worked hard to focus on Rose. What had she ever done without friends? "Would you please?"

After Rose pried away the letter, Georgie held Mellie's hands in hers.

Rose opened the letter, unfolded it, and scanned it. Her expression softened, and she glanced up. A gentle smile curved her lips. "He's alive."

Mellie's chest heaved. Her thoughts whirled. "He's . . . he's . . . ?"

"Alive. Yes. He's at Santo Tomas, a Japanese prison camp for civilians. He's alive, Mellie. He's alive. Here's his address and instructions to write him."

A year of tension welled up and escaped in giant, laughing sobs. On either side, her friends embraced her, comforted her, supported her weight, and rejoiced with her.

She wasn't alone after all.

Assi-le-Meur, Algeria
February 27, 1943

"I can't believe we only get one quart of water each day for washing." Alice Olson filled her helmet with water from the Lister bag, which hung like a giant udder from a wooden frame.

"We also get two showers a week." Mellie unbuckled her helmet, which barely fit over her hair.

Vera glared at her. "That's fine if you're used to living in primitive conditions."

Mellie gave her a sweet smile. "I am." Lieutenant Lambert encouraged her to share her knowledge of living in the field. Some accepted it, others didn't.

The bivouac area near Oran, nicknamed Mud Hill, was definitely primitive. Standing in line for chow, eating from mess kits, sleeping in tents under mosquito netting, latrines, slit trenches, and limited water.

When Alice and Vera finished, Mellie knelt, opened the spigot, and filled her helmet with her daily quart of disinfected water. She chewed her lip. The shower time was too short for a shampoo. Somehow she had to figure out how to wash her mass of hair in one quart.

Mellie closed the spigot and picked her way through the mud toward the tent she shared with eleven other nurses.

In the jungle she could wash in rivers and streams, but not in Algeria.

She glanced down at her helmet. A quart was barely enough to dampen her hair. She knew better than to complain, but her scalp itched from dirt and bugs, and she longed for a good scrubbing and thorough rinse.

She passed a group of nurses washing their hair in their helmets. They managed, but they wore their hair nice and short. Practical. And cute.

Mellie worked her fingers under her braids and scratched. For the first time in her life, she wanted to hack it all off.

What about Papa? He'd be so disappointed, so worried. Her long hair reassured him she wouldn't turn into her mother.

Mellie stopped and stared over the sea of khaki canvas tents under the leaden sky. Or did she wear her hair long to assure herself she wouldn't turn into her mother?

That was ridiculous. Wild living never tempted her. Papa knew that. Mellie knew too. Did it run deeper?

She scrunched her eyes shut and swayed. Telling her mother's story to Ernest opened unexplored compartments in her mind. Had she truly forgiven? Was her long hair nothing but a rejection of her mother?

Would a haircut, in some tiny way, act as a badge of forgiveness?

She opened her eyes and looked around. Hundreds of ward and flight nurses, none with hair below their shoulders. Short hair wouldn't make the women like her, but would it show the women that she liked *them*? That she was willing to identify with them?

What about Papa?

Mellie strode forward, careful not to lose a drop of water. Had she clung to her long hair in a subconscious attempt to keep him alive? Why, that would be silly and superstitious. Besides, after what Papa had endured, he would be thrilled to see Mellie even if she were bald.

Outside her tent, Georgie and Rose played cards, their hair wrapped in towels.

"Hi, ladies." Mellie burrowed her helmet down into the mud so it wouldn't spill. Before her friends could ask questions, she ducked into the tent, heavy with the scent of damp, dirty canvas.

She opened her carved mahogany box, set it on her cot, and yanked out dozens of bobby pins. Determination filled her chest, and a smile flicked up. No more poking bobby pins.

Her braids swung down almost to her knees. "Georgie, may I borrow your sewing scissors?"

"Sure," she called from outside. "You know where they are. What do you need them for?"

"Just need to trim something." She grasped a braid in one hand and the scissors in the other and paused. *Lord, it's just hair. It needs to go for hygienic reasons. It needs to go so I can forgive my mother. It needs to go so I can be part of the group. And it needs to go if I've made it an idol.*

With her jaw set, she sawed at the braid. Too thick. She poked the scissor point between the plaits and cut them one at a time. One, two, three.

A long, black braid dropped to the dirt like a dead snake.

Mellie grabbed the metal mirror from her toiletry kit and stared at her dim image. On the left side, her hair unwound, popped free of the braiding, and sprang up just below her chin.

"Oh my goodness." She'd cut it shoulder length, but it had wave—more wave than she knew. It was short. So short. She pawed at the locks, the springy ends, the curls, the void below her shoulders. Her head felt light and lopsided.

"I've done it now," she whispered. Now she could ask for help.

She wrinkled her nose. She hated to draw attention to herself and have everyone make a fuss, but it couldn't be avoided.

"Rose," she called. "You're good with haircuts, aren't you?"

"Yeah, sure. Why?"

Georgie gasped. "You don't want to cut your hair, do you?"

Her cheeks flamed. "Already have. I need help evening it out."

The women burst through the tent flaps. Their mouths hung open.

Mellie gave them a shrug and a wink, and fluffed the short side of her hair. "Being a lady is overrated."

Rose laughed. "Goodness. What did you do? Why?"

"It's heavy, it itches, and it isn't practical here." Mellie grabbed her towel and edged past her friends and out of the tent. She sat on a camp stool and held out the scissors to Rose. "Please. I look ridiculous."

Georgie squatted in front of her with wide, concerned eyes. "You never said anything."

"You might have talked me out of it. Now you can't." She wiggled the scissors in Rose's direction. "Please. Would you please even it out?"

"Love to." Rose fingered Mellie's cut hair. "When I'm done, we'll have to beat off the boys."

A little laugh popped from Mellie's lips. "A miracle worker, are you?"

"You know I am." Rose put one hand on her hip, tilted her head, and snipped the scissors in the air. "Watch and be amazed."

Georgie took Mellie's hand. "But why? You said long hair was important to your father."

"It is." Mellie closed her eyes as Rose chopped off the other braid. Her head felt as if it would float away. "He didn't want me to turn out like my mother."

"Your mother?" they said together.

The story came more easily now that she'd told Ernest. "She was raised in the Philippines. Her father was stationed there in the Army, married to a Filipina. Papa met her on one of his botanical excursions. After I was born, they came to California. My mother had never been to the States, and she decided she'd never really lived. She bobbed her hair, went to the speakeasies, and neglected Papa and me. One night when I was two, she crashed a car into a tree and died."

"Oh no." Georgie squeezed Mellie's hand. "I'm so sorry."

Rose's scissors kept snipping. "That's why he never wanted you to cut your hair."

Mellie nodded.

Rose clamped a hand on her head to stop her. "If you don't want it any shorter, sit still."

Georgie rubbed her thumb over the back of Mellie's hand. "You're not your mother. You know that, don't you?"

Mellie gave her a smile. "I know. That's why I cut my hair."

Rose snipped away. "You tell your old man you've got two gals to keep you out of bars. We'll keep you straight."

"You'd better," Mellie said with a laugh. "You know what a wild woman I am."

Georgie's eyes glistened. "Wait till you see. You're as cute as can be. Let me get a mirror."

Her hair tickled her neck and cheeks. "Are you done, Rose?"

"Hold your horses, missy. You've got gobs of hair." Scissors snipped. "A little more."

Georgie returned and handed Mellie the mirror. "See? You look like Rita Hayworth but with black hair."

Mellie blinked. She didn't recognize the face in the mirror. It looked so modern. Nothing like the movie star, nothing at all, but she did look almost . . . almost cute.

Rose fiddled with her hair. "See, you roll it like this, up from your forehead. My, you have a nice hairline. And you pin it here. I am so jealous. Your hair is so thick and wavy. Just gorgeous."

Mellie fingered the fluff of curls around her jawline. Somehow it minimized the severity of her mouth. She ventured a partial smile and startled at the sight. For the first time, she saw a hint of exotic beauty.

"You look so pretty," Georgie said. "But then I always thought so."

What would Ernest think? Mellie peered at her image, fuzzy and dark in the metal mirror, and she sighed. She'd never find out, and that was best.

18

Youks-les-Bains Airfield
Algeria
February 28, 1943

Tom forced himself to lift his chin as he stood at attention in the crowded company headquarters tent.

Captain Newman addressed the group with stern words.

How could Tom look his CO in the eye? Weiser and Lehman were demoted to corporal and transferred to Quincy's platoon. Sergeants Ferris and Kovatch, who headed squads in Quincy's platoon, were transferred to Tom's platoon to replace them. Two corporals were promoted to replace Ferris and Kovatch.

A mess. And all Tom's fault.

If he'd been a better leader, Weiser and Lehman would have obeyed orders when evacuating Thélepte.

Shame burned in his chest. His engineering degree saved his position, but Newman's grace only extended so far.

Tom had to change. But how? He didn't want to be cruel like Quincy or aloof like Reed. Newman wasn't the best example either. He was pleasant and excellent at logistics, but he couldn't contain Quincy or teach Tom.

The wind ruffled the canvas, just as Annie's last letter had ruffled Tom. She suggested looking to Jesus Christ as an example of the perfect leader.

Yeah. Perfect. How could he draw parallels? The disciples had chosen to follow. Tom's men had been drafted.

"Company dismissed," Newman said.

Salutes snapped up, and field jackets rustled. The men filed out of the tent.

Weiser shot Tom a dirty look, as if Tom had imposed the discipline rather than Newman. And he should have. Instead the captain did the hard work.

Quincy hitched the strap for his carbine higher on his shoulder and gave Tom a look loaded with disgust.

For once, Tom didn't smile. He looked away, his heart heavy as if full of black tar. Quincy would bear the brunt of this. He'd lost his best squad leaders, he had to train new ones, and he got saddled with Weiser and Lehman.

Tom pushed his way through the tent flap with Larry behind him. Sergeants Ferris and Kovatch stood to the side, and a gust of wind tossed their voices into Tom's ear.

"Stuck in the misfit platoon." Ferris lit a cigarette and sheltered the lighter with his hand.

Kovatch borrowed Ferris's flame for his own cigarette. "We'll whip it into shape."

Tom swallowed a sticky mouthful of shame and raised a smile. "Sergeant Ferris, Sergeant Kovatch, glad to have you in my platoon."

Ferris puffed on his cigarette. He was a small man with dark hair, dark eyes, and an even darker look. "Yeah, thanks, Gill."

"Lieutenant MacGilliver." Right on the spot he made that decision, but it felt right. More distance, less fraternization.

Larry's gaze whipped to him. Yeah, that would be a surprise.

"Sure thing, Lieutenant." Kovatch's square face, perpetually red from the weather, wrestled down a smile. "What's our first assignment, Lieutenant?"

Tom ignored the mocking tone. He'd earned the disrespect. "Your boys are down at the runway with Moskovitz's squad, replacing the planking ripped up in the last air raid. I'll take you down, introduce you."

"Why? We know the men." Ferris blew out a gray cloud of smoke.

Kovatch slapped Ferris on the back. "What do you say? Think we can find the runway?"

They were challenging him. Mom's training told him to back down, but something deep inside told him not to. For once, he'd listen. "I'm going down there anyway." He marched toward the runway.

Larry trotted to catch up. "What's that about, Gill? Or can I call you Gill?"

"You can. No one else. Things have to change around here. I have to change."

"Nonsense." Larry glanced behind him, where Ferris and Kovatch lagged. "Don't let this get you down. You're a great engineer."

The gray sky pressed down on him, heavy with the threat of German attack. Rommel had retreated back through Kasserine Pass two days before, but was he just regrouping for another thrust?

"Come on, Gill." Urgency laced Larry's voice. "Where's the grin everyone loves?"

"Everyone loves." Tom blew air between his lips, making them flap. "I'm smart, I'm talented, I'm friendly. But it's not enough. The men don't follow me."

"It doesn't matter anymore."

"What?"

Larry motioned with his thumb back at Ferris and Kovatch.

"Newman took care of it. Those guys will do the dirty work, and you can be the nice guy. It's brilliant."

Tom shifted his carbine strap. "It's not right."

"Why not? Don't good leaders delegate? You're delegating."

"Delegating." That didn't sit well. He was delegating leadership itself. Or serving as a conduit for Newman's leadership. Either way Tom was a figurehead.

"You don't have a choice." Larry's voice flattened. "You and I don't have a choice."

Laughter floated from behind. Kovatch bowed to Ferris, his arms folded across his stomach, his teeth in an exaggerated overbite.

"See what I mean?" Larry said in a low growl.

Heat flamed in Tom's stomach. "Hey, Kovatch! Drop something? Or are you sick?" Half a smile, but he didn't let it go to his eyes.

Kovatch snapped upright, his eyes wide. "Um, no, just—"

"Don't let it happen again." Tom strode toward the runway, his insides tumbling.

"What's gotten into you?" Larry said. "Keep smiling and ignore them."

Sounded like Mom. If only it worked. "It's one thing when someone picks on me, another when they pick on my men."

"I can take care of myself."

"I know." Tom gave him a warm smile. "But we can also stick up for each other."

Larry dipped his chin. "Yeah. We can."

The gray steel runway stretched across the rocky tan soil from northeast to southwest. A mountain range jutted up in the east, the only barrier from Rommel's panzers.

Tom's platoon laid planking at the northern end of the runway. "Afternoon, Moskovitz."

"Hiya, Gill."

"Lieutenant MacGilliver, please."

Moskovitz's bushy eyebrows rose to the rim of his helmet. "Um, sure, Gi—Lieutenant."

Tom gestured to the men behind him. "Sergeants Ferris and Kovatch will replace Weiser and Lehman. Introduce them to their men and let them know what to do."

"Sure. Wow. A lot of shaking up around here."

Tom nodded. "Things are going to change."

Moskovitz searched Tom's face. "Oh."

Cheerful but firm. "It'll be good."

"Sure, boss." Moskovitz shook hands with the replacements and made introductions.

The men's faces registered shock, worry, but mostly annoyance. They'd have to work hard from now on. That churned up more shame in Tom.

He and Larry headed back to HQ. Paperwork awaited them.

Larry nudged him with his elbow. "Anything new from Annie?"

Tom shrugged. "Her last letter was written February 6. She's in transit."

"What if she came here? You could meet her."

"Uh-uh. Don't want to do that."

"Why not? Afraid she isn't pretty?"

"I don't care about that, but I still don't want to meet her."

"Why not? You two have something good. I bet she's falling for you."

"Girls don't fall for me."

Larry stopped in his tracks and flung his arms wide. "Where'd gloomy Gill come from? You're not bad looking. You've got a college degree. Girls fall for stuff like that."

Tom gave him half a smile. "You read too many pulp magazines."

"I like happy endings. You'll have one too."

"First of all, she doesn't want romance. She told me up front."

"She could change her mind."

Tom hooked his thumb over his pistol belt. "Even if she did, girls don't want anything to do with me. They like me as a friend. Nothing more. They're afraid of me, or their parents and friends are. Don't forget the name. Who wants to be Mrs. Thomas MacGilliver?"

Larry tipped his head and looked away.

"Exactly." Tom shifted his weight to his other leg. "The only girls who are attracted to me just want to annoy their parents. But when they realize I'm not a bad boy, they lose interest. And why would I want to be with a girl like that anyway?"

Larry huffed. "Come on, Annie sounds like a swell gal."

"Which is why she wouldn't be interested. Remember, she doesn't know my name, doesn't know anything about my father." A twinge of guilt. Annie told him about her mother, which took guts, but he'd only told her his father was dead.

Larry resumed walking to platoon HQ. "So tell her."

Tom followed in step but not in thought. Any details about his dad's crime and execution would chip away at the wall of anonymity. He didn't want to lose her.

He'd never felt this way about another human being. A mutual need had drawn them together. They'd opened up to each other and exchanged advice. He loved watching her grow and develop. But she was more—his first real friend, the first person who had seen inside him and still liked him.

Tom looked up and drew a deep breath, and the gray clouds filled his soul. Whether or not she was falling for him, he was definitely falling for her.

19

Maison Blanche Airfield
Algiers, Algeria
March 3, 1943

New sights and smells wafted around Mellie. What could be better? A few years before she'd seen the movie *Algiers* with Charles Boyer and Hedy Lamarr, and now she was there. The C-47 cargo plane had flown over the glittering white city on the Mediterranean and landed a few miles southeast.

Mellie hauled her barracks bag across the gravel-surfaced runway. Airplane engines roared in the distance, and the scent of citrus and olive groves mingled with the smell of aviation fuel. Papa loved the olive tree in their front yard in Palo Alto. Whenever Mellie had scraped her knee, he'd apply a poultice made from olive tree leaves to prevent infection, and whenever she ran a fever, he'd brew tea from the leaves.

A gust of wind blew her hair into her face. She directed a puff of breath to get it out of her eyes. Wasn't shorter hair supposed to be easier?

It was definitely more fun. Her head felt so much lighter, and she loved how her hair swung when she turned her head and bounced when she walked.

And it was worth it. After a few days of too much attention, things settled down. Now men looked at her, smiled, and tipped their caps. They didn't look twice, but Mellie didn't mind.

"Right this way, ladies," Lieutenant Lambert called. "We'll leave our gear in the barracks and meet in the briefing room at 1400."

"The briefing room?" Georgie nudged Rose. "Will we have to synchronize our watches?"

"The target for today," Rose said in a deep voice, imitating a newsreel announcer.

Mellie realized she was smiling. Fully. She reined it in to a more acceptable expression. Still, her step bounced. Maison Blanche Airfield would serve as the home base for medical air evacuation in North Africa. Finally they'd get to practice flight nursing.

The women passed hangars, administration buildings, and workshops. Behind the buildings, khaki tents fanned out into the distance. A bulldozer rumbled along the far edge of the runway.

Mellie's heart shimmied up into her throat. Was Ernest there? Would she recognize him? Part of her thought his soul would shine like a beacon, but the other part realized that was romantic twaddle.

"Here we are." Lieutenant Lambert swung open the door of an old French barracks, an attractive tile-roofed building with a stone façade. "There's a dayroom and an indoor bathroom."

"Thank goodness," Alice Olson said. "Hot water?"

"No, but at least you can wash your hair in the sink." The chief gave Alice a stiff smile.

Rose and Georgie exchanged some message spoken with eyebrows. Mellie still couldn't translate the intricacies of their language, but she got the gist of it.

The lieutenant led the women down a hallway, and at each door she read names from her clipboard for room assignments. Four to a room.

Mellie's face tingled. Their flight divided into solid groups of three. One of the threesomes would be broken up. What if she had to room with Vera, Alice, and Kay?

Lieutenant Lambert tapped on the second door on the left. "Mellie Blake, Rose Danilovich, Kay Jobson, Georgie Taylor."

Georgie and Rose grinned at Mellie. She smiled back with a twinge of discomfort for Kay. But Kay wore a neutral expression as she stepped into the room and plopped her barracks bag on a lower bunk. "You don't mind," she said to Mellie.

"I like the top bunk." Mellie gave her a little smile.

"Good, and with all the flyboys here, I won't be around to bug you." Kay sauntered out of the room.

Georgie hooked her arm through Mellie's. "Off we go to the briefing room. Do you think we'll get leather flight helmets? Goggles? Silk scarves?"

"If we're going to be flygirls, we have to learn to swagger," Rose said.

"Some of us already do," Georgie said in a low voice.

Mellie glanced out the door, where Kay chatted with Vera and Alice. "They deserve our prayers, not our gossip."

Georgie sighed. "You're right. But they make it so easy."

A few minutes later, the nurses of the 802nd MAETS filed into the briefing room. A dozen men rose to their feet and saluted. Most looked thrilled to have women in their midst, but some wore stony expressions.

Capt. Frederick Guilford greeted them. The flight surgeon had organized air evacuation in the theater and had recruited thirty-five enlisted medical technicians. Captain Guilford was taking over as the new commanding officer of the 802nd and bringing his techs with him.

In his early thirties, the CO stood at the front of the room in an olive drab service jacket and khaki trousers. "In December, Major Tompkins, the flight surgeon with the 14th Fighter Group, was stationed at the airfield at Youks-les-Bains. He didn't have a hospital. An ambulance ride to Algiers takes fourteen hours over rough roads, so he sent out his wounded on returning C-47s. Other medical officers followed suit."

Guilford clasped his hands behind his back. "The Twelfth Air Force made it official and assigned air evac to the 51st Troop Carrier Wing. We've run flights since January 15, over eight hundred patients this week alone. Most of our men are on flights right now."

"Yeah," a man grumbled behind Mellie. "That's why we don't need no skirts telling us what to do."

Mellie's stomach churned. Oh dear, he would be a challenge. He had a long face and a prominent chin, and he raised that chin at Mellie. She spun back to face front, cheeks hot.

Guilford cleared his throat. "Colonel Woolford with the Air Surgeon's office just visited. The hospitals desperately need nurses. The colonel says it's a shame to use nurses in air evacuation when technicians have proven themselves."

"Yeah," came the voice behind Mellie, but she didn't rise to the bait.

"However, I think it's a shame to waste your training. A trial is warranted."

A trial? Had their truncated training prepared them? Back at Bowman Field, squadrons underwent a new formal training program, but if the 802nd failed, flight nursing would be doomed.

As they left the building, Georgie smiled at Mellie and Rose over her shoulder. "I'm glad we get a trial. They could have shuttled us straight to the nearest field hospital."

"That's my optimist," Rose said. "First they've got to send

us on flights. Real flights, to the front. Then we have to show we add something valuable."

"Well, look who's here." Outside the building, a man stood to the side, wearing a leather flight jacket and the "crush cap" favored by airmen. "Saw you ladies and wondered if my rose had arrived. She has."

The ladies stopped and stared. Mellie's jaw dropped. He was the man they'd met in the theater in Louisville.

"How . . . how did you know my name?" Rose whispered.

"Your name?" He walked over and took off his cap. Blond curls sprang free and so did his grin. "I don't know your name—not for lack of trying. Don't tell me it's Rose."

Georgie laughed. "It is. How did you know?"

"I didn't." He gave Georgie a quick smile then turned the fullness of his attention back to Rose. "It's what I've called you in my mind. You drew me like a flower, but oh, those thorns."

Rose's face blanched. Every freckle stood out. "To keep pests away."

His face sobered. "Listen, let's start over. I'm Lt. Clint Peters. I'm a C-47 navigator. We'll spend time together, so we might as well get acquainted."

"I see I'm not needed." Georgie strode away. "Come on, Mellie."

"Oh no, you don't." Rose grabbed Mellie's arm.

She gave Clint a sheepish smile. "Looks like I'm the chaperone."

"Hi, chaperone. What's your name?" He shook her free hand.

"Mellie Blake. The escape artist is Georgie Taylor, and this is Rose Danilovich."

"Danilovich. Nice. But Rose Peters sounds better."

"That's it." Rose spun away and dragged Mellie with her.

She scrambled to keep her feet under her. Who knew chaperoning could be dangerous?

"Hey, now." Clint trotted around and blocked their path. "Give me a chance. I'm not usually like this. Really, I'm not. Something about you makes me bold."

Rose tried to edge around him. "If you find out what it is, tell me so I can turn it off."

"Please don't. Don't ever turn it off. It's wonderful." His brown eyes softened. "Never have I met a woman and thought, 'Boom! She's the one.' Then I met you and boom, boom, boom! You're the one."

"This is nonsense." Rose's voice wavered. "Come on, Mellie. Let's go."

Although Rose's fingers dug into her arm, Mellie hung back. Clint seemed sincere, and hadn't Rose wanted a man to treat her as precious?

A soft yearning pulled inside Mellie. Would any man ever look at her like Clint looked at Rose? How would Ernest look at her? Would he see who she was inside or only the broad mouth?

"One chance." Clint held his hands in front of his chest like a linebacker blocking the attack. "How about coffee at the officers' club? Big crowd so you'll feel safe. Bring your friends if you want. Give me a chance."

Rose lifted her chin. "Why should I?"

A slow smile turned up his lips. "Because the Lord brought us together. I know it, and you know it. That's why you're flustered."

"I'm flustered because you're a pest. Good day, Lieutenant."

"Good day, my Rose." He bowed his head and set his cap back in place. "We'll meet again."

"Not if I see you first." Rose hauled Mellie away.

She glanced back. Clint wore a smile so big anyone would think Rose had agreed to a date.

"Insufferable." Rose let go of Mellie's arm and marched at a brisk pace. "Conceited. Rude. How dare he bring the Lord into this? If this was God's will, don't you think God would have talked to me too? Huh?"

"Maybe. Maybe not. I don't know anything about romance."

"Neither do I. I'm the tomboy, the sidekick. No one pursues me."

"Clint's pursuing you."

"Exactly." Rose's eyes lit up. "What's wrong with him? I'm not that pretty. I'm not sweet and bubbly like Georgie. What on earth does he see in me? He's deranged."

"Deranged?" Mellie laughed. "Because he likes you? Nonsense. You're prettier than you think, and you have strength and spirit."

"Guys don't like that. They like girls soft and sweet. They see me as a buddy, their pal Danny, someone to talk to about the girls they really like."

Mellie brushed back her hair and peeked at her from the corner of her eye. "Like Ward did?"

Rose sucked in her breath. "And every other fellow I've known."

"Clint's different. Isn't that good?"

"Hardly. Something's wrong with him."

Mellie stopped in front of the north hangar, which towered over her. The desire to be liked told her to stop, but something else lurched inside, something that felt like true friendship. "So, any man who likes you is deranged, and you can only love a man who doesn't love you?"

Rose tucked a strand of dark blonde hair behind her ear. "I wouldn't know. I've never been in love."

"Never?" Mellie fidgeted with the strap for her purse. "I see how you light up when his letters come."

"His letters?" Rose scrunched up her face. "What are you talking about? The only men who write me are my dad and brothers. Not even Ward writes and he's my oldest friend."

"I know." She gave her the soft look reserved for patients in pain.

Rose stared at Mellie. She gasped. "You don't think . . . ? That's crazy. How could you think that?"

Mellie glanced away to a C-47 taxiing down the runway. "I don't talk a lot, but I listen and observe. When you talk about him, when Georgie talks about him—"

"Ridiculous." Rose's voice wavered. "They're my oldest and dearest friends."

"And he chose Georgie instead of you." Mellie turned back to her friend.

Her eyes reddened. "I wouldn't—I'd never hurt either of them."

"I know, but that doesn't change how you feel."

Rose snapped her head to the side and sniffed. Her chin worked back and forth, and the redness spread over her face. "You know, when I was little, I always thought we'd get married someday. We had so much in common. I never pictured myself with anyone else."

An ache traveled through Mellie's chest. Her feelings for Ernest were the closest she'd come to love. How would she feel if he loved someone else? Could she rejoice for him as a friend? Or would it break her?

Rose rubbed her cheeks and wiped her fingers on her skirt. She turned frantic red eyes to Mellie. "I'd never come between them. You know that, don't you?"

Mellie handed her a handkerchief. "I know. That's why you've never told her."

"Of course. I don't want to hurt her, and can you imagine how awkward, how miserable . . . ?" Rose raised her shoulders and shuddered. "I'll keep that ugly little truth hidden."

"Or you could change it."

"Excuse me?"

Mellie gazed over the rocky ground toward the briefing room. "If you dated someone else, you could take your mind off Ward."

"Oh, that's just wrong. Clint may be annoying, but I couldn't use him like that."

"Well, yes, if that's the only reason you went out with him. But what if you liked him, even a little bit?"

"He's rude and obnoxious—"

"And he adores you, and he has a nice face, and he's smart and responsible enough to be a navigator."

Rose sniffled and blew her nose. A smile twitched around the edges of the handkerchief. "He does have great hair."

Mellie laughed. Her gaze swept the airfield, a place of new beginnings. "The Twelfth Air Force gave us a trial period as flight nurses."

"A trial." Rose wadded up the hankie. "One single evening in the officers' club. Friday night. You and Georgie will come. He can bring his friends. Find him and tell him."

"What?"

"Yes, now. Quick. Before I change my mind."

"All right." Mellie laughed and walked back the way she came. True friendship required more than being pleasant. It meant being there for the hard times and even confronting if necessary.

She'd done it, and she grinned.

Compared to the palace of friendship, the forest of solitude seemed dull and lifeless.

20

Youks-les-Bains Airfield
March 12, 1943

Wreckage from a German Ju 87 Stuka dive-bomber littered the ground near the runway. Privates Earl Butler and Bill Rinaldi shoveled bits of debris into the path of the M1 tractor fitted with a bulldozer blade.

Tom frowned at the scene. "Butler, watch out. You're too close."

Sergeant Ferris cussed. "I can handle my own squad." He cupped his hand over his mouth. "Faster, Butler, you lump of—"

"Please don't insult the men. Doesn't help."

"That's right. This is the sunshine platoon." Ferris flicked ashes off the tip of his cigarette. "Never mind, Butler. You're perfect. Perfectly useless."

Granted, Butler moved slower than the dozer and had his back turned to the machine. Not smart. Tom stepped closer. "Butler! Watch the dozer. Get out of the way!"

"What?" he called over the rumble of the machine.

"Keep working, you nitwit," Ferris shouted.

The dozer rolled closer to Butler. Tom motioned him to the side. "Watch out."

Butler looked over his shoulder to the dozer, and he startled. He lunged out of the way, caught his foot on the wreckage, and fell.

"Stop!" Tom ran forward and waved his hands over his head to Kendrick, the driver. But Kendrick looked out the other side of the dozer and shouted something at Rinaldi.

The machine lumbered closer and closer.

Butler screamed and tugged at his leg—right in the path of the dozer.

Tom sprinted forward, grabbed Butler's arms, and yanked. No good. His foot was jammed tight.

The dozer blade struck. Butler cried out. A horrid cracking sound, and Butler's body flipped to the side.

Tom let go of his hands. "Butler!"

The private's right leg bent at a grotesque angle. He screamed and groped at his mangled leg. At least he still had his foot.

"Ferris!" Tom yelled. "Get the doc!"

For once the man obeyed. Tom snapped open the first aid pouch on his pistol belt, opened a tin, and pulled out a morphine syrette. "Hold still. Let me give you some morphine."

Butler clamped his mouth shut and gave a stiff nod.

Tom flicked off the cap over the needle, plunged it into Butler's thigh, and squeezed the little tin tube to release the morphine. "You're gonna be okay."

"My leg. My leg."

"I know it hurts, but you'll be okay. Doc will truss you up and send you to a hospital. You get a little vacation."

A strained smile. "Nurses."

Tom laughed. "Yeah. Lots of nurses."

The dozer had finally ground to a stop. Kendrick and Rinaldi ran up, and a small crowd hurled questions and accusations.

"It was an accident," Tom said. "We work with powerful equipment. We've all got to keep our eyes open."

"Clear the way. Everybody out of the way." The battalion doctor, Captain Abrams, ran up with two medics. He knelt beside Butler. "What have we got here?"

Tom tried to back up, but Butler grabbed his arm and held fast. "Private Earl Butler. He fell in front of the dozer. His foot was trapped. He couldn't get out of the way in time."

The doctor did an examination, applied a splint to Butler's leg, and loaded him onto a litter. "Good timing. An evac flight's coming in a few minutes. Take him to the flight line."

"Don't leave me." Butler's voice slurred from pain and morphine. He looked up at Tom with anguish all over his beefy face. "Please don't leave me, Gill."

Tom shot Doc Abrams a questioning look, and the doctor nodded his consent. Tom turned to Ferris. "Finish the job. We'll talk about this later."

"Yes, sir." Ferris dropped his gaze, his face pale. Good, maybe he had learned his lesson. But Tom couldn't let it slide, not when a man had been injured.

The litter-bearers took Butler away, and Tom followed down the runway toward the large hospital tent. The 9th Evacuation Hospital served as a holding unit for wounded from the front lines awaiting transport to the rear.

Outside the tent, a couple dozen patients on litters and in wheelchairs waited for the planes. Doc Abrams talked with another officer, and they gestured to set Butler's litter down.

Tom squeezed Butler's hand. "Looks like you get an airplane ride."

"Stewardesses?"

Tom laughed. "No. Just a bunch of fellows, but they'll get you out of here."

"Good." Sweat beaded on his forehead, although it was no more than fifty degrees.

Tom pulled out his handkerchief and wiped Butler's face.

Planes droned overhead—C-47s from the sound of the twin Wasp engines. Survival on the front meant distinguishing friend from foe. Even Sesame knew the difference. Smart dog. He'd earned a day off. Tom had tied him up in the tarpaulin-covered dugout the men called home, with a long tether so he could explore and hunt. His skill at catching rats added to his popularity.

Three C-47s landed and taxied to the hospital tent. Trucks drove up to meet them, and men piled out to unload the supplies.

The cargo door of the first plane swung open, and a man hopped to the ground. Another figure emerged. A curvy figure.

"That's a woman!" someone cried.

It sure was. A dark-haired woman stood in the doorway wearing a blue jacket, trousers, and garrison cap. She shielded her eyes from the sun and looked into the distance, over the buildings and tents. As her gaze swept the landscape, a smile spread.

A smile unlike anything Tom had ever seen in his life, wide and brilliant, filling her face, filling Tom's eyes.

One of the patients whistled. The woman glanced down, as if she'd just noticed the men before her. Her smile contracted, and Tom blinked.

"Holy cow! Look at that dame." A soldier pointed to the next plane down, where a striking redhead disembarked and waved to the crowd. All the ambulatory men ran or wheeled to the second plane and hooted and hollered.

Tom stayed. The dark-haired woman jumped to the ground, her face relaxed again. She headed toward the tent, toward

Tom, and his heart rate picked up. At the last minute, he remembered to take off his helmet. A lady was present.

He saluted her. "Good afternoon, ma'am."

She returned the salute. "Good afternoon, sir. Are you . . . ?" She glanced at the lapels of Tom's olive drab wool shirt, partially hidden under his field jacket. He wore silver first lieutenant's bars and the gold castle insignia for the engineers. "No, you're not. Do you know—"

"Looking for the physician?" He grinned at her.

"Yes, sir." She smiled back, soft and modest. Her complexion was darker than most girls he knew, and her coffee-colored eyes had a hint of an almond shape.

Exotic. Compelling.

"Well?" The corners of her eyes crinkled.

He was acting like a fool. "I'll help you find him." He scanned the area and waved over the doctor.

The physician and nurse exchanged salutes. "Capt. Marvin Richards."

"Nice to meet you, sir. I'm Lt. Mellie Blake."

Mellie Blake. Mellie Blake. Her hair shone like obsidian and curled below her chin.

The doctor led her away. "I heard you gals were in the theater. Not sure about this. It's a dangerous place, and the hospitals could really use you."

Mellie Blake was of average height, but she stood tall and assured. "You want the best for your patients, sir. That's my job. I'll give these boys first-rate, uninterrupted care from here to Algiers. And I've been in more dangerous places than this and done just fine."

Captain Richards hiked up his eyebrows.

Tom clamped off a laugh. That little nurse could take care of herself. He'd love to get to know her better.

He scrunched his eyes shut. What was he doing? What

about Annie? They knew each other well. He cared for her deeply enough to wonder if he loved her. And she was in North Africa now, the same soil. Maybe God wanted them together. What if she could overlook his name? What if she could love him? He wanted to give that a chance.

Besides, all he knew about Mellie Blake was he liked her smile and her pluck. And she didn't know anything about him, except that he was a bit daft.

"Gill? You think I'll go home?" Butler's eyes roamed in lazy circles.

Tom squatted by the litter. "Maybe. No matter what, you'll get a few months' vacation. Algiers, she said. By the shore in the sun. Not bad, huh?"

"I wanna go home."

"Tell me about home. What's it like?"

Butler rambled about the farmhouse in Indiana, his Ford with the rumble seat, and his parents and brothers. When he mentioned the cute little gal who liked to meet him in the barn, Tom diverted conversation back to family and crops.

His gaze kept hopping to Lieutenant Blake. She made her rounds, listened to Captain Richards's reports, made notes on a clipboard, and questioned each patient in a warm voice. Richards prodded her onward, but she resisted and gave each wounded man her full attention.

She came closer and closer, and Tom's throat swelled.

Captain Richards stood at the foot of Butler's litter. "Last man. Private Butler. Just arrived. Closed complete fractures of the right tibia and fibula, needs surgery. Had half a grain of morphine at 1300."

Lieutenant Blake wrote on her clipboard and knelt beside Butler. Beside Tom. Inches from him. She smelled . . . he couldn't place the scent, but it tickled the edges of memory. Clean. She smelled clean. How long since he'd been around someone clean? And how much did he stink?

The nurse patted Butler's arm. "How are you feeling, Private?"

"You . . ." He pointed at the nurse, but his finger made a wobbly circle. "You're a girl."

"Clever one, aren't you?" She winked at him and made another notation. "I see half a grain of morphine is plenty for you."

"I gave him a syrette." Tom wanted to be included for some stupid reason.

Her dark eyes shifted to him. "Thank you, sir. Are you . . . ?"

"I'm his platoon leader. He wanted me to stay."

"Don't go, Gill. Don't leave me."

She glanced at Butler's grasp on Tom's hand and she smiled. "I see."

"He's the best," Butler said. "Ferris is mean. Mean, I tell you. But Gill, he cares."

Lieutenant Blake shot Tom a brief smile, not nearly enough. "You can accompany him onto the plane and stay until it's time to depart."

"Thank you, ma'am." He gave her a smile in the hopes she'd return it. She did, but only a smidgen.

She looked up at the doctor. "I need help loading the patients. May I borrow some of your hospital staff?"

"I'll send out some medics." The doctor went into the tent.

"You don't need to do that." A sergeant swaggered over from the plane and pointed his long chin at the nurse. "I can handle it. Always have."

Lieutenant Blake got to her feet and lifted her own chin. "Thank you, Sergeant, but we were trained to load patients as quickly as possible. Someday we may need to do so under fire."

The sergeant snorted. "Don't see no planes."

Fire rose in Tom's belly and pulled him to his full height.

Thank goodness he had a few inches on the sergeant. He turned his back on the man and addressed the nurse. "We have air raids almost daily. Loading quickly is smart. I'd be glad to help." Then he sent a smile over his shoulder to the sergeant. "And you'll address the lieutenant with respect, as an officer but also as a lady. I'm sure your mother taught you right."

The sergeant's eyes flicked back and forth. "Yes, sir." He turned to leave.

Would she be angry at Tom for interfering? He faced her.

She had a keen gaze fixed on him, her lips in a slight curve. "Thank you, sir."

"You're welcome. Now, put me to work, boss."

A flash of that smile he'd first seen, but she hauled it in as if ashamed. "Come with me, please."

Gladly. He bent down to Butler. "I need to help the lady. I'll be back."

Butler flapped his hand at Tom. "Bye-bye."

Tom followed the nurse, who instructed the medics in a voice of authority.

A voice of authority. He needed that. Once again he looked to a woman as an example. Mom had taught him all his life, he sought Annie's advice, and now he studied the way this young lady spoke.

She didn't scream. She didn't toss out cold orders. She didn't cuss or insult. But she didn't apologize or bribe or ingratiate herself. She just told them what she wanted as if she expected them to obey. And they did.

So did Tom. He carried litters onto the plane and held them steady while that snake of a sergeant fastened clamps. As the men worked, Lieutenant Blake tucked blankets around her patients and sang "His Eye Is on the Sparrow." Her voice flew like a bird, rising high, gliding, and landing with a calming touch on each man on the plane.

Tom tried not to watch her, but her voice soaked through his skin and warmed his blood. An enchanting voice had been the downfall of man since the Sirens and the Lorelei.

Before long, twelve litters lined the sides of the cargo plane, stacked three high, and another half-dozen men sat in seats toward the front. Butler's litter was on the lowest level nearest the cockpit, and Tom sat on the floor beside him.

Finally Lieutenant Blake knelt beside Butler. "How did this happen?" she asked Tom.

"Got mowed down by a dozer. I couldn't get him out of the way in time."

"He tried," Butler said. "He tried."

"I'm sure he did." She examined the splint on his leg.

"S'working as fast as I could. Gotta keep this runway in shape. S'what we do."

"What do you do here?" She eyed Tom's lapels again. "I don't know all the insignia. What's the castle for?"

"Engineers," Tom said.

"Really." She searched Tom's face. Her gaze roamed his eyes, his forehead, his mouth, and gripped him in its intensity. "You—you build things?"

He couldn't speak. With a sharp move, he nodded and broke the hold she had on him. "Airfields. I'm in the 908th Engineer Aviation Battalion. I build airfields. And fix them."

"That's important work." She flipped pages on her clipboard and got to her feet. She wobbled and grasped the litter rack.

Her clumsiness relaxed him and loosed his grin. "I'd rather build bridges. That's what I want to do after the war. I want to build bridges all over the world, bring people together, help people explore new places."

A small smile, almost sad. "That would be lovely."

The door to the cockpit opened, and a man in a leather flight jacket leaned out. "We're about to start engines."

Tom squeezed Butler's arm. "Okay, I've gotta go. Enjoy your vacation."

"Uh-huh." His eyes drifted shut. "Say bye to Sesame. Love that dog."

"I'll do that."

The nurse headed to the cargo door, grasping the poles as if the plane were in turbulent flight.

He followed her down the aisle. "Thanks, Lieutenant Blake. I know you'll take good care of him, of all these men." He held out his hand.

She hesitated, then shook his hand, her fingers small and warm and alive in his. Their joined arms swooped like the cable of a suspension bridge, and a sense of connection raced through Tom's arm and straight to his heart.

"Thank you." She gazed at their clasped hands. "Thank you for your help, Lieutenant Gill."

He could leave it at that and have her think highly of him. But truth welled up inside him and forced itself out as always, and for the best, now more than ever. He had to shatter his illusions. "Actually, it's MacGilliver. Lieutenant Tom MacGilliver. And let's get this over with. Yes, I'm his son."

Her eyes widened with the shock he was used to, but a tempered shock, and she searched his face again, almost as if she recognized him. "Tom. Tom Mac—"

He cracked a smile. "Not every day you meet a celebrity, huh?"

Lieutenant Blake nodded, and her eyebrows arched with compassion. Her full lips worked. "I—I've always prayed for you."

It was Tom's turn to be shocked. "You have?"

"When your father . . . when he was convicted, I saw your picture in the paper. So sad. I cut it out, and I've prayed for you ever since."

Tom's mouth drooped open. How many years? How many years had this fascinating woman prayed for him? For him?

She wriggled her fingers.

He still held her hand. He released it. "Thank you." His voice came out thick.

"I always thought it must have been hard for you." She gazed out the door, a distant look, and she pulled those lips in between her teeth.

"You did?"

"Everyone hated your father so much. But you were just a little boy. You must have loved your father. You must have sweet, warm memories. How difficult to be torn between the man you loved and the man the world hated."

Tom's heart spun and stopped, hung up on the truth. Nothing good about that man, his mother said. He was a bum, a wino, a murderer, and Tom couldn't be anything like him, anything at all.

Lieutenant Blake's eyes rounded. "I'm sorry. That was too much. I shouldn't have—"

"No. No. It's fine." He jumped down to the ground. The jolt started his heart again. He tried to smile at the nurse but failed. He lifted a salute. "Thank you. Thank you for your prayers."

She looked down at him, forehead knit together. "Goodbye."

"Bye." Tom walked away. He'd never see her again, thank goodness. That woman could do serious damage to his heart.

21

Mellie leaned her forehead against the cool aluminum of the closed cargo door, and her pulse thrummed in her ear. An engineer. In the 908th. Sesame. He was Ernest.

Her world swirled about her. Oh goodness, she'd met Ernest. Did he know? Did she say anything, anything at all, that would link her to Annie?

"Please, Lord," she whispered. "Don't let him figure it out."

She pressed her palms to the door, fingers splayed wide. Ernest was Tom MacGilliver, the son and namesake of a convicted murderer, the boy she'd prayed for. She took all she knew of little Tommy and all she knew of Ernest and tried to match them like two ripped pieces of paper. Did they form a whole? A soft moan slipped out. She never thought she'd meet either man, certainly never dreamed they'd be the same man.

An engine sputtered to life, and Mellie jerked up her head.

She needed to focus. A planeload of patients needed her. The next two hours would be critical. In New Guinea the 801st MAETS had yet to fly, so the 802nd led the way. A failure today would jeopardize the flight nursing program.

Today of all days, why did she have to meet Ernest?

Tom.

From his newspaper picture, she'd always imagined him with dark eyes, but he had blue eyes, the same bright blue as the Mediterranean, shaped like teardrops. When he smiled, which was often, they narrowed into commas.

"Lord, help me."

"I told them. Dames can't handle this."

Mellie jumped. Why did they have to send Sergeant Early today? Captain Maxwell paired Vera and Kay with friendly technicians, but Mellie with flight nursing's most vocal opponent. As if the surgeon wanted her to fail.

However, Mellie knew how to deal with condescending men, from jungle guides to physicians. Be cool and firm and professional.

She leveled her gaze at him. "I like to start with prayer. Now, excuse me, please. I'd like to talk to the men." She strolled down the aisle and patted the patients' arms. "We're ready for takeoff, gentlemen. Everyone is strapped in. Sergeant Early and I need to take our seats, but once we're in the air, we'll tend to your needs."

Vibrations from the two engines rumbled the length of the plane and tickled Mellie's feet in her black nurse's pumps. Completely impractical for use in a combat theater.

She returned to the rear of the cabin and sat on the floor against the cargo door as she'd been trained. Early perched on the medical chest against the back wall, smoking a cigarette. None of the patients needed oxygen, so Mellie didn't say a word.

The plane rolled forward, turned, then accelerated down the runway. Mellie held on to a metal litter support so she wouldn't slide.

She fixed her mind on the bleak, rugged beauty of the landscape that had enthralled her when she landed, so different from the coastal region. But Tom's face popped up. Such a nice face. That contagious grin. Not movie-star handsome but boy-next-door handsome, and far too good-looking to notice her in a romantic way.

Mellie's stomach squirmed. His character in person matched his character on paper. His kindness to Private Butler, his chivalry to her, his willingness to help, how he confronted Early with a smile. Everything matched.

And everything made sense. Ernest said he had to be sunny for reasons he couldn't mention. Why, of course. With a shameful legacy of violence, he'd chosen to erect an inoffensive façade. His letters showed her the man behind the façade, safe in anonymity, never knowing the anonymity would be demolished.

Mellie pressed her free arm over her roiling stomach.

The only time he hadn't smiled was when she mentioned his father and presumed to know how he felt. Anger sparked in his eyes.

What a fool she was. She scrunched her eyes shut, then forced them open in case Early watched and judged.

Tom never mentioned his father in his letters, yet Mellie babbled about his happy memories. Maybe he didn't have any. Maybe his father had been a raging drunk who beat his son. Mellie had no right to project her childhood stories about scrapbook Tommy to the real man.

He was so real. The streak of dirt across one cheek. How his sandy blond hair stuck up at all angles when he removed his helmet. The smell of earth and oil and hard work about him.

Her eyes slid shut, and everything inside her turned as soft and warm as his gaze. If only she'd had more time with him.

"Sleeping on the job?" Early prodded her calf with his combat boot. "Or just scared?"

"Neither." Mellie scrambled to her feet, picked up the flight manifest, and scanned it. Eighteen patient names were listed, with columns for time, the plane's altitude, and the patient's temperature, pulse, and respiration. "Time to do TPRs."

"It's better to do them at the end of the flight."

"Yes, but I'd like to take care of the litter patients now as well." Mellie headed for the front of the cabin and asked the ambulatory patients if they had any needs. Some wanted a cigarette lit or a drink of water, and she motioned for the sergeant to take care of them.

At the first tier of litters, Mellie checked her manifest. Top patient on the right, Corporal John Fordyce, stepped on a land mine while retaking Sbeïtla. He'd lost his right leg below the knee.

Mellie used the stirrup-shaped foot under the middle litter to hitch herself up. She smiled at her patient. "Good afternoon, Corporal Fordyce. Are you enjoying the flight?"

"Sure." He stared at the fuselage curving over his head. Mud from the battlefield speckled his hair, and dark stubble covered his cheeks. The forward hospitals didn't have time to clean the whole patient before surgery, only the affected area.

Nineteen years old, but the corporal looked much older.

Mellie settled her hand on his blanketed arm. "How does your leg feel?"

"It's gone," he said through clenched teeth.

"I know," she said softly. Now was no time for platitudes.

He turned to her, dirty eyebrows raised.

"Are you in any pain?" She folded back the blanket to examine the bandages around the stump. Clean, dry, no signs of bleeding. He'd had a dose of morphine an hour before and wouldn't need any until they landed at Maison Blanche, but she liked to ask.

"No," he said. "No pain."

"Good. When you get to the hospital in Algiers, they'll give you a bath and a shave. Won't that be nice?"

The corporal gazed over her shoulder. "Haven't had a bath since . . . I dunno."

"To think, when you were a boy, your mother probably had to wrestle you into the tub."

One corner of his mouth twitched. "I liked to hide in the cellar."

Mellie laughed. She recorded his vital signs, all within normal limits. "Anything you need in flight, anything at all, flag us down."

She eased herself to the floor to check the middle patient, Private Harry Jones, who took a machine gun bullet in his gut in the battle for Kasserine Pass. After his initial surgery, complications set in, and he needed further surgery in a specialized hospital.

The broad grin on the private's face didn't reveal how serious his condition was. "Hiya, nursey."

"Lieutenant," she said, but she smiled back. "How are you feeling?"

"Depends. How many girls you got at that hospital in Algiers?"

"Oh, not one of them is good enough for you."

"She wears a skirt, she's good enough."

Mellie clucked her tongue. "Too bad. All the women wear trousers."

The door to the cockpit opened, and Clint Peters entered the cabin. "Hi, Mellie."

"Lieutenant Blake." She inclined her head toward her patient. She had to maintain professionalism. "Do you need something, Lieutenant Peters?"

He rested his elbow on the top litter pole. "Your opinion on Rose."

Mellie groaned and examined Private Jones's dressings. "I hate to keep you from your navigation."

"Ten minutes before I check our heading again. What do you think? About Rose?"

"She's a good nurse and a great friend."

"I know that, but what do you think? It went well last Friday, didn't it?"

Mellie sent him a sidelong glance. "She didn't slap you and she only insulted you a dozen times."

"Yeah." Clint let out a dreamy sigh. "Isn't she swell?"

Mellie wrapped her fingers around her patient's wrist. "So do you—"

"Ssh." She tapped her ear and looked at her watch to time Private Jones's pulse.

Clint jiggled his leg while she worked. Oh dear, he had it bad.

After she finished timing respiration, Clint spoke up. "What do you think? She let me sit with her in church. I talked with her three times this week, and she didn't punch me. Do you think I can ask her out, just the two of us?"

"Oh, why do you want to drag me into this?"

"Come on. I'm not asking you to break a confidence. I just want to know if my life's in danger."

Mellie laughed. "It wouldn't hurt to wait."

"Another group date?"

Goodness, no. The first one had been painfully awkward. Clint brought two friends, but not the men from Louisville. Mellie couldn't think of a thing to say to them, and when they learned Georgie had a boyfriend, they looked ready to bolt.

"Well . . . ?"

Mellie sighed and noted her patient's vitals on the manifest. "I suppose so. No need to bring your friends. As long as Georgie and I are there, Rose will probably agree."

"Swell." Clint turned for the cockpit. "Thanks. You're the best."

Jones grinned at Mellie. "I'm no doctor, but that man's got a bad case of it."

"He sure does." She knelt down to take care of the man on the bottom litter. Private Butler. The man under Tom's command, the man he'd cared for so tenderly.

She smiled at her patient, but all she could see was Tom's kind face. All she could hear was his deep laugh. All she could feel was his strong hand in hers.

Oh dear. She had a bad case of it too. And he could never know.

22

Rain tapped on Tom's helmet and his thigh-length mackinaw. "Come on, men, a little more." He attacked the mud with his entrenching tool. Only a rookie would call it a shovel. Slowly he carved space around the nose wheel of the P-39 Airacobra.

Another rookie mistake. A replacement pilot parked the fighter plane on low ground, ignored his ground crew, and got the plane stuck knee-deep in Algerian mud.

"Ready for the planking." Sgt. Lou Moskovitz handed scraps of pierced steel planking to his men, who wedged it under the P-39's wheels.

Two men secured rope around the plane and hooked it to the winch on the dozer. At Moskovitz's signal, the dozer churned into reverse and spat out dollops of mud.

Tom wiped his face and went to work with the entrenching tool. Only the white bar painted on his helmet differentiated him as an officer, and he was fine with that. He didn't mind dirt or hard work like some of the officers, and it fit his emerging leadership plan.

At Annie's suggestion, Tom had searched the Gospels for a picture of Jesus as leader.

Sure, Jesus had divinity on his side, but the human side of his leadership showed Tom something striking—balance.

Jesus as the servant leader called the disciples his friends and washed their feet. Tom understood that.

But Jesus also rebuked his disciples when they erred, and the original misfit platoon erred frequently. Tom needed to work on that.

"Faster, Rossi. That's the way," he yelled to the man digging around the right wheel.

The plane's nose tipped up, lifted by the winch, and the wheels slurped out of the mud and climbed the planking ramps. A cheer went up from Tom's men, and he clapped them on the back.

The dozer towed the muddy fighter plane to a higher spot paved with steel planking.

The ground crew watched with arms crossed and muttered to each other. The rookie's mistake meant more work for them.

Off to the side, the pilot stood smoking. He wasn't in Tom's line of command, but Tom addressed him with a grin. "You'll clean her up, all by yourself."

The flyboy's jaw dropped.

Tom set his muddy hand on the pilot's shoulder. "Wouldn't be fair to the ground crew to clean up your mistake." He tilted his head toward the crew. "They're your best allies, keep your plane in top shape. Do right by them."

His thin lips pressed together. "Fine."

"Good man." Tom patted his shoulder. He left a muddy handprint on the pristine leather flight jacket and he'd do it again.

Tom followed his men toward the control tower, where they needed to repair the roof. The buoyancy of his heart counteracted the mud tugging down on his feet. He'd been firm. He'd been gentle. He'd rebuked. Annie would be proud of him. "Thanks, Lord. Maybe I can do this."

Sesame trotted toward him with his working-dog belt in place.

"Hey, buddy." Tom squatted and gave the dog a rubdown. "Got something for me?" One of the pouches on the belt bulged, and Tom pulled out a slip of paper. He leaned forward, using his helmet as an umbrella to keep the rain off the note.

Larry wrote, "It's happening again. Quincy's giving orders to Kovatch."

"Great. Just great." Tom crumpled the note.

"Come on, Sesame." He marched toward the hospital tent, where Kovatch's squad dug trenches. Tom had given thorough instructions. Why did Quincy have to interfere again? Payback? Arrogance? Disrespect?

A prickling sensation, and his buoyancy drained away.

Not only was Quincy undermining him, but Tom preferred to avoid the hospital. In weather like this, no evacuation flights would come, but what if a flight had arrived two days before in clear weather and had gotten grounded at Youks-les-Bains? He didn't want to run into Mellie Blake.

He couldn't get her face out of his mind or her words out of his head. Even thinking about her felt disloyal to Annie. For a brief moment, he'd entertained the hope that Annie and Mellie were the same. After all, both served as nurses in North Africa. But Annie's painful shyness contrasted with Mellie's confidence.

Too bad. Tom drew a deep damp breath to clear his mind. Kovatch and Quincy stood next to the hospital tent and shouted orders at the men. Larry stood to the side.

An acknowledging wave to Larry, and Tom approached Kovatch. "How's it going?"

"Almost done."

"Almost done?" Tom scanned the length of the tent complex. A narrow trench ran through the center of each tent. "I told you to dig them three feet wide."

Quincy snorted. "Busy work."

The muscles in Tom's arms contracted, and he jammed his hands in his mackinaw pockets to conceal his fists. He looked Quincy in the eye and reminded himself not to smile. "It's not just for drainage. The hospital staff wants shelter for the patients in case of an air raid."

"Since when have we taken requests? And haven't you heard?" Quincy's misshapen lips curled. "Patton's on the move. We'll push the Jerries into the sea within the week."

Tom kept his gaze locked on his rival. "Never underestimate your enemy."

Quincy drew back his chin and hiked up one eyebrow.

A belt cinched around Tom's heart. What was he doing? That sounded like a challenge, like an invitation to a schoolyard brawl. Like danger.

He switched his gaze to Kovatch. "You have your orders. You need to finish before dinner, and you don't want cold hash. It's bad enough hot. And Quincy, I know you'll be glad to return to your own platoon. Kovatch is under my command." Tom walked away.

Quincy's snort caught up to him. "That's what he thinks."

A chill snaked around Tom's gut. He forced himself to walk away from conflict and catastrophe.

Did Quincy want to take over his platoon? Was that even possible in the Army? Sure, Ferris and Kovatch were used to Quincy, but he couldn't muscle his way in.

What would his dad have done? Cussed the man out and pummeled him with his fists? That's what a murderer did. That was the image he'd been fed. But what was the man really like?

He did have good memories of his father. Mellie Blake's words had pierced holes in a wall blocking them from view.

When he peered through that wall, he saw his father playing with him, reading to him, singing with him, dancing with Mom, twirling her around, kissing her, making her laugh. He remembered a couple of spankings, well deserved. Nothing negative. Nothing at all.

As he walked, Tom's arms rubbed against the bulk of his mackinaw and made a chuffing sound like a locomotive. It had to be an illusion. Another wall farther back must have hidden the bad things. Or had his mother shielded him and sent him to his room when Dad was violent?

He had to know. But who would tell him? Not Mom, and he hadn't seen his MacGilliver grandparents since he was five. They'd sent at least one birthday card. Tom had found it in the trash, memorized the address, and replaced the card among the potato peels and eggshells.

He understood. His mother didn't trust people who'd raised a bum.

But maybe . . .

If they were alive. If they lived at the same address. Maybe they could fill in the holes.

"Hey, Gill! What's the hurry?" Larry jogged up behind him with Sesame at his heels.

Tom worked up a smile. "Take your pick—anticipation of tonight's dinner or a painful reminder of yesterday's."

Larry laughed. "No kidding." Dysentery kept the battalion dispensary busy.

"Actually I've got to do the weekly report."

"You need me, remember?" Larry's face got as stern as it ever did. "Kicking me out of my job?"

"Lot of that around here." Tom headed toward company headquarters.

"Yeah." Larry glanced over his shoulder toward Quincy. Tom grumbled. "I should tell Newman."

Creases formed in the slim space between Larry's eyebrows and his helmet. "He and Quincy came over to Kovatch together. He left Quincy here."

The cold, snaky feeling returned to Tom's belly, and it had nothing to do with last night's stew. Was this Newman's idea?

"That reminds me." Larry patted his chest. "Newman gave me a letter for you. From Annie."

"Yeah?" He held out his hand.

A smile crept up. "Shouldn't you wait until we're inside so the ink won't run?"

"Yeah. Of course."

Larry laughed. "Can't fool me. Waiting is killing you."

Tom glared at him. "So's my platoon sergeant."

"So's the food."

"Don't even get me started on the mud."

"And the neckties. General Patton's in charge now, and suddenly we've got to wear neckties."

"What does he think this is?" Tom spread his arms wide, imitating the whiners on the base. "A bank?"

"If it were a bank, we'd get a decent paycheck." Larry raised his voice in mock outrage.

"That we would, brother. That we would."

The men laughed together. Grousing was a full-time sport in North Africa.

At headquarters, Tom flipped back the flap and entered the tent. The smell of damp canvas and cigarette smoke pressed in. He took off his mackinaw, and then unbuckled Sesame's belt and toweled him off. Sesame shook off the residual moisture and curled up on the towel.

Although his fingers itched for Annie's letter, he had to

look unaffected. He sat at his field desk and pulled out a form for the weekly report. His platoon had worked hard this week and might catch up to the others. But was it due to his leadership or Quincy's?

Larry stood in front of his desk and swung an envelope like a pendulum. "What could this be?"

Tom held out his hand. "Orders for the demotion of an annoying sergeant?"

"Ferris? Kovatch?"

"Fong." He beckoned with his fingers.

"Yeah, yeah." Larry handed over the letter. "I liked the old Gill better."

"The old Gill died when Rommel rolled into Thélepte." Tom sliced open the envelope with his pocketknife.

"So when are you going to meet her?"

"Annie?"

"No, Betty Grable."

"I'm not. Don't start on this again." Tom opened the letter and immersed himself in the music of Annie's words. She told of an unnamed officer who serenaded her friend in a cracking voice. He sang "These Foolish Things Remind Me of You" with his own lyrics. Annie's friend had to be a spitfire, because the foolish things included his black eye, the glove she smacked him with, and a bottle of iodine.

Annie also described a stork nesting on the roof of a nearby building, and she drew a picture.

Then she told of her confidence in him, how his kind heart and strong spirit could allow him to become the finest kind of leader. With Annie's encouragement, he believed it too.

Tom's leg jiggled. He rubbed the stationery between his thumb and fingers, needing more than words.

The correspondence began with his craving for openness, which had been met. A new craving took shape.

He could see Mellie's dark eyes, hear her song lift from that captivating mouth, feel her small hand. Feel the connection.

He wanted that with Annie. He wanted to see her, to hold her, to feel her warmth, to smell the fragrance of her hair and taste her mouth.

Once he'd been resigned to a life alone, imprisoned by his name. Now he wanted to break out. Now he wanted to be a man.

Tom squeezed his eyes shut. His name remained. His father's legacy.

If he told her, he might lose her.

He stuffed the letter in his shirt pocket, rolled the weekly report form into the field typewriter, and pounded out his frustration on the flimsy keys. In anonymity he had only part of her. In disclosure he could lose all of her.

His fingers stilled on the keys. Anonymity didn't satisfy him anymore. To gain her love, he'd have to risk losing her friendship.

"It's worth it," he whispered.

23

Maison Blanche Airfield
April 6, 1943

Lieutenant Hughes, the pilot of the C-47, leaned in the open cargo door and laid down a string of cuss words as long as Mellie's day. "What did you do? Your patients retched all over my bird."

"Sir, I used every grain of sodium bicarbonate in my supply." Mellie picked up her clipboard and her service jacket, a victim of the vomiting epidemic.

One patient's tank had gone up in flames, and his wounds still stank of burning flesh. The hot, stuffy plane hit every pocket of turbulence over Algeria. Ten patients threw up. Even Sergeant Early looked green.

Mellie edged past the pilot and lowered herself to the ground. "After I turn in my reports and restock my meds, I'll come back to clean."

"You'd better." He walked away, profanity in his wake.

Mellie drew a deep breath of warm fresh air and blew it out hard. The only good part of her day was not seeing Tom at Youks-les-Bains.

Or was that the worst part?

She headed toward squadron headquarters. With all the

fighting on the Tunisian front as the Allies pushed forward at Maknassy and El Guettar, Mellie's workload had increased. So had her chances of running into Tom.

Why couldn't Captain Maxwell send her to Bône or Telergma? Why couldn't he send someone other than Vera, Alice, and Kay to Casablanca with patients heading stateside? She couldn't concentrate at Youks-les-Bains.

What if she saw Tom again? She couldn't mention any of the details she'd written in five months of correspondence. Maybe she could follow his advice and ask him questions.

She groaned. Was it dishonest to pretend she didn't know his identity and to conceal her own? Tom needed this anonymous correspondence. How could she take away the one thing that allowed him to be candid?

Or was it selfishness? A man with Tom's All-American good looks wouldn't fall for an orchid like Mellie. Especially after she presumed to know how he felt about his father. If he knew Mellie was Annie, would he stop writing? He'd be polite. The letters would continue for a while, then shorten, diminish, and fade away.

"Oh, Lord, help me." She gazed at the sky, as blue as the stones in the brooch Tom had sent her from this very country. "Help me do what's right, what's best for Tom."

Outside the squadron headquarters building, Captain Maxwell stood talking with Vera, his favorite. Vera glanced over the surgeon's shoulder to Mellie, then pointed to her.

Maxwell spun around. His handsome face transformed from congenial to annoyed. He marched straight to Mellie.

Her stomach felt queasier than it had on the flight. "Good evening, Captain."

"Good evening, Lieutenant. Or should I call you Captain? You seem to think you're a doctor."

"Pardon?" Mellie searched his reddening face.

He sank his hands into his pants pockets. "The physicians have noted some green jellylike substance on their patients' burns. We narrowed it down to your flights."

That was all? Mellie broke into a smile. "Yes, sir. That comes from the prickly pear cactus. It grows at Youks-les-Bains. Nothing feels more soothing on a burn."

"Cactus?" His upper lip curled. "You put cactus on our patients?"

"The gel inside the leaves. It has a marvelous cooling effect."

His jaw shifted forward. "You're a doctor now? You can make these decisions for yourself?"

Mellie edged back, and her mouth dried. "Sir, I just want to make the patients comfortable. My father's a botanist. He kept a cactus plant. I've used it all my life."

"This isn't the jungle. We have modern civilized medicines. Leave your witch doctor mumbo jumbo at home. And don't ever step outside your scope of practice again, or I'll ship you home so fast the U-boats won't be able to keep up."

Mellie's eyes and her heart stung. Why would he deny the wounded such a benign treatment?

She nodded. "I won't, sir."

Three hours later, Mellie trudged back to quarters in her coveralls. She'd changed out of her service uniform for cleaning duty. Exhaustion pressed on her eyelids and her feet. She'd missed dinner, but she didn't care.

She stopped in front of the barracks. Golden light and laughter spilled from the open windows and deepened Mellie's fatigue. All she wanted was quiet and solitude.

She sat in the dirt and leaned back against the wall under a window and pulled out Tom's latest letter. Twilight glimmered like a mirage, promising light but failing to deliver. She angled the stationery to catch the beam cascading from the window and she reread her favorite parts.

> Sesame's turned into quite a soldier. He wears his uniform with pride and performs his duties with diligence. He's getting brave too. The last air raid didn't make him flinch. By the end of the month, he may outrank me.

Mellie smiled at the sketch of Sesame standing on his hind feet and saluting. He wore a cartridge belt and a helmet with a general's star. But the end of the letter drew her eyes and her heart.

> You probably wonder why I never talk about my dad. My conscience niggles me, and I think you need to know what kind of fellow you're writing. So here goes. I have more to be ashamed of than you do.
>
> My mom left my father due to his drinking. Things got tough, he turned to crime, and he paid for his crimes. I can't share more and maintain anonymity, but I wanted you to have some idea.
>
> I've spent my life trying to be the opposite of my father. My mother says he was no good. But I wonder. My memories of him are few and vague, snippets of film edited out of my life and tossed aside. But they're here, on the floor of my brain, and they're good memories.

Most boys long to be like their fathers. Not
me. But what if he had good in him? What if
he has something to teach me, even now? Who
was he?

I know he loved me. I know he had a laugh
deep as a locomotive that rumbled in my
tummy and made me laugh too. I want to know
more.

Mellie's eyes brimmed with tears. He trusted her enough
to share part of his legacy. Considering Georgie and Rose's
negative reaction to his identity, he had reason to hesitate.
But he must have known she'd understand because of her
own legacy.

Papa said nothing about her mother. What she knew would
fit on the back of the single photograph she owned of the
woman who bore her. Her mother was fickle. Her mother loved
fun more than family. Her mother didn't love Mellie enough.

She and Tom were in the same bind. They'd each been
blessed with the deep love of one parent, but each groped
for someone to emulate.

Laughter from the barracks tinkled down on Mellie. Georgie and Rose, who had proven worthy of emulation. Mellie
closed her eyes and smiled. "Thanks, Lord," she whispered.

Her name pricked her ear. She sat up straighter and lifted
one ear closer to the open window.

"This weekend." That was Kay's voice. Since when had
Georgie and Rose gotten chummy with Kay?

"Uh-huh. Clint found a French restaurant in Algiers."
Rose's voice lingered on Clint's name. His persistence was
paying off. "I admit, I like the idea of a date, just the two of
us, but we have to get Mellie fixed up."

Mellie shuddered, tired of their matchmaking.

"Who's left?" Georgie asked. "We've tried half the men in his squadron. She's a wonderful girl, but we need the right sort of fellow."

Mellie's mouth tightened. Georgie didn't mention her looks, but that's what she meant, and Rose and Kay murmured in agreement.

"I don't get it," Kay said. "I thought she had something going with that pen pal."

The skin on Mellie's face went taut. She'd never told Kay about her correspondence with Tom. How did she know?

"That's why we need to get to work," Georgie said. "She's falling for him, and that would be disastrous."

"Afraid he won't like her when he meets her?"

Mellie clutched her arms around her middle, the letter from Tom pressed against her rib cage. How could they gossip about her? How could they share her fear and insecurity without her permission? Behind her back?

"Well, yeah," Rose said. "But it gets worse. She's already met him. He doesn't know who she is, but she certainly knows who he is. Everyone does." Her voice dipped low and dark.

"You make it sound like he's Al Capone."

"Close enough," Georgie said. "His dad's MacGilliver the Killiver."

Mellie's breath came hard and fast. Now they were gossiping about Tom. How could they? What had he ever done to them?

"You're kidding me," Kay said.

"Named after him and everything. We have to get her away from him."

"Why?" Kay's voice went harsh. "Just because his dad's a rat doesn't mean he is too."

"But what if he is?" Georgie's voice quavered. "It's too dangerous."

"Besides, can you imagine wearing that name for the rest of your life?" Rose said. "Mellie can't let infatuation drive her into a stupid mistake."

Mellie's thoughts swarmed and crashed into each other. She'd trusted them. She'd let them into her life, her scrapbook, her letters, and her heart.

She'd followed them out of her nightingale's refuge into the glittering palace of friendship. In time, the nightingale in the story had been neglected in favor of a mechanical singing bird. Mellie hadn't been neglected. She'd been betrayed. She sang her song for them, and they used it against her.

Her breath puffed out in bursts. Georgie and Rose told Kay. She had thought they were different, but they weren't. They were just like her mother, like the girls in school. Fickle and mean.

Mellie pushed herself to her feet. Her knees wobbled and her head swam. She pushed the door open. The ladies sat on the floor of the dayroom in a triangle, playing cards in hand.

"There you are," Rose said. "Good. We need a fourth."

Georgie peered at Mellie. "Honey, are you all right?"

Her mouth opened and closed, grasping for words. "How . . . could . . . you?"

"What?" Georgie scrambled to her feet. "What's the matter, honey?"

"I heard you." Her breath sucked in. "Outside. Every word."

"What do you mean?" Rose asked, her voice fake.

Mellie crossed fisted arms over her roiling stomach. "How could you? How could you talk about me like that? About Tom?"

"We were just . . ." Georgie's eyes turned into Blue Willow saucers. "We want to help you. We're your friends."

A bark of a laugh. "Friends? Do friends gossip about each other?"

"We didn't—"

"I told you all that in confidence. My letters, Ernest, Tom. You had no right to tell Kay. That's mine to tell."

Kay huffed and slapped down her cards. "Oh, that's really nice, girls."

Her words ran a righteous thread of steel into Mellie's anger. "How many other people have you told? Vera? Alice? Lieutenant Lambert? Why not track down Tom and tell him?"

Rose's face contorted. "We wouldn't do that."

"How do I know?" Mellie's vision blurred. "How do I know that? You're like every woman I've ever known—fickle, mean little gossips."

"Wait a minute," Rose said. "That's not fair."

"Sure, it is." Mellie kicked at the pile of cards on the floor. "You played games with my heart, dealt out my secrets in exchange for popularity."

"Mellie . . ." Georgie wiped tears from her face.

But Mellie let hers flow, her Purple Heart. Wounded in action. "You talk about me to Kay. You talk about Kay to me. You talk about Vera and Alice. You pass around secrets behind people's backs. How would you like it if people talked about your secrets?"

"Why don't you sit and calm yourself down?" Rose patted the ground. Her face stretched long, and her freckles stood out.

Something hardened in Mellie's heart. "Why? Afraid I'll tell your secrets?"

"Mellie . . ." Georgie's voice wavered.

Pain and fire coursed through her soul, and a primitive, irresistible urge burned inside. To return pain with pain. "Friends? You told me friends don't keep secrets. You made me bare my heart, but you keep secrets from each other."

Rose's face turned white. "No, we don't."

"Is that right?" Mellie turned to Georgie. "Want to tell her the truth? That you don't want to be here? That you never wanted to leave Virginia? Not for Alaska and certainly not for Africa."

"Mellie!" Tears streaked down Georgie's bright pink cheeks.

"Don't be ridiculous," Rose said. "She wanted to come."

Georgie's face scrunched up, and she glared at Mellie. "How could you?"

"What?" Rose stared up at Georgie. "You wanted to come." Her shoulders sank. "I wanted to be with you."

"You said—"

"You were so excited. I can overcome a little fear to be with my best friend. You need me."

Rose pressed her fingertips to her forehead. "What? You think I can't get along without you?"

"We need each other, honey. And you wanted me to come."

A wedge in Mellie's throat tried to block off poisonous words, but she dislodged it. "Now I know why. I know why she wanted you to come."

"Because we're friends." Georgie spat out her words. "You wouldn't know anything about that."

"And you two don't know anything about each other. For heaven's sake, you're smack-dab in the middle of a love triangle, and you don't even know it."

"A love triangle? What on earth are you talking about?"

Rose's eyes turned to cold, dark stones. "How dare you?"

Mellie's words spilled in a poisonous puddle, and she stepped back instinctively. Her fingers groped in front of her, but the words, the venom, couldn't be retracted. What had she done?

"Dare what?" Georgie looked down at Rose, who didn't break her murderous glare at Mellie.

She held her breath as the pool rose around her, green and noxious.

Georgie's gaze darted about. "Ward?" she whispered.

Rose's mouth pursed, and air puffed from her nostrils.

"What?" Georgie's voice broke into a dozen pieces. "That's ridiculous. You're not in love with Ward."

Rose tossed back her hair and sniffed. "Of course not. He's yours." But the snap in her tone told the truth.

Mellie gasped from the pain. She'd hurt them as they'd hurt her. So where was the pleasure? Where was the satisfaction?

"Ward?" Georgie asked. "You're in love with Ward? How could you?"

Rose got to her feet and brushed off her trousers. "Nonsense. It's just a childhood crush. I'm getting over it."

"You're in love with my boyfriend? How could you do that to me?"

Rose crossed her arms and stamped her foot. "It's not like I did it on purpose. I'm getting over it. And I'd never get between you."

"Never?" Georgie stepped closer, her arms in stiff poles by her sides. "You dragged me out here, dragged me away from him. You think he'll forget me, don't you?"

"Nonsense. I did no such thing."

"Some friend you are." Georgie whirled around and ran out the front door, averting her gaze from Mellie.

"Georgie, wait!" Rose followed, passed Mellie, and shoved her to the side.

Mellie stumbled but didn't fall.

"Thanks a million, Philomela." Rose strode outside and banged the door behind her.

Mellie rubbed her sore shoulder and stared at the floor. Fifty-two cards lay strewn before her, the wreckage of friendships and hearts and confidences.

"Well, well, well."

Mellie startled and glanced at Kay. She'd forgotten she was in the room.

Kay got to her feet and walked over, her head inclined. "So, you think women are mean and fickle?"

Mellie snapped a nod.

Kay patted Mellie's cheek. Or was it a slap? "Congratulations. You're one of us."

The door slammed again as Kay left.

Mellie's hips, her knees, her ankles gave way, and she sank to the floor, her stomach churning. She was just like the others.

24

Youks-les-Bains Airfield
April 8, 1943

"Sesame, want some dinner?" Tom held out a cube of Spam.

Sesame sat on his haunches and lifted one paw.

In the officers' club tent, a dozen officers gathered around Tom murmured their approval. Men from the 908th, fighter pilots, and C-47 crewmen formed an audience for the debut of Sesame's new routine.

Tom fed the Spam to the dog. "Want some beef stew from the mess?"

Sesame lay down and flopped one paw over his nose.

The men laughed.

Rudy Scaglione, the battalion transportation officer, slapped his knee. "This from a dog who eats rats."

Tom waited for the laughter to recede, motioned for Sesame to sit up again, and paused to let the anticipation build.

One of the C-47 pilots, Roger Cooper, beat a drum roll on the table with drumsticks and grinned at Tom.

He held up a K ration tin. "Sesame, want some hash?"

The little dog flopped to the ground, rolled onto his back, and his tongue lolled out of his mouth. Dead.

Lubricated by beer, the men roared with laughter. Cooper

beat out a rimshot and whacked the lantern overhead, a substitute cymbal.

"Take a bow, Ses." Tom sat on a camp stool by the table and fed the dog more Spam.

Sesame turned in a circle twice and curled up behind Tom's stool.

"Did you hear we got the Jerries trapped?" Scaglione said.

"Yeah." Clint Peters, Cooper's navigator, took a swig of beer. "Time for the final push."

Tom nodded. The U.S. II Corps had broken out of El Guettar in southern Tunisia. Yesterday they linked with Gen. Bernard Montgomery's British Eighth Army, which had driven the Germans across Egypt and Libya. "You fellows will be busy, won't you?"

Cooper ran his hand through his dark red hair. "We're always busy, not like these glamour boys in their Cadillacs." He nodded to a trio of fighter pilots but with a good-natured smile.

"You're just jealous 'cause you're stuck in a dump truck of a plane."

Peters leaned forward, his elbows on the table. "You're just jealous 'cause we carry passengers of the feminine persuasion."

Tom chuckled. The rivalries between bomber, fighter, and cargo pilots never ended.

"Say, Coop." Peters tapped his pilot on the arm with the back of his hand. "Speaking of the gals, where are they?"

Tom tensed but kept his smile fixed. The gals had to be the flight nurses. The cargo planes had landed too late in the day for the return flight, so the entire bunch had an RON—Remain Overnight. Tom swirled his cup of coffee to get the grit back in solution. *Please, Lord, don't let Mellie be here. Can't stop thinking about her.*

Cooper sipped his coffee. "I hope they don't come. Women are nothing but trouble."

One of the fighter pilots let out a long low whistle. "What pretty little troubles they are."

Three women stood in the entrance to the tent, wearing the blue trouser uniforms of the flight nurses. Not Mellie, thank goodness, but a blonde, a brunette, and a redhead. Any one of them alone would cause a stir, but together . . . ?

The men cheered, whistled, and made catcalls.

Tom stayed silent, as did Cooper, and they exchanged a look. Cooper must have had bad experiences with women. Tom had none.

"Boys! Boys!" the brunette called out until the men quieted. "I don't hear any music, do you, Alice?"

"How can we dance without music?" The blonde pressed one finger to her cheek, but Tom had a hunch she wasn't as dumb as she was trying to look.

The redhead swept a flirtatious look over the men. "And I want to dance."

A whoop rang out, and several of the men dashed to the record player "liberated" from some Frenchman in the early days of the occupation. Soon, Louis Armstrong crooned "I'm in the Mood for Love" from a scratched record.

The brunette raised her hand. "Line up, boys. Everyone gets one dance, no more."

"I'll take less," Cooper grumbled. "Nothing but trouble."

One of the fighter pilots gulped some beer, wiped his mouth, and got to his feet. "I'm in the mood for trouble."

"There's Rose." Peters darted through the queuing crowd to the side of another blonde, who looked thrilled and relieved to see him.

Tom downed his coffee. Time to go. His audience had dispersed, and he didn't dance. At high school dances he en-

tertained the wallflowers on the sidelines, but there wouldn't
be any wallflowers tonight.

A petite curly-haired brunette stepped into the tent. She
fiddled with her hands, and her gaze hopped around the tent.
She and Rose glowered at each other.

Tom blew out a breath. She might need rescue, but he
really wanted to leave.

Before he could take another breath, half a dozen men
surrounded her.

"Good." Tom drained the last drops of coffee from his
canteen cup, nestled it back in its pouch under his canteen,
and got to his feet.

Then Mellie Blake came in, and Tom sagged back onto the
stool. He needed to leave. He loved Annie. If he spent time
with Mellie, he'd feel disloyal to her.

Another woman held Mellie's arm. A nurse with silver first
lieutenant's bars on her shoulders, the chief nurse, most likely.

Mellie's brow bunched up. She said something to the chief,
but the chief pointed into the tent and issued an order.

Tom leaned forward, but he couldn't make out the words
over the music and crowd. All he knew was Mellie did not
want to be there, and her CO made her stay.

The chief tapped her watch, gave Mellie a stern look, and
left her alone. Very alone.

No crowd surrounded her. No friends pulled her into their
group. And Tom felt her loneliness in his gut.

Her chin down, she glanced around, probably looking for
a friendly face or a seat.

Tom's muscles went taut, but she didn't meet his eye.

"Found my target." At a table to Tom's left, Martin Quincy
pointed his beer bottle toward Mellie.

"Her?" An officer Tom didn't know pointed his bottle at
the other gals. "Those three—they're the lookers."

"Exactly. With those dames, I'll get one dance, not even a kiss. I don't stand a chance. But with her, a few dances, a little sweet talk. She'll be grateful. You know what dames are like when they're grateful."

The pilot laughed. "You're in like Flynn."

"Betcha five bucks I'm the only man in this outfit gets action tonight." Quincy stood and set down his bottle.

Tom found himself on his feet. He strode across the tent, a few paces behind the other platoon leader.

Quincy pulled up beside Mellie. She inched to the side and glanced at her watch.

"This song," Quincy said. "'And the Angels Sing.' They're playing it for you, angel-face."

Tom closed the gap. "Say, Mellie, there you are."

She looked up, startled, and her lips parted. "Oh. Tom. Hi."

Quincy loomed closer, and Mellie glanced at the big oaf.

"Good to see you," Tom said. "How've you been? Haven't seen you for a while."

Mellie's gaze bounced between the men. Her eyes widened, and then she turned a bright smile to Tom. "I'm fine. It's good to see you too."

"Why don't we catch up? Want some coffee?"

"Yes, please."

"Let's get you some." Tom held out his arm for Mellie, and he nodded to Quincy. "See you later."

Quincy's lip curled, he spread out empty hands, and he mouthed a curse.

Tom would pay later, but it was worth it. He led Mellie across the tent to the makeshift bar. Her little hand rested in the crook of his elbow, the warmth seeping through the olive drab wool of his shirt.

"What was that about?" she said in a low voice. "Is he bad news?"

"I'll say. Pearl Harbor bad news. Crash of the stock market bad news. Pirates losing to the Cubs bad news."

She laughed, a trill of a birdsong. Then she turned a serious face to Tom. "Thank you."

"You're welcome." He dipped his cup into the five-gallon bucket of brewed coffee and wiped it with his handkerchief. "Here you go."

"Thanks." She stared into the cup. "Listen, I appreciate what you did, but you don't have to stick around. That wouldn't be fair."

Fair? Where was the take-charge nurse he'd met a few weeks before? "I'll tell you what isn't fair—your chief making you stay."

Her gaze popped up to him. "You saw that?"

"How long is she making you stay?"

A flicker of a smile. "An hour."

"How long do you have left?"

"Um . . ." A glance at her wrist. "Fifty-four minutes."

Tom motioned to the table he'd sat at earlier. "I'm not the best-looking fellow in the room, but I can introduce you to someone."

Mellie's mouth sagged open. "I—I don't want to meet anyone."

"You'll want to meet this fellow." He took her arm—stiff as pierced steel planking—and led her to the table, where Sesame lay behind his stool. Tom squatted. "Isn't he the handsomest fellow?"

Mellie laughed and knelt beside Tom. "Oh, he is. Is this— what's his name?"

"Sesame. He's my dog."

At the sound of his name, Sesame opened his brown eyes, lifted his head, and thumped his coiled tail.

Mellie smiled, reached out a tentative hand, and rubbed Sesame behind the ears. "How cute."

SARAH SUNDIN

"He's the best." Tom stood and pulled out a camp stool for Mellie. Fifty-two minutes to go. What was he doing? This woman intrigued him too much. He wasn't being fair to Annie.

Mellie took her seat and turned worried eyes to Tom. "I have to apologize. For what I said when we met. About your father. I had no right to make assumptions."

Tom raised half a smile. "Don't apologize. Sure, I was shocked, but not the way you think. You see . . ." He scanned the table. Nothing to pick up and fiddle with. Instead he leaned his elbows on the table. "You see, everyone thinks my father was a monster. You're the first person I've met who realizes he was human."

"Of course."

Tom kneaded the muscles around his elbow, sore from today's job. "They expect me to hate him. But he was my dad. I loved him. I wanted to be like him." He let out a little laugh. "Now that's my worst fear."

Mellie frowned at the cup. "I know we just met, but I can't imagine that happening."

"Thanks." His voice came out too thick. He had to change the subject and fast. "Where are you from?"

She gave him a blank look as if she didn't know the answer. "Um . . . California. And you—you're from California too, aren't you?"

"When I was little, but we moved to Pittsburgh. My mom's family lives there. She thought they'd help, but they didn't want anything to do with us."

"Oh dear. That's horrible."

"Yeah, but some of her friends stood by her. They found her a job and a little house to rent, so we were okay."

"What's she like, your mother?" Mellie sipped some coffee, her gaze on Tom.

"She's the best." He grinned, pulled out his wallet, and slipped out a snapshot.

Mellie smiled at the photo. "You look like her. Especially around the eyes."

"She's a good woman. Hardworking, strong, and godly. And she loves me to pieces."

Her smile stretched wide, making her eyes crinkle, but she hauled the smile back in. "I'm glad you have each other. She must be proud of you."

"More than I deserve." He tucked the photo away.

"Do you like Pittsburgh?"

"Yep. The Pirates, the rivers, the bridges, even the snow. But I like variety. I want to travel, live different places."

"Me too." A soft smile. Had she leaned closer? "I even like it here. It's different, exciting, exotic."

"Yeah." Tom's mouth dried out as he gazed into those different, exciting, exotic eyes.

"The bridges in Pittsburgh—is that what led you into engineering? The other day you said you wanted to build bridges."

He nodded to break the hold she had on him. "Pittsburgh straddles three rivers, so we need bridges to keep us connected. Worked on some to put myself through engineering school."

"Where did you go to school?"

Tom couldn't remember anyone ever asking him so many questions. That was usually his job. "University of Pittsburgh. Where else?" He winked.

She smiled and drank her coffee. "What's it like?"

"It's great. Pitt's got a beautiful campus, high over the city. We've got the Cathedral of Learning, over five hundred feet tall. Looks like a skyscraper on the outside—but Gothic-inspired—and the ground floor looks like a real cathedral with stone arches and grottoes everywhere."

Her smile was so warm and encouraging, he felt four inches taller. He never talked about his life. Except with Annie.

Tom leaned back a bit. He had to watch himself. "So, is Mellie a nickname? I've never heard it before."

Her smile dipped. "Yes. It's short for Philomela."

"There's got to be a story behind that." He leaned forward again. Now he had to encourage her.

She kept her chin low but raised those dark eyes to him. "It means nightingale. I've always loved music, even in the womb. Apparently I kicked in time to music. My father has a gorgeous tenor and he decided I'd be his little nightingale."

"Good thing you can sing, huh?"

She laughed. "Yes, it is."

"And you're a nurse. Well, that fits you perfectly. I like it."

"You do? But it's so different."

"Didn't I tell you I liked variety?"

"You did." She gave him a relaxed little smile.

If he could just get her to give him that full smile and convince her to keep it.

"Hey, Gill." A heavy hand clapped onto his shoulder.

He glanced up into Quincy's rumpled face. "Hey, Quincy. What's up?"

"We've got a serious shortage of dames. Rationing is the only way to handle it."

"Rationing?" He looked at Mellie. "She's a woman, not a sack of sugar."

"You look sweet to me, angel."

"Leave her alone, Quince."

"Maybe she doesn't want to be left alone. Maybe she wants to dance. You're hogging her so the poor thing can't jitterbug. You like to dance, angel?"

"Sometimes." Mellie shot Tom a look he couldn't make

out—part fear, part . . . was it longing? As if she wanted to dance with Tom.

That couldn't happen. He stood on a narrow bridge buffeted by high winds. Dancing with her could push him over the edge, away from Annie.

"She wants to dance. You gonna ask her . . . MacGilliver?" Quincy drew his name out, stretched it on a rack in preparation for execution.

Tom's stomach crumpled under the burden. He stared at the rapid succession of expressions on Mellie's face. As understanding as she was, she didn't deserve to be linked to him, even for the length of a song.

"So, angel, how about it? Wanna cut a rug?"

"All right," she said and she left.

His shoulders slumped. He'd failed to protect her from Quincy. He'd hurt her feelings. And his heart was in worse shape than before.

25

Mellie loved the song "Deep Purple," but she wouldn't anymore. Quincy held her too close, his breath stank of beer, and he kept calling her "angel." Just because no one else wanted to dance with her, he thought she was easy.

And Tom didn't want to dance with her. The ache constricted her lungs so she could barely breathe. As a gentleman, he'd rescued her and conversed with her. But as a man, he wasn't interested.

The other nurses danced too. Rose and Georgie wouldn't meet her eye, Vera and Alice smirked at her, and Kay gave her a humiliating look of pity. Lieutenant Lambert looked less cross but hardly happy. Mellie had shredded all harmony in her flight.

She'd never felt lower in her life.

Only careful measured breaths kept her together.

She couldn't even pray. How could she approach God? How dare she ask for forgiveness when she'd wounded others deeply and maliciously?

Tom was smart to reject her.

But it didn't relieve the pain.

At least she'd followed his advice and asked questions so

she didn't reveal any telling details. Thanks to anonymity, her name was a safe topic.

Anonymity would be more vital now that she knew he didn't find her attractive. The pained look on his face when Quincy asked if he wanted to dance with her.

Her throat clogged, and her eyes watered.

"You don't talk much, do you, angel?" Quincy asked.

"No. And please don't call me that. I'm no angel."

"Even better," he said with a growl and pulled her closer. She resisted. "Please don't."

"Loosen up, have some fun. Here we go. 'Little Brown Jug.'" He shoved her away, holding one hand, then yanked her back into his arms.

The music had changed. "I don't know how to jitterbug."

"It's not hard." He spun her around.

"I'd rather not."

"What's wrong? Pining over lover boy back there? You know who his father is?"

"Yes, I do." Mellie planted her feet and stared him down. "But I don't know who your father is. What's he like? Ever done anything wrong?"

"You're a strange dame. Forget it. Not worth the effort." He flung her hands down and marched away.

Mellie stood alone among the dancing couples. No one wanted anything to do with her, not that she blamed them.

She stepped back and bumped into someone. Vera dancing with Captain Maxwell.

Vera shook back her glamorous hair. "Typical Mellie. Out of place as always. Don't you know you need a partner on the dance floor?"

"I . . . I'm sorry." Her hour wasn't up, but she didn't care. She charged for the tent entrance, pushed aside the flap, and burst into the cool night air. Let Lambert send her home. Let them kick her out of the Army Nurse Corps. She would not stay to be laughed at.

Her vision blurred. Where was the tent they'd put the nurses in for the night? How could she find it in the dark? How could things get any worse?

A triangular flash of light from the tent. Someone left. "Mellie? Where are you going?"

Tom. That was how things could get worse. "I'm turning in."

His footsteps thumped behind her. "Are you okay? Is it Quincy? Did he try something?"

"No. I just need to go."

"You still have . . . twenty-two minutes. You should stay."

"No, thank you." Her shaky voice sounded like a lovesick schoolgirl's. Oh goodness, she'd give herself away.

Tom caught up and walked in step with her. "May I explain something?" His voice softened and lowered.

She ventured a glance, thankful any redness in her eyes wouldn't show in the pale moonlight. "Explain?"

He touched her arm, tilted his head, and stopped in his tracks. Mellie stopped too. How could she do anything else?

Tom looked deep into her eyes. A furrow formed on his forehead, and he dropped his gaze to her shoes. Two breaths expanded his chest. "I don't dance."

Men never wanted to dance with her—except that snake Quincy—so why did she expect Tom to? How silly of her. At least he was polite enough to make an excuse. Mellie forced a small smile. "That's all right. A lot of fellows don't know how to dance."

"I know how. I just don't. It's not fair to the girls."

"Not fair? What do you mean?" But a thought ballooned, and the pain in her heart wrenched from her situation to his, a fresh, jabbing pain.

His jaw worked from side to side. "People talk. I couldn't do that to a girl's reputation."

"I'm so sorry, Tom. You shouldn't be judged for your family. That isn't right."

He raised his gaze, and his eyebrows bumped into each other. "I should have known you'd be different. From everything you said. But I assumed. I didn't give you a chance."

Mellie laughed it off, a nervous twitter. Oh dear, he knew she wanted to dance with him. One more mistake and she might reveal her love. "I understand. It's all right."

"No, it's not all right." One side of his mouth crept up, and he lifted his hand to her. "Would you please dance with me?"

Oh goodness, no. How could she? How could she bear being held by the man she loved, knowing he'd never love her? Concern for her reputation explained only part of his reaction, not the initial appalled look. Mellie let out a light laugh and headed in the general direction of quarters. "Thank you, but I'm rather tired."

"Are you afraid of me?" His voice hardened.

Mellie spun around. "No. How could I? How could I be afraid of you?"

Pain she had inflicted etched his face. "Everyone else is."

"I'm not."

"So dance with me." He held out his hand and a challenge.

She glanced at the tent. "I don't want to go back in there."

"Then don't. We can hear the music. We can dance out here. Unless you're chicken." Humor returned to his voice.

"I'm not chicken." But chickenlike flutters consumed her heart.

"Bawk, bawk, bawk." He grinned and stepped closer.

She had to laugh. "How old are you anyway?"

"Old enough to know a chicken when I see one." He beckoned. "Come on."

Mellie gazed into his face, handsome even in the dark, and she stepped forward. What could she do? Mercy compelled her. Friendship drove her. Love stirred her.

"That's better. I prefer nightingales to chickens." He took her hand in his and circled his arm around her waist.

Mellie's hand rested on his shoulder, his muscles hard and defined from manual labor. He was about Papa's height—just right. And the scent of him flooded through her—coffee and wool and hard work and kindness.

"Here we are, ready to go, but where's our music?"

"Oh?" Mellie hadn't noticed. She pulled her gaze from Tom's shoulder to his face, only inches away, and she drew in her breath. She'd never been that close to a man before. She made herself smile back. "I've heard of a cappella singing, but a cappella dancing?"

His laugh rumbled deep like a locomotive, as he said his father's had. Like that sound, Tom's laugh offered travel and adventure. What would it be like to spend her life with this man with his ready smile, his deep faith, and his love of variety?

It would be bliss.

But it would never be. Friendship beyond the scrapbook exploded in her face. Romance would never move beyond paper either.

Tinny notes from the record player started up, and Tom led her in a foxtrot. "You've got an admirer in there."

"Me?" But a few bars of music made her laugh. The record played "A Nightingale Sang in Berkeley Square."

The lyrics told of a couple in London sharing a kiss under the stars, and Tom was too close and too real and too attractive. And too quiet.

"You're a good dancer," she said. "I'm sorry most girls—"

"Hey, now." He went into double time and spun her in

a circle. "You'll think I'm one melancholy fellow. I'm not. It does no good to dwell on things that can't be changed."

"True." Once again she needed to heed his advice.

"How about we talk about something that can be changed? Your smile."

"My what?" Mellie's jaw went slack.

"You heard me. When you smile, you yank the leash and haul it in like a bad dog."

A laugh hopped out of her mouth. "Well, it doesn't behave. My smile cracks my face in half like a coconut."

"Nonsense. It's beautiful, and it's part of who you are. You should never be ashamed of who you are."

Mellie tapped one finger on his shoulder and gave him the teasing look she gave Papa whenever he delivered a long botanical lecture. "Listen to yourself, Lieutenant."

He moaned and clapped their clasped hands to his chest. His solid chest. "You wound me. You think I should follow my own advice?"

"Absolutely. Never be ashamed of who you are." Why was it so much easier to say that about him than about herself?

His eyes—the moonlight obscured the blue but not the pale glow. "I'll work on that. You're . . ." He pressed his lips together. "Thank you."

"I'm a nurse. I like to fix people."

He laughed and whirled her around. "I'm a civil engineer. I like to build people up."

"Then we're well—" Well matched? How could she say such a thing? They might be well matched as friends, but never anything more. "I'm—I'm glad we met."

"Me too." He cocked his head and squinted one eye. "Well, milady, the song's over." He stepped back and bowed.

She curtseyed. "Thank you for the dance, kind sir."

He held out his arm. "Let's get you inside so you won't get in trouble with your chief."

She took his arm but didn't move. "Tom, wait."

He lifted his eyebrows.

Her heart beat faster than the rhythm for "Bugle Call Rag" in the background. What on earth was she doing? But she had to do it. For him. "Would you like another dance?"

Tom stared at her. Unblinking. Lips parted.

She shrugged. "I like this song. The air is fresh out here. No cigarette smoke, no beer fumes, no one to step on our toes."

His head dipped in the slowest nod she'd ever seen. "One condition."

"Condition?"

"You have to smile. All the way."

Why didn't he ask her to strip off her uniform and do the hula? She'd feel less exposed.

"Come on." An irresistible grin. Even more irresistibly, he moved closer. "One smile. One dance."

One smile to be in his arms again? One smile to convince him of her unattractiveness? He said he liked her smile, but he'd never seen the stark fullness.

"Come on. Smile." He wagged his head in front of her as if coaxing a baby to laugh.

It worked. She released her smile. She rolled her eyes to let him know how she felt about it and let her smile crack her face in half. The full monkey smile. "Happy?"

"Yep. That was nice. Let's see if I can make you smile again." He pulled her into his arms and danced.

"That wasn't the deal. One smile, one dance. Oh dear. I can't keep up. I'm no jitterbug."

"Neither am I. But who's to know? Just kick your feet around, swing your arm." Tom burst into a kicking, swinging frenzy. "See, it doesn't have to be good. It just has to be wild."

She laughed. He definitely wasn't good. Why not join in? She tried some kicks and swings.

"There you go." He twirled her under his arm.

She struggled to coordinate her feet with him so close, with his arm firm and warm around her waist. "Oh dear. I don't want to kick you."

"Good. We're on the same side. Kick the enemy."

"How about Quincy? Want me to kick him?" Giggles burst out.

"What's with the violence? I thought you were a lady." He spun her so fast her feet left the ground.

Mellie gasped and clung to his shoulder. "Oh my goodness. Dancing's dangerous."

"You said it, angel-face."

Laughter bounced through her, lifting the monkey smile, but for the first time since first grade, she didn't haul it in.

"That's it. Now I push you away. Get your feet going any old way." He held her right hand as if shaking hands. "Now wag your finger at me. Scold me for making you smile."

She raised one finger and wagged it at him. "Scold me for making you dance again."

They circled, scolding each other, their feet shuffling over the dirt, laughter swirling around them.

Tom lifted their joined hands. "Twirl under and come back to me."

She did as he said, and she was back in his arms, the arms of the man who knew her best, the man she knew best, the man she loved. He looked down into her eyes, and his smile seemed warmer, deeper, as if it permeated his whole being.

Her smile grew too, from someplace far inside she could barely remember, a place where she felt understood and appreciated and loved.

The music stopped. Tom rocked gently and didn't release her from his arms or his gaze. He pulled their clasped hands closer, down to her waist, and his expression softened. Intensified.

Mellie's breath came out choppy, her cheeks warmed, and her body relaxed into his. This couldn't be happening, could it?

His gaze meandered over her face, and she could almost feel the caress of it, and it landed on her mouth.

Her monkey mouth.

Tom eased back. "I—I should take you inside. I don't want you to get in trouble with your chief."

A heavy molten mass pressed on Mellie's heart. He liked her as a person, but not as a woman.

She backed out of his arms. "You're right." Her voice sounded tinny.

Tom tilted his head toward the tent and they walked back. He didn't offer his arm this time. "I never asked. What's going on with your chief? Why'd she force you to come here?"

The chill of the night made her shiver. "The nurses aren't getting along. She thinks a fun evening will help. She also thinks it's our duty to improve morale among the men."

"Well, you ladies increased morale 1,000 percent." He looked at his watch. "And your hour's over."

A dismissal, and for the best. "All right."

"I'll get you back in the chief's graces. What's her name?" He held the tent flap open for her.

"Lieutenant Lambert." She ducked inside and breathed a sigh of relief that she'd never mentioned names in her letters.

Tom led her to the table where Lieutenant Lambert sat with a dark-haired man. "Captain Newman, may I have the honor of addressing your guest?"

A chill raced up Mellie's spine. Captain Newman? The man she addressed her letters to? The man who forwarded Tom's letters to her? He knew which squadron she served in. He'd recognize her name.

"Absolutely," he said. "Lieutenant Lambert, this is Lieutenant

MacGilliver, one of my platoon leaders. Gill, Lieutenant Lambert is the chief nurse of the 802nd Air Evac Squadron. She and my wife are dear friends."

"Pleased to meet you, ma'am." Tom saluted her. "Thank you for bringing your nurses tonight. Lieutenant Blake indulged me in several dances outside in the fresh air and has been a delightful companion. You're blessed to have her in your squadron."

Lambert gave Mellie a surprised glance, then smiled at Tom. "Thank you."

"Now, I know the lady's tired and wishes to retire." He turned to Mellie and offered his hand. "Thanks for your company, Mellie. I've had a wonderful time."

She shook his hand, his fingers rough and strong. "I have too. Thank you."

"I'll walk you to your tent. Let me get Sesame." He headed for the table.

Captain Newman tilted his head and narrowed his eyes at her. He knew.

The chill deepened and convulsed her stomach. He couldn't tell Tom. He just couldn't.

Lieutenant Lambert looked away and called out to Alice.

Mellie leaned closer to the captain. "He doesn't know," she said in a fierce whisper, begging him with her eyes. "Please don't tell him."

He frowned and raised one eyebrow. "All right, miss. If you're certain."

Tom walked over with the sleepy dog in his arms, a barrier between him and Mellie.

The molten mass oozed into every corner of her heart. She'd never been more certain in her life.

26

Tunisia
April 11, 1943

Tom's jeep bumped along the road across an arid plain. Camels munched prickly pear cactus, Arabs in long robes herded goats, and giant fields of poppies flamed on rugged hills in the distance. The decimation of war shouted from every village reduced to rubble, every animal carcass, and every palm tree snapped like a matchstick.

Larry drove today, behind the platoon's trucks crammed with men who scanned the morning sky for strafing German planes. Their vigilance allowed Tom to read Annie's most recent letter, dated April 6. One thing he'd miss about Youks-les-Bains would be the quick exchange of letters. Her hospital had to be close to an air base. Still it was best if he left and never saw Mellie Blake again.

He was a heel. The heeliest type of heel, who said he loved one woman and flirted with another. For heaven's sake, he almost kissed her. Never, ever had he wanted to kiss a woman more. Those luscious lips. Only the thought of Annie stopped him at the last minute.

He groaned. His efforts to make Mellie feel better ended up hurting her feelings. She'd been quiet when he walked her back to her tent.

He stroked Sesame, asleep on the seat beside him, and dove into Annie's letter to remind himself of what he could have lost.

> It's late, but I need to write. I need to get this down, although you'll despise my heartlessness. You're the only one I have left to talk to.
>
> Tonight I heard my two friends gossip about me. Oh, Ernest, I've often been the target of gossip and mockery, but never from a friend. It hurt more than anything.
>
> In my anger I did something horrid. Each had confided a secret in me, a secret she'd kept from the other. I hesitate to tell you, but I betrayed them and revealed their secrets. I hurt them terribly.
>
> I don't know if they'll forgive each other, and I'm certain they'll never forgive me.
>
> What sort of person am I? I claim mercy as my greatest virtue, but I chose vengeance over mercy.
>
> Ernest, you seem to understand me, but can you understand this? Can you offer any advice? Do you even want to? How can you trust someone who betrayed two of the dearest people in her life?

His sweet, dear Annie. Thank goodness he'd penned a reply yesterday before the convoy departed.

Had he consoled her enough? Reminded her that the greater the intimacy, the greater the chance for hurt, but the greater the reward?

Had he pointed her firmly but kindly to seek forgiveness from the Lord, her friends, and herself? The worst thing she could do would be to retreat into her shell again. Had she experienced enough of the joys of friendship to know it was worth fighting for?

Just as Annie was worth fighting for.

After the thrilling, disastrous evening with Mellie, he'd decided to pursue Annie fully, with all the risk of revelation and rejection. The letter he'd written the next day—had she received it? What would she think?

Larry nudged him. "What'd she say?"

He folded the letter. "Problems with her friends."

"And she has competition and doesn't know it."

Tom winced. He'd run into Larry while walking Mellie back to her tent and later told him too much about the evening.

He squinted toward the sun rising ahead in the east. Stuka dive-bombers liked to attack from the sun so you couldn't see them until it was too late.

Annie didn't know his name, but Mellie did. She showed him compassion and understanding and something else. Oh boy, she was something else. So vulnerable, so strong, so attractive, so kissable.

Tom slammed his eyes shut. What was wrong with him? He'd almost thrown away a deep relationship for a mere acquaintance. "No competition. Annie's the one for me."

Larry hit the brakes.

Tom braced one hand on the dashboard and held Sesame with the other. He peered around the truck in front of him. "Convoy stopped. Must be at Kairouan."

"Now we'll see how much damage Jerry did on the way out."

"And how much damage we did on the way in." The Luftwaffe field eleven miles south of Kairouan had been a favorite target for the RAF and the U.S. Twelfth and Ninth Air Forces.

In a few minutes the company's vehicles parked and the troops prepared for the assault. The Germans had evacuated Kairouan in their massive retreat up the eastern coast of Tunisia, but they had a nasty habit of leaving mines, booby traps, and snipers.

Tom let Sesame out of the jeep to relieve himself, then tied him back up in the jeep and filled the cup from his canteen for the dog. "You be good while I'm gone."

Sesame lifted his nose and wagged his curly tail in acknowledgment.

The men of the 908th climbed out of the trucks. The platoon and squad leaders met to review plans. Air reconnaissance photos showed a concrete runway from north-northwest to south-southeast with buildings on the west side. Infantry would clear the buildings and a ravine that ran southeast of the field. Quincy's platoon would accompany the infantry and search for booby traps. Reed's platoon would clear mines outside the buildings, while Tom's platoon surveyed the runway.

The men clumped together, checking helmets, rifles, grenades, charges, spools of detonation cord, and mine detectors. Their joking had a sharper, louder edge. Although trained for missions like this and veterans of dozens of air raids, they hadn't followed an assault wave since the November Torch landings.

Tom whistled, and the men gathered around. "Okay, boys. You know your duties. This is what we trained for, where we show what makes engineers the best. Follow your orders, keep an eye out for snipers and aircraft, and stay on cleared pathways. I'm convinced half the Nazi economy is dedicated to manufacturing mines."

"No kidding," Bill Rinaldi said.

Newman caught Tom's eye and waved him forward.

"Okay, men, let's go." Tom gave them a grin and headed out. Although prepared for a firefight, the men would most likely have a tedious and nerve-wracking day under a hot sun.

Still, he held his carbine at the ready. *Lord, don't make me use it.*

At the northern perimeter, the squads separated and the men jogged south onto the field, hunched over, rifles in hand. Tom and Larry led Ferris's squad.

To his right, infantry slunk beside buildings, flung open doors, and charged inside, rifles leading the way.

As he ran, Tom scanned the field. Deep craters would keep the company busy. Half a dozen wrecked planes littered the runway, blackened by fire. Each would receive a hand grenade to set off any gifts from the Germans.

No gunfire yet, but Nazi snipers were sneaky. Tom had heard reports of snipers opening up from well-disguised caves several days after the front passed by. Anything to breed terror.

Tom hung around as Ferris's men swept mine detectors over craters and blew up the remains of an Me 109 fighter plane.

After a few minutes, Tom and Larry headed down the runway toward Kovatch's squad. Around the buildings to his right, white tape already marked safe passages. Infantrymen continued to barge into buildings.

Tom and Larry passed a burning Me 109, tipped onto its nose.

"Looks good," Larry said, but he swung his rifle in an arc before him.

"Yep, sure—"

A whine, a zing. A blow to Tom's right hip shoved him to the side.

"A sniper!" he yelled. "Take cover!"

He dashed back for the burned-out plane. Hot moisture oozed down the outside of his thigh. Oh swell, he was hit. Why didn't it hurt?

Another zing.

Larry cried out, spun to the ground. His rifle skidded away across the pavement. "I'm hit! I'm hit!" A furious red stain formed on his shin.

"Hold on to me." Tom grabbed him around the waist and hauled him up to his good foot. "Gotta take cover."

A bullet pinged off the pavement in front of them, but Tom plowed forward, heart thumping, sweat beading under his helmet.

Shouts rang out around the airfield, and men scrambled for shelter.

Tom eased Larry down behind the Me 109's crumpled nose, not much protection, but it had to do. "How bad is it?"

"I don't know." Larry's voice came out cramped. He shoved down his legging and pulled up his pants leg. "Flesh wound, looks like. Get him, Gill. Get that sniper."

The sniper? "Gotta do first aid."

Larry opened his first aid kit. "I'll take care of it. Get him."

His own wound. That was his excuse. Crouched behind the plane, Tom examined his hip. Dark, damp, warm, but no pain, no blood. "Huh?"

Something dripped on the ground beside him in a steady beat. His canteen. The sniper punctured his canteen. A ragged breath tumbled out.

A bullet dinged off the plane's nose. Tom sheltered Larry with his body.

"Get him, Gill. Before he kills someone."

Tom rose slowly to his knees behind the fuselage and propped his carbine on the wreckage. He mentally followed the bullets' trajectory to the center building, the only two-storied structure, probably the control tower.

A pile of concrete rubble lay on the flat roof, an unlikely place for rubble, but a clever spot for a sniper. Tom just had to aim for the center of that pile, the dark hole where a German lay, rifle pointed at him.

Infantry eased up to the building and exchanged hand signals. They'd get to the roof in a few minutes. But now Tom had a perfect line of sight.

"Lord, no," he whispered.

"Shoot, Gill! What are you waiting for?"

Hot sweat dripped down his temples. Down the neck of his shirt. Down his sides.

He could take that sniper with a single bullet. He was a good shot. Too good a shot.

MacGilliver the Killiver. MacGilliver the Killiver.

A yellow flash from the rubble. A bullet kicked up chunks of pavement by Tom's knee.

Behind him, Larry screamed and grabbed his thigh. "Stinking Kraut. Get him! Get him!"

Tom's breath came fast and hard. He squinted down his gun sight, lined up with the source of that muzzle flash. How could he take a life? Destroy? Kill?

Larry writhed behind him, groaned, and swatted Tom's combat boot. "What are you waiting for? Get him before he kills us. He'll kill us, you know."

Tom could shoot, aim high, scare the sniper, slow him down, make himself look busy. But his fingers locked in position.

"Gill!" Larry hit his ankle. "What's wrong with you? Shoot him!"

A bullet skittered past, too far to the left. Tom was a better shot than that German.

"I understand." Larry curled up in a ball and looked up at Tom with accusing eyes. "You don't want to be like your dad. So you'll let me die."

"What? No! That's not—"

Another shot. Tom ducked. Larry cried out and clutched his calf. Three hits.

His friend, his colleague, a good man was wounded. Three times he was wounded. Because Tom wouldn't shoot.

He stared down the barrel of his carbine, willed himself to squeeze the trigger, to kill, to fulfill his destiny and become his namesake.

A loud whack. A trapdoor sprang open on the roof. Men surged out, shouted, kicked at the rubble, and prodded it with bayonets. A man stumbled to his feet, hands raised high.

Thanks to Tom, he lived.

Thanks to Tom, Larry was wounded.

"Medic! Medic!" Tom turned to his friend. "How bad is it?"

"Don't touch me." Larry's voice sent icy chills into Tom's heart. He rocked back and forth, clutching his bloody leg. "Your reputation means more to you than my life."

A team of medics and litter-bearers ran up, and Tom sat back on his heels. His carbine clunked to the ground. What kind of man was he?

27

Sergeant Early hooked up a litter rack in the back of the C-47. "That's all. We only have enough parts for four litter patients."

Standing on the tarmac below, Mellie sighed and leaned her head against the rim of the cargo door. The litter racks had to be disassembled to make room for cargo, then reassembled for air evac, but with each flight they lost more parts.

There had to be a better way. If only she could run the problem through Tom's engineering mind. She could picture his blond head bent over paper, sketching designs, his blue eyes bright. But she couldn't ask in a letter without revealing herself as a flight nurse, and she couldn't ask in person since his battalion had left Youks-les-Bains.

Would she ever see him again? Pain squeezed her heart. What would be more miserable—seeing him again or never seeing him again?

Once she'd been content to live her life alone, but now her contentment had been destroyed by letters and an evening of dancing that gave her a tantalizing taste of romance. But love eluded her. Like trying to catch a hummingbird.

"What did I do to get stuck with you?" Early jumped to the ground and glared at Mellie. "Every stinking flight."

She pulled her lips between her teeth and shook her head. The other nurses worked with different techs each day, but Maxwell never switched Mellie and Early.

"Doc hates you." Early jerked out his big chin. "And I pay the price. The worst nurse, the worst flights, and the worst planes."

"Sorry." She strode away in the midday heat. It was all her fault. The friction in the squadron had caused even more problems with the flight surgeon.

"Hiya, Mellie." Kay Jobson approached from the next plane down. Ever since the argument with Georgie and Rose, Kay had been oddly friendly. "Ready for the flight?"

Mellie struggled to smile. She couldn't afford to alienate the only woman who was nice to her. "We can only take four litter patients. Too many missing parts."

"We can only take eight." Kay lifted her strawberry blonde hair off her neck. "Ugh. Can't believe how hot it is. When we get back to Algiers, how about you and I head to the beach for a dip?"

Mellie stopped and waited until Kay faced her. Her mouth crumpled. "Why are you being nice to me?"

Kay glanced away and shrugged. "Why not?"

"You were there." Mellie wrapped her arms around her stomach. "You saw what I did to Georgie and Rose. I'm a lousy friend."

Kay turned back, her green eyes intense. "On the contrary. Now you're finally ready to be a friend."

A rivulet of sweat ran down her breastbone. "I don't know what you mean. I've never had friends, then when I finally get friends, I ruin everything." Her jaw tightened and wobbled.

"That's why you're ready." Kay tapped one finger into

Mellie's shoulder. "Now you know you're no better than the rest of us, and you can be genuine friends with someone."

Mellie's throat swelled. "Georgie and Rose still won't talk to me."

"They're talking to each other again."

"Thank goodness," she whispered. They needed each other.

"Keep apologizing, and in the meantime, come to the beach with me."

The image of bombshell Kay and frumpy Mellie together at the beach brought up a strangled, damp giggle. "I don't understand. Why do you want to be friends with me?"

Kay looked off into the distance, and a twinge of hurt contracted around her eyes. "You're different. I have more in common with you than I do with Vera and Alice."

How could that be? Mellie's mouth drifted open. "Well . . . I . . ."

Kay glared at her. "Fine. I understand. You think I'm a slut. You think I'm not good enough for you." She marched off, her slim hips swaying in practiced rhythm.

What had she done? How could she make things worse? Mellie ran after her. "Wait, Kay! That's not what I meant, not what I think."

Kay didn't slow down. She flipped a hand over her shoulder. "Don't bother."

Mellie stopped and tipped her head back. Would she ever learn how to get along with women?

———

Mellie filled in the last of the vital signs on the flight manifest and made plans for the rest of the flight. The men needed distraction. With the plane's interior temperature close to one hundred degrees, the griping would escalate. If only the C-47 could climb to a cooler, higher altitude.

She tried to think, but Sergeant Larry Fong lay on his stomach on a midlevel litter, and his morose presence addled her thoughts. She'd met him when Tom walked her back to her tent after dancing, and he recognized her.

Larry had been hit by a sniper. Had Tom been hurt too? Or worse?

She shook off the thought and sang "When Peace Like a River." Maybe the lyrics about peace and water would calm and cool the men and herself. As she sang, she checked her patients' canteens and replaced wet compresses.

She finished the round by Larry's litter. "How are you doing, Sergeant?"

He shrugged and stared ahead, his chin resting on his forearms. Not the cheerful man Tom described in his letters.

Mellie folded back the blanket to check his dressings and provide an excuse for conversation. Three bullets had punctured his right leg, but the bones hadn't been damaged and infection hadn't set in. A few weeks of convalescence and he'd be back to work.

"A sniper did this?" she asked softly. "You were at the front?"

"The airfield at Kairouan."

Kairouan lay close to Tunisia's east coast and close to the front. "Was Lieutenant MacGilliver with you? Is he all right?"

A harsh laugh. "Of course he's all right, the rat."

The rat? Mellie frowned. Tom and Larry were friends. "What do you mean?"

Larry swiveled his head to look at her. "Stay away from him. He'll pretend he's your friend, but when it really matters, forget it."

Mellie's legs went numb and tingly as if she'd sat on them wrong. "I don't . . . what do you mean?"

"I got hit, dropped my rifle. Sure, he got me to safety, but he didn't fight for me. He had a great line of fire on the sniper, didn't shoot. I got hit again. And again. And he didn't shoot. When it comes down to it, he only cares about his reputation." Hurt and anger glittered in Larry's black eyes.

Part of her wanted to defend Tom. She knew why he didn't want to kill. But another thought choked off her defense. Tom let down a man under his command and a friend.

Could he be trusted? If he didn't stand up for his men, would he stand up for her?

She thought she knew Tom, but perhaps she was mistaken.

The plane banked sharply to the left, and Mellie grabbed the litter rack for support.

Were they under fire? None of the evac flights had been attacked since the nurses arrived.

Mellie headed for the tail of the plane, now an uphill climb. The C-47's twin engines roared as the plane picked up speed and dropped altitude. She swung around the tier of litters and pressed her face to the window.

Six Spitfire fighter planes escorted the three cargo planes. In the distance, five fighters darted and spun. Three Spitfires and two single-engine fighters, similar in shape to the Spits. One zipped past, and she backed up and sucked in her breath. A cross was painted on the side, the black cross of the Luftwaffe.

The C-47 banked again, to the right this time, and the men talked all at once.

Sergeant Early worked his way up from the front of the plane. "Okay, boys, nothing to worry about. The fighter jockeys got it under control."

If only it were that simple. The plane carried patients, but cargo planes couldn't bear the Red Cross of protection. Allied fighters made a game of shooting down Axis transports, starving the Germans and Italians of troops, fuel, and food. These Luftwaffe pilots would want revenge.

Black smoke flowed from one of the planes bearing the U.S. Army Air Forces' blue star on a white disc. "Oh no," Mellie said.

The little plane climbed as if aiming for the sun, hovered for an excruciating moment, then plummeted toward the earth.

Mellie gasped and stepped back.

"See?" Early grumbled behind her. "Combat's no place for a sniveling woman. Now they'll ground you dames and let us get back to work."

Mellie pulled herself tall. "I'm not afraid, Sergeant. I'll give these men the care they deserve."

She headed down the aisle and assessed the patients. Some looked terrified, some looked angry, and some called out shots as if the fighter pilots could hear their advice. All needed a calming touch.

Once more she sang "It Is Well with My Soul," too overcome to think of a new song.

Somehow she had to find that peace like a river again.

28

Kairouan Airfield
Tunisia
April 14, 1943

The tent for company headquarters stood before Tom, canvas flapping in the hot breeze. Inside his future would be destroyed.

He drew a deep breath and tried to pray, but he couldn't get past "Lord." He had no right to pray for mercy from Captain Newman after he'd failed Larry and the whole company.

No one respected him anymore.

He thought killing a man would ruin his reputation. Rather, sparing a man had killed his reputation.

"'Bout time you get what you deserve." Quincy's voice.

Tom groaned and walked toward the tent.

"Newman will ship you home, back to pansy-land where you belong." Quincy whacked the carbine that hung over Tom's shoulder. "That's a gun. You're supposed to use it."

Tom stiffened but kept walking. Confrontation would do no good.

Quincy barked out a laugh. "Your father was more of a man than you are. At least he fought for what he wanted. Even if all he wanted was booze."

Fire coiled up Tom's spine and spun him to face Quincy. Tom's breath chuffed out, but he couldn't speak, didn't trust himself with words. His fingernails dug into his palms, and he restrained his muscles. If he didn't, his fists would add more damage to Quincy's warped face.

That face broke into a narrow-eyed smile. "Just once I'd like to see you lay into me. I'd beat you to a pulp. That'd feel good."

Tom turned on his heel and marched toward the tent, breathing hard. Part of him wanted to take Quincy's bait and get the beating he deserved. Instead he'd let Newman do the beating with a demotion or transfer.

Tom ducked inside the tent, Quincy right behind him. Newman sat at his field desk, and Corporal Reilly tapped on a typewriter at another desk. Sergeant Moskovitz sat on a camp stool and shot Tom a disdainful look. The squad leader used to like Tom.

In the stifling heat, Tom saluted the captain and held his chin high.

Newman motioned for Quincy to pull up a camp stool but gave Tom no such courtesy. Tom stood stiff and waited for the deathblow to his career and dreams.

The captain leaned an elbow on the desk, pinched the skin between his eyebrows, and sighed. "I don't know what to do with you, Gill."

"Yes, sir." He understood.

Newman thumped a pile of papers. "I need your engineering expertise, but the Army has structure. There's no room in the Tables of Organization for an officer who can't lead."

A slap to Tom's face. "I know, sir."

"I thought you were getting better, taking charge. But then you failed to protect Sergeant Fong. All because you don't want to kill."

A solid punch to Tom's chest. "I'm sorry, sir."

Quincy snorted. "Pansy."

"That's enough, Quince." Newman's gaze probed into Tom with a flicker of understanding, but he shook his head and set his lips in a hard line. "That won't do. This is the Army. We're at war."

"I know, sir." Shame shuttered his eyelids, but he forced them open.

Newman rubbed the back of his neck. "The military isn't set up for flexibility. I'll do what I can to keep your expertise while protecting the men."

"Aren't you shipping him home, Captain?" Quincy said.

Newman turned a hard gaze to the platoon leader. "I need a trained engineer in this company. He's the only one. You and Gill will have to work together."

Quincy rocked forward. "What?"

"Excuse me?" Tom said.

Newman held up one hand. "It's the only thing I can think of. Quincy, you'll command both platoons and work with the men. Gill, you'll do the paperwork for both platoons and stay away from the men. I can still use your expertise. You keep your title, but only in name."

Tom nodded although his neck felt like a steel girder. He could still serve his country. He wasn't demoted. He wasn't going home. But he had a humiliating blemish on his record.

"No disrespect, sir." Quincy's tone contradicted his words. "But why couldn't you pick Lieutenant Reed to work with him? Why do I have to be saddled with this—"

"No. I trust you to lead these men. Kovatch and Ferris are used to you, and you can pick the man to replace Moskovitz."

Tom glanced at his favorite squad leader. "What's happening to Moskovitz?"

"He's replacing Fong as your platoon sergeant."

Moskovitz's gaze drilled holes into the base of Newman's

desk. Tom's heart sank even lower. Who would want to replace Larry after what Tom had done—or hadn't done?

"It's only temporary," Newman said. "Three months, no more. Gill, if you can earn back the men's respect and my trust, I'll put things back to normal. If not, I'll send for a replacement."

"Thank you, sir." Tom's mind whirled. How could he earn back the men's respect if he couldn't work with them? How could he earn trust doing paperwork?

And how could he save his dream? Adding a tarnished military record to his tarnished name would destroy his engineering career. He'd never be able to build. He'd never be able to support his mother and allow her to retire. He'd never be able to—oh, who was he kidding? What woman would marry him anyway? Annie deserved better.

"Quincy, Moskovitz, you're dismissed," Newman said. "Reilly, you too. I need a few minutes in private with Gill."

He reminded himself to keep his shoulders square. What more could Newman say to him? He couldn't be brought any lower.

Newman shuffled papers on his desk. After the men left, he lifted his gaze to Tom. "It's about the letters."

"The letters?"

"Those stupid anonymous letters. I won't do it anymore."

Tom was wrong. He could be brought lower. "What do you mean, sir?"

"It's too much time and hassle. I've done it for six months. That's enough. The other men stopped writing or they correspond openly. You're the only one left."

A jagged hole ripped open in his gut. He couldn't lose Annie, not now. Her friends had abandoned her, and he needed her as never before. "But sir, we both need this correspondence."

"You can still write her. I'll give you her name and address. But I won't play postman anymore. I've had it." Newman pulled out a notepad.

Annie's name. Her address. Tom leaned forward and peered at the notepad, willing the words to form. Finally he could have a real relationship with a real woman.

Newman lifted the pen. With a few scratches, he could shred the anonymity that cloaked them both.

"No, sir," Tom said. "Not now."

Newman glared at him. "You don't understand. I won't do this anymore. I'm fed up with you and I'm fed up with these blasted letters."

Tom's eyes closed. "I understand, sir. But we promised each other. We promised to keep it anonymous. I can't take her name and address without her permission. That wouldn't be fair."

"I won't do this—"

"One more letter, sir." Tom fixed his gaze on the captain. "Please send one last anonymous letter from me. I'll explain the situation, ask for her name and address. But it has to come from her, sir. I won't betray her trust."

Newman's eye twitched.

Tom winced from the irony. He'd betrayed Larry's trust and Newman's as well.

"One letter," Newman said in a clipped tone. "Only one."

It would be the hardest letter Tom ever had to write. What would he do if Annie said no?

29

Mellie laid her head on her pillow with Tom's letter beside her. Her mood matched the day—the Saturday after Good Friday when Jesus's body lay dead in the tomb. The disciples had lost all hope with no knowledge of resurrection around the corner.

"Where's my Easter?" Mellie rolled onto her stomach and raised herself on her elbows.

Tom wrote the letter the day Larry was shot. Mellie picked it up again.

> I have no excuse. All I could think about was not becoming a killer, a fear that I'm just like my father. I froze. I could hear the taunts and see my mother's dismay that all she'd taught me had gone to waste.
>
> So I let my friend get hurt, again and again. I put my reputation above another man's welfare. A hero does the opposite. What does that make me? A coward. A congenial coward.

Mellie sat up on the top bunk and gazed out the barracks window. A hot sunny day outside made the room as oppressive as her thoughts.

In the letter Tom had written before this, after the Remain Overnight, he'd expressed a desire to meet her and see if something more could develop. As a prerequisite for meeting her, he'd even admitted his father was executed for murder. He took a romantic interest in Annie at the same time he found Mellie wanting.

She wrote a firm letter of refusal coupled with the assurance that his father's history didn't affect her decision. But what if she *should* reject him? His kind heart had drawn her, but kindness wasn't enough. A man—a human being—needed strength as a foundation for kindness. Papa was both strong and kind.

Her chest, her throat, her eyes swelled shut. She missed Papa so much. He'd give her wise advice. But the Japanese allowed only twenty-four words in the body of letters to their prisoners, and she still hadn't received a note from him. Not uncommon with the Japanese.

Mellie pressed her hands over her face. "Lord, show me what to do. Show me how to respond to Tom. He needs me, but do I need him? And please give me someone to talk to. I miss Georgie and Rose. Could you see fit to let them forgive me? I need a friend. I need to talk—"

Someone laughed out in the hall. Mellie wiped her face and stuffed Tom's letter back in its envelope.

"If they won't let us fly to the front, the beach is the next best thing," Georgie said.

"Better hurry. We've got ten minutes before the truck leaves." Rose flung open the door.

Neither of them glanced at Mellie. They burrowed in their bags, laughing and pulling out bathing suits.

More than ever, Mellie longed for a friendship like theirs. A lifetime of shared joys and hurts allowed them to forgive each other. Rose had to be pleased that Georgie overcame her fears to follow her to Alaska and Africa. Her sacrifice showed true friendship. And Georgie overlooked Rose's attraction to Ward. Of course, Rose's romance with Clint helped.

But Mellie? They didn't share a history with her. The benefits of her friendship didn't balance out her betrayal.

In the suffocating heat of the barracks and loneliness, the fresh air of the beach and friendship beckoned. "The beach trip," she said. "Can anyone go, or do you need an invitation?"

Rose kept her back to Mellie and snapped the straps of her bathing suit onto her shoulders. Silent.

Georgie's gaze flitted up to Mellie, soft but guarded. "Anyone can go."

Rose huffed and grabbed her towel. "Come on, Georgie, let's go."

Mellie climbed off the bunk. A day of solitude on the beach would be better than moping in the barracks. But she wanted more.

"I really am sorry." She clenched her hands in front of her stomach. "What I did was unforgivable, but could you . . . could you ever forgive me?"

"We've already forgiven you." Rose wiggled into a skirt, not meeting Mellie's eye. "It's the Christian thing to do."

Mellie's chest caved in. They'd already forgiven her? This was as good as it would get? This was forgiveness? To be banned from the palace of friendship?

"Let's go. We'll miss the truck." Rose left the room.

Georgie followed but cast a glance over her shoulder at Mellie, her eyebrows pinched together. Regret flowed from her gaze, but not enough regret to lead to action.

A hideous whimper bubbled in Mellie's throat. "This is what forgiveness looks like?"

Georgie flinched as if Mellie had slapped her. She ducked her head and shut the door.

Mellie pressed her hands over her face. Without restoration, what good was forgiveness? Meanwhile, she'd forgiven them and longed for restoration, although they'd never apologized for betraying her confidence.

A sob bulged in her chest, but she swallowed it and unbuttoned her blouse so fast the buttons strained on their threads. Whether they liked it or not, she was going to the beach.

She threw on her bathing suit, slipped on her uniform blouse and skirt, and picked up a book. Her hand hovered over Tom's next letter, still sealed in its envelope. He'd failed a friend.

So had she.

Mercy flooded through her, and she slid the letter inside the book. He needed forgiveness and restoration, and who was she to hold back? He'd offered such sweet words when she confessed what happened with Georgie and Rose. He deserved likewise.

Mellie dashed outside to an open Army truck. A grinning corporal helped the nurses into the back. Mellie took the last seat, next to the tailgate.

All alone. Again.

Mellie lowered her head. This was her new life.

After the truck lumbered away and the ladies returned to their conversations, Mellie opened Tom's letter.

Annie, this is the hardest letter I've ever had to write.

First, I'll bring you up-to-date, so you can decide if you want me for a friend.

Newman didn't send me stateside for the sniping incident. Instead he combined my platoon with "X's" platoon. X will be in command, and I'll do the paperwork. I have three months to regain respect or home I go. But how can I regain respect holed up with a typewriter while X spreads the truth about me?

The truth is, I'm not the man I should be.

Did you ever see the newsreel footage from the collapse of the Tacoma Narrows Bridge in 1940? As an engineer, I've studied that collapse. The bridge was well designed, but not for its location. The winds howl through the Narrows. When they hit the bridge, a wave fluttered through the steel and concrete. That wave built into a giant, heaving oscillation that snapped the suspension cables and sent the bridge plummeting into the waters below.

That's how I feel. My character was designed for calm breezes. But life sent me howling winds, which proved me lacking. When the winds hit, I snapped, collapsed, and plummeted.

I need the Lord's help to rebuild my bridge with stronger cables, bigger bolts, and plenty of trusses. I'm thankful I have you to talk to, my Annie.

Mellie's vision blurred. The truck lurched to the side, and she yanked up her gaze. No one looked at her, but she had to be careful.

Poor Tom. He was falling apart. But he recognized his failures and was determined to change. That meant a great deal. She returned her attention to his beloved handwriting.

That said, I'm afraid we have a problem. Captain Newman won't transfer letters anymore. He offered me your name and address so we could correspond openly, but I refused. That wouldn't be fair without your permission.

I'd hoped to have an open relationship with you someday when both of us were ready.

I believe I'm ready. I'm willing to reveal my name to you, even though the name itself could drive you away forever. If you're willing, please reply with your name and address.

If you aren't willing—and I understand why—then this is the last letter you'll receive from me. Captain Newman will not send any more. He'll forward your letters for another two weeks so you can send your name or your farewell.

Anonymity is the foundation of our friendship, and I feel like I've broken a promise by asking your name. But I have to ask for the sake of our relationship.

I'll give my final good-bye just in case. Your friendship means a lot to me. We've helped each other through difficult times. No matter what, I'll continue to pray for your safety, your friendships, your father, and for you to

continue to blossom as the woman you are—
giving and thoughtful and beautiful.

Yours always, Ernest

Mellie's breath came hard and fast. No. No. She couldn't lose him. Not now.

The only way to keep him would be to reveal herself, but that was out of the question. She could still see his face when Quincy asked if Tom wanted to dance with her.

He might see beauty in her soul, but not on her face.

Mellie's eyes filled. Perhaps it would be best to cut things off now before Tom knew who she really was.

A void formed in her heart and swamped her with darkness and emptiness. Without Tom, she'd have no one. Georgie and Rose shut her out. Her father was locked up. Yes, the Lord was enough, and yet he wasn't. He'd created people to live among other people.

And all were stripped from her.

A tear slithered down her cheek. She rubbed it away and sneaked up a glance.

On the bench seat across from her, Kay eyed Mellie, one eyebrow raised.

Mellie dropped her gaze, heart pounding, and she reread Tom's letter. His last letter.

No. The timing was wrong. They were both going through horrible times. He was all she had, and she was all he had.

The truck stopped. The nurses bumped into each other, laughing.

The Mediterranean stretched before her, the Bay of Algiers curving like a hug. Mellie took the corporal's hand and jumped out of the truck. A few steps, and her bare feet eased into the sand. A breeze wrapped around her. Sunshine spilled over her.

Her eyes drifted shut, and she soaked in the warmth. *Lord, please help Tom and me. We need anonymity, even if he doesn't realize it. But we need each other too. Please show us a way.*

Sand struck her shins as a group of nurses passed.

"Who's tonight, Kay?" Alice asked.

"Grant, that new C-47 pilot. Doesn't the name fit him? He looks like Cary Grant."

Alice and Vera murmured their appreciation.

Mellie opened her eyes. C-47s flew supplies to airfields all over North Africa. Tom was stationed at airfields. Kay Jobson knew practically every pilot in the 51st Troop Carrier Wing. Surely some of those pilots knew Tom.

As one, Vera, Alice, and Kay lifted their towels, let the wind fluff them out, and laid them on the sand. They stripped down to their bathing suits and stretched out on their towels.

Mellie crossed the sand to an isolated spot, so no one would think she'd imposed on them. She rolled her clothing around her book, but she didn't lie down.

A dip in the sea. That would help her sort things out. Or would it wash away her determination? No, she had to act now.

Soldiers circled Vera, Alice, and Kay, but the three nurses lay with eyes shut. Only the hint of smiles indicated they knew the effect they had.

Mellie chewed on her lower lip. If she did this, she had to open herself again to genuine friendship with all its bumps and bruises. She set her jaw and strode forward. "Hi, Kay. May I please talk with you?"

"Huh?" Kay lifted her head and shielded her eyes from the sun.

"May I please talk with you? Alone?"

Kay shrugged and sat up. "Sure. What's up?"

Mellie ignored the giggle Vera and Alice shared and headed down the beach toward the turquoise water. A lace-edged wave crashed at Mellie's feet, cooled them, and sucked the sand out from underneath, making her feel two inches shorter.

"Well, what's up?" Kay stood behind her, feet dry.

"I'd like to be friends."

Kay's expression softened, but she crossed her arms. "Is that right?"

Another wave hissed around Mellie's feet. "That's right. I want to get to know you. I want to find out what we have in common. I'm not much good as a friend, you know that, but I'm willing if you are. You have Vera and Alice, but—"

Kay cracked a smile. "Vera and Alice are fun, but they're superficial little snobs."

Mellie let a teasing smile climb up. "And you're not?"

Kay laughed. "Would I want to be *your* friend if I were?"

"No, you wouldn't." Mellie offered her hand. It felt like the right thing to do. "Friends?"

Kay tilted her head and squinted at Mellie's hand, then she shook. "For what it's worth."

It was worth a whole lot more than Kay knew. Mellie winced and turned back to the ocean. A wave smacked into her shins and made her stumble. "I have to be honest. I want to ask a favor too."

"Does it have anything to do with the letter that made you cry?"

"Everything." Mellie waded in to her knees. "Come on in. The water's warm."

"Yeah?" Kay leaned down and swept an armful of water out at Mellie. "So what's the favor?"

Mellie set her hands on her hips, while hope as warm as the Mediterranean splashed into her heart. "How would you like to play postman?"

30

Tabarka Airfield
Tunisia
May 7, 1943

"Come on in. The water's great." A wave whooshed past Tom's knees. "Don't be a sissy."

Sesame shook his head and dropped his stick on the dry sand. He did not like water.

Tom sloshed out and heaved the stick down the beach. Sesame loped down the empty expanse of white sand.

The other men in his company spent their day off in the nearby town of Tabarka, hoping its beaches would be populated by females. They'd earned the break after their hard work laying a new airstrip a stone's throw from Tunisia's north coast. A fine strip. The sandy soil drained well, and good drainage allowed for a stable airstrip. But Tom's knowledge of soils and surfaces didn't buy respect.

He waded into the surf and ducked under the salty waves. He stood up and slicked back his hair. Solitude felt good, but he also welcomed Sesame's company to keep him from slipping beneath the dark waves in his soul.

Sesame returned with the stick, his tail curled over his back. He cocked his head at Tom.

"I know, boy. I'm not myself." But who was he anyway?

A wave bumped into the back of his knees and threw him off balance. Yesterday's letter from his MacGilliver grandparents had thrown him even more off balance.

They loved him and missed him and rejoiced over his letter. All his life he could have received more than his mother's love.

Tom chucked the stick down the beach. That would have been enough to digest, but their information about his father sat in nauseating, indigestible lumps in his stomach.

Even though his father drank, he lost his job for another reason. Some men on the demolitions site had cut corners. His father knew about it but didn't speak up. Something went wrong. Men died. Those who cut corners were fired and so was Tom's father.

That night he got drunk and smashed the kitchen chairs, the first time he'd done anything dangerous. Furious, Tom's mother left.

Understandable, his grandparents said, given her background.

Turned out her own father was a violent drunk. Tom had never known that.

That night, Mom took Tom and left. She couldn't forgive her husband. No second chance. No mercy.

That's when booze became his life. He couldn't pay his rent. He couldn't find a job. He ended up on Skid Row.

Then that fateful night, he begged Max and Lucille DeVille for money. And it was over.

Tom ran his hands back into his hair and groaned. Granted, his grandparents could be biased, but the story held the shattering, illuminating glare of truth.

All his life he had avoided becoming a violent drunk. But his father's true fault, his tragic shortcoming was that he didn't stand up for right.

Tom had rejected one flaw and embraced another. Just like his father, he'd chosen not to act when action was right, and someone got hurt. Unwittingly he'd followed his father's path.

Tom plunked down onto the wet sand, and a spent wave washed around him.

All his life, he'd placed his father in the gutter and his mother on a pedestal. But he wasn't all bad and she wasn't all good.

Tom rested his head in his hands. "Who am I, Lord?" He had to be more than not-his-father. He had to find balance between godly kindness and godly boldness. "Lord, help me be the man I should be."

Sesame whimpered and bumped Tom's side.

"Hey, boy." Tom stroked the dog's back and uncoiled his tail. It sprang back into position. "I'm glad I have you."

And Annie. He'd write her tonight. Thank goodness she'd figured out how to maintain anonymity. He'd put his letter in its usual blank envelope inside an envelope addressed to Kay Jobson, one of the flight nurses, with his name and mailing address enclosed for Kay's use. He'd hand it to one of the C-47 pilots to deliver to Kay, and Kay would pass the letter on to Annie. Then Annie would give her letter to Kay, who would slip it in an envelope addressed to Tom and hand it to a pilot who knew him.

Seemed strange that Annie knew Kay Jobson, of all people. Annie just said they were acquainted and stationed near each other. Once again, he entertained a wish that Annie and Mellie were the same person, but Annie had never mentioned flying or planes. However, she had given him one clue—she was stationed near Algiers.

Tom gazed down the shore, as if he could see down the hundreds of miles of coastline.

Anonymity seemed wiser than ever. With his history and

faults, why did he think she'd want a romance with him anyway? Her last letter had a sober tone and reminded him of the importance of strength as a foundation for kindness.

Annie claimed another reason for anonymity. She said most men didn't find her attractive and she apologized for not telling him sooner. He'd never pictured her like a cover girl, but he couldn't erase the exotic image he'd formed in his mind. How much did looks matter to him? He wanted to say he didn't care, but he wouldn't really know until he met her.

Tom traced a stick figure in the wet sand. "Guess we both need anonymity awhile longer."

Sesame yipped and dashed up the beach. A wave soaked Tom's legs, up to his waist.

He pushed himself to standing. "Aren't we a pair? You're afraid of water. You're made of water, know that? And I'm afraid of . . . well, I'm afraid of what I'm made of too."

He crossed the sand to a goat path through the gray-green scrub that coated the dunes. He hadn't brought a towel. The heat would dry him fast, and the air tingling on his damp skin felt great.

Sesame romped through the brush and nosed around, searching for something edible.

A shot cracked the silence, splintered the peace.

Tom dropped flat to the ground. His heart thumped against the sand. What on earth? They'd cleared Axis troops from this area ages ago. The Allies were on the march. The Americans were supposed to plow into Bizerte that day, the British into Tunis.

Laughter rang out about a hundred feet ahead. "You call yourself a good shot?"

Tom's eyes slipped shut and a sigh leached out. Americans. Stupid Americans out for a hunt. He racked his brain for the current parole and countersign. "Fibber McGee!" he yelled.

"What?"

"Fibber McGee!"

"And Molly."

Tom got to his feet and brushed sand off his chest and swim trunks. "Before you shoot, make sure there aren't any men around." A sharp edge sliced through his words.

Two officers stood on top of the dune, carbines in hand. Reed and Quincy.

Quincy laughed. "I don't see any men around."

"Funny." Tom marched up the goat path, head down.

Something rustled in the brush about twenty feet to Tom's left. A curly white and brown tail popped into the air. Sesame dug after some unfortunate rodent.

"There's one!" Reed leveled his carbine. At Sesame.

"No! Don't shoot!"

Quincy pushed out his lower lip. "Afwaid we'll hurt a widdle bunny?"

A flash from Reed's gun. The whine of a flying bullet.

Sesame yelped.

Tom sprinted to him. "That's no rabbit. That's my dog! Sesame!"

Sesame yelped, writhed on the ground, and tried to nip his tail. His red tail.

"Sesame!" Tom skidded to his knees. Sesame's beautiful tail didn't curl. It formed a jagged, cruel, red angle.

"It's okay, boy. It's okay." Tom scooped Sesame into his arms. "Come on, boy. I'll get you some help."

He hurdled bushes, back to the path, up the dune, past Reed and Quincy, not meeting their eyes.

"Hey, Gill, I'm sorry," Reed said. "I didn't know."

"You should've listened." Tom sprinted up the path, which led to the northwestern corner of the airstrip. The pierced steel planking was great for planes but not for bare feet, so

Tom ran beside the runway toward the tents of the 10th Field Hospital.

Sesame twisted in his arms.

Tom tightened his grip. "It's okay, boy. I'll get you some help."

He passed three C-47 cargo planes on the runway, and he slowed his pace. Tabarka had opened for medical air evacuation that day. Another reason Tom had escaped to the beach.

How could he worry about seeing Mellie Blake when Sesame depended on him?

His bare feet protested the beating, but he ignored them and pressed on to the main tent closest to the airfield.

He shoved through the tent flap like a linebacker.

"Whoa!"

He smacked into someone who blocked him with small cool hands to his bare chest. A woman. A dark-haired woman. Mellie Blake.

Of all the people in the world.

"Tom?" Her eyes went round.

Like looking into two warm cups of coffee and he wanted to drink them right up. "Mellie," he said over his thick tongue.

Her hands. How could such cool little hands shoot fire through his chest?

He stepped back.

She looked at her hands, suspended in air, and dropped her gaze. Then she gasped. "Sesame?"

Tom breathed. Yes, Sesame. He'd come for Sesame. "He's hurt."

Mellie's hands went to work, stroking, probing over the dog's fur. Much too close to Tom's skin. "What happened?"

"He was shot. Some idiots out hunting."

"Just the one wound? His tail?"

"Uh-huh."

"Thank goodness. He'll be all right. Follow me." Mellie strode down the aisle of the tent hospital past rows of men on cots. "Dr. Sayers?"

Tom followed and cooed to Sesame.

"Dr. Sayers?" Mellie tapped the shoulder of a tall, skinny man. "We have a dog that's been shot."

"A dog?" The physician eyed Tom. "Put your clothes on, get your gun, and put the beast out of its misery."

"Sir!" Mellie cried.

Tom stepped forward, and steam expanded his chest. He hadn't stood up for Larry, but he'd stand up for Sesame. "Excuse me, sir, but it's just his tail."

Dr. Sayers walked away and waved one hand over the cots. "Do I look like a vet? I have real patients. Get that cur out of here before you give these men fleas."

Tom charged forward. "Sir, all I need is—"

A small hand clamped onto his arm. Mellie swung around and stepped into his path. "Tom, wait." She looked up at him with the strangest expression, her eyes narrowed and probing.

His jaw hardened. "I will not fail him. He depends on me."

Mellie's gaze melted, the sweetest curve turned up her lips, and she swayed closer. Just a bit, but his pulse pounded like a jackhammer.

"I have—" The words turned to powder in his mouth. Why couldn't he function in this woman's presence? He swallowed hard and moistened his lips. "I have to help him."

She gave a few slight nods, then looked to the back of the tent where the doctor had gone. "I'll see what I can do. Wait for me outside."

Tom nodded. He couldn't speak anyway. He headed outside, back into the fresh hot air. Sesame struggled in his arms. "Ssh, boy. It's okay. We'll take care of you."

A few minutes later, the tent flap rustled, and Mellie came

out with a white bundle. "Come with me." She walked at a brisk pace toward a C-47.

"A doctor over there?"

Mellie shook her head. "Dr. Sayers is the only one working today. I'm not a surgeon, not a vet, but I'll see what I can do." Her voice wavered.

Tom caught up and looked hard at her until she turned her gaze to him. "I trust you. I know you'll do your best."

Her smile twitched in a vulnerable way. "Thank you."

He winked, anything to relax her. "Don't you have *real* patients?"

She shook back the black waves of her hair to reveal a mischievous glint in her eyes. "Sesame isn't real? I didn't know you had imaginary friends."

Nope, anonymous friends. And he'd better watch himself.

Mellie climbed through the cargo door of the C-47, and Tom followed. She unrolled a bundle of towels wrapped around a canteen of water and an olive drab canvas pouch. Then she opened the chest in the back of the plane. "They weren't ready for us when we landed. We won't load patients for two hours, so I have plenty of time."

"Okay." Plenty of time. Up to two hours. The thought frolicked in his heart, then skidded to a stop in his brain. He jerked his gaze to the hurting little dog in his arms. "It's okay, Sesame. Everything will be okay."

"Absolutely." Mellie laid a towel on the floor of the plane. "Lay him here, but keep a good grip on him."

Tom did so. Sesame's legs scrabbled around, but Tom held him down and cooed at him.

Mellie poured water over the wound and worked away dirt. "His tail is broken."

"You'll put a cast on it?"

One side of her mouth bent up. "No. It'll have to come off."

"Come off? His tail? You can't do that."

Mellie leveled her gaze at him. "It's broken clean through. Only a hinge of skin and soft tissue holds it in place. If I don't cut it off, he'll chew it off."

Heaviness pressed on his chest. He rubbed Sesame's head. The dog panted and looked up at him with trusting eyes. "Poor boy."

"He'll be fine. It could have been much worse." She dabbed the wound with an iodine-soaked gauze pad.

With one hand firm on Sesame's head, Tom stroked his shoulders. Tawny fur covered his back and sides and the top of his tail, while the underside of his body and tail were white. His tail used to swirl like cream being stirred into coffee. But no more.

Mellie sprinkled powder on the wound. "Sulfanilamide, to prevent infection."

"Uh-huh." The men carried sulfanilamide in their first aid packets, although few could pronounce it.

"You'll need to hold him down." Mellie filled a syringe. "I'm giving him something to sedate him, maybe make him sleep so he won't chew out his stitches."

"Okay." Tom sat with his full weight on his left leg and threw his right leg over Sesame's haunches. His bare, hairy leg. Why did this have to happen when he was half-naked?

Mellie drew her lips between her teeth. "Medications don't always have the same effect on animals that they do in people. I guessed on the dose, based on his weight, but I honestly don't know how it'll affect him."

Tom's hands dug into the fur over Sesame's shoulders and neck. What would he do without his dog? He cleared his throat. "But he needs it."

"Yes." She sent him a tentative glance.

He nodded his permission.

She injected the medication. Sesame yipped, and Tom exerted steady pressure to restrain him.

Mellie unrolled the canvas pouch and lifted a pair of gleaming scissors.

Tom jerked his gaze to the side. "It's okay, boy. I'm right here."

Scissors snipped. Tom braced himself against the sound and held his dog in place.

Sesame looked up at him with wild, questioning eyes. His tail. His beautiful tail.

Tom stroked his dog's head. "What will he do without his tail?"

"Excuse me?"

"He loves his tail. It's who he is, his identity."

Mellie stayed quiet so long, Tom shot her a glance. He must have sounded stupid. She gave him a soft, sweet look, full of understanding. "That's not all his identity, is it?"

"I—I don't know."

She bent down to her stitchery. "You love him and he loves you. Isn't that a big part of his identity?"

Sesame's gaze fixed on Tom, seeking guidance and protection and answers. "Yeah."

"And he's got his—" She frowned. Her forehead bunched up. "Well, does he do anything around here? Any roles, any jobs?"

"Yeah. He does a lot around here, carries messages, things like that."

"He doesn't need his tail to do that, right? He's loved. He has a purpose. He'll be fine." She gave him a penetrating look and the subtlest of smiles.

As if she'd seen. As if she understood.

Understood that his question about identity didn't apply just to Sesame but to him.

31

Tabarka Airfield
May 13, 1943

"Everything looks great." Mellie tugged on the litter rack in the back of the C-47.

Sergeant Early huffed. "I know what I'm doing."

She gritted her teeth, then relaxed her jaw so her voice would come out softly. "I know. I'm impressed with all you men do."

"The feeling ain't mutual. You dames do nothing but get the men hot and bothered." Early jumped out the cargo door and marched away.

She lowered herself out of the plane. It was almost time to load patients. Over the last few days, the Allies had swept over the German and Italian armies in Tunisia. Yesterday they had signed an official surrender, effective today. The hospitals teemed with patients, both Allied and Axis, and air evacuation ran in earnest.

Mellie crossed the runway, careful to walk the seams of the planks so her shoe heels wouldn't fall through the holes that perforated the steel like ticker tape. Tom said the holes made the planks lighter, helped in drainage, and provided grip for the planes' wheels. She smiled. Had Tom touched this plank? Why, she could almost hear his voice in her head.

"Thanks, Grant. Appreciate it." About two hundred feet away, one man addressed another. He sounded like Tom. He looked like Tom.

"No problem," the other man said. "Any excuse to see Kay."

"Yeah. Well, thanks again."

Mellie's breath caught. She'd witnessed Tom pass a letter for her. Even better, he walked in parallel with her.

Her heart angled her path toward his. When he looked her direction, her tongue froze, but she raised her hand in a tentative, ridiculous little wave.

He tipped his hand to the rim of his helmet, nodded, and continued on his way.

Mellie halted and gaped at him, her heart as pierced as the planks. He didn't want to talk to her? The man she loved didn't even acknowledge her? She was a fool, a deluded fool.

She strode toward the hospital tent. Maybe he didn't recognize her from that distance.

Yet she recognized him, the way he walked in his gray-green herringbone twills, the way he held his shoulders and chest. She knew how those shoulders felt in her arms. She knew the feel of his bare chest under her hands, the heat and strength.

Her cheeks warmed. He'd pulled away from her that day, and now he didn't even say hello.

Who was she kidding? He could never love her.

Her right foot wrenched to the side. She cried out and crumpled to the ground.

Her stupid heel had gotten stuck in the planking. Why didn't the Army Nurse Corps supply practical shoes?

Footsteps pounded toward her.

Oh no. Tom. He'd consider her a silly female who feigned injury so men would come to her aid.

She wiggled her foot out of the shoe. Her ankle throbbed.

"You okay?" Tom knelt beside her. "Mellie? Oh, it's you."

"I'm fine." She didn't meet his gaze, afraid her eyes were red. She swiveled her ankle. Not broken. A strain, maybe a mild sprain.

Tom chuckled. "That's why you waved. I didn't recognize you. The sun was in my eyes. Sorry. You must think I'm rude."

Mellie ventured a glance into his eyes, even bluer against a tan. He must have had more days at the beach. In his swim trunks. She lowered her head and rubbed her ankle. "Perhaps a bit rude."

"Sorry." Tom worked her shoe out of the hole. "Maybe you should keep the high heels at home."

His grin prodded up a shaky laugh. "If I did, I'd be barefoot."

Tom brushed dirt off the shoe and handed it to her. "I'll loan you some combat boots."

"I'd accept if they came in my size." She worked the shoe back onto her foot and winced at the pain.

"Are you hurt? 'Cause I could reserve a spot for you on this flight."

Why did he have to smile? It was the most glorious, agonizing thing. She forced herself to play along and send him a wink. "I already have a reservation."

"Smart woman." He got to his feet and offered his hand.

Nothing to do but take it, although the feel of his warm, callused strength sent shivers through her more painful than the twinges in her ankle.

She tried not to favor her right foot. "How's Sesame?"

"He's great." Tom pulled off his helmet and ran his hand over his sweat-damp hair. "He slept real well that day, and I kept him busy. He didn't pull out his stitches. Doc Abrams will take them out in a few days. He admired your handiwork."

"Doc Abrams?"

Tom motioned with his thumb over his shoulder as if a physician stood behind him. "Our battalion doctor. Anyway, thanks for all you did."

"I'm glad I could help." Mellie couldn't tear her gaze from his determined expression. When he fought for his dog with Dr. Sayers, he showed he'd learned from his mistakes. Strength bolstered his kindness, and she loved him deeply.

Tom plunked his helmet back in place. "I'd better get back to work. Good seeing you."

"Same here."

He saluted and left her.

All alone.

———

"Sing it loud, boys." In the bottom litter on the left, Sergeant Benson launched into "The Star-Spangled Banner."

As she made her way down the aisle, Mellie cringed, and not from the pulsing pain in her ankle. On any other flight, she'd welcome singing. On this day, with the war in North Africa at an end, the men deserved to celebrate.

But not when their celebration taunted the defeated enemy.

Irritated murmurs in German rose from some of the litters. Mellie didn't think it wise to mix Allied and Axis patients on the same flight, but two armed MPs stood guard in white helmets at the front of the cabin.

Mellie knelt beside Benson's litter. "Excuse me, Sergeant. I appreciate your patriotism and understand your joy, but please wait until we're on the ground. Things are tense."

Benson added a smile to his handsome face. "To the winners go the spoils."

"Yes, sir." Mellie patted his arm. "But save the spoils for later."

He waved her off with a glint in his brown eyes and sang "Praise the Lord and Pass the Ammunition."

Mellie sighed and straightened up. She'd never seen the enemy so close. Other than their unfamiliar uniforms and languages, they could be American boys. One looked scared, one looked sad, and two Italians seemed thrilled to be done with the war. But a German soldier in the litter above Benson gave icicle looks that chilled Mellie to the bone.

She returned to the rear of the plane to get the flight manifest for the final round of vital signs. Every bump burrowed into her ankle. She'd need to elevate it tonight so she wouldn't miss work.

"Hey, boys, get your raspberries ready," Benson shouted. "You know it—'Der Führer's Face.'"

Mellie's hands fisted. That was too much. It was one thing to rejoice over victory, another to make fun of the enemy.

"*Schwester! Schwester!*" The icicle-eyed German motioned for Mellie.

She didn't speak a lick of German, but she knew he wanted silence.

The man lay on his litter, his hand clamped over his mouth. Not his ears. The ice melted from his eyes. "*Schwester, ich werde mich übergeben.*"

The man's green skin tone communicated clearly. "I'll be right back, sir." She added some hand motions.

Early was helping patients in the front of the cabin, so Mellie dashed to the medical chest in the back, grabbed a rubber basin, and returned to her patient.

He grabbed the basin in both hands, leaned over the side of the litter, and retched.

Mellie stroked the blond hair on the back of his head and spoke soothing words he wouldn't understand.

All around, men made noises of disgust and turned away.

"What's the matter, Kraut?" Benson said from right below. "Can't stomach defeat?"

Laughter rewarded him, and he belted out the next verse of "Der Führer's Face."

Mellie ducked down to meet his eye. "Stop it, Sergeant."

"Just having fun. Join in." Benson waved his arms and conducted his GI chorus.

Mellie rolled her eyes. But the plane would land in half an hour and she'd be rid of this lot. She addressed her patient, who seemed to be finished. "Do you feel better? *Gut?*"

He lifted his head. Mellie wiped his blotchy pale face with a gauze pad. His eyes gave her the shivers, so cold, so hard, so hateful. She knew what the Nazis thought about half-breeds. Thank goodness she'd been born an American. Her racial heritage earned teasing, not death.

"May I?" She held out her hands for the basin.

His eyes narrowed, and his upper lip curled. He leaned over the side of the litter and dumped the basin onto Sergeant Benson.

Benson cried out and sat up, spewing curses as vile as the basin contents.

Mellie glared at the German and pressed his shoulders. "Lie down."

She bent to clean up Benson, but he'd unfastened his securing strap. He swung his legs to the ground and stood.

"No, sir! You shouldn't stand."

He shoved past her, flung his body on top of the Nazi, and pressed his fouled blanket over his enemy's face.

"Sergeant, no! You'll smother him." Mellie tugged his arm. "Help! MP!"

A crowd blocked the aisle and cheered Benson on. The MPs carried guns, but they couldn't shoot the men in the aisle. Sergeant Early barked commands over the crowd, but no one listened.

Panic scrambled in Mellie's chest. The German thrashed beneath Benson's weight, but he wasn't strong enough to throw him off. Mellie wasn't strong enough either. She searched the crowd for one man who would fight for what was right.

She found none.

Benson tightened his grip. "This is for Yates and Caruthers and Jacoby and all the other good men you filthy Krauts killed."

A strange idea filled her, nothing she could have thought of herself, so unnatural and illogical it had to come from above. She obeyed. She laid a firm hand on Benson's shoulder. "That's right. He deserves it."

Benson turned wild eyes to her, eyebrows twisted.

She leaned closer. "He deserves to die. He's a barbarian."

"Yeah," Benson chuffed out, arms firm over the struggling man's face. "Barbarian."

"I've heard what they do." Mellie locked the strongest gaze she could muster on Benson's red face. "They shoot their prisoners."

"Yeah! They do."

"They shoot their prisoners. Unarmed men who surrendered honorably. They show them no mercy. We wouldn't do that."

"No." His voice came out clipped. Horror jolted through his eyes.

"We wouldn't do that. We're better than that." With gentle pressure, Mellie eased him to the side. "We aren't barbarians. We treat our prisoners honorably. And this man is our prisoner."

A wash of emotions flooded over Benson's face. He stared at his hands.

Disappointed cries resounded through the plane.

Mellie guided Benson down to his litter. The German lay limp.

"Sit down! All of you!" Mellie swept the blanket off the man's face and pressed her fingers to his carotid. Still had a pulse, and his chest rose and fell. "What do you think this is? A prize fight? This is a man's life."

Early and the MPs shouldered their way through the crowd.

Mellie addressed the MPs. "Get these men seated and quieted." Then she turned to Early. "Get the oxygen equipment. Now."

She knelt down to check on Benson. "Are you all right?"

He held his hands in front of his face. "I'm a . . . I'm a . . ." Blood soaked through his pajamas over his abdomen.

Mellie folded back his pajama top and the gauze dressing over his gunshot wound. He'd burst his incision. She headed toward the medical chest for gauze and plasma.

She squeezed past Early coming down the aisle. "Give the oxygen to the German. He's still breathing, thank goodness."

Early studied her, eyes wide, mouth parted. "You defused a riot. All by yourself."

Mellie glanced upward. "I had help."

"Well . . ." Early dipped his chin and slowly raised a salute.

"Thanks." She gave him a quick smile, then went back to work. Adrenaline pulsed in her veins and would aid in the mop-up, but once it defused, she'd collapse.

Maison Blanche Airfield

"A riot on your plane?" Captain Maxwell ran his hand through his sleek black hair.

Mellie sat on the edge of a chair in the squadron head-quarters building, her arms and legs weak from the ordeal. "Yes, sir. But we put a stop to it."

"Put a stop to it? You never should have let it start."

"Be fair, Frank." Lieutenant Lambert rested her hand on the back of Mellie's chair. "Emotions run high on those POW flights. You know Sergeant Early does not give praise lightly, and he said she did a brilliant job and stopped it all by herself."

Maxwell spun and looked out the window to the darkening sky. "That's her problem. She thinks she's still in the jungle. She wants to do everything by herself."

Mellie blew out a breath. "Independence is an important trait in a flight nurse, isn't it?"

He turned, planted his fists on the desk, and leaned on them. "Within limits, Blake. Within limits. Vera and the others know their limits. They don't smear cactus on wounds, try to stop riots single-handedly, or perform amputations."

"Amputations?" Lieutenant Lambert circled the chair and stared down at Mellie. "You never performed an amputation."

Mellie looked back and forth between Maxwell and Lambert. Her mouth opened and closed. She'd never discussed Sesame's procedure with anyone.

The surgeon cocked an eyebrow at her. "Captain Abrams of the 908th Engineers told me how lucky I was to have such a skilled little nurse in my squadron. Seems you chopped off a dog's tail and did some pretty embroidery."

The chief nurse groaned. "Mellie . . ."

She leaned forward. "Sir . . . ma'am, the dog had been shot. The tail was broken clean through. The doctor on duty refused to treat the dog, and it seemed cruel to let him chew it off and get infected. I only needed to snip through some skin and soft tissue."

Maxwell crossed his arms and looked down his nose at her. "So you performed a surgical procedure. You used valuable supplies on a dog. And you didn't have a doctor's order, much less a vet's. That's just a little outside your scope of practice, isn't it?"

Tingles zipped through Mellie's cheeks. "Yes, sir. I suppose it is."

"What did I say would happen if you stepped outside your scope of practice again? I'd send you home."

Lambert twisted her hands together. "Don't be hasty, Frank. And remember, that's my decision, not yours."

"So make it. She doesn't know her place."

The chief turned to Mellie. Her brown eyes alternated between scolding and pleading. "You know better. Please don't do anything like that again."

Mellie's throat thickened, and she swallowed hard. "I won't, ma'am." But how could she allow the sick and wounded to suffer when she knew how to help them?

"Thank you. I don't appreciate being in this position. I shouldn't have to defend my nurses."

"I'm sorry, ma'am."

"You're dismissed." She waved her hand to the door.

"Thank you, ma'am." Mellie darted for the door and gasped from the stab of pain in her ankle.

Kay stood outside the building and waved. "Hiya, Melliebird. Heard you had a riotous day. I'm so proud of you."

Mellie ventured a smile although her muscles quivered like jelly. "Maxwell doesn't share your opinion."

"Never mind him. He's frustrated from a lack of marital relations."

"Kay!"

She laughed, and her green eyes glittered. "You know it's true. But it's fun to shock you."

"Glad I amuse you." Mellie gave her half a smile.

"Are you limping?"

"I sprained my ankle at Tabarka."

"You poor thing. Let's get you back to the barracks." She dangled an envelope in Mellie's face. "This will make you feel better."

The letter Tom passed to Grant. It seemed so long ago, but fresh pain at Tom's rejection ripped through her. He might have had the sun in his eyes, but if he had any interest in her, the conversation would have lasted longer.

Kay held the barracks door open. "Want some privacy?"

"Privacy? Around here?"

"I'll keep the girls out. Get that foot elevated. You know what to do."

"Thanks. I appreciate it." Mellie climbed onto her bunk, bunched the blanket over the railing at the foot of the bed, and propped her leg on top.

Tom's writing filled less than a page. Mellie suppressed disappointment and read the letter.

> My own dear Annie,
>
> Pardon the lack of small talk, but I have to get right to the point or I'll lose my nerve. Annie, we've been writing for seven months. I've seen into your heart and let you into mine. I've never met a woman like you.
>
> I've been in love—unrequited love—before, but I've never felt like this. I've never seen your face or heard your voice or watched your gestures, but I feel I know you well. Annie, I think I'm in love with you.
>
> This tears me up inside. If my feelings

don't drive you away, what I'm about to say
next probably will. I want to meet you. In the
meantime, I want to come clean. I want to tell
you my name and send my picture, and I want
to know your name and see your picture. You
say most men don't find you attractive, but
I'm not like most men. I know I'll love what you
look like.

"Oh, sweetheart." Mellie leaned against the whitewashed wall. Her heart throbbed in aching rhythm with her ankle. "No, you don't."

32

El Aouina Airfield
Tunis, Tunisia
June 8, 1943

Quincy tossed paper scraps onto Tom's desk and headed to the tent entrance. "Have fun with your report."

"Sure." Tom sorted the scraps. As always, Quincy gave him disjointed, incomplete, and sloppy information for the platoon reports. Each week it got worse. Tom only had one more month to regain respect, and Quincy knew it. What good was Tom to the battalion if he couldn't even put together decent paperwork?

He drummed his fingers on the desk. The solution meant bending Newman's rules.

Tom glanced down at Sesame curled up beside his desk. "Let's do some bending."

Sesame lifted his head. His stump of a tail tapped the dirt floor, a heartbreaking sound. At least the wound had healed well, thanks to Mellie's expert, cool little hands.

Tom shook his head hard, got to his feet, and grabbed a notebook. He headed outside and welcomed the hot, dry breeze.

The engineers had their hands full at El Aouina. Allied

bombers had pockmarked the former Luftwaffe airfield. Almost a month after the surrender, and carcasses of German and Italian aircraft still littered the base. But the Allies needed the field soon. The scuttlebutt pointed to an invasion of Sicily.

A roar built up to the south. Tom turned to watch.

A B-17 Flying Fortress zoomed down the dirt runway, a cloud of tan dust in its wake. The graceful four-engine bomber lifted off the ground and tucked up its landing gear. Most likely headed out to bomb Pantelleria, the Axis-controlled island halfway between Tunisia and Sicily.

Tom passed the burned-out hulk of a German cargo plane.

Cargo planes. Thank goodness El Aouina wasn't a site for medical evacuation. Mellie Blake tempted him too much.

He grimaced. He hadn't seen her for almost a month, and he hated the fact that he knew how long it had been. The last time he saw her, he'd been careful to limit their interaction. So why did he feel bad?

How could he have explained his shortness? "Sorry, Mellie. I find you too attractive, so I can't talk to you. I don't want to betray the woman I love. What's her name? I don't know."

Yeah. That would sound crazy.

Maybe it *was* crazy. Tom skirted a large bomb crater. Several men scampered inside. On the rim a man with a movie camera scanned the depths of the crater, where an aircraft engine poked out of the soil.

Tom let out a low whistle. That must have been some blast. He'd survived enough air raids to picture the scrambling men and burning planes and screaming wounded and geysers of flame and dirt.

He gazed east, as if he could see across the straits to Sicily. What awaited him there?

Sesame bumped his leg.

Tom ruffled his ears. "Thanks for keeping me alert, boy."
He continued on his way.

Ferris's squad worked on a runway, filling and grading.
Tom hailed him.

"Hi, Lieutenant. What are you doing out here?" Suspicion
lowered Ferris's voice.

Tom flipped open his notebook. "Filling in details for the
weekly report. Quincy gave me the data, but you know how
bad his handwriting is." Why disparage Quincy by telling
everyone he sabotaged Tom with flimsy data?

Ferris chuckled. "His handwriting stinks."

A few minutes, and Tom had everything he needed. He
thanked Ferris, clapped him on the back, and headed for the
next squad's area, farther down the runway. Felt good to be
around the men and the work, to be part of the operation
again, even if he just gathered numbers.

He'd tell Annie in tonight's letter. The pace of the correspondence had increased since he declared his love. She
even said she "entertained the notion of similar feelings."

When he read that, he'd let out a loud whoop and startled
Sesame and all the officers in the mess. He made some feeble
comment about the Pirates' latest victory. Last time he read
Annie's letters in public.

Granted, she was cautious and concerned. One section
of the letter he read last night wouldn't leave him: "How
can it really be love if we've never met? What if you can't
stand my hair, or I'm too fat or skinny, or I have an annoying gum-smacking habit, or my voice grates on your nerves,
or we don't have that chemistry everyone talks about? If we
aren't attracted to each other, I'm afraid our friendship might
become extremely awkward, and I couldn't bear to lose your
friendship. No, it's best if we never meet."

Tom couldn't imagine that happening. Maybe his mother

was right and he'd set himself up for a broken heart, but he doubted it. He loved the woman inside, and he had a gut feeling he'd like the outside as well.

He approached Kovatch's squad. A roller compacted the earth from a recent repair, and Tom had to shout his request twice. The sergeant grumbled about having to provide data he'd already given Quincy, but Tom persisted and prevailed.

The minor victory put a bounce in his step as he strolled down to the next work site. Sesame stopped, snapped his head to the side, and loped off to the hunt.

Two men walked in Tom's direction along the runway: Lieutenant Reed and—

And Larry Fong.

Tom's breath caught. He'd heard Larry had returned to the battalion yesterday, reassigned as Reed's platoon sergeant. Reed's former sergeant had been seriously injured by a land mine the week before.

The longer Tom waited, the harder this would get. "Lord, give me the right words."

Larry didn't limp, thank goodness, but when he saw Tom, his step faltered.

This wouldn't be easy, but it was the right thing to do. Tom raised a hand in greeting.

Reed responded. Larry didn't.

"Hi, Reed. Hi, Larry. I'm glad you're back." Tom wiped his free hand on his trousers and swallowed hard. "May I have a word with you?"

Larry's mouth flattened into a thin line, but he glanced to Lieutenant Reed.

"Go ahead, Fong, but make it snappy. Or as your people say, 'Chop, chop.'" Reed clapped his hands and walked away.

Larry's shoulders tensed, and Tom winced.

Once Reed was out of earshot, Tom addressed Larry. "It's good to see you. How're you feeling?"

"Fine." Larry directed his gaze somewhere beyond Tom's left shoulder.

Tension ate like acid into his stomach. "I can't believe what Reed said. I'm sorry you have to work with that."

"At least I know where I stand."

Tom absorbed the punch. "Listen, I can't begin to tell you how sorry I am for what I did. I could have killed that sniper. But I was afraid I'd turn into my father, MacGilliver the Killiver. That paralyzed me. But I wasn't thinking straight. This is combat, not Skid Row."

Larry's gaze skewered Tom. "So I'm supposed to feel sorry for you? Excuse what you did?"

"Absolutely not. There's no excuse for what I did. I put my reputation over your life. That's unforgivable."

"I'll say." His gaze skittered away, but his mouth relaxed.

"Irony is, my reputation is in worse shape than if I'd shot that sniper."

"Good."

Tom sucked in a breath between clenched teeth. Always helped the pain. "The worst part is knowing you suffered because of me. I might as well have pulled the trigger myself."

Larry directed an intense look at him.

Too intense. Tom studied the low foothills to the west, the hills many good men died to claim. "The Lord forgave me, and I hope someday you'll forgive me, but I'll always regret it."

"God keeps telling me I need to forgive you." Larry's voice came out low and gravelly.

Just as Annie's sin had consequences, so did Tom's. "Forgiveness doesn't have to mean restoration. This cost me your friendship, the friendship of the best man in this outfit. I know that. I understand."

Larry's boots shuffled in the dirt. He let out a long breath. "You aren't smiling."

A weight dropped off Tom's shoulders. "Neither are you."

"Yeah? It's hard to smile with three holes in your leg." A hint of humor colored his voice.

Tom turned back to him. "Ever try to smile with a big whopping hole in your head? I must have one. My brains fell out."

A quick smile crinkled Larry's eyes. Then he dropped to his knees and clucked his tongue. "Hi, Sesame. I missed you, boy. Say, what happened to your tail?"

Back from a fruitless hunt, Sesame put his front paws on Larry's knees and licked his face.

"Reed. That's what happened. Out hunting. Thought Sesame was a rabbit and shot him."

Larry gave the dog a good rubdown. "Poor boy."

"Second time in two months someone I cared about got shot. Least this time it wasn't my fault."

Larry pressed his forehead to Sesame's and rubbed the dog's ears. Not a word.

Tom shifted his weight from one leg to the other. "It'll never happen again. I promise."

One last scratch for Sesame, and Larry stood. "I'd better get to work."

"Yeah." Tom's right hand twitched and lifted, but one glance from Larry screamed it was too early for a handshake. Instead, Tom gave him a deep, respectful nod. "See you around. It's good to have you back."

"Thanks." Larry saluted so fast it looked like he swatted a mosquito on his forehead. And he was gone.

Tom drew a long, shaky breath. Not easy, not the best result, but he'd done the right thing.

33

Casablanca, French Morocco
June 12, 1943

Officers from the 802nd MAETS and the 64th Troop Carrier Group clambered out of Army trucks onto the palm-lined sidewalk of the Boulevard de Paris.

Finally a flight to Casablanca. Mellie savored the contrast of white buildings, green palms, and blue sky. The cool weather in French Morocco contrasted to the heat of Algeria and Tunisia, and it energized her, as did the promise of seeing the ancient walled town and the modern French section.

A Remain Overnight rewarded the demands of the long flight. From Casablanca, their patients would catch a hospital ship stateside for convalescence. No one knew where or when the next invasion would come, but first the hospitals in North Africa had to be cleared.

Captain Maxwell put two fingers in his mouth and blew a sharp whistle.

All chatter stopped.

"Thank you." He held his hand high. "It's five-thirty. Be back here at nine o'clock. We return to Algiers early tomorrow."

"Phooey. There goes my fun," Kay said, and Vera and Alice giggled.

The surgeon swept his hand over the boulevard. "As in all cities, safety is an issue here. Stay in groups of six or more. Every lady needs at least one male escort for safety as well as a female escort for propriety."

Mellie's fingers went cold. Groups? What if she couldn't find one?

The crowd divided into thirds. Vera, Alice, and Kay attracted a crowd of men eager to escort them, including Captain Maxwell. The word *nightclub* bounced around.

Kay shot Mellie a glance and bit her lip. "Join us?"

Mellie managed a crooked smile. A nightclub held no appeal, nor did the company with the exception of Kay. Besides, Kay shouldn't feel obligated to babysit her when she deserved a night out. "It's okay. I'd rather see the sights."

Kay's gaze circled the remaining groups, and she frowned. "If you change your mind . . ."

"Thanks. I appreciate it." She patted Kay's arm and stepped away, but her stomach flopped around. No group would welcome her.

The six nurses from the other flight and their boyfriends formed a tight-knit clique even Georgie and Rose couldn't crack, and Georgie and Rose . . .

Mellie gripped her hands together to stop the shaking. Georgie and Rose stood with Clint Peters, Roger Cooper, and Bill Shelby, Cooper's copilot. They studied a map and chatted about sights. Just the group Mellie would enjoy.

If she were welcome.

Georgie sent her a furtive look, and Mellie's cheeks heated. Unlike Rose, Georgie spoke to her occasionally.

Mellie stepped closer to the group from the other flight. Perhaps she could follow them closely enough to satisfy Captain Maxwell and then set off on her own.

"Hey, everyone!" Clint called out. "We're at five. We need one more."

One of the men gestured as if shoving them away. "No good. Both dames are taken."

"I have an idea." Georgie got a determined and triumphant look on her face. "We need someone who speaks French."

A bubble of hope rose in Mellie's chest. "I speak French."

Georgie marched over and took her arm. Her blue eyes carried an unusual mix of regret and joy. "You'll join us, won't you?"

Rose groaned, and Clint whispered something in her ear.

"Ignore her," Georgie said in a low voice. "I miss you. I can't nudge Rose, so I'll kick her in the seat."

The mischievous glint in Georgie's eyes made Mellie smile. "It'll be awkward."

"I don't care. It's time." Georgie hooked her arm through Mellie's and hauled her over to the group. "We have our sixth person and a translator to boot."

Rose groaned and marched down the road, map in hand. "Come on. We don't have much time. You wanted to go to the waterfront first."

"Don't worry," Georgie whispered. "She'll warm up."

"Perhaps." But restoration of even one friendship would be a gift.

Clint caught up to Rose, Roger Cooper and Bill Shelby fell in behind them, and Georgie and Mellie followed. They passed a building labeled La Poste, the post office, a three-storied white stone structure with an arcaded façade.

Georgie nudged Mellie. "I'm glad you came with us. Clint and Rose are inseparable, and Coop and Shell—they're nice, but they stick to themselves. Shell's married, you know, and I think he sees all women as threats, even though he knows I have my Ward. Coop? Well, you know him. He keeps his distance from anything feminine."

No, Mellie did not know all this. "Oh?"

"Oh dear," Georgie said. "Am I gossiping? That's what got me in trouble last time."

"Perhaps a little." Mellie gave her a slight smile. "But it's good to talk to you."

Georgie glanced up at a building covered with little arched windows. "That's what happens when you like people and you like to talk and you don't always take time to think."

Mellie drew a deep breath of salty air, laced with exotic smells and the warmth of mutual mercy. "Your heart's in the right place. I know that. I'm really sor—"

"Please don't apologize again. Not when I've never apologized to you. Not once. And our gossip started it in the first place. You were right. We had no right to discuss you and To—" She clapped her hand over her mouth. "Why, there I go again. And Clint and Coop know him."

Mellie eyed the men walking about ten feet in front of her under the palm trees. She kept her voice low. "Everyone knows him. Not just because of his name but because he's fun and friendly."

"Let's call him Ernest." Georgie turned a hesitant gaze up to Mellie. "If you even want to talk about him. I'll understand if you don't."

Emotions swelled inside. The pain of broken trust and the uncertainty of opening her heart didn't compare to the joys of friendship. She blinked hard. "I do. I do want to talk."

"Thank you." Georgie's eyes misted over. "I'll be more careful."

"So will I."

Half a block ahead, Cooper beckoned. "Stick close, ladies. We're going into the old quarter."

"The Ancienne Medina." Mellie studied the high stone walls, hundreds of years older than anything in the United States.

They passed through the gate into narrow streets wafting with a mix of strange, delicious, and unpleasant odors. Men in long robes and little fez caps sat in stalls under colorful awnings. Veiled women guarded baskets of grains and produce, and children with dark curly hair and short dirty robes darted between the stalls.

Georgie clutched Mellie's arm a bit tighter. "Isn't this wonderful? I was scared to come here, but I'm glad I did. There's so much more to the world than my lovely little square of Virginia." Her mouth twisted. "I wish Ward understood."

"He doesn't?"

Georgie flapped her hand in front of her face. "I'm probably too sensitive. He never asks about life over here. He just talks about the crops and the weather and asks when I'm coming home."

Mellie stepped around something dark and questionable on the ground. "Does he feel bad that you're overseas and he's safe at home?"

"He shouldn't. His work is important to the war effort."

"But yours is more dangerous, and you wear a uniform. Maybe he has a hard time with that."

Georgie sighed and gestured to a woman selling olives. Only her large eyes showed over her veil. "Does he want me to live like that? God gave me a gift and an opportunity. I'm doing good things over here. I wish Ward understood."

Mellie squeezed Georgie's arm. "Romance isn't any easier than friendship, is it?"

"No, it isn't." She stopped at a stall with bolts of bright fabrics and fingered a swath of turquoise cotton decorated with delicate azure swirls. She stretched it under Mellie's chin and squinted. "So, how are things with To—Ernest?"

Mellie nudged her friend onward. "A mess."

"A mess?"

A merchant stepped in their path and held up an egg.
"*Oeuf? Oeuf?*"

"*Non, merci.*" Mellie circled past him. Local traders kept
Maison Blanche well supplied in eggs.

Georgie giggled. "Can you imagine eggs in our shoulder
bags? That would really be messy. And how—how are things
with Ernest a mess?"

"In his letters he insists he's in love with me."

"Oh dear. That is a mess. You don't . . . how do you feel
about him?"

Mellie rolled the strap of her shoulder bag in her fingers.
She'd never said it out loud. "I love him."

Georgie's eyes widened. "Oh. Is that wise?"

"No, it isn't, but not for the reason you think. He's a good
man. He's kind and strong and he loves the Lord."

"You feel safe with him?"

Mellie could feel his muscled arms around her, see him
leap to rescue her from Quincy, and hear his determination
as he fought for his little dog. "Very much."

"Oh dear. You have it bad."

"That's why it's a mess."

Georgie frowned. "I don't understand. If you love him and
he loves you, why—"

"He loves Annie, not me. He thinks I'm unattractive."

Georgie gasped. "He said that?"

"Well, no. He's never been anything but sweet and chiv-
alrous."

"So why do you—"

"I can tell." Mellie turned the corner and picked up the
pace to catch up with the group. She let out a long sigh,
drowned by GIs yelling in English at a trader, as if volume
would increase comprehension.

"Tell me. That is, if you trust me." Georgie's voice lowered
with shame.

"I do. I'm trying to figure out how to explain it." Mellie gave her a reassuring look, but it descended into a frown. "At our RON at Youks-les-Bains, he only danced with me when he realized he'd hurt my feelings. And last time I saw him, he got away as fast as he could."

"Hmm." Georgie's brow bunched up. "He loves Annie, right? And he doesn't know you're Annie."

"I hope he never does."

"Maybe he's like Shell."

"Shell?" Mellie glanced at the airman in front of her. A small, thin, pale blond man, and Mellie had never exchanged two words with him.

"He loves his wife, you see. To protect his marriage, he stays away from other women. I respect that."

"I understand, but how—"

"Maybe Ernest does the same thing. He loves Annie, so he keeps his distance from you to protect that relationship."

Mellie raised one eyebrow. "So he avoids me because he loves me?"

Georgie laughed. "Something like that."

She tried to smile, but Georgie didn't know what rejection looked like. Mellie did.

They passed through another gate in the ancient wall. The Atlantic Ocean lay before them.

Georgie waved. "Hi, Mama! Hi, Daddy! Hi, Ward! Hi, Freddie and Bertie!"

Rose chuckled. "They can't hear you."

"Yes, they can." Georgie shook back her curls in the sea breeze. "They hear me in their hearts."

Mellie gazed over the azure sea to where it curved down into darkness. No one awaited her on the other shore, and her father sat in a prison camp far in the other direction.

But she had a friend. She had the Lord. And for now, she

had Tom's paper friendship. She refused to give in to melancholy.

She strolled down the path until she could see past the walls of the old quarter. Casablanca lived up to its reputation for beauty and mystery. White buildings glittered in the afternoon sun, punctuated by minarets and tall square towers. With a little imagination, she could picture Humphrey Bogart and Ingrid Bergman strolling arm in arm.

She lifted her chin and sang "As Time Goes By."

After the first line, Georgie's alto joined in, sweet as caramel. Then a rich baritone from Cooper. Then a surprising bass rumbled from Shell's small body.

Clint stepped forward and sang in an off-key tenor.

Everyone stopped and laughed for a second.

When they resumed, Rose joined in. Softly. Her gaze reached out to Mellie, hesitant and cautious, and Mellie gave her a shaky, apologetic smile.

Rose nodded, snuggled closer to Clint, and added her rough voice to his.

Mellie's voice wavered. Forgiveness and restoration at last.

34

Tom peered over the side of the LCVP—Landing Craft, Vehicle or Personnel.

Gray smoke from the pre-invasion bombardment of Sicily billowed behind the town of Gela. Artillery fire whined through the air. Axis shells shot up fountains of saltwater. Allied shells sent up plumes of dirt.

Tom checked his watch—0740. His LCVP had loaded from the troop transport over an hour before for Operation Husky, the invasion of Sicily.

"Should be there soon," he called to the thirty-five men in the boat. "Weapons ready?"

"Of course," a voice snapped. "Sir."

The muscles in Tom's back tensed. He had not regained respect. Due to the demands of Husky, Newman had returned Tom to actual command, but only for the assault phase. His last chance.

If Tom didn't make significant progress in the next few days, he'd be replaced.

His fingers slipped over the grip for his carbine, and he wiped his sweaty hands on his trousers. He knew the stakes.

His military career. His engineering career. His chance to meet Annie. If he went stateside before he wore her down, he might lose the opportunity forever.

Most importantly, he had to lead these men well to accomplish the objective. If they took the Gela-Farello landing ground today, Allied planes would have an emergency landing strip. Sicily would be conquered sooner. The liberation of Europe would be hastened.

Today the Allies set foot in the homeland of an Axis nation for the first time. Paratroopers dropped before midnight, and now the British landed on the southeastern coast near Syracuse while the new U.S. Seventh Army landed on the western coast at Licata, Gela, and Scoglitti. Company B of the 908th accompanied the 1st Infantry Division to Gela.

Tom surveyed the men in the LCVP. They required a strong leader. But could he build that bridge between the man he was and the man he needed to be?

He muttered 2 Timothy 1:7, muffled by the sound of lapping waves and the boat motor. "God hath not given us the spirit of fear; but of power, and of love, and of a sound mind."

That's how Jesus led and how Tom wanted to lead.

The pitch of the boat motor altered, and he poked his carbine and his head over the edge. The beach drew near.

Tom faced his men. "Okay, boys. When Joshua took his army into the Promised Land, God told him, 'Be strong and of a good courage; be not afraid, neither be thou dismayed: for the Lord thy God is with thee whithersoever thou goest.'"

He'd have to thank Annie for quoting that verse in her last letter. She knew him so well. "Well, boys, those words apply to us too. Be strong. Be of good courage. God will be with us."

"Amen," someone said. No note of sarcasm.

A shell rustled overhead, and the men ducked. A loud watery explosion, and a wave tipped the landing craft hard to the left.

Tom banged his shoulder on the side of the boat, and Lou Moskovitz tumbled against him.

Curses filled the boat. She rocked to the right, and a wave sloshed over and drenched Tom's right side. Thank goodness he'd left Sesame with Rudy Scaglione, the transportation officer. Scaglione would bring the dog over later in the day with the equipment.

"Hold on, boys. We're almost there." The hull grated over the sandy bottom, and the bow ramp thumped onto the sand.

"Follow me." Tom charged down the ramp, carbine ready. He'd use it if necessary.

Soft sand slowed his steps. No rifle or machine gun fire greeted him. Aircraft engines throbbed high above, the unique sound of American P-38 Lightnings.

Tom approached a group of soldiers around a field desk near a high dune, a sign the beach was already secure. "Lieutenant MacGilliver, 908th Engineer Aviation Battalion."

An officer flipped through papers. "Engineers. 908th. Gela-Farello, right?"

"Right. We're following the 26th Regimental Combat Team."

The officer pointed northeast. "Two battalions from 26th RCT headed that way. The Italians aren't fighting, just surrendering. You boys are in for a quiet day."

"Good." It was wrong to hope for a fight just so he could prove himself, but still his heart felt strangely heavy.

Ponte Olivo, Sicily
July 12, 1943

Tom huddled in a rocky ravine on the hill slope with Sesame. Artillery shells whistled above, and explosions thundered in the early morning light.

Today they had a fight.

On D-Day, they'd taken the landing field at Gela-Farello without a shot. The next day, the Germans counterattacked. Naval bombardment and American stubbornness prevailed, but blackened carcasses of panzers rendered the airstrip unusable.

Today's objective was the Ponte Olivo Airfield, a major base a few miles north of Gela. After the infantry cleared the field, the 908th would fix it up.

If they ever got there.

A shell burst about a hundred feet up the slope of the hill. Tom shielded Sesame with his body, and dirt rained on his back.

His platoon hid in a ditch just west of Highway 117 on the southern slope of Il Castelluccio, named for the square Norman tower at its peak.

Larry Fong dropped into the ditch. "Take cover. They're calling in fire from the USS *Boise*." Larry didn't meet Tom's eye but made his way down the trench, repeating the warning. Fine way for Reed to use his sergeant—as a messenger and running target.

When Larry left the ditch and scrambled for the next trench, Tom signaled his platoon to fire. "Cover him!"

The men obeyed and sent a barrage of bullets up the slope.

Larry leaped into the next ditch.

"Good job, boys. Now, dig yourselves deeper." Tom pulled out his entrenching tool. Soon the sound of metal scraping dirt filled the ravine. One thing they'd learned in North Africa was how to dig and fast.

Sesame joined in, and Tom smiled. "Good boy. Good digger."

Streaks of light whizzed above, and the ground shook. Tom pressed against the dirt wall and covered his ears. Sesame worked his head between Tom's side and the wall.

He tried to count the naval shells but lost track after a hundred. The *Boise* did her job.

When the naval guns fell silent, so did the Italian artillery.

A great shout rose to Tom's left, and the 2nd Battalion of the 26th RCT charged up Il Castelluccio, rifles firing. On the far left flank, out of Tom's vision, the 1st Battalion was supposed to head up Monte della Guardia overlooking the airfield.

Once the two mounts were secure, the 908th would follow the 2nd Battalion of the 18th RCT to Ponte Olivo.

Rifle shots zinged on the hill above Tom, voices shouted in English and Italian, and before long, GIs marched a column of Italian soldiers out of the castle and down the hill.

Tom unfolded his cramped limbs, climbed out of the ravine, and gathered his platoon into marching order.

Newman came over. "Your boys ready?"

"Absolutely," Tom said. "Did we get our equipment?"

Newman grumbled. "Lost the grader in the surf. The heavy equipment's still down at the beach. Got a DUKW with mine detectors and hand tools."

"Okay." Tom looked behind him to the strange amphibious vehicle that made its first appearance with the Husky landings.

Corporal Reilly jogged up and saluted Newman. "Got word from infantry. Field's clear."

"Great." Newman lifted his hand high. "Field's clear, boys. Let's move in."

Tom hooked Sesame's leash to his belt, signaled to his platoon, and they marched up Highway 117 onto a flat treeless plain.

"Should have known," Moskovitz said to Tom. "The Eye-Ties have no fight in 'em."

Tom didn't like the derogatory word, but confusion between the words *Italian* and *battalion* had led to disastrous incidents of fratricide in North Africa, so the nicknames were mandated. "Don't count them out. They put up a fight on that hill."

"Sure did." Sergeant Giannini, who had taken over Moskovitz's squad, hooked his thumb under his rifle strap. "But they want out of this war. They hate Mussolini more than we do."

Sergeant Ferris snorted. "Patriotic for the motherland?"

Giannini's face darkened. His jaw jutted out. "I was born in the Bronx."

"Yeah," Ferris said. "Eating garlic and speaking that Wop language."

Giannini sprang at Ferris, fists flailing.

"Stop it! Break it up!" Tom thrust himself between the men, absorbed a couple of punches in his ribs, and pushed the men apart.

Moskovitz grabbed Ferris's arms from behind. Sesame barked, curses stained the air, and the platoon circled.

"Enough!" Tom shouted. "You're fighting the wrong people. The enemy's that way."

"Says who?" Ferris strained against Moskovitz's grip, his narrow face red. "Got the enemy right in our midst. Japs and Wops and Krauts."

"That's enough." Tom got right in Ferris's face. "They're Americans, you fool. Have you forgotten what makes America strong? It's people from every country and culture. You want a nation where everyone looks alike and sounds alike?"

"Sure do." Ferris spat onto the ground.

"Swell. Hitler started one. You can go there."

Ferris jerked back, his dark eyes large.

"Yeah, Ferris," someone called out. "That's what you want? I'll get you a ticket."

"All right, enough." Tom raised his hands. "We're all on the same side. I won't put up with any baloney. We've got a job to do. Let's do it."

"You tell 'em, Lieutenant."

Tom stared down Ferris and Giannini. "Shake hands. Now. We'll talk later."

The men's handshake looked more like an arm-wrestling match.

"Come on, boys. Move on out." Tom threw an imaginary fastball toward Ponte Olivo, and the platoon marched forward.

Tom's heart beat too fast and his arms quivered. But his heart slowed to a stop when Captain Newman approached from the front of the column.

Newman pulled Tom to the side of the road and eyed his platoon. "Quincy reported a fight back here."

"Yes, sir." Tom's shoulders sagged, but he squared them. "Ferris called Giannini a Wop. Giannini threw punches. I broke it up."

"He did, sir," Moskovitz said. "He sure told 'em."

Newman turned a scrutinizing gaze to Tom. "You did?"

"Yes, sir. They'll dig some extra ditches tonight."

"Good. Keep it up." The captain clapped Tom on the back and returned to his position.

Tom's shoulders relaxed. He'd done it. He'd shown leadership, the strong kind.

Sesame gave him a wide doggy smile.

"Good job." Moskovitz's black eyes sparkled. "Gill."

A smile twitched up. Maybe he'd finally earned respect. "Thanks for helping, Mossy."

Moskovitz scrunched up his face. "Don't call me that. I hate it."

"I know." He grinned and jogged toward the head of the platoon.

"You said no name calling."

"I also said call me Lieutenant."

"Yeah, yeah, yeah."

Tom jogged with a light step. He put down a fight. Moskovitz liked him again. Newman might let him stay. Tonight's letter to Annie would be full of good news, the kind of news that might convince her to meet him.

The airfield lay on a plain ringed by low hills covered with golden grasses and green scrub. A short stone wall ran around the perimeter.

"Take cover!" The shout rippled down the column.

Tom led his men to a ditch beside the highway. Men clambered down. Gear clanked.

"They said it was clear," Moskovitz said.

"Yeah." Tom peered over the edge.

An Italian soldier walked through the main gate and waved a white flag. Dozens of men followed, all waving something white and grinning. *"Viva Americani! Viva Americani!"*

"Well, I'll be." Tom wiped sweat from his upper lip. "Guess the field's clear after all."

A small detachment herded the jubilant prisoners toward the rear, and the rest of the men prepared to work.

Newman divided the airfield into sectors, with Tom's platoon in the northern sector. Tom assigned Ferris to the west, Giannini to the east, and Kovatch separating them in the center.

They didn't need mine detectors. The Germans had strewn five-hundred-pound demolition bombs all over the field, interconnected with a maze of detonation cord. The mine detector teams inched forward and cut the det cord.

Right outside the perimeter wall, Tom sank a tent stake into the ground and tied up Sesame in the shade. "I'll get you when the field's clear, boy." He filled his mess kit cup with water from his canteen and went back to work.

Within half an hour, narrow paths edged by white tape crossed the field. But they still needed to remove the booster charges and haul away the bombs. They'd have to stay up all night. The airstrip needed to open the next day.

Tom followed the path to check on progress and finished with Giannini's squad.

Giannini tipped back his helmet and wiped sweat from his brow. "What a mess."

"Yep." Tom surveyed the field. Could they have left snipers?

Quincy's squad had checked the buildings, but Tom frowned at the northern edge of the field. The stone wall butted up against an earthen embankment, and a slit ran the length of it. A bunker, partially collapsed by bomb damage.

Tom turned around. Quincy talked to one of his squads not far away. "Hey, Quincy! Did you guys check out that bunker?"

Quincy waved him off. "Don't be a granny. It's bombed out. And didn't you see how they pranced out to surrender like pansy girls?"

"So you didn't check the bunker."

"What? You think they're taking a siesta in there? They'd have opened fire by now. Think, Gill. Think."

Tom's jaw set hard. He was thinking. Thinking maybe the Italians had learned lessons from the Germans about lying low and waiting for a moment like now, when dozens of men filled the field, guard down.

He squinted at the dark slit in the bunker. Was it his imagination, or did he see movement?

"Giannini, let's make sure the bunker's clear. Rossi, Lopez, bring a satchel charge in case we have to blow the door. Lucas, Simon, Ambrose, you're with me." Tom led the men toward a bombed-out section of the eastern wall about a hundred feet away. He watched the bunker.

Was that movement? A thin shadow formed below the slit.

The shadow of the barrel of a machine gun.

"Get down!" Tom shouted. "Everyone down!"

A flash of light. The gun pock-pock-pocked. Bullets skittered over the asphalt, and men leaped into bomb craters.

"Go! Run! Now!" Tom motioned his team past him to the break in the wall.

Crouched over, he bolted for the break. In front of him, bullets zinged past the men's feet. Giannini, Rossi, and Lopez made it through the break.

Lucas screamed, arched his back, and went down.

"Lucas!" Ambrose dropped to his knees beside his friend. "No!"

"Get up, Ambrose. Keep going." Tom ran hard. Not only was it dangerous to stay in the open, but they had to clear the bunker before others were hit.

Ambrose stumbled to his feet and ran through the break, followed by Simon.

Bullets whined closer and closer. Tom leaped over the rubble in the break.

Something slugged him in the shoulder, spun him midair. He flopped to the ground outside the wall.

Tom grabbed his left shoulder. Warm and wet. He groaned.

"Lieutenant! You're hit."

"I know," he said through gritted teeth. But he wiped his hand and pushed himself up to sitting. He refused to send his men into danger while he sat in safety. He tossed his carbine aside and drew his pistol, which he could use with one hand. "Just my shoulder."

Giannini fumbled with his first aid packet. "Let's get a bandage—"

"Later." Tom managed a smile. "Apparently that bunker isn't clear."

A few nervous laughs.

"We can't get close enough to toss in a grenade from the front. We might have to blow open a door."

"I'll toss in the grenade." Ambrose scowled. "If they killed Lucas, those—"

"No grenade," Tom said. "Let's see if they'll surrender. Giannini, you speak Italian?"

"No." His face darkened again.

"I do," Rossi said. "And I ain't ashamed of it."

"Great. How do you say, 'Hands up. Surrender'?"

"*Mani in alto. Arrendetevi.*"

"Everyone say it." Tom stood, careful to keep his head below the wall. "*Mani in alto . . .*"

"*Arrendetevi,*" Rossi said.

"*Arrendetevi.*"

"You gotta roll your *r*'s."

"I'm not rolling my *r*'s." A dagger of pain jabbed into his arm. He winced but kept going.

Tom paused at the corner, then darted out, pistol drawn.

No one there. A metal door cut into the slope of the embankment. Machine gun fire swept the field, answered by rifle shots from the Americans.

Tom motioned the demolitions men forward. Rossi hung a satchel charge from the door handle, while Lopez spooled out detonation cord. They retreated behind the corner and lit the det cord.

Tom studied the five faces before him, smeared with dirt and fear and determination. "Soon as it blows, we go in. Follow me."

"*Mani in alto,*" the men mumbled. "*Arrendetevi.*"

Tom squeezed his eyes shut. *Lord, give me strength. But please don't let me kill anyone.*

An explosion whomped through the air.

"Follow me!" Tom charged forward, pistol ready. "*Mani in alto! Arrendetevi!*"

The door lay twisted in the entrance, surrounded by chunks of dirt and concrete.

Tom climbed through and picked his way down a concrete tunnel, his heartbeat so loud it had to announce his presence.

A man sprang into the tunnel.

"*Mani in alto!*" Tom cried.

The man leveled a rifle at him.

"No! *Arren—mani in alto!*"

"No!" The Italian's finger cocked around the trigger.

Tom fired first.

The man reeled back, thumped to the ground. Eyes glazed.

Tom gasped. What had he done?

Shouts in Italian, footsteps pounded.

"*Arren . . .*" Why couldn't he remember the word?

"*Arrendetevi!*" Rossi cried. "*Arrendetevi!*"

Another man ran into the tunnel, fired his rifle.

Tom squeezed the trigger. The Italian crumpled to the ground.

"Lord, no!" His chest constricted. Why wouldn't they surrender? "*Mani in alto! Mani in alto!*"

He stepped over his victims and into the main room of the bunker. A rifle pointed at him. Tom shot. A man fell.

A gunshot. Tom turned, fired. Another man dropped.

One man remained. He maneuvered the machine gun, turned it to face inside the bunker instead of outside.

"No, don't. No." Tom shook his head. His eyes stung. "*Mani . . . mani . . .*"

The man's eyes—black. Liquid. Hate. The machine gun barrel rotated closer and closer. Bullets spat out, ricocheted off concrete.

Tom pulled the trigger.

Silence flooded the bunker, a rushing sound like water, rising to drown him.

He dropped the pistol and collapsed to his knees. His breath came in bursts as hard as the bullet fire only moments before.

A quiet curse behind him. Rossi shuffled in, Giannini, Lopez, Simon, Ambrose.

The men held their rifles in the victims' faces, prodded the bodies with their feet, knelt to feel for a pulse.

No pulse. He'd killed them all. His lips tingled. He licked his lips, tasted salt.

Giannini stared down at him, a strange look, part admiration and part fear. "They're all dead. One shot each. Right through the heart. All of 'em."

Tom's breath huffed out in rhythm, in a jump-rope rhythm.

"Thank God he's on our side," Ambrose said, then cussed. "MacGilliver the Killiver."

35

Foch Field
Tunis, Tunisia
July 17, 1943

The lid of Mellie's stationery box barely fit anymore, thanks to the profusion of Tom's letters. Before she shut the lid, she held a postcard to her heart and thanked God for the thousandth time since it arrived the night before.

Papa had written. Well, he had checked off the little boxes on the pre-printed card the Japanese supplied. But his hand had marked the boxes that he was happy and healthy and well fed, and his signature graced the bottom, as strong and masculine as ever. And in the bottom corner, he'd drawn a tiny orchid. He might not be allowed to write the words that he loved her, but he'd drawn it.

"Sorry I haven't had any letters from Tom lately." Kay packed her nightgown in her barracks bag.

"It's not your fault." Mellie slid the box into her musette bag with her other necessities. "Everything's topsy-turvy since the invasion."

"You don't know where he is, do you?"

"Nope. But he'll find me. Or rather, the pilots will find you."

Kay fluffed her hair off her shoulders. "I hope so. My date schedule's topsy-turvy too."

Mellie laughed and peered under the pair of bunk beds. "Looks like we got everything."

"Only here a week. Barely time for Georgie to make curtains and matching pillows."

"What'll she do when we're in tents?"

Kay swung her bag off her bed. "Oh, we'll have the cutest tent in Sicily."

Mellie pressed her finger to her lips. "We're not supposed to know." But anticipation rippled through her at the thought of quaint Sicilian villages and sun-drenched vineyards.

"Goodness gracious, where *could* we be going?" Kay batted her eyelashes.

"Berlin. We'll evac Adolf."

Kay burst into laughter. She led the way out of the old villa and toward the airstrip. "So what's the plan with Tom?"

"Plan? Hold him off and extend the correspondence as long as possible."

"That's not a plan. What's your goal? Do you want to be with him?"

"I've told you. He loves Annie but he finds me unattractive."

"But do you want to be with him? Just dream."

Mellie didn't have to dream to picture his grin, his deep laugh, and his strong arms around her. "I do."

"So make a plan. Now, when you're with him, which Mellie are you?"

"Which Mellie?"

"Yep. Confident nurse Mellie or pitiful wallflower Mellie? Which are you with Tom?"

She groaned and tilted her face to the hot African sun. "He's seen both."

"Well, leave mousy Mellie in Africa. Men don't find self-pity attractive. Be confident in who you are. They like that."

Mellie gave her a grin and a nudge. "Easy for the pretty girl to say."

Kay rolled her very pretty eyes. "Honestly. When you relax and smile, you *are* pretty."

"When I smile?"

"Yeah. When you try not to, you look like you're sucking a lemon."

Mellie sighed. Why did she have to be so self-conscious?

A C-47 waited for the nurses of the 802nd. They were supposed to take a hospital ship to Sicily on July 13, but when casualties were lighter than anticipated, the ship didn't sail.

Meanwhile, the flight nurses were grounded. The brass agreed on the importance of air evacuation, but the past few days, they'd sent planeloads of patients to Tunisia without the benefit of nursing care.

The wounded deserved better, and Mellie wanted to be a part of it.

She climbed onto the C-47. Vera Viviani greeted Kay with a squeal and pulled her into the seat next to her. She shot Mellie a sidelong look coupled with a quick curl of her upper lip.

Oh brother. Why was Vera jealous of her friendship with Kay? Georgie and Rose weren't. Mellie tucked her hair behind her ears and sat in a canvas seat next to Georgie.

Her friend ran a needle through turquoise cloth she'd bought in the Casablanca bazaar. The more nervous she was, the faster her stitches, and today her needle flew. On July 11, in a horrid incident, American ships and artillery accidentally shot down twenty-three C-47s carrying hundreds of paratroopers. And the airfields in Sicily lay mere miles from the front. Georgie had reason to fear.

Mellie patted her friend's arm. "The dress is coming along nicely. You do beautiful work."

"Thank you. You'll look darling." Georgie had already

made similar sundresses for herself and Rose. "You can wear it to the beach, to parties, anytime Lambert lets us dress up. With the little bolero jacket, it'll work for spring and autumn too."

Mellie fingered the soft cotton decorated with cobalt blue swirls. What would it be like to wear the dress on the beach under the stars, with Tom holding her close, gazing into her eyes, murmuring his love into her ear, brushing his lips over hers?

An empty dream without a plan. But with a plan? With mousy Mellie and lemons and monkeys left behind in Africa?

Her hand closed around the fabric. *Lord, give me a plan.*

Ponte Olivo Airfield

Mellie set her gear on the cot in the canvas tent. "Just like Mud Hill."

"Ah, happy memories," Georgie said with an exaggerated lilt. No one missed their first week in Algeria.

"Did you ladies save some plasma cans?" Mellie pulled four from her barracks bag. "Set the legs of your cot inside and fill the cans with water. That'll keep bugs out of your bed."

Alice shuddered. "That's disgusting. Why do you always talk about bugs?"

"She likes bugs. They're her friends." Vera brushed off her cot. "Ugh. Filthy."

"Get used to it, princess." Rose fiddled with the rigging for mosquito netting. "The girls in the field and evac hospitals always live like this. They never get posh barracks like we did."

"Nope." Mellie inched toward the tent flap. "I'm going to explore before lunch."

"Don't take long," Kay said. "You heard Lambert. We might get flights today."

"All right." She ducked outside before anyone could join her. The soldier who showed them to their tents mentioned engineers fixing up the base. Tom said ten Engineer Aviation Battalions worked in the theater, which meant a 10 percent chance he was at Ponte Olivo. If he was, Mellie wanted to implement her plan.

What if Kay was right? What if confidence made her attractive? If they were stationed together and spent time together, maybe Tom could come to see her in a new way. And if he did, she could reveal her identity.

Besides, her heart yearned for him. She hadn't seen him for two months.

A crew of men dug a slit trench between tents. Mellie paused, drew a deep breath, and approached. "Excuse me, gentlemen?"

"Say, it's a dame." A short man leaned on his shovel and puffed out his bare chest.

"Hiya, dolly, whatcha doing tonight?"

"No fair. I saw her first."

Mellie laughed as the men gathered around. They must not have seen a woman in months. If only she could get Tom's attention this easily. "I wanted to ask a question."

A red-haired man winked at her. "Why yes, I'm free tonight."

Mellie wagged her head at him, but she smiled. This group helped her confidence. "I wanted to know what unit you're with."

"The 908th Engineer Aviation Battalion. Best unit around."

Her chest expanded with hope. "Is Lt. Tom MacGilliver around?"

"Gill? Figures. Everyone wants to see Gill."

Mellie nodded. "Is he around?"

"Sure." He pointed down a few tents. "Over there with the dog."

She restrained her smile so she wouldn't look too lovesick. "Thank you."

The man she loved stood outside a tent and read from a clipboard. Unlike most of the men on the airfield, he actually wore a shirt.

Mellie stopped, her heart full. She'd be content to watch him all day and memorize his gestures and expressions.

He ran his hand down over stubble on his cheek, shifted from one leg to the other, sniffed, and flipped a page on the clipboard.

It almost felt wrong to know him as she did, inside and out. He didn't know she'd read all his letters and had seen into his heart.

Sesame sat beside Tom, his head pressed to Tom's knee and tipped up to watch his master, as if worried about him.

Mellie straightened her shoulders. Time to take her own advice and be strong and of good courage. Confident. She could do this.

She put on a smile and walked up to him. "Well, hi, Tom. What a nice surprise."

He startled. His mouth hung open. "Hi. Hi, Mellie."

"And hello, Sesame." She leaned down and held out her hand to the dog. "Do you remember me, little guy? You probably don't want to."

Sesame nosed her hand and let her scratch him, but he didn't budge from Tom's side.

"What are you . . . ?" His Adam's apple dipped to his open collar. "Why are you here?"

He didn't want to see her, but Mellie propped up her smile and pointed toward the runway. "Evacuating the wounded, of course."

His eyes looked strange, almost cloudy. "We're only twelve miles from the front."

Mellie relaxed. He was only concerned for her safety. "All the more reason to be here." She tilted her head. It looked flirtatious when Kay did it, but Mellie felt silly.

"This isn't a good place to be." His cheeks were pinker than usual.

"They said it was safe." Her stomach twisted. This wasn't working.

"They say a lot of things." He looked past her, toward the far end of the field. His body swayed in a circle.

Something didn't feel right. Mellie shoved aside her disappointment and studied him. "Tom, are you all right?"

His gaze turned back to her but didn't latch on. "I'm fine. I need to get back to work." He stepped to the side and stumbled.

Mellie grabbed his arm to brace him.

He cried out and flinched.

She let go, but heat radiated through her hand, and not the pleasant heat she'd felt when dancing with him. "What happened? You're hurt."

He hugged his left arm to his abdomen and scrunched up his face. "Okay, I got wounded the other day. Just a scratch."

Mellie pressed her hand to his forehead. "You're burning up. Let me see."

"See?" He opened bleary eyes.

"The wound. Let me see."

His chest caved in, and he sighed. "Bossy woman."

First nice thing he'd said all day, and she smiled. "That's right. Now, let me see."

His eyes drifted shut. He fumbled with buttons and shrugged his shirt off his left shoulder. A gauze bandage covered his deltoid, bunched up and soiled.

"Tom! When was the dressing last changed?" She gently unwound the gauze.

He shrugged his good shoulder. "Don't know."

She leveled her gaze at him. "*Has* it been changed?"

Another shrug. He looked to the side.

"This is more than a scratch." Mellie inspected the wound. A ditch ripped through the mass of the deltoid muscle. "How did this happen?"

"Securing the field. Sniper."

"Oh my goodness. Thank God you're alive." But the wound was red and inflamed.

"I need to get back to work."

"You need to see a doctor right now. This is infected. It's in your blood. You should be in the hospital."

His eyes sprang open. "Hospital? No. I can't. Got work to do."

She laid her hand gently on his forearm and gave him a soft smile. When men were sick, they were either babies or stoics. "How can you work like this? You're in pain. You have a high fever. You can barely stand up."

"I'm fine. Can I have my bandage back?"

She held it behind her back. "Absolutely not. It's soiled. We're going to the doctor right now. At the very least you need a clean bandage and some sulfa pills."

Tom pulled his shirt back onto his shoulder but didn't button it. "Doc gave me some pills." His gaze skittered away.

"Are you taking them?"

He pressed his fingers to his temple. "I gotta—I gotta get back to work."

Cold fear oozed into her heart. This was more than manly stoicism. He wasn't taking care of himself. As if he didn't care. "Tom, you need to take those pills."

"I know." He headed down the path between the tents.

Mellie felt dizzy. Something horrible had happened. Something worse than the injury and infection. Even though he refused her help, she wouldn't let him lose his arm, wouldn't let him die.

"Lieutenant Blake!" The chief nurse waved from the entrance to Mellie's tent. "Hurry up! Get to the plane. We've got an evac flight."

Mellie grimaced. Not now. She had to help Tom. "Be right there."

She dashed back to the crewmen who helped her earlier. "Excuse me. Please have the doctor see Lieutenant MacGilliver. It's urgent. He's very sick."

"Sick? Why?" The red-haired man sauntered up to her. "Did he turn you down for a date? Must be sick if he did that."

Her cheeks warmed. Did they think her that forward? "Excuse me?"

A tall skinny man nudged his pal. "Figures, Red. The hero gets all the dames, doesn't even appreciate it."

"Hero?"

"Sure, dolly. Haven't you heard? The other day, clearing out that bunker." Red pointed to the end of the field. "Shot five Italians—boom, boom, boom, boom, boom. Got them each right in the heart. Five bullets, five corpses. Lived up to his name."

The tall man laughed. "Got our own Killiver."

Mellie gasped and whipped her gaze toward where she'd last seen Tom. He'd killed five men in battle? Oh dear, what he had to be going through.

Her fear solidified into ice. "Lord, help him."

36

Ponte Olivo Airfield
July 18, 1943

Tom crept down the concrete tunnel, a pistol in each hand.

He darted into the bunker. Larry curled on the floor, clutching his leg. Tom shot him.

Annie sat in the corner, writing a letter, her face shrouded in darkness. He shot her.

"No, Tommy! Stop! Smile!" His mother walked to him, arms outstretched. He shot her.

His father twirled a pistol in each hand like a Wild West gunslinger. "That's my boy. My son's just like me."

Tom shot him over and over, both guns, but he wouldn't, he wouldn't, he wouldn't die.

"No!" He jerked awake, breathing hard, tangled in his bedroll, clammy with sweat.

Sesame whimpered beside him in the half-shelter rigged next to the perimeter wall.

"Sorry, boy." Tom lifted a leaden hand and patted the dog's head. All he wanted was sleep, but Luftwaffe bombing kept him awake, and when sleep came, it only brought nightmares.

He pushed himself up to sitting. His arm and head throbbed, and his skin felt on fire.

The bandage slipped down to his elbow, and he scooted it up and tightened it. He'd used the gauze in his first aid kit rather than see Doc Abrams. The doctor would send him to the hospital, and Tom couldn't let that happen.

He checked his watch, strapped around his good arm. Already 0745? He needed to report to duty in fifteen minutes, but first he had to deliver his letter.

Tom eased his shirt on. He hated the extra layer of heat but he had to conceal his wound.

He crawled out of the half-shelter and stood. The world swirled about, and he braced himself against the wall.

Sesame bumped his knee, as if to push him back to bed.

"Sorry, boy. Stuff to do." Tom shoved his feet forward, but his knees wobbled. If only he could keep some food down. Regardless, he had a letter to deliver and men to lead.

Down at the runway, medics loaded patients onto C-47s. Going there was risky but necessary. He had to find a pilot.

Grant Klein inspected the tire of one of the planes.

"Hi, Grant. Could you deliver another letter?"

"Hey, there's the man of the hour." He grinned. "Glad you're on our side, Killiver."

Only decades of hiding his emotions kept him from screaming. "The letter?"

He shrugged and pointed to the next plane. "Just give it to Kay. She's over there."

"All right." But the distance stretched long before him. His gelatinous legs refused to walk in a straight line.

"Tom! Tom!" a woman called behind him. Mellie.

He turned too fast. Vertigo overtook him. He collapsed to his backside and flopped onto his back like a dead cockroach.

"Tom! Oh dear. Oh no." Mellie dropped to her knees beside him, along with a man.

Doctor Abrams.

"No." Tom rolled to his side and pushed up on his good elbow.

"No, you don't." Doc Abrams pressed Tom's chest so he lay flat on the ground.

Tom groaned and closed his eyes, trapped on the rough, gravelly asphalt. "Asphalt. Good surface."

"Thanks for finding me, nurse." The doctor unbuttoned Tom's shirt.

"Oh dear. I'm glad I found you when I did."

Tom forced his eyes open. Mellie leaned over him, black curls shining around her face. She looked so pretty. So worried.

He lifted his hand to pat her cheek, but he still held Annie's letter.

The letter! "I need to—I need to give this to Kay."

"Kay?" Mellie stared at the envelope.

"The flight nurse. You know who she is?"

Mellie nodded and took the letter. "I'll give it to her."

"Thanks." At least she didn't ask questions. Then he'd have to explain the woman he loved to the woman he was attracted to.

Not that it mattered anymore. Nothing mattered. He was going to die.

The doctor swabbed the inside of Tom's elbow. So wonderfully cold. Then a needle poked through. "He needs to be hospitalized immediately."

"No." Tom rolled away from his grip. "No hospital. Leave me alone."

Mellie pushed him back down. "The 93rd Evacuation Hospital?"

"No. He'll need at least two weeks of treatment. Can we evac him today?"

"Um, yes." Mellie pulled her lips between her teeth. "I have room on my plane. But you'll need to clear it with Captain Maxwell."

"I'll do that right now; send a medic with a litter. Go ahead and load him up. I gave him morphine to calm him down, ease the pain."

Tom grabbed the sleeve of Mellie's blouse. "No. You can't do this. I can't leave."

She gave him a gentle smile. "How can you stay here? You're almost delirious with fever. You're no good to your battalion."

"No good." He flopped back to the asphalt. Pebbles poked the back of his head. "I'm no good at all."

"Hush. That's not what I said." With an icy hand, she smoothed his hair back from his forehead. Felt really good. "You can't work now. You need to heal and rest."

"No good. No good at all."

"That's not true."

"It's true. I'm a killer. You know that?" He tried to fix his gaze on her. "You hear I killed five men?"

"I did." Her hand cupped his cheek, as cool as water. "I heard the enemy shot at you and your men, you begged them to surrender in their own language, but they refused. You single-handedly cleared a bunker. They give out medals for actions like that."

"No. No." He shook his head, grinding gravel into his scalp. "Don't deserve a medal. Deserve to die."

"Don't talk like that. Ssh. Ssh." She sat up straighter. "Oh good, the litter. Thank you, gentlemen."

The medics rolled Tom to the side, slid the litter under, then hefted him on. They fastened straps across his chest and thighs.

"No." Tom pulled at the straps. "Don't. I gotta work. Sesame. What about Sesame?"

Mellie took his hands in hers. "I'll get someone to watch Sesame. You need to get well."

Tom squeezed his blazing eyes shut. "I don't want to get well."

"Think, sweetheart, think. You need to get well for Sesame. He loves you. So does your mom. And so . . . you need to get well for them, for the people who love you." Her voice cracked.

He couldn't open his eyes against the heavy weight of morphine. Sweetheart? Why did nurses talk to patients like they were children?

Something wet on his forearm. He cracked his eyes open. Sesame whimpered and licked his arm. "Hey, boy. Someone will . . ." Who? Who would take care of him?

The medics lifted the litter.

"Mellie! Mellie!"

"Right here." She walked beside him. "What is it?"

"Larry. Sgt. Larry Fong. He likes Sesame even if he doesn't like me."

"I'll tell Dr. Abrams. Don't worry. We'll take care of him."

"Good." And his mom would get by. She'd be better off without him to worry about.

"I'll be back in a minute." Mellie winked at him. "Don't go anywhere."

Tom managed a smile. Between the morphine, the straps, and the burly medics, he wouldn't be going AWOL, as much as he wanted to.

The litter rose, jiggled, and Tom entered the dark, stuffy interior of the plane, filled with the smell of unwashed bodies, blood, and a touch of vomit.

The medics clamped the litter in place along the right side of the plane, with two litters below him. Morphine surged warm and drowsy in his veins. Why couldn't it be cool instead of warm?

"How are you doing, Lieutenant?" The big-chinned medic spoke—the man who'd been rude to Mellie the day Tom met her. "Got a fever, huh?"

"It's nothing."

"Yeah. Well, we're out of aspirin. Everyone is. Chew this." He held out something that looked like wood. "Willow tree bark. Lieutenant Blake's a genius. Did you know the first aspirin came from willow tree bark?"

Tom's gaze swiveled around, uncooperative. "Lieutenant Blake?"

"The flight nurse. She's the best." He prodded the bark between Tom's lips and sent a furtive glance down the aisle. "Chew. And don't go blabbing about this in Tunisia. We don't want to get her in trouble."

"No." Apparently Mellie had won the fellow over. Tom bit down. The bark tasted dusty and bitter.

"She's back." The medic headed for the front of the plane. "Say, Lieutenant, I gave him the bark."

Tom made a face and gazed up into the nurse's brown eyes. "It's worse than his bite."

Mellie let out a chime of a laugh. "Oh, you'll be just fine, Tom."

He shook his head. He didn't want to be fine.

"Comfortable?" She pressed her hand to his cheek. "I don't think you need a blanket."

Tom tried to smile, but his cheek only twitched under the coolness of her hand. Why did she have to be sweet to him? "My dog?"

"Sesame's with the doctor, and he'll get him to Larry."

"Good. I can die in peace."

"Don't talk like that." She squeezed his hand. "You're not going to die. We'll get you fluids and sulfa. A few days, and you'll be fine."

He turned his head away. "I don't wanna get well."

"Of course you do. The fever's talking."

"No. No. It's a bad line, my father's. Needs to end."

"Nonsense. You're a fine man."

He fought against the comfort of her shaking voice and her hand stroking his cheek. He didn't deserve comfort. "Just like him. Never thought I was. Same. Needs to end."

"Tom MacGilliver, look at me." She turned his head and got within six breathtaking inches of his face. "Look at me. Listen to me. You're not your father. You're a wonderful man, full of compassion and strength and honor."

He covered her hand with his. Her gorgeous mouth twisted in concern. Even now with his lips on fire—even now he wanted to kiss her. What kind of man was he? "Honor? No."

"Yes, honor."

"Uh-uh." He told Annie he loved her, but he couldn't get Mellie out of his mind.

"Hush. Now, you rest. Don't worry about anything. Just go to sleep."

"Sleep." Tom's eyelids slid shut. Sesame was taken care of. Annie would receive his last letter. Now he could die.

37

3rd General Hospital
Mateur, Tunisia

"Next." The physician motioned the medics to bring Tom's litter forward.

Mellie flipped the page on her clipboard and stole a glance at Tom's sleeping form, at peace at last.

"Yes . . . ?" Captain Donaldson raised a pale eyebrow.

"Lt. Thomas MacGilliver, age twenty-five." Mellie used her professional voice despite her raging emotions.

Both pale eyebrows shot up. "Thomas MacGilliver? Like—"

"Yes, sir. But that's irrelevant." Mellie read the medical information, although she knew it by heart. She relayed how she gave him five grains of sulfanilamide, though not how she cajoled him to swallow. After the morphine had taken him away, she hung fluids, cleansed the wound, and applied sulfanilamide powder and a fresh bandage. And she sang him hymns of comfort.

The physician shifted the bandage and whistled. "Bit longer and he might have lost his arm, maybe his life."

"I know, sir." Her voice tripped over the lump in her throat.

"Admit him to the medical ward," he said to the nurse at his side then turned back to Mellie. "Any more?"

"He's the last one." More than anything, she wanted to press a kiss to Tom's fevered forehead, but two medics raised his litter and carried him away. At least the 3rd General was in Mateur, so she could visit him on her stops.

Mellie stepped out into the Tunisian sun and whipped Tom's letter from her trousers pocket. No drawing adorned the letter, and his handwriting scrawled all over the page.

Dear Annie,

This is my last letter to you. I got shot the other day, and I'll be dead by the time you read this. It's best this way.

You see, Annie, I'm just like my father. Worse. I killed five men. Five. I want to build but I destroy, just like him. I can't stand how people sing my praises as if I'd scored a grand slam, I can't stand myself, and you shouldn't stand me either.

This is a bad line. My dad's killer blood flows in me. It needs to stop. I should never have children, never get married. I should never have let myself fall in love. And Annie, my sweet Annie, how could I let you fall in love with me?

Forget me and fast. You deserve better.

Please don't mourn me. Remember I'll be with Jesus in heaven, where my name won't matter. Rejoice for me, darling.

All my love, Tom

Mellie rubbed away tears. Delirium colored every word, even how he signed his real name.

"Oh Lord, he needs you. He needs your healing in his soul even more than he needs it in his body. Show him how much you love him."

She would have time on the return flight to pen her reply, and she'd need it. At least he voiced the same issues in the letter as he had in person so she could address them without revealing her identity.

Mellie turned her face to the blazing African sky. "Lord, give me your words."

Ponte Olivo Airfield

"That is enough." Captain Maxwell thumped his canteen cup down onto his field desk. "Twigs? You made the patients chew twigs?"

The stuffy tent and the pressure of another reprimand made Mellie's head throb. The doctor hadn't told her to take a seat, so she stood behind the camp stool. "It's bark, sir. Willow tree bark, a natural source of salicylic acid."

"Oh, Mellie." Lieutenant Lambert sat on another stool, arms crossed and brow furrowed. "We warned you."

Mellie gripped her hands together. "Pardon me, ma'am, but I was told not to use prickly pear—"

"Do I have to spell out every little thing to you?" Maxwell stepped right in front of her, green eyes burning in the glow of the lantern overhead. "None of these quack remedies. None."

"Sir, we're out of aspirin, you know that. We have nothing else for fever."

"That doesn't mean you can use jungle juice."

Mellie drew a deep calming breath and ventured a slight

smile. "Sir, willow tree bark is the original source of aspirin. I used the same medication, just in different form."

"You don't understand, Blake. You may only use the approved medications in your medical chest. Anything else is forbidden. Understood?"

"Yes, sir." She looked down to her white knuckles. He'd let patients burn with fever? What kind of care was that? She swallowed hard. "It won't happen again."

"You're right. It won't. You're done here."

"Sir!"

"Frank," Lambert said in a firm voice. "Once again, you do not make those decisions. I'll take care of it."

"Like you took care of her other offenses? I'm going to Major Guilford on this. I've had enough. We can't let rogue nurses practice medicine without a license."

Mellie's heart ricocheted in her chest. She wanted the best for her patients. How could that be wrong? How could that lead to her dismissal?

The chief nurse sighed and stood up. "All right. Let's have a talk tomorrow with the major. But I think she deserves one more chance. Come on, Mellie. Let's go."

Mellie left the headquarters tent. Her legs and hands shook.

Vera Viviani stood right outside. How much had she overheard through the canvas? She passed Mellie, gave her a sly look, and leaned into the tent. "Excuse me, Captain Maxwell? I have a question about acceptable treatment."

"Come on in, Vera." Now his voice was sugary sweet. "I'm glad one of our nurses understands proper physician-nurse relations."

Mellie groaned and followed Lieutenant Lambert toward the nurses' tents, careful with her step in the dark.

The chief nurse paused under the Sicilian stars. "Oh, Mellie, when will you learn?"

"I'm sorry, ma'am." Her lips dried out. "We had no aspirin, I had half a dozen febrile patients, and—"

"And you made a mistake." Lambert held up her elegant hand. "I defended you in there, but I'm fed up too. You should have known better. You know what Maxwell's like. He can barely tolerate nurses breathing without a physician's order."

"I'm sorry, ma'am." Mellie gave a feeble smile. "I thought we were pioneers."

Lambert let out the shortest laugh. "Pioneers, yes. But we have to move slowly. They're men."

"Yes, ma'am."

The chief swatted at a mosquito. "I'm sure I can get you one more chance. Guilford's been wonderful for us. But don't waste it. Stay within your scope of practice."

Mellie blew out her breath over her rough throat. "I'll be good."

"Do you have more of that bark?"

"Yes." Mellie patted her musette bag. "I promise I won't use it."

"Better yet, turn it in to him. Right now."

"What? Right now?"

"Yes." Her voice brightened. "I think that'll work. Oh, I know you could get more, but that's not the point. You just have to show him you're contrite. Show him you're serious about changing."

Mellie grimaced. She didn't want to face him tonight. And what if Vera was still there? "Can I do it tomorrow?"

"No. Right now. He'll go to bed with a softened heart." Lambert took her by the shoulders and turned her toward the flight headquarters tent. "And you're going to ask in your very sweetest voice what he'd recommend for fever. Show him respect. Show him you know he's in charge. It'll do a world of good."

"Ma'am . . ."

"Don't make me doubt my faith in you."

Mellie tipped back her head and drew a deep breath of the cool night air. "All right, I'll go."

Dread pooled in her stomach, but she peered at the ground in the dark and made her way back to the tent. After what had happened with Tom and with Captain Maxwell, all she wanted was a good night's rest.

Something nipped her neck, and she slapped. She took her Atabrine every day, but she needed to retreat under her mosquito netting. With all her worries, she didn't want to add malaria to the list.

Lantern light glowed through the canvas of the headquarters tent, and Mellie huffed. So much for her hope that Maxwell had retired for the night. At least the silence meant Vera wasn't there to watch her humiliation.

"Excuse me, sir." Mellie slipped through the tent flaps. "I wanted to—"

In the lantern light, Captain Maxwell and Vera stood in an embrace.

Kissing.

They sprang apart.

"Mellie!" Vera cried. "How dare you?"

Blood rushed into Mellie's cheeks. Oh goodness, no. He was married. He had two children. How could he do such a thing? How could Vera?

"What are you doing here?" Maxwell shook his hands in the air as if shaking Mellie's shoulders.

"I—Lieutenant Lambert—she asked me to turn in the bark. I'm leaving." She inched back. Was this what he meant by proper physician-nurse relations?

"Are you spying on me? Trying to blackmail me?"

"No, sir!" She stepped back to the exit, her pulse galloping. "Why would I—"

"I know why." Vera smoothed her tousled hair. "She's in trouble again, so she wants to get you in even bigger trouble."

"No! That's not—"

"Of course it is," Vera said. "You've always hated me. Now you can get both of us in one shot."

"I don't hate you, and I wouldn't do that." Mellie lowered her voice. "What you're doing is wrong. Captain, you're betraying your wife and your position of authority, and Vera, you're no better."

"Oh, what do you know?" She stomped her foot. "You're just jealous because you can't get a man."

Mellie clamped her lips together. "Better no man than a married man."

"I knew it. I knew it, Frank. She'll ruin us both."

"No, she won't." He ran his hand through his hair and stared at Mellie, hard and determined. "She can't. Everyone knows she's being disciplined. If she goes to Guilford with this—with no evidence—it'll look like petty retribution. In fact, she'll be guilty of slander and in worse trouble than before."

"You have my word. I won't say a thing." Mellie dashed out of the tent, her head spinning. He was right, of course. What he didn't say, didn't have to say, was that he'd work harder than ever to send her home.

38

3rd General Hospital
Mateur, Tunisia
July 19, 1943

"Please, sir. You need to take your pill." The nurse poked it between Tom's lips.

He shoved it out with his tongue and rolled his head to the side. "Don't want it."

"So, you just want us to let you die, huh?" She sat on the cot by his knees.

Tom forced his eyes open. Lieutenant Steinmetz had thin brown hair and an angular face. Not the prettiest nurse he'd seen. Could she be Annie?

She patted his knee and gave him a soft look. "What is it? Lose your best buddy? Get a Dear John letter?"

His eyelids burned, and he let them slip shut.

"Live or die, it's up to you," she said. "Just don't die on my shift. I hate the paperwork."

A smile twitched on Tom's lips. He brought it under control. "I'll wait."

"Thank you. But let me tell you, dying won't bring your buddies back. And will it matter if your girl beats herself up and moans about her tragic mistake? You'll be dead and you won't get to enjoy the melodrama."

"Wise woman." The words rasped over Tom's parched throat. Wise, but not like Annie.

"You know it." She got up, grabbed some envelopes on the up-turned crate by Tom's bed, and sat back down. "If you won't take the pill, how about some letters?"

"Letters?" Tom hitched himself higher in the bed, but dizziness overtook him. He slid back down to the pillow. "Can you read them for me?"

"Sure. I'm bored." She ripped open the first envelope. "From Staff Sergeant Larry Fong."

Tom groaned. That couldn't be good. "Go ahead."

Lieutenant Steinmetz unfolded the letter.

Dear Gill, I knew you'd worry about Sesame, so I wanted you to know he's safe with me, a bit concerned, but he caught a nice fat mouse, so he'll be fine. Doc Abrams said you're distraught about the sniping incident.

The nurse lifted one eyebrow. "Sniping incident, huh?"

He waved his hand in a loose circle. "The letter?"

"All right. No more editorial comments." She drew a breath.

Let's get this straight, Gill. The men say you're a hero because you killed five men in combat. I know better. I know your heroism runs far deeper. You had the courage to set aside your reputation, overcome your fears, and protect your men. Those machine gunners injured *three of our boys, but they would have injured many more if you hadn't acted. The outcome was tragic for those five men, but your actions were justified. Giannini told me everything. You did your best to save those men's lives, but you put our lives first. I respect you and thank you.*

Tom stared at the khaki canvas above him, his throat tight and hot. Thoughts struggled not to drown in the boiling pool of his brain. A thought gasped for breath—he'd done the right thing? No, it couldn't be. Five men died. Another gasp—how many would have died if he hadn't acted? And another—he wasn't his father.

"Are you all right, sir?" Lieutenant Steinmetz folded back the blanket over his chest. It was too hot anyway.

Tom nodded. "You said there was another letter?"

"Special delivery. Pretty little redheaded flight nurse. She your girl?"

"Nope. Courier." He scooted a bit higher, closed his eyes until the dizziness went away, and reached out his hand. "I'll read this one myself."

"All right." She pulled it out of the envelope and passed it over. "How about some water?"

Tom nodded and laid the paper on his belly. He took a canteen from the nurse and swallowed warm metallic water with the faint taste of chlorine. It absorbed into his dry mouth and throat. Why had he deprived himself of fluids?

Across the top of the page, Annie had drawn a bridge. Not a structurally sound bridge, but still, she'd thought of him, more refreshing than that water. He squinted at the drawing, his vision blurry from the fever. Worked into the design of the bridge were dozens of little birds.

His Annie. So creative and thoughtful. She deserved better than him. He read the body of the letter.

> Along with your letter, I received the news that you are very sick and headed for the hospital.
>
> My dear Ernest, my prayers go out to you. Your illness worries me, but not as much as your letter. I tell myself you wrote it while delirious. I know the shooting incident rattled you, but darling, you must not let it consume you.
>
> Kay told me some of the details, while maintaining your anonymity. You did what a good soldier would do to protect his men. You acted with both courage and compassion, demonstrating your growth.
>
> You despair that you've turned into a killer like your father, but you haven't. You worry about destroying like he did, but you build. Oh Ernest, in everything you do, you build. Not only on the airfield, but you've built me up more than you know. Someday you'll build great and glorious bridges.
>
> Sweetheart, remember what God's Word tells you in 2 Corinthians 5:17. "Therefore if any man be in Christ, he is a new creature: old things are passed away; behold, all things are become new." You are a new creation! Even if every sin of your father's flowed in your veins, Jesus's blood washes them away. You

are a new man, with a vibrant life waiting for
you.

Look at Colossians 3:10: "Put on the new
man, which is renewed in knowledge after the
image of him that created him."

You're doing this in your life. You've taken
the best parts of your earthly father, put aside
the rest, and filled in the gaps by emulating
your heavenly Father.

You have a ways to go, as do I, as do all who
love the Lord. But my beloved Ernest, you must
not give up. You have so much to live for.

Tom rested his head back on the pillow. Annie's letter
merged with Larry's and with the memory of Mellie's touch
and words and songs. "I'm not my father," he whispered.
"I'm a new creation."

And he had a lot to live for.

"Lieutenant Steinmetz?" Tom raised himself on his good
elbow and caught the nurse's eye. "I'm ready for that pill."

Ponte Olivo Airfield
July 24, 1943

Mellie brushed dirt off her stationery box. Thank goodness
it hadn't opened when her musette bag got dumped next to
her cot.

Rose picked up Mellie's toiletry kit. "Those slobs. Couldn't
they pick up the mess they made?"

"We don't know how it happened." Mellie picked up her
scrapbook and inspected it for damage. She'd found everything on the ground after breakfast.

Kay poked her head in the tent. "Lambert says to get your tails to the trucks. Heading up to Agrigento, and it's a long way to walk."

The front had moved north, and so had the evacuation holding unit. "I'm not ready. My bag tipped over. It's a mess."

"I'll say." Kay frowned. "Well, hurry, 'cause Lambert's in a tizzy."

"We'll be there." Georgie whacked Mellie's hairbrush on the cot to shake out the dust.

"You'd better." The tent flap closed. "It's a real big tizzy."

Mellie grimaced. "Georgie, Rose, I appreciate your help, but why should all three of us get in trouble? Go."

"Mellie . . ."

She picked up Georgie's barracks bag and thrust it into her arms. "No. It'll go faster if I'm not bumping into the two of you. Go. You can explain. Lambert will understand."

Rose's mouth shifted to one side. "You know what she thinks of tardiness."

"I don't care. Go."

To her amazement, they obeyed. Mellie picked hairpins out of the dirt and put them back in her carved wooden box. How had things gotten so scattered when her bag fell only eight inches off her cot?

A sick feeling squeezed her belly. It hadn't fallen. Someone had done this on purpose. She'd been the victim of too many mean pranks not to recognize one.

"Mellie." Lieutenant Lambert stepped into the tent, eyes snapping. "I told you to be at the truck ten minutes ago."

"I know. There's been an accident." She closed her bobby pin box.

The tent flap opened. Vera stepped in. "Excuse us, ladies. Just need to get our gear."

Alice wrinkled her nose at the mess. "Unlike some people, we packed ages ago."

Mellie pressed her lips together and scooted out of the way. She couldn't even look at Vera since discovering her with the flight surgeon, but the other nurse acted as if nothing had happened. Had she no shame?

Vera gasped. "Who did this?"

"Did what?" Lieutenant Lambert went over. "What on earth?"

Mellie peeked around them. A pile of dirt sat on Vera's barracks bag, as if someone had emptied a bucket on top.

"Well, I got a present." Alice smiled and picked up a little cardboard box from her cot. She untied a ribbon, opened the box, shrieked, and tossed it aside. Bugs skittered out in all directions.

Vera screamed and stamped on them. Mellie joined in the stamping.

Lieutenant Lambert set her hands on her hips. "What is going on here?"

Alice smoothed her blonde hair and sniffed. "I can't imagine who would do such a thing."

"I can." Vera's brown eyes honed in on Mellie. "I complain about the dirt. Alice complains about the bugs. You think you're better than us because you like dirt and bugs. As if a jungle were a good place to be raised."

Mellie's jaw hung low. "You think . . . but I didn't . . ."

Alice poked out her chin. "You're getting back at Vera because she told Captain Maxwell about the twigs."

"What? I didn't know that was Vera."

"Don't lie. I told you myself." A challenge quirked around the corners of Vera's eyes. She had framed Mellie because Mellie knew about the affair, even fabricated a reason for Mellie to pull the prank.

"I'm not lying. You never told me." But truth spun in her head. To defend herself would require revealing Vera's motivation—her affair. That would open Mellie to charges of slander.

"Oh, Mellie." Lambert shook her head slowly. "I can't believe you'd do such a thing."

"I didn't." Her fingers worked together in front of her stomach. "You have to believe me."

The chief rubbed her forehead. "I don't know what to believe anymore. All I know is I'm tired of having to defend you."

Mellie's heart plummeted to her knees and made them wobble.

Vera spun and faced the chief. "I don't blame you. The nonsense with Georgie and Rose, a riot on her plane, using cactus and bark and cutting off a dog's tail, all that know-it-all jungle talk, and now this. Why is she still here?"

"Oh! The jungle talk." Alice waved her hand in front of her face. "Don't forget to take your Atabrine, girls. Your mosquito netting isn't right. Set your cot legs in cans of water. Heaven's sake, who put her in charge?"

"I wanted to help." Mellie fought for breath as cruelty burned up all the oxygen in the tent.

Vera looked down her nose at Mellie. "Well, save it, sister."

"No one wants her here." Alice leaned in close to the chief. "Georgie and Rose, even Kay, they try to be nice, but it's hard. She just doesn't fit in."

Mellie sucked in a breath, hating the sobbing sound. She wrapped her arms around her belly to hold herself together, as if she could, as if she could keep her world intact.

Pity covered Lambert's face. "Back at Bowman Field I told you we had to work together, that I couldn't let one nurse drag us down. When will you learn?"

Mellie shook her heavy head back and forth, grasping for words, for breath. She had learned. Couldn't the chief see?

"I have to think about this." Lieutenant Lambert marched out of the tent. "Hurry up, ladies."

"We will." Vera tipped over her barracks bag and poured the dirt onto Mellie's things on the ground. "A little dirt won't kill you."

On her way out, she and Alice shared the shortest, meanest smirk.

Mellie dropped to her knees and poked through the mess. Tears left dark divots on the ground.

Why did it have to be this way? She'd been set up. Vera and Captain Maxwell wanted her gone, and they'd get their way.

She lifted the brooch from Tom out of the dirt, and a sob hopped out. Was he improving? Were the antibiotics working? She brushed off the colorful stones and blew dust from the delicate setting. Never once had she worn it. Jewelry didn't belong on the front lines.

Just as Mellie didn't belong in the 802nd. She was a good nurse. She'd become more open and taught herself to smile. She'd made friends. She'd even cut her hair.

But it would never be enough. She'd never belong.

39

"Which one of you is the Killiver?" A man in fatigues leaned in the hospital tent, wearing an arm brassard with C for Correspondent.

Tom sat cross-legged on the hospital cot with his stationery box on his pajama-clad knees, and he sighed.

In the next cot, a tank officer with malaria pointed his thumb at Tom. "That fella."

The reporter's face lit up and he rushed to Tom's side. "Fred Freeman, *Stars and Stripes*. Got a few questions for you."

"Sorry." Tom gave him a polite smile. "I don't do interviews."

"Ah, come on. I've already got my headline." He formed his hand into a bracket and painted a banner in front of him. "'Son Uses Father's Murderous Skills for Good.' Whaddya say?"

"I say no thank you."

"Ah, please?" He pulled out his notepad. "Everyone's glad you're on our side. Hey, they even say the Italians deposed

Mussolini yesterday 'cause they're scared of you. Why bother fighting when the U.S. has MacGilliver the Killiver?"

Tom opened his stationery box. "Sorry to disappoint you. The U.S. has Tom MacGilliver, an engineer who happened to be at the right place at the right time and did the right thing, same as any of our boys would do."

"That's swell." He scribbled on his notepad. "Right place . . . right time . . . right thing."

He rolled his eyes. He hadn't meant to be quotable.

Lieutenant Steinmetz stood at the foot of the bed in her belted GI coveralls. She put her hands on her hips. "That's the problem with tents. They don't keep out the rats."

Freeman turned to her. "Say, toots, how about a quote from you? What's he like?"

"My quote?" The nurse put her finger to her cheek and batted her eyes at the ceiling. "Get lost before I give you an enema."

Tom burst out laughing.

"Hey, now, baby, you wouldn't do that to me." The reporter draped his arm over her shoulder.

She grasped his draped arm and marched him away. "I would. There's the door."

"Please, baby. I'm the first one to get in here."

"And the last." She gave him a gentle shove outside.

He leaned back in. "Come on, MacGilliver, at least tell me one thing. Did you enjoy it?"

Tom scrunched his eyes shut. Had the reporters tortured Dad before his execution? As horrid as his father's crimes were, Tom knew he didn't enjoy murdering the DeVilles.

"Get lost. Now," the nurse said in a firm voice.

"All right, all right." Footsteps shuffled away.

"He's gone." Lieutenant Steinmetz smiled down at Tom. "Better?"

He worked up a grin. "With nursing care like this, how could I not feel better?"

She flapped her hand and walked away. "My mama warned me about charmers."

"Smart mama." But he meant every word about nursing care. He had no doubt the Lord sent Annie and Mellie and Lieutenant Steinmetz. Without Mellie's physical intervention, he might have died. Without all three women's spiritual intervention, he might have withered.

Tom rolled his left shoulder, pushing against the pain to regain strength and mobility. He would live for Sesame, for his mom, for Annie, to honor Mellie's faith in him, and for the Lord.

To live, to really live, he had to make changes.

He pulled his mother's latest letter out of the box and scanned her familiar script. After he heard from his grandparents, he'd taken two weeks to write his mother. Likewise, she'd delayed in replying.

It must have been hard for her to write. In her letter she confirmed her love for Tom's dad, her fears due to her father's violence, her lack of mercy, and her failures as a mother. Regret flowed with every loop of her handwriting. She meant only the best, but she'd failed him. Could he forgive her?

Tom laid a fresh sheet of stationery on the box and pulled the cap off his pen.

My dearest, most beloved Mom,
    Of course I forgive you for wanting to protect me, even though you made some mistakes doing so. I don't hold you accountable for my father's failures, crimes, or death. Each man lives his own life and is responsible for his own deeds.

Likewise, I must live my own life, responsible for my own deeds.

I understand why you raised me to always smile and be cheerful. You meant to show the world I wasn't my father so I could succeed.

All my life, I've suppressed sadness, anger, and distress, striving to be inoffensive. Yet I offended because I would not be strong when strength was required, or angry when anger was warranted.

This is a way to function, not to live. I want to live.

From now on, I will mourn and rage and laugh like everyone else, true to how God made me. I will stand up for what's right, even if I lose every friend. I will seek love, even if my heart is shattered. And I will—

"Tom?"

He looked up. A smile rose, natural and unforced. "Mellie. What brought you here?"

"An evac flight." A twitch of a smile, which melted into a real one. "Goodness, you look so much better."

"I feel better too. Come, sit down." Tom scooted his rump back to the head of the bed, set aside his stationery box, and patted the foot of the bed. "I'm glad you came. I wanted to thank you."

"Thank me?" She bent to sit. She had curves in all the right places and plenty of them.

Tom jerked his gaze back to her face where it belonged. "Yeah. Thank you. For bullying me into the hospital."

She smoothed her blue trousers and winked. "All in a day's work."

Why did she have to be so cute? "Well, you earned your pay and then some."

"It's worth it to see you healthy again." She leaned a bit forward. "I stopped by Ponte Olivo yesterday. Sesame says to get back soon. Larry takes good care of him, but no one spoils him like you."

"He said that, did he?"

"Sure did." She gave a serious nod. "I'm multilingual."

Tom laughed. "Well, tell him bark, bark, woof."

"I don't speak that dialect."

"Nothing to it. It's all in the *r*'s. You've got to roll them around in your throat like you're gargling." He demonstrated.

Mellie laughed, a lilting soprano that made him want to pull her close and kiss that fascinating mouth. "I think you need medication for that throat condition," she said.

Tom sat back. No, what he needed was restraint.

She looked around, a few chuckles still escaping. "How do they treat you here?"

"They treat me well."

"I'm glad," she said.

"How are things in your squadron?"

The playfulness drained from her face. She pulled her clasped hands closer to her stomach. "Overall, they're going well. We've had lots of flights. The commanders have finally seen the value of air evacuation."

"But . . ."

She sighed and looked up to the canvas ceiling. "But it looks like I'm going home."

"Home? Why?"

Mellie shook her head. "To explain would require revealing secrets, and I refuse to do that."

Tom leaned forward on his knees. "You don't want to go."

"No." She blinked several times. "It's not my choice. But I think it's for the best."

Tom's breath grew choppy. How could it be for the best? Mellie was an outstanding nurse, and she always managed to be there when he needed her. And if she left . . .

If she left, he'd lose any chance he had with her. The thought made him squeamish, but he couldn't deny the hope that if things didn't work out with Annie, he could pursue Mellie. Annie resisted him. What if he was wasting time in his imagination when he could hold reality? A spark of anger parched his lips.

He swabbed his mouth with his tongue. "What do you mean 'best'?"

Her liquid gaze melted into his. "It just is."

"That doesn't—"

"That reminds me. I have letters for you. Kay asked if I could deliver them." She opened her purse and pulled out four envelopes. "You're quite the letter writer, aren't you?"

Mellie's hands—hands he'd held, hands that had touched him—wrapped around Annie's letters. Guilt contorted his insides.

"Thanks." He took the letters. "Sorry to inconvenience you."

"It's no inconvenience." Mellie glanced toward the tent opening. "I should go."

Tom shuffled in his stationery box and pulled out three envelopes. "If it isn't an inconvenience, I have a few letters myself. Would you mind giving them to Kay?"

"Not at all." Her eyelashes fluttered on her cheeks.

"Thanks. I appreciate it."

"Bye, now." Mellie got up and headed to the tent entrance.

What if she left the theater? What if he never saw her again? He didn't even have her address, her hometown. "Mellie!"

"Yes?" She turned, one hand holding back the tent flap, the other grasping his letters for Annie.

His heart went down, but his smile went up. "Thanks again. Bye."

She smiled, waved, and left.

He groaned and leaned back. The metal head rail jabbed his spine. All these years he'd mentally beaten up his father for his failings, when Tom had plenty of failings of his own.

Annie. Annie. He loved Annie.

To remind himself, he spread her new letters before him. One a day. In her concern and her love, she took time from her busy life to write him every day. Beautiful letters that built him up as much as she claimed he'd built her up.

Had he really loved her before he was injured? He thought he had, but new passion pulsed in his heart. She knew him and loved him and encouraged him. If anything, she was far more real than Mellie, whom he knew only superficially.

He wanted Annie in his life always. To have and to hold. No matter what she looked like.

It was time to act, to force things to a head.

He closed his eyes, shutting out the crowded, noisy, muggy hospital tent. *Lord, let her see how much I love her. Convince her to trust me.*

40

Agrigento Airfield
Sicily
July 30, 1943

Mellie paused outside the tent that served as squadron headquarters, drew a shaky breath, and gazed up to the brilliant
morning sky. Lambert had summoned her.

She didn't want to leave. Sicily enchanted her with sparkling beaches, olive groves, winding roads lined with stone
walls, and homes with trays of tomato paste drying on the
roofs. A few days before, she and Georgie and Rose had visited
the Valle dei Templi south of Agrigento and its ruins of seven
Greek temples. She wanted to see more and to build these
sweet friendships into something deep and lasting.

Three nurses from another flight passed and shot Mellie a
dirty look. Since Mellie couldn't defend herself without exposing herself to charges of slander, Vera and Alice's story held.

She sighed, opened her purse, and pulled out Tom's most
recent letter, written after her visit to the hospital.

She skipped to the last page.

> When we started this correspondence, you
> and I stood at opposite ends of a bridge. I was

everyone's friend. You kept to yourself. Over the past nine months, we've both found balance in the center.

I've learned the only person I need to please is the Lord. I'm determined to be genuine and strong and stand up for what's right, and I'll smile only when I feel like it. In the process, I will not please everyone. That is as it should be.

You've learned you can only please the Lord when you step out of yourself and offer friendship to others. You've had to learn to please people. But some people can't be pleased, nor should they be.

My love, be friendly and open, but stay true to how God made you. He created us all unique. Delight in your differences while reaching out to others.

We both stand in the middle of the bridge, where we must meet. I hold my hand out to you and long to draw you close. It's time, darling.

Mellie slammed her mind shut against the final, inviting, heart-melting paragraph, and focused on the fortifying words before it.

"Good. We get to watch her comeuppance." Vera brushed past Mellie into the tent. Alice bumped Mellie's shoulder as she passed.

Mellie lifted her head. *Lord, help me be merciful and kind, truthful and strong.*

Inside the tent, Lieutenant Lambert sat at a folding desk and motioned to three camp stools. "Have a seat, ladies."

Mellie saluted then sat, glad her hammering heart couldn't be seen. Why wasn't Captain Maxwell present? He'd enjoy this too.

The chief nurse's gaze settled on Vera, then Alice, then Mellie. A dark and inscrutable gaze. "You know why you're here. Or you think you do. Mellie, you've been strangely quiet about this incident. Do you have anything to say?"

Mellie wrapped her hands around the black shoulder bag containing Tom's words of encouragement. "No, ma'am. I told the truth. I didn't do it. What else is there to say?"

"For heaven's sake." Alice's chest heaved. "Everyone knows you did it."

"Popular opinion." Lambert's mouth disappeared into a thin line. "Popular opinion is only proof of gossip's power."

Mellie blinked to clear her vision. Had Lambert taken her side?

Vera brushed her hair off her shoulder. "Maybe, but popular opinion usually reflects the truth. And the truth is, Mellie pulled a childish trick on us. She doesn't belong here."

Lieutenant Lambert smoothed out papers on her desk. "Immediately after the incident, I sent for her replacement, as well as one for Sylvia, since she still suffers from malaria."

The confirmation should have sent Mellie reeling, but somehow it straightened her spine. "I think that's best, ma'am."

The chief's head jerked up. "Pardon?"

"Vera's right. I don't belong. I've tried to fit in. I cut my hair and made friends and I'm overcoming my shyness. But I'll never be able to change enough to please these two. I was raised primarily in the jungle among men and didn't have friends until I joined this squadron. I can't cover differences like that with lipstick."

"I'll say," Vera mumbled.

Lieutenant Lambert stared at the desktop, and her mouth shifted from side to side. "From the start, I placed the responsibility for the squadron's harmony on Mellie, but I should have looked to others as well." Her gaze locked on Vera and Alice.

A quick thrill of vindication rushed through Mellie's lungs, but confusion shoved it aside.

Alice sat back. "Excuse me?"

The chief picked up a piece of paper. "Does the name Private Judson mean anything to you, Alice?"

"I should say not. We aren't allowed to fraternize with enlisted men."

"I had an interesting conversation with him yesterday." The paper crinkled in Lambert's hands. "He asked if the nurses had more odd jobs for him. 'More?' I asked, and he said you paid him five dollars to collect bugs. You wanted them in a little box with holes so they'd stay alive."

Mellie's lips parted. That's how they did it. She couldn't imagine either of them touching insects.

"Nonsense," Alice said. "Mellie must have put him up—"

Lambert raised one hand to silence her. "Everyone saw Mellie at breakfast that morning, but not you two. Kay said you skipped breakfast."

"We weren't hungry," Alice cried. "Mellie had plenty of time. She was alone in the tent when we came back for our gear."

"Stop it." Lambert's face reddened. "I ran into Georgie and Rose not ten yards from your tent. She wasn't alone long."

"She could have—"

Vera huffed. "It's over, Alice. Stop it."

Alice glared at her. "Don't you dare pin this on me. This was your idea."

Mellie's thoughts tumbled into dizziness. Although she couldn't speak the truth, the Lord brought it into the light. She might—she might be able to stay.

Vera raised a slight shrug and smile. "We didn't mean anything. It was just a little prank."

"A little prank?" Lieutenant Lambert thumped her hand on the desk and made it rattle. "You connived, you framed her, you lied, you gossiped, and you almost got her sent home. That is not a little prank."

Mellie's breath came faster, in joyful little hops. She could remain a flight nurse and travel and support herself no matter what the future held. She could nurture friendships with Georgie and Rose and Kay. And she might occasionally savor Tom's company.

Alice pressed her fist over her mouth and whimpered. Vera stared at the ground in front of her, eyes round and eyebrows drawn together. They would be reprimanded. They would be replaced.

A wave of compassion swelled in Mellie's heart, but she wouldn't let the wave break. Didn't Micah 6:8 say, "What doth the Lord require of thee, but to do justly, and to love mercy, and to walk humbly with thy God"? They had failed in all three.

But Mellie's mind snagged on the word *mercy*.

Lieutenant Lambert stood, crossed her arms, and turned to the back of the tent. "I can't begin to tell you how angry and disappointed I am. And humiliated. You used me like a pawn on your little chessboard, and I don't appreciate it."

Tears flowed down Alice's blotchy, twitching cheeks.

"I had high hopes for the two of you." Lambert tilted up her head and sighed. "Your experience and poise made you naturals. But you treated your fellow nurse worse than you'd treat the enemy."

Vera leaned over her knees, her back rising and falling quickly. Her black hair hung like curtains beside her head and swung in rhythm with her hyperventilation.

Another wave of compassion threatened Mellie, and she shifted her gaze to the chief nurse.

Lieutenant Lambert's eyes glistened. "I've discussed the situation with Major Guilford. Sylvia should improve soon. I'll keep her here and Mellie too. Vera and Alice will return stateside."

Vera expelled a long, soft moan. "My dad. My dad will kill me."

Something twisted inside Mellie. She knew nothing about them beyond the superficialities. Had she ever reached out to them? Deep inside, they had dreams and fears.

"For if ye love them which love you, what reward have ye? do not even the publicans the same?" She hugged her pocketbook to her stomach. Mercy meant more than compassion for the sick or forgiving friends who hurt you. Mercy meant loving your enemies.

A strange stirring wound through Mellie's soul. Mercy meant sacrificing your dreams for the sake of others. For the sake of flight nursing. For the sake of Georgie and Rose and Kay.

For the sake of Vera and Alice.

"Lord, help me," she whispered. The stirring worked through her legs and propelled her to her feet. "Ma'am, please give them a second chance. Let them stay. Send me home instead."

"Excuse me?" the chief said.

Alice gaped at her. Vera raised her head and peered around the wall of dark hair.

Mellie's eyes moistened, but she held her chin high. "Give them a second chance, ma'am. You've given me second, third, fourth chances. They deserve the same. They're excellent flight nurses, competent and caring and professional."

Lambert cocked her head to the side, and furrows raced up her forehead. "That doesn't change the fact—"

"The fact? The fact is, I don't belong in this squadron. You gave me so many chances, but I still don't belong. Vera and Alice get along with everyone but me. If I leave this squadron, your problems will be solved. No more squabbling and gossip and nastiness."

"It's not that simple. I can't trust them."

Mellie gazed down at the two stunned nurses through watery vision. "You won't have problems with them anymore. They're smart enough to learn their lessons. Give them another chance."

Vera shoved back her hair. "Why . . . why would you . . . ?"

"Because I'm odd." Mellie raised one eyebrow, but that loosened a teardrop to slither down her cheek.

"This isn't your decision to make." Lambert sat at her desk.

Mellie stepped closer. "It should be. Please show them mercy. They didn't do anything illegal. Make them dig latrines or something, but don't make them leave. Send me. I've used up my second chances."

Lambert's gaze wavered.

Mellie pounced on the opportunity. "Please, ma'am. Send me. It's best for the squadron, best for the future of flight nursing. Send me to Bowman maybe. I could help with training. A teacher doesn't have to be popular. She just has to be good."

The chief pursed her mouth and studied Mellie. She nodded.

"Thank you, ma'am." Mellie spun away and fled the tent.

The Sicilian sun blazed down and evaporated her tears, leaving prickly tracks on her cheeks. Her dreams, her friendships, everything she'd worked for over the past year—gone.

Her chest collapsed from the weight of it. If she'd done the right thing, why did she feel so miserable?

41

Boccadifalco Airfield
Palermo, Sicily
August 2, 1943

The C-47 banked, and Tom looked out the window to Boccadifalco Airfield. A good solid runway, originally used by the Italian Air Force, and for the past three days by the United States.

His uniform felt strange after two weeks in pajamas, but his arm felt better. Sore, weak, but ready to work.

The plane leveled off for landing. The Mediterranean sparkled greenish blue to the north. Palermo was General Patton's prize, a key port on Sicily's north shore to funnel in supplies. The Seventh Army surged east toward Messina on the northeastern tip of Sicily, where the busy port cringed, waiting for the kick from Italy's boot.

The ground neared, and Tom gripped the canvas edge of his seat. All those months working on airfields, but he'd only flown twice. Fever and morphine wiped out all memory of his first flight except Mellie's sweet voice singing over him.

Tom puffed out a breath, and the plane bumped as if to

punish him for his unfaithful thoughts. The ride got rougher, and he glanced out the window. "Hey, we landed."

The crates behind him didn't respond.

The plane taxied for a minute, swung to the side, and stopped. The two engines built to a loud roar then died.

Clint Peters opened the door in the front of the cabin, a leather map case slung over his shoulder. "How was your flight on Cooper Air?"

"Sure beats how I arrived in Sicily last time—in a landing craft under artillery barrage."

"High compliment. I'll pass that on to Coop."

"Speaking of the man, I need to talk to him." He needed a courier who was motivated to find Kay Jobson, and Peters had eyes only for his Rose.

Clint pointed with his thumb toward the cockpit. "Head on in."

"Thanks." He passed through a door into the navigator's compartment and opened the door to the cockpit. He'd never asked Roger to help before, but his C-47 came alone, and Tom needed this letter to go out today.

In the cockpit, Roger Cooper and Bill Shelby turned dials and flipped switches.

"Hey, Coop. Hey, Shell."

"Hiya, Gill." Roger slipped off his headphones from over his pilot's crush cap. "How was the flight?"

"Swell. I was conscious this time."

A smile cracked Roger's square face. "If you'd asked, I could have knocked you out."

"Excuse me, boys." Shelby squeezed past Tom. "Gotta find a bush."

Roger pulled off his cap and ran his hand through his dark red hair. "Go ahead, peanut bladder."

"Better than a peanut brain."

"Too bad you got both."

Tom grinned, but he didn't know them well enough to join the fun. "Say, Coop, can I ask a favor?"

"Sure. What do you want?"

Tom pulled out the envelope holding his hopes and dreams. "I need a letter delivered to Kay Jobson."

Roger stared at the envelope, then gave Tom an incredulous look. "Should have called you the peanut brain. How'd you get mixed up with a dame like her?"

"It's not really for her. She's the go-between, knows the girl I'm writing to."

"Leave Kay out of this. Who's it for? I'll give it to her."

Tom raised half a smile. "Don't know her name. We're anonymous pen pals."

"Anonymous? Like in *The Shop Around the Corner*?"

"That's how this whole thing started. So, could you give this to Kay?"

Roger loosened his tie and got up from his seat. "I keep my distance. That girl's bad news. Can you mail it to her?"

"Yeah, but it takes so long." Tom followed the pilot out of the cockpit, his throat constricting. He needed this done now. "How about Mellie Blake? Do you know her?"

Roger turned and pointed a finger at Tom. "Now, there's a nice girl."

Relief turned up the corners of Tom's mouth. "Yeah. Could you give it to her? She could give it to Kay."

"Sure." He opened his hand. "Agrigento's one of our prime stops."

"Thanks. Have her tell Kay I'll be at Termini Airfield." Tom held out the letter, and Coop plucked it from his fingers. Part of him wanted to grab it back and keep things the way they were, but the other part of him—the new, strong part—released it. Even if it devastated Annie and ended their friendship, he had to do this.

"Termini. All right." Roger ambled down the valley of crates in the cabin and tapped the envelope into his palm. "Complicated way of doing things."

"It's going to change." One way or the other, everything would change.

Termini Airfield
Sicily

Tom climbed out of the back of the two-and-a-half-ton truck and stretched his limbs. Thirty miles over winding coastal roads pocked by bomb craters took a lot out of a man.

Three other passengers hopped down after him, while a crew from the airfield approached to unload the cargo.

In the late afternoon sun, Tom took the lay of the land. A good, flat field overlooked the Tyrrhenian Sea to the north, the town of Termini Imerese lay to the east, and farther east a mountain stood sentinel. Olive trees and prickly pear cactus dotted rugged hills to the south.

All he wanted was to find Larry and Sesame, but first he had to report to Newman. He headed into the city of tents beside the runway, following signs written on scrap wood and stuck into the ground.

"Go find Mossy. Good boy. Find Mossy."

Tom turned to the side. That was Larry. And Sesame trotted in his direction.

"Sesame! Hey, boy!"

The dog stopped and cocked his head.

Tom squatted and spread his arms wide. "It's me, boy."

Sesame chortled and ran to Tom, his legs skittering in all

directions. He leaped into Tom's arms and knocked him on his rear end.

Tom laughed. "Hey, boy. Calm down."

Sesame's nose and tongue competed with each other, sniffing and licking.

"I know I smell funny, but so do you." Tom burrowed his nose in his dog's short, smooth fur and grinned at the familiarity.

"Well, look who's back." Larry stood over him. He was smiling.

Tom struggled to his feet as twenty pounds of squirming canine flesh threw off his balance. "Hi, Larry. Thanks for taking care of Sesame. He looks great."

"He's a swell dog." His expression grew serious. "I'm glad you're back."

"Me too. Say, thanks for that letter you sent. You don't know how much I needed it." Tom's voice deepened too much, so he coughed to cover up.

"It needed to be said." He raised a sharp salute. "I appreciate what you did that day."

Tom's throat thickened. Larry's respect meant more than anyone else's. Did he dare hope for friendship again? He shifted Sesame to one side and extended his hand. "Thanks."

Larry studied his hand, then grasped it, shook it heartily, and gave Tom a grin he'd missed.

"About time you showed up, Gill." Captain Newman's voice sounded behind him.

"Sorry, sir." Tom turned and saluted. "My limousine driver called in sick."

Newman smiled. "I'll walk you to your tent, get you up to speed. Fong, you're dismissed."

"Yes, sir. Excuse me a second." Larry unsnapped a pouch on Sesame's belt. "Better deliver this message to Mossy in person. Sesame's done for the day."

"I'll say." Tom hugged the dog tighter. He did not want to let go.

Newman walked at a fast clip down a tent-lined path. "Here's the situation. Got here a week ago, laid down square mesh track, rolled PBS over it."

"Good." Prefabricated Bituminous Surfacing, jute impregnated with asphalt, came in large rolls, easy to lay, easy to repair, and easy to pack up when the front moved forward.

"One squadron of the 31st Fighter Group relocated here yesterday, their HQ joined us today. We need to expand the field, get installations in place."

Tom's blood ran faster. Newman wouldn't brief him if he planned to send him stateside. "I'm ready to work, sir."

Newman gave him a cautious look. "I'll keep things the way they were. Quincy gets the men working, you can handle the paperwork, and I can still use your expertise."

"Sir, I'd like—"

"I switched sergeants around again. Fong will return as your platoon sergeant—special request—Moskovitz will get his squad back, and Giannini will fill Fong's spot with Reed."

All good news, but Tom wanted more. "Sir, I'd like my platoon back."

Three men from Ferris's squad approached.

"Hey, the Killiver's back!" Conrad Davis shouted.

"Bang, bang, bang, bang, bang!" Bernie Fitzgerald slapped Davis on the shoulder. "That's our man."

Bill Rinaldi stepped forward, a gleam in his eye. "Say, Gill, I gotta get a picture with you. My old man won't believe I know such a hotshot."

Tom's heart spiraled down into his stomach.

"Later, boys." Newman guided Tom past. "You see what it's like, Gill? Reporters swarm all over this place. The men think you're some sort of murderous superhero. You'll distract them from their work. You can't get your platoon back. Got to wait for this to blow over. If it ever does."

"Yes, sir." Heat expanded his chest. If any other man had done what Tom did at Ponte Olivo, things would already have blown over. But they didn't bear the MacGilliver name.

42

Over Sicily
August 5, 1943

The headlines of the *Stars and Stripes* blurred to gray in Mellie's eyes. How could they print such things about Tom? They made him sound like an unfeeling killing machine rather than the kind soul she knew so well.

If only she had conversation to keep her occupied, but Sergeant Early dozed in the seat beside her, and the plane carried litters, blankets, and splints. Air evacuation drained these vital supplies from the front. When sea shipping wasn't available, they had to be returned by air, one planeload for every ten evac flights.

Down by her feet, her musette bag drew her gaze, and Mellie's stomach and heart went into twin palpitations. She flipped the page of the North African edition of the servicemen's newspaper.

The Soviets had defeated the Germans at the Battle of Kursk and had them on the run. The Americans had invaded New Georgia in the Solomon Islands, slowly gaining lands from the Japanese. The U.S. Eighth Air Force had finished a Blitz Week of heavy bombing against German industrial targets. And Lt. Ruth Gardiner, a flight nurse with the 805th MAETS, had been killed in a plane crash in Alaska, the first American nurse killed in a combat theater in World War II.

Mellie sighed. The 805th had arrived at Bowman Field right before the 802nd left. Mellie hadn't met any of the nurses, but everyone felt the loss keenly.

Bowman Field now offered a formal six-week program at the newly designated School of Air Evacuation. Mellie would see it firsthand and soon.

"That'll be good." If she said it often enough, she'd believe it.

The C-47 tilted into a wide right turn in preparation for landing.

Mellie stared at her bag and then shoved away the newspaper. She'd have no peace until she read Tom's letter. She'd put it off all day since Roger Cooper handed it to her in Agrigento. Tom's letters had become more romantic and more adamant that they should reveal their identities. Her arguments held no sway with him.

She unstrapped the bag, opened the envelope, and unfolded the letter.

A photo and a piece of newsprint fluttered into her lap. Tom's service portrait and the *Stars and Stripes* article about the Ponte Olivo incident. Mellie gasped.

Tom's photo . . .

Oh, he had the most inviting smile, the most pleasant face. She'd never seen him in dress uniform before, and he sure looked handsome. She pressed the likeness to her lips, the closest she would ever come to kissing him.

And the clipping. The article included Tom's name and picture.

He was revealing his identity to her, and her fingers went numb. Somehow she focused on the letter.

My beloved,

    This is the last letter I'll address to Annie.

"What?" Mellie's vision clouded over. Oh goodness, it was over. It was already over. She blinked hard and returned to the letter.

From now on, any letters must be addressed to our real names. It's time, my love. I know this letter will devastate you. You don't believe I'll love the real you, but please give me a chance. I'm taking a big chance too. My name has the destructive power of dynamite.

    I need to formally introduce myself. My name is Thomas MacGilliver Jr. I go by Tom. The men in my unit call me Gill. It sounds like an affectionate nickname, but it's really a way to avoid my full name.

    Now you know. Even though you spent a great deal of your life abroad, I'm sure you've heard my father's story and probably jumped rope to the rhyme, never dreaming someday you'd write to his son.

    As you can see from the news clipping, my father's reputation will never leave me. You've heard my version of the story, but this is what the rest of the world sees. You need to know exactly what you're getting into.

    Annie, can you see my heart splattered all over the page? I'm trying to convince you to

reveal yourself, knowing my name could drive
you away forever.

Mellie fumbled in her trousers pocket for her handkerchief.
Her dear, brave Tom. He hadn't written anything she didn't
already know, but it took great courage to tell her.

With a quivering hand, she turned to the second page.

For some reason, I want to laugh. I want to
burst into the deep, joyful laughter of freedom.
Whatever you decide, I've done it. For the first
time in my life, someone knows the real me,
inside and out.

Everyone knows the outside me—the killer
name and friendly personality. I've shown you
the inside me. Not even my mother knows my
heart as you do. In this letter I've bridged the two
sides. No matter what, I claim this victory.

I'm asking the world of you—to trust the son
of a notorious criminal. But I must do this. If
our relationship is to grow, I must know your
identity, and someday we must meet. I want
to know you better. I want to see your smile
and hear your laugh and feel your hair in my
fingers.

Given my name, what I'm about to say will
terrify you, but I'll say it anyway. I want
more. I want a genuine relationship with a
real woman I can hold and kiss and maybe
someday marry. I can't marry a letter.

I've failed to persuade you, so now I'll force things to a head. If you reveal your identity, I will continue to write. If not, I won't.

I don't know where in the theater you're stationed, and I can't tell you where I am due to censorship, but Kay knows where I am. If you're nearby and willing, I want to meet you. If not, respond with your name, address, and picture. Yes, your picture.

I've never asked more of another person. I'm asking you to overlook my heritage. I'm asking you to trust me to love you no matter what you look like. I'm asking you to open yourself to the possibility of real love.

But please, darling, take this step.

No matter what you decide, I'll treasure the memory of our friendship. You prodded me to openness, strength, and freedom. I will love you for that always.

With my undying
love, Tom

Mellie choked back a sob, covered her mouth with a trembling hand, and shot a glance at Early. No, he was still asleep.

If she didn't reveal herself, she'd lose their correspondence—Tom's warmth and humor, his understanding and insight, his friendship and love.

But if she did reveal herself, it would be even worse—the slow, agonizing death of rejection. So kind and polite, he'd let her down gradually, but he would let her down.

Either way, she'd lose him forever. Either way, her heart and his would be shattered.

The greatest mercy for both of them was the quick dagger, the sudden shock, and the immediate transition to healing.

Mellie hugged Tom's letter close to her heart. She couldn't bear to inflict pain on him, but this was for the best in the long run. "Lord, give me the right words. And be with him, help him through this."

Wheels bumped along the ground, and Mellie jerked her head up. They'd landed? Early roused, then snorted and settled back to sleep.

Mellie pressed her palms to hot, wet cheeks. How could she pull herself together? She dried her face with a handkerchief and drew deep breaths that hitched on her swollen throat.

The 802nd had left Agrigento that morning for a new, unspecified field. The three teams that had flown today's evac mission to Tunisia had taken their gear with them.

Mellie gazed out the window. Craggy amber hills studded with olive trees in one direction, a smooth slope to the Mediterranean in the other. Beautiful like all of Sicily, but she wouldn't be here long.

Would leaving ease her heartache? It might. But Tom wouldn't have that luxury.

Clint Peters swung open the door to the cabin. "Hi there. How was the flight? Rise and shine, Sarge."

"Just fine." She wrangled up a smile and shook Early's shoulder.

The sergeant grunted, stretched, and groped for his belongings. He might be rising, but he wouldn't shine for at least an hour.

Clint looked out the window. "Say, I wonder if the others are here yet."

Rose and Georgie hadn't flown a mission today but had

traveled by air with the rest of the squadron. "We'll find out. Where are we?"

"*Benvenuto a casa,*" he said in an exaggerated Italian accent. "Termini Imerese."

"Termini." Appropriate. A terminus, the end of the line for her flight nursing career. Or terminal, like her relationship with Tom.

"On the north side of the triangle, about thirty miles east of Palermo and a hundred miles west of Messina." Clint charged down the aisle. "Come on. I need to find my girl."

Mellie lifted a sad, soft smile. At least Rose had a happy ending.

Roger Cooper ducked through the door to the cabin. "Funny thing, Mellie. That letter I gave you is back where it started. Gill could have waited and handed it to you or Kay in person."

Mellie's breath rushed in. "He's here?"

"Yeah." He raised one eyebrow.

Oh goodness, if she weren't careful, she'd give herself away. She forced out a laugh and headed down the aisle. "Kay will be glad to hear that."

"They're not an item, are they?" Disdain tinged his voice.

"No, the letters. It'll be easier." Her cheeks warmed from her own babbling and from the painful truth that only one more letter would be passed.

Clint helped her to the ground, and Early hopped down after her. She gazed around the airfield, not sure if she wanted to see Tom or not. One last time to look into his eyes—would it make it easier or harder?

"Clint! Clint!"

"There's my girl." He jogged to Rose, swung her in a circle, set her down, and kissed her.

"Clint," she said in half a dozen syllables. "Not in front of everyone."

"Everyone had better get used to it. I don't plan to stop." He leaned in for another kiss.

Rose ducked her head to the side and shot Mellie a sheepish look.

Mellie smiled at her and headed across the airfield, a strange surface, black like tarmac but squishy.

Georgie greeted her with a wave. "I'm glad you're back. Rose and Clint will be sharing a romantic meal of C rations."

"Mess isn't open yet?"

"They're working on it." Georgie's face looked puffy, and red rimmed her blue eyes.

Mellie's heart flipped from her own concerns to Georgie's. A year ago, she wouldn't have known what to say and would have been too shy to speak up. "Have you been crying? What's wrong? Bad news from home? From Ward?"

Georgie gave her head a little shake and walked toward rows of khaki tents like sand dunes in the desert. "Nothing like that."

Mellie fell in beside her friend. "Well, what is it?"

A sigh collapsed Georgie's chest. "I overheard Lambert talking to Guilford. The replacement nurses arrived in Oran. They'll be here in a few days."

"Oh." She glanced back to the olive drab C-47s, representing all she'd worked for the past year. Would she make any more flights?

"It's not right." Georgie's voice shook.

Mellie would only have a few more days with her friends, and then she'd return to Kentucky. Georgie and Rose would write, maybe even Kay, but it wouldn't be the same. However, a peaceful feeling told her she'd make new friends.

"I can't believe you aren't fighting this." Georgie faced her with fire in her eyes—an unusual look for her. "It isn't fair."

Word of Vera and Alice's prank and Mellie's decision had spread with no help from Mellie. "It was my choice."

"I don't understand. It doesn't make sense."

"Yes, it does. Don't you see? I'm that square peg aiming for the round hole, twisting and turning and not fitting. It's best for the squadron if I leave."

"Best for the squadron?" Georgie leaned closer and stared into Mellie's eyes. "Do you really believe that?"

A solid nod. "I know it for a fact."

43

Termini Airfield
August 7, 1943

Out on the airstrip Captain Newman spoke to Company B's three platoon leaders. Since Tom already knew the status at Termini, his gaze slipped over his CO's shoulder. In the distance, washed in peach-colored early morning light, men carried litters to C-47s.

He let out a silent groan and returned his attention to his CO. He hadn't seen Mellie at Termini and he'd probably never see her again. Yesterday, when he asked Kay Jobson whether Annie had written—she hadn't, which fed his worry—Kay told him Mellie was going home and why. Anger simmered inside him at the cruelty and injustice. He didn't quite understand Mellie's decision, but it had a noble ring to it, and he admired her all the more.

Tom puffed out a breath and nodded at Newman's words. Part of him would be glad to see his little temptation leave, but part of him wanted her to stay. What if Annie couldn't come to grips with his identity? What if she never wrestled up the courage to show her face? What if he lost his chance with the intriguing flight nurse while Annie dithered?

His stomach wadded up into a little ball. What if he was the biggest heel in the world?

"In summary," Newman said, "runway and access road are complete, so are the electrical grid and water system. Just need to shore up the dumps for supplies, ammo, and gasoline. One detachment will stay behind for maintenance, and the rest of us will head to the next airfield when it's secured."

"That could be awhile," Lieutenant Reed grumbled.

The Americans had taken Troina in the north, and the British had finally taken Catania on the east coast, but both armies had to battle around the rugged base of Mount Etna to the flatlands near Messina where good airfields could be built.

Newman shielded his eyes from the rising sun. "We'll be ready when it's time."

"Not me," Quincy said.

"Excuse me?" The CO turned back, his eyebrows lifted.

"How can I get any work done in the middle of a circus? Not only do I got two platoons to lead, but the reporters won't leave my men alone. They want the scoop on him." He jerked his chin toward Tom. "They call us the Killiver Battalion."

Tom grimaced. He'd heard that too.

"It won't last forever," Newman said. "They'll lose interest."

"How can they when the Killiver won't stay away from the field like he's supposed to?"

The tone of the morning light changed, from soft and peachy to harsh and hot. Tom wet his lips. "I have paperwork. I need the data. You don't bring it to me, so I go get it."

Quincy hitched his carbine strap higher on his shoulder. "Captain, you told him to stay away from the men, from the field."

Newman huffed out a sigh. "Gill, I did tell you that."

"But he doesn't. When he's around, the boys don't work. They fuss over him like he's a Hollywood star."

"Yeah," Reed said. "I've seen it."

Hot air pressed around him and stole his breath. Without the data, he couldn't complete the paperwork, the only reason for his presence. Quincy could snuff out his career. "I need the numbers, sir."

"Why's he even around?" Quincy flung one hand into the air. "His three months are over."

"He does a good job," Newman said in a low voice. "He's a skilled engineer."

"But he distracts the men." Quincy raised one stubby finger. "All they talk about is the killer."

Tom's hand clenched around his web pistol belt. "You should be glad, Quince."

A scoffing laugh. "What?"

"You used to call me a pansy because I didn't shoot." Tom kept his voice firm and low. "This time I shot. You should be glad."

"That's another thing." Quincy stepped up to him. "I think you snapped. Pansy to killer. You're unstable."

Tom hardened his stance. Heat pulsed through his body, seeking an outlet. "I'm not unstable. I did what any of you would've done—or should've done. I acted. I protected my men. Can I help it if I'm a better shot than you are?"

"You're unstable." Quincy bored his gaze deep into Tom's eyes and soul. "You used to smile all the time like an idiot. Now you don't."

"That's not unstable. That's normal. Everyone gets scared and angry and sad. Guess what? Me too. I'm not going to plaster on a smile all the time just to prove I'm not my dad."

"With a dad like yours . . ." Quincy turned to Reed and let out a laugh.

"Come on. Your dad ever done anything you're ashamed of? Does he have a hard time keeping a job? Maybe he smells bad or tells stupid jokes. Does he drink too much? Gamble too much? Cheat on your mom?" He stepped right in front of Quincy, a man so mean he must have learned it from someone. "Did he beat you?"

Quincy's gaze jerked away, then returned, darker than ever. "My dad ain't a murderer."

"I'm not either."

"You're just getting started. Someday you'll go berserk and shoot us all in our sleep."

"That's enough," Newman said. "Gill won't go on a rampage."

Tom sucked in a breath. No, but he'd always be his father's son.

The heat of his anger sizzled out on the cold stone slab of truth. Things would never change. People would either fear his name or be overly fascinated by it. For the rest of his life, his father's reputation would color Tom's every action.

Quincy shot Tom a snide glance, then turned to Newman. "Sir, you have to do something. He distracts the men, he attracts those lousy reporters, he gave our battalion a bad name, and he might even be dangerous."

With his anger gone, Tom felt strangely disconnected. His career could be smashed. He'd probably never find love. Yet all around him, the land shimmered in the heat of a new day, fresh with possibilities.

God made all things new. He was a new creation.

Only Annie believed it. And Tom. But he wouldn't let that stop him anymore. He'd act like a new man whether they liked it or not.

He marched up to his CO. "You told me if I gained the

men's respect, you'd give me back my platoon. They respect me now, maybe too much. I want my platoon back."

Newman retracted his chin. "Pardon?"

Quincy laughed. "You're making demands? You can't do that."

He'd made a lot of demands lately. First with Annie, now with Newman. Both would lead to disaster, but he didn't care. Tom didn't break his gaze with Newman. "Here's the situation. If you order me to stay away from the field, and Quincy doesn't give me the data, I can't do the paperwork. Then I fail. There's no reason for me to be here. You make that order, my career is dead. Quincy knows that. So give me back my platoon or get it over with and send me home."

"Send him home," Quincy said. "The man's dangerous."

"You think so, Quince?" Tom sloughed his carbine off his shoulder and dropped it to the ground. "If you're too chicken, I'll work unarmed."

"I'm no chicken, you jerk."

Newman raised one hand. "Gill—"

"If I'm unarmed, I won't be a distraction. I can't be a murderous superhero without a gun." He handed Newman his pistol.

"Gill, that's not—"

"Let me work." Tom drilled a strong look into his shocked commander. "I want to lead and I need to build."

"Send him home," Quincy said, and Reed murmured his approval.

Newman's face twisted through a dozen emotions.

Words burned holes in Tom's throat, but none would help. If he didn't get his platoon back, he'd go home one way or the other—through an immediate order or due to slow failure as Quincy's secretary. Either way, he was done here.

Tom shoved his way past Quincy and marched toward quarters.

"Gill, come back here," Newman called.

He lifted a hand to block the command and continued on his way.

"Lieutenant MacGilliver, that's a direct order."

His feet thumped on the compacted dirt. He'd never disobeyed an order before, but what did it matter? He was going home. His career was over.

44

"Hiya, ducky. You the gal training me?" A nurse approached Mellie outside the airfield tent hospital. Her broad grin revealed pronounced buckteeth.

Even though the woman would replace her, Mellie smiled. "If you're Lieutenant Gerber, I am."

The nurse stood several inches taller than Mellie, and her unruly blonde curls made her look even taller. "Call me Goosie. Everyone does."

Childhood nicknames could be so cruel. "Is your name Lucy?"

She let out a peal of laughter. "Nah, it's Mary. They call me Goosie 'cause I call everyone ducky. Me mum's British," she said in a fake accent. "Dad brought her home as his trophy from the last war. For her looks, you know."

Mellie nodded and gave her a sympathetic smile. It had to be hard to be plain if your mother was beautiful.

"Thank goodness I look like her and not my dad." Goosie wiped pretend sweat off her brow. "You think I'm ugly, you should see him. Whoa, Nellie!"

Mellie laughed. If only she could joke away her looks. If only she could stay and get to know Goosie better. "Well, I think you're fine."

"Get some eyeglasses, ducky." She strolled among the litters and wheelchairs lined up for loading. "What's this about air evac-a-tu-a-cation?" she said in a loud voice. "You mean, we go on one of them there air-e-o-planes?"

Mellie stared at her. Goosie wore the official new flight nurse uniform the women in her squadron craved—gray-blue trousers, a matching waist-length "Ike" jacket, and black Oxfords. Low-heeled Oxfords. She'd come through Bowman Field's School of Air Evacuation and probably knew more about flight nursing than Mellie did.

Goosie clapped her hands on top of her garrison cap, which made her curls spring higher on the sides. Then she dropped to her knees beside one of the litters and leaned toward the patient. "An air-e-o-plane? In the sky? I ain't never flown before. Will you help me? Will you be brave for me? Will you hold my hand?"

The soldier laughed. "Sure thing, toots."

"Oh!" She hugged his arm. "I'm indebitacated to you forever and ever. Indebitacated."

A smile of wonder crept up Mellie's face.

"You know what that means?" Goosie sprang to her feet and pressed her hands over her heart. "We're engagitated. Soon's we land, you and I are getting hitched. Yahoo!" She danced back to Mellie as her "fiancé" shouted his protest over his fellow patients' laughter.

"You've done this before," Mellie said.

"As often as I can." She hooked her arm through Mellie's. "You going to show me the ropes?"

"I think you should show me the ropes."

"Just relaxing the fellas, taking their minds off their troubles. Sorry, ducky. I didn't get your name."

"Mellie Blake."

"Mellie Blake?" A serious look darkened Goosie's pale gray eyes. "You're the one going home?"

She nodded.

"They say it's because you don't fit in." Goosie set her hands on her hips. "Well, if you don't fit in, what'll they do with me?"

Mellie gazed at a woman who'd been dealt as bad a hand as she had—but chose humor. "What'll they do with you? They'll bake you in a moderate oven with a nice orange sauce. Goose à l'orange."

She whooped with laughter. "I'd look good in orange."

Sergeant Early poked his head out of the cargo plane. "Lieutenant Blake, we're ready to load."

"Thank you." Theirs was the last plane to load.

Medics brought patients to the cargo door, and Mellie showed Goosie how she greeted each patient, checked his Emergency Medical Tag against the flight manifest, and decided where he would be placed based on his medical needs. Then the medics and Sergeant Early assisted the patient to his seat or clamped his litter in place.

After the last patient was loaded, Mellie and Goosie climbed into the plane to make sure the patients were secured and comfortable.

"Lieutenant Blake!" Captain Maxwell beckoned her from the door with a concerned look on his face. He'd been disgustingly nice to her since her decision. He got to keep his mistress and be rid of the one person who knew of their affair.

"Yes, Captain?" She joined him outside the plane, where a patient lay on a litter, his torso swaddled in white gauze.

"Do you have room for one more litter case? The other planes are full."

"Yes. Two actually." She stared at the unconscious patient. Bloody streaks painted his face, arms, and khaki pants.

"Emergency situation. Private Jenkins and a buddy were playing football in a local field, fell headlong on a land mine. His buddy didn't make it. The nearest hospital's in Cefalù, a long ambulance ride over rough roads. By air he'll be in Mateur in two hours. He needs a thoracic surgeon."

Mellie frowned. "Is he stable enough for flight?"

"Honestly, no. His left lung's collapsed, shrapnel dangerously near his inferior vena cava. We gave him whole blood, hung plasma for the flight, patched him up a bit, put in a chest tube."

"Chest tube?"

"Yes. He's a lousy candidate for air evacuation, but this is not a normal circumstance."

"We're his only hope." Mellie gazed down at the young man with his matted sandy-blond hair and solid build. If Tom were in a similar situation, she hoped someone would give him a chance. "I'm training a nurse on this flight, so we have extra hands. We can 'special' him."

"Knew I could count on you." He clapped a hand on her shoulder and gave her a cheesy smile.

Although bile rose to her throat, she managed to thank him. She never thought she'd miss the old antagonistic Maxwell.

During takeoff, Mellie talked Goosie through in-flight duties. While Mellie gave Private Jenkins the special one-on-one care he needed, Goosie would care for the others.

After the plane leveled off, Mellie went down the aisle and knelt beside Jenkins's cot. She wrapped her fingers around his cool wrist and had to shift them twice to find his pulse—rapid and thready. His respirations were shallow.

Although the patient's cot was tilted in the Trendelenburg

position, with his feet higher than his head to promote blood flow to his heart and brain, he was going into shock.

Mellie sang "Abide with Me" while she adjusted his oxygen mask and the flow of oxygen from the yellow tank.

She sang "Softly and Tenderly" as she opened two plasma cans, transferred sterile water from one bottle into the other, dissolved the life-giving flakes, and exchanged the new bottle for the almost-empty one hanging on the litter rack above.

She sang "He Leadeth Me" as she used a rubber bulb to suction the chest tube, and then administered more morphine and adrenaline.

But Private Jenkins was dying.

Both his heart rate and respiratory rate grew irregular and faint. His eyes were open and glassy. And Mateur still lay an hour away.

Mercy led to the death of her career and dreams. Mercy would lead to the death of her relationship with Tom. And mercy couldn't save the young man in front of her.

An ache grew in her chest, a gaping raw hole as if she'd fallen on the land mine herself, but no matter what, she'd choose mercy again.

She gazed around at the other patients. Goosie occupied most of them with her antics, but the man across the aisle eyed her movements carefully. The most merciful thing she could do was to keep Jenkins's condition secret.

"Here. Let's clean you up a bit." Mellie moistened a gauze pad with water from her canteen, turned Jenkins's head toward the fuselage wall so no one could see his blank expression, and cleaned his cheek and neck. His carotid pulse fluttered beneath her fingers. "I'll be right back with more fluids."

She passed Goosie and Sergeant Early. "Come with me, please, so I can hear report."

At the rear of the plane, Goosie flipped pages on her clipboard. "Everything looks—"

Mellie held up one hand. "Private Jenkins is dying," she said in a low voice.

"Oh no." Shock registered on Goosie's face, but her voice remained low too. Behind the comedienne lay a competent nurse.

Early cussed under his breath and wiped his hand over his mouth.

"I don't want the patients to know," Mellie said.

"Yeah," Early said. "Don't want that."

"I'll pretend to tend to his needs. You two keep the men distracted."

Goosie raised half a smile. "I'm good at that."

Early cast a glance down the aisle. "We'll unload him last so no one can see."

"Thank you." Mellie pulled gauze pads and a bottle of normal saline from the medical chest and filled a rubber basin with water from a spare canteen.

She returned to her patient. His arms twitched, and his respirations hopped around. The end would come soon.

Mellie sang "O Love That Wilt Not Let Me Go" and replaced the empty plasma bottle with normal saline. Then she bathed the young man, gently cleansing his arms of dried blood.

Some twenty years before, another woman had cleansed these limbs, then small and pudgy and pink. In a few days that woman would receive a telegram that would rip her heart inside out.

As she sang, Mellie prayed for that woman and the boy's father and his brothers and sisters and sweetheart and friends. With so much death around, she wanted to remember, needed to remember, that each man was precious and cherished.

The life of Private Jenkins eased out with a long breathy whisper and a relaxation of muscles and the extinguishing of light in his eyes.

Still Mellie sang. She didn't even know what she sang, but she had to continue for the other men, for those who lived. She adjusted oxygen flow and IV flow and bathed his limbs, now muscular and limp and pale. Never again would he throw a football or clap to music or hold the woman he loved in his arms.

A quiver entered Mellie's voice and she stretched her neck to clear her vocal cords.

Tom said he wanted to hold the woman he loved in his arms. Mellie had chosen to deprive him of that.

Mercy yanked her in two directions. Was it more merciful to give him the chance he wanted, even if it meant deep disappointment for him and devastating rejection for her? Or was a sudden end more merciful?

Mellie cleansed blood from the sandy blond hair framing her patient's face.

Yes, a fast death was best. She couldn't put it off any longer. Tonight she'd unsheathe her dagger and write her final letter.

Termini Airfield

Inside the pyramidal tent he shared with three other officers, Tom stuffed his belongings into his barracks bag. Sesame sat at his feet and whimpered.

He rubbed the top of the little guy's head. "Get to go home now. No more rats and air raids for you, boy." He shoved aside the concern that dogs would be banned from the troop transport. Somehow Tom would sneak him on board.

Sesame cocked his head and whimpered again. He could always see behind the smile.

Tom huffed, tired of faking it, even for a dog. "All right. It stinks. It all stinks. No matter what I do, I can't succeed. I can't be a normal leader, Annie probably won't write back, and I don't know what I'll do for a job when this war's over."

Sesame wagged his tail on the dirt floor as if pleased with Tom's honesty.

He stared at the stump. When Mellie amputated his tail, Tom had worried about Sesame's identity, but Mellie had reassured him. *"He's loved. He has a purpose. He'll be fine."* And he was.

Tom was loved too—by the Lord, by his mother, and by Sesame. He had a purpose—to build, whether as an engineer or in construction. And he would be fine.

"I will," he mumbled. "I'll be fine."

He laid the stationery box with Annie's letters on top of his belongings. He wouldn't get to meet her. Kay had his APO number so she could mail Annie's reply if it ever came. If Annie did reveal her identity, their relationship would be limited to letters for the duration of the war.

But her silence screamed.

"I'll be fine." He yanked the drawstring shut.

The tent flap opened, and Captain Newman stepped inside. "Gill, I gave you an order."

Tom's shoulders sagged, and he folded his bedroll. "Quincy said everything he needed to say. I said everything I needed to say. Why stick around?"

"So you could hear what I had to say."

Tom shook his head and rolled the bedding. "I'm going home. I know that."

Newman fiddled with something in his hand. Silent.

Out of the corner of his eye, Tom sneaked a look.

Newman had a carbine slung over his shoulder and he inspected a pistol in his hands. Tom's pistol. "How often have you fired this?"

"Five times, sir."

"No more than that?"

"No, sir. I was afraid of what I'd become. Completely unnecessary. I was also afraid of how people would react. That was well grounded."

The CO polished the barrel of the gun with his thumb. "You're a good shot."

"Excellent, sir."

"Good." He held out the gun to Tom. "I need fine marksmen with personal control."

Tom's mouth drifted open. He closed it. It opened again. "But, sir, I thought—"

"You asked for your platoon back. I'm giving it to you."

"But, sir—"

"Arguing with me?" One side of his mouth twitched up.

Tom blinked, but the sight remained—his commander returning his pistol, his platoon, and his future. "No, sir. But what about the men?"

"It'll blow over. The reporters will find new prey. Do your job, make the men work, and they'll forget all about it. Even if they don't, they'll obey."

Tom nodded, but his mind swarmed with questions. "Why are you doing this?"

"Because of what you said. I waited all year for that. I deliberately remained quiet to see what you'd do. And you did it. You stood up for yourself. You stood up to Quincy. You got angry with him when he deserved it, and no one died."

A smile tugged at Tom's lips. "Not even Quincy."

"I've wanted to strangle that man a dozen times myself. Didn't I tell you he respected vinegar? You dumped a whole vat of vinegar on his head."

He rubbed his hand over the stubble on his chin and chuckled. "I suppose I did."

"He had it coming. And watch, he'll respect you now." Newman jiggled the pistol in his hand.

Tom took it and slipped it back in its leather holster. "I'll use it wisely, sir."

"I know." He returned the carbine. "Now get out there and yell at those men when they're lazy, mope over a girl, laugh at the jokes, grumble about the chow, and *lead*."

"Yes, sir." Tom stood taller than he'd ever stood in his life, his chest and heart full. "I'll do that."

45

"Hode shti' or I shtick you," Georgie mumbled over the sewing pins clamped between her lips.

"Sorry." Mellie stood still on top of an empty crate in the four-man tent while Georgie pinned up the hem of the turquoise sundress. Georgie was determined to finish before Mellie left.

Kay lounged on her cot. "That turned out cute."

"I know," Rose said from her bed. "Wait till Tom sees you in it."

Mellie groaned. A dress, no matter how cute, would not make a difference.

"There. All done," Georgie said in her normal voice. "Here's a mirror. What do you think?"

Mellie tilted the hand mirror up and down to get a complete view. The fitted bodice and slightly gathered knee-length skirt complemented her figure, and the square neckline and wide shoulder straps provided plenty of modesty. "You do excellent work. It's beautiful."

"*You're* beautiful," Georgie said. "And that color looks great on you."

Mellie had to admit she looked nice. An image popped in her mind—Tom seeing her in the dress, admiring her with that tremendous grin, holding her, kissing her. Nothing but a fantasy, and she shook it out of her head. She'd made her decision and written her letter the night before. She only had to hand it to Kay.

"All right. Take it off so I can get to work." Georgie unbuttoned the back of the dress. "Now that we all have sundresses, we need a party to wear them to."

"What are you up to?" Suspicion lowered Rose's voice.

"Victory's coming any day, and we'll need to celebrate. Wouldn't a beach party be fun? For all the officers around here?"

"A party?" Kay rolled onto her side and propped her head in one hand. "I like that idea."

However, Mellie smelled a setup. Tom was an officer around here. She stepped carefully out of the sundress so as not to dislodge the pins.

Georgie took the dress. "We could set up a barbecue pit on the beach, have some fellows play dance music, and I had another idea."

"Uh-oh." Rose grinned. "I know that tone of voice."

"Hush, you." Georgie flapped a hand at her friend and arranged the fabric on her lap. "Did you meet that pharmacist at the 93rd Evac? Hutch, they call him. Very sweet but quiet and lonely. He misses his fiancée and isn't happy in his job. But he has a telescope and knows all the constellations and their stories. And I heard the 93rd is at San Stefano now, just up the road, so I'll finagle him over here to show us the stars during our party."

Rose rested her chin on her forearms. "Watch out, Mr. Pharmacist. Georgiana Taylor has a new project."

"A project?" Mellie buttoned her light blue uniform blouse.

"I need one." She knotted the end of the thread. "I'm done with Rose, done with you."

"I'm a project?"

"Sure." Georgie gave her a fond smile. "And now look at you. No matter where you go, I know you'll make friends. But I hope you'll stay. You have to come to the party. We'll get Tom there, and he'll see you in that dress, and you'll tell him who you are. Isn't that romantic?"

Mellie rolled her eyes and zipped up her trousers. That would be a disaster.

Kay flopped onto her back. "Speaking of Tom, you got a letter for him? It's been days, and he keeps bugging me."

"I do." Mellie's voice came out leaden. She forced herself to walk to her cot and pull out the letter. She stared at it, hating how the words would break Tom's heart. "This is the last one."

"The last one?" Rose said. "Y'all have a fight?"

"No." She fingered the envelope. "He gave me an ultimatum. If I don't reveal my identity, the relationship is over."

"Oh my goodness. Are you telling him?" Georgie said.

Mellie shook her head. She hadn't told the girls because she wanted to make the decision on her own. Now she'd printed the decision in ink. "It wouldn't be fair to him. He says he'll love me no matter what I look like, but I know he doesn't find me attractive. Can you imagine how embarrassed he'd be? He'd feel obligated to put up a pretense, but eventually he'd tell the truth and break it off, and we'd both end up heartbroken."

Georgie shoved the sundress off her lap. "But you're so cute. We'll set up a meeting, and he'll be pleased as punch."

"Remember what happened with me?" Rose said. "I thought Clint had to be deranged to like me. Maybe Tom's deranged too."

"I wish." Mellie managed a tiny smile. "No. I know how he feels, and I want to protect him. I don't want to embarrass him."

Kay snorted and got to her feet. "Oh brother. You're not protecting him. You're protecting yourself."

"Excuse me?" The letter crinkled in Mellie's grip.

"Come on, Kay," Rose said. "Didn't you hear her?"

"I heard her." She pulled out her compact and flipped it open. "She said it's less painful to reject him than to watch him reject her."

"That's not what—" Her breath caught. Yes, that was exactly what she said.

Georgie pulled the material back onto her lap. "That wasn't what she said at all. She said she wants to protect him. She loves him."

"Love?" Kay dabbed powder on her nose. "If you loved him, you'd want to please him. He wants to meet you. If you loved him, you'd give him that."

"But I—"

"Yeah. But you." Kay snapped her compact shut. "It's about you. About you not getting hurt. You're being selfish."

Rose and Georgie gasped.

"I'm not," Mellie whispered. "I do love him. But he can't love me."

"You know what? You're right." Kay strode to Mellie and snatched the letter from her hand. "You feel sorry for yourself. Of course he can't love you. Who would?"

"Kay!" Georgie said. "How could you?"

Kay marched to the tent entrance and flipped a hand over her shoulder. "If you can't pull yourself together and see yourself as we do—well, I don't want to hear it. I spent years feeling sorry for myself, but I pulled myself together. I have no patience for it in others." She flounced out of the tent.

Mellie gaped at the tent opening. Rose and Georgie voiced protests behind her, but Mellie could only hear Kay's words.

Truth rang in those words.

"Hey, ladies." A nurse peeked into the tent. "Lambert called an emergency squadron meeting. Let's go. Where's Kay off to in such a hurry?"

To deliver the letter to Tom, and Mellie's heart writhed in agony.

"We'd better get going." Georgie hooked her arm in Mellie's and dragged her outside.

Rose took Mellie's other arm. "Don't listen to a word she said. With a face like hers, she's never had a reason to feel sorry for herself."

As they walked to headquarters, Rose and Georgie comforted her, bolstered her, and supported her decision. But Mellie couldn't speak. Was her decision kind or selfish? Was she trying not to inflict pain or avoiding it?

Rose and Georgie hauled her into the stuffy headquarters tent, crowded with the nurses and technical sergeants stationed at Termini, all seated on crates.

Lieutenant Lambert stood. "Looks like everyone's here. I wanted to introduce our new nurses, Lieutenants Mary Gerber and Evelyn Kerr."

Goosie and Evelyn stood. Evelyn gave a polite nod, but Goosie waved maniacally.

Lambert smiled. "They've already made an impression and will be a welcome addition to our squadron."

Mellie held back a sigh. Yes, they would. Evelyn was sweet, and Goosie was—well, Goosie. Mellie wouldn't be missed.

"We're sending Sylvia home to recuperate fully, and another nurse will also leave—for a very happy reason."

Happy? Mellie frowned. Nothing happy about it.

But Lambert smiled at Wilma Blake Goodman. "We were

honored to attend the wedding of Wilma and Jim back at Maison Blanche, and now that marriage has been blessed. Wilma will return stateside to care for that blessing."

Wilma blushed and lowered her gaze, and the room erupted in joyful murmurs.

Mellie's mouth hung open, and her tongue dried out. What did this mean?

The chief nurse held up some papers. "I'm pleased to announce Mellie Blake will stay."

Georgie and Rose squealed and squeezed Mellie's arms.

Lambert thumbed through the papers. "I have a petition circulated by Georgie Taylor, and signed by every nurse and tech in the squadron, including those in Mateur and Palermo, asking for Mellie to be retained."

Mellie swiveled her gaze to Georgie.

Her friend wore an expression filled with warmth and triumph. "Everyone."

"Most of the signers included comments—that Mellie's hardworking, kind, knowledgeable, and never complains. Sergeant Early said she's the only nurse he'll fly with, and underneath that, a nurse wrote, 'Please keep Mellie so we don't have to fly with him.' Several women seconded that comment."

Laughter resounded through the tent. Early's face reddened, and he shot Mellie a grin.

She could only stare. Everywhere women and men smiled at her. They wanted her here?

Georgie put her arm around Mellie's shoulders. "You said it would be best for the squadron if you left. I proved you wrong."

"Everyone?" Mellie's voice hiccupped.

"Even Vera and Alice," Rose said.

Georgie enveloped her in a hug. "I'm so glad you're staying. Are you?"

Mellie nodded on Georgie's shoulder and hugged her back. "I am. I'm so happy." A year before, if someone had told her an entire squadron would sign a petition for her, she never would have believed it. Even now, she could barely comprehend.

After the meeting was dismissed, Kay walked over. She dangled Mellie's letter for Tom between her fingers. "Still think he could never like you?"

Mellie's mind reeled. She pushed herself up on quivering legs and wiggled out of Georgie and Rose's grasp. "I need to think. I need some time alone."

"We'll go with you," Georgie said.

Mellie patted her friend's shoulder. "Honey, alone means alone."

She escaped from the tent into the morning sun. A dozen air base bicycles stood outside the tent, available for anyone.

Mellie mounted one and pedaled a wobbly course through the base. When was the last time she'd ridden a bike? Probably not since grade school.

By the time she reached the access road, her course straightened. But the course of her thoughts wavered.

She'd earned the friendship of Georgie and Rose. Even Kay. If Kay didn't care, she wouldn't confront her. And the squadron liked her. So she wasn't unlovable, and she had to stop seeing herself that way.

Mellie rode through an olive grove, and the shade of the trees speckled her vision. Her decision to refuse Tom's ultimatum seemed right, but was it selfish at the core?

She loved Tom. But what was best for him? What did he need most of all?

Tom didn't think anyone could love his complete self. He already knew Annie loved him—inner self to inner self. But he didn't know that all of Mellie loved all of Tom.

Didn't he deserve to know? Didn't he deserve to know he'd earned someone's love, name and all?

Mellie wiped the sheen from her eyes and turned left onto the road into town. Somewhere there had to be a turnoff for the beach, where she could sit in the sand and pray. "Lord, what's best for him? Please help me make the right decision."

Tom's face swam in her mind. He needed to know he was capable of winning a woman's heart.

A sob burst out. But the price. To give him what he needed, she had to set her heart before him. She had to offer the look of love in her eyes while absorbing the rejection in his.

"It's too much, Lord. How can I?" The bike sped downhill past low stone walls draped with magenta bougainvillea. "It's too much."

She stopped and planted her feet. Too much what? Too much mercy?

Hadn't the Lord shown the greatest mercy of all? Hadn't he offered the world the depths of his love while absorbing the ultimate rejection in his beaten and crucified body?

Mellie buried her face in her hands. If Jesus bore the cross to show his love, couldn't she bear Tom's polite rejection to show her love? He deserved the gift, whether or not he chose to accept it.

She pedaled down the road and navigated a series of hairpin turns toward the Mediterranean. Offering Tom her love was the right thing to do. It was merciful. And it would be the most difficult and painful thing she'd ever done.

Mellie rounded the last turn and stopped short. She stared at the sight and imagined the wonder on Tom's face if he saw it.

A plan bubbled in her mind, a tiny spring, and it flowed in a little ribbon, meandering and widening and gathering strength from other streams.

She turned her bicycle around and pedaled hard, up the road, across the access road, and onto the base. Her lungs screamed for air and sweat dribbled down her sides, but she kept going.

Outside the mess tent, Kay chatted with Vera and Alice.

Mellie hopped off the bike, let it clatter to the ground, and strode up, panting hard. "Do you . . . have that . . . letter?"

Kay's green eyes widened. "Um, yeah." She pulled it from her trousers pocket.

Mellie ripped it in half. "Would you . . . please help me?"

Kay smiled. "Again?"

46

Milazzo Airfield
Sicily
August 17, 1943

"What a mess." Tom took off his helmet, ran his fingers through his hair, and plunked his helmet back on.

"Made perfect sense to me." Sergeant Ferris jutted out his chin, but the hollow look in his eyes told the truth. He'd made a whopping mistake.

Tom inspected the bomb crater on the runway they'd built only the day before. Milazzo lay at the base of a narrow spit of land that thrust north into the Tyrrhenian Sea less than twenty miles from Messina. The flat terrain made a perfect location for an airfield complex close to the Italian mainland. Today both American and British troops converged on Messina, and the Twelfth Air Force was fit to be tied that their brand-new airfield was down on a crucial day.

Larry kicked a rock into the crater. "What do you think, Gill?"

Tom shook his head and clipped Sesame's leash to his belt. The bomb severed the telephone line that ran in a culvert under the runway from the control tower to the tent complex. If the line had been left in place, they could have spliced it together and used it to pull a new line through. But Ferris had ordered his squad to pull out the old line.

Larry groaned. "We'll have to cut away the PBS, lift the square mesh track, lay new line, put it back together again. Good thing PBS is easy to mend."

"Yeah," Tom said. "But that's half a day's work." They couldn't afford to have the runway down when the men at the front needed coverage by fighter planes.

"Better get started, huh?" Larry said.

"There's got to be a better way." Tom squatted at the end of the culvert and peered through. Too narrow for a man.

Sesame nudged him. Whenever Tom got low to the ground, it meant playtime.

Light filled his head. "It's not playtime, boy. It's work time."

Tom beckoned to a Signal Corps man standing by a spool of telephone line. "Rosen, isn't it? Bring the line here. Ferris, get your men to clear the rubble from the culvert. I need a straight path."

Larry squatted next to him. "What's up?"

"Sesame." He unhooked the leash from the collar and tied telephone line in its place. "He'll fit in there."

"You think he'll go in?"

"He'll need a nudge. But he'll come to you. Go to the other end of the culvert and call him when I tell you." Tom opened a ration tin and cut Spam with his pocketknife. "Ferris, fetch some square mesh track. Enough to cover the crater so Sesame won't take the easy way out in the middle."

Head down, Ferris recruited a handful of men to roll over a seven-and-a-half-foot wide roll of square mesh track.

Tom checked the line on Sesame's collar. "Want some Spam?"

His stubby tail wagged like a metronome.

"Yeah, that's a good boy." Tom looked over to the center of the runway. Ferris's men rolled SMT over the crater. "Ready?"

"Ready."

"Okay, boy. Here's the Spam." Tom tossed a couple of cubes into the culvert.

Sesame licked his chops and ran into the tunnel. Now to keep him in and coax him through.

"Call him, Larry." Tom held his clipboard over the entrance, leaving a slit for the line to pass through. "Rosen, give him plenty of slack."

"Here, boy!" Larry called from the other side of the runway. "Here, Sesame!"

Tom beckoned to Bill Rinaldi and had him hold the clipboard. "Don't let him out."

"Here, Sesame," Larry said. "Who loves you? Larry loves you, not mean old Gill."

Tom grinned and jogged to the covered crater. No openings big enough for little dogs. He clapped Davis and Fitzgerald on the back. "Looks good. Don't let him escape."

"Here, boy!" Larry called. "I'll get you a steak, not that Spam mean old Gill gives you."

"Where are you going to get that?" Tom joined his friend.

"I'll carve it out of Ferris's behind."

Tom laughed. "I'll help. We'll have a fine barbecue."

Soon a little nut-brown face poked out of the tunnel, and Sesame scrambled into Larry's arms. The dog gave Tom a wounded look and licked Larry's face.

Tom brushed dirt off the white stripe down his dog's nose. "Yeah, Ses, you love him now. Wait till you ask for your steak, and he's in the brig for cannibalism."

"Not cannibalism. Ferris is a weasel not a human."

Tom glanced at his squad leader across the runway. He might be a weasel, but he was a humbled weasel.

Rinaldi ran over with Tom's clipboard. "Let's hear it for the lieutenant, boys! He saved us hours of work."

The men cheered, and even Ferris joined in, if halfheartedly.

The applause felt good. Instead of cheering bloodshed, they cheered a job well done. Things were shifting. Tom raised Sesame's paw. "Here's your real hero."

"Yeah," Rinaldi said. "And he's a whole lot better looking."

"I'll say." Tom walked out to the crater. "Okay, Ferris. You know what to do. Fix the culvert wall, fill in the crater, lay new SMT and PBS. Let's get this strip up and running."

"You heard the man," Ferris yelled. "Get to work, you clods."

Yep, Ferris would take out his frustrations on his squad, but the runway would open soon.

Tom gazed to the west, where toast-colored hills met blue sky and blue sea. Would any cargo planes come today? Any mail?

Each day another layer of resignation settled heavy on his heart. Over two weeks had passed since he'd sent his ultimatum. Annie didn't want to meet him or tell him her name. She wouldn't even say why. Almost a year of friendship was just fading away.

"Gill, I need to speak to you." Captain Newman stood at the side of the runway with a stern look on his face.

Tom frowned. What had he done now? Things had improved. He walked over to his CO. "Yes, sir?"

From the nose down, Newman looked fierce, but humor played around his brown eyes. "I told you I wouldn't deliver any more letters."

Tom searched his commander's face, the odd mix of humor and ferocity. His mind turned to mush. "Letters?"

Newman pulled an envelope from behind his back.

The stark white jolted Tom's heart. "A letter?"

"She addressed this to me. There's an envelope for you, but most of it's for me, instructions, requests. Does she know I outrank her?" Newman lifted one eyebrow but failed to look imposing.

"Requests?" Tom eyed the breathtaking white. What had she written? A kind excuse why she wouldn't reveal her identity? Or did she sign her name and send her picture?

"I've had it for a few days."

Tom's gaze jerked up to his commander. "A few days?" Did Newman know how he'd suffered the last few days?

"Her idea. She told me to give you the letter the day we secured Sicily. We just got a telegram. Patton entered Messina at 1000—beat the Brits to the prize. It's over. Sicily's secure."

"Great news." Tom held out his hand for the letter. His fingers twitched.

"Your little nurse pleaded for you to have a forty-eight-hour pass, arranged a plane ride for you. What could I say? You've got a pass, starting tomorrow at 0800. Use it well."

A pass? A plane ride? That could only mean one thing.

"She wants to meet me?" Tom's breath came out in little bursts. He grabbed the letter, ripped it open, and broke out in laughter. "She wants to meet me!"

August 18, 1943

Tom wiggled his nose under the blindfold. About fifteen minutes before, Clint Peters had come back to the C-47 cabin and tied a bandanna around Tom's head. Tight.

His hands slapped out a nervous beat on his thighs. Smooth khaki cotton greeted his fingers rather than the herringbone twills he'd lived in for almost a year. Deep in the recesses of his barracks bag, he'd located his khaki dress shirt and trousers, and his olive drab service coat and garrison cap. Rinaldi, a barber in the real world, gave him a good cut and shave.

In a few minutes he'd meet his Annie.

With the stupid blindfold, Tom couldn't see his destination, and he couldn't read Annie's letter for the hundredth time. She'd meet him at the plane, wearing a civilian dress, welcome him, and invite him to a party. That's how he'd know who she was.

She hadn't written what would happen next, but Tom knew. He'd take her in his arms and kiss her long and hard.

Or would he? Something hitched in his gut. What if she'd only invited him here to let him down face-to-face, the honorable way? Or what if her fears were founded, and they didn't share a mutual attraction? Was it enough to love her heart and soul?

Her letter warned him strongly. She worried that he'd built an unrealistic image in his mind and she'd disappoint him.

"She's unattractive," he said. "Not pretty. Not at all."

He contorted his mental image of her, changed dark hair and eyes to pale, padded her figure, stretched her a foot taller than him, gave her black teeth and a hunchback and warts on her nose.

He groaned. A useless exercise. He wouldn't know until he saw her.

The plane wheels bumped onto the runway, and Tom's heart thumped along in rhythm. In just a minute. Just a minute.

In the blindfold's blackness, Tom squeezed his eyes shut even harder. "Lord, if it's your will for us to be together, let us see each other with your eyes. If it isn't your will, show us now."

The plane shuddered still. The engines whined, then sputtered to a stop.

Tom ran his sweaty hands up and down his thighs. Clint gave him strict orders not to move until told. Annie went through a lot of work, and Tom wanted to follow her plan. His insides warmed. She planned this out of love for him.

And out of caution.

The door to the navigator's room opened. "You ready?" Clint asked.

"Absolutely. When can I take this thing off?"

"When I tell you. Come on, let's go. I've got your bag."

"Thanks." Tom had packed his half-shelter and bedroll, a change of clothes, his toiletry kit, and his swim trunks, at Annie's intriguing request.

Clint guided Tom down the aisle and opened the cargo door. Fresh hot air replaced the stuffy heat of the plane, and sunshine lit Tom's eyelids.

Clint laughed. "Wow. Wait till you see."

"Can I take this thing off yet?" Tom strained against the blindness. The woman he loved stood below him, and his pulse galloped out of control. "I want to see her."

"Just you wait." He chuckled and untied the bandanna.

Tom stretched his eyes open and blinked away the blur. A riot of colors lay below him like a garden. He blinked again. A garden of women?

About two dozen ladies stood by the cargo door, each wearing a civilian dress. Reds and pinks and yellows and whites and blues and greens.

Why were there so many women? Which was Annie?

Tom scanned the smiling faces. Some he recognized but most he didn't. "Annie?"

His gaze landed on Mellie Blake.

Everything spun within him, as his two conflicting desires collided one last time and merged into one bright hope. Could Mellie be Annie?

At that moment, Mellie was the only woman there. Her dark eyes rounded, and she held one hand over her heart as if pledging allegiance. She wore a dress as blue as the Mediterranean.

Tom searched her face, her expression, willed to see under that hand and straight to her heart. Hope rose from his chest and curved up his mouth. "Oh, please," he whispered.

Mellie's eyebrows sprang high.

What if she wasn't Annie? What if the real Annie watched his connection with Mellie, her heart breaking?

Tom jerked his gaze away, spread his hands wide, and smiled at the crowd. "Is anyone going to explain?"

Clint motioned outside with his thumb. "Out of my plane, Gill."

Tom hopped to the ground, into the bewildering garden.

Kay Jobson sauntered over in a green dress. "Welcome to Termini. We're having a party tonight. You'll come, won't you?"

The welcome. The invitation. That was his clue, and his face sagged. Kay Jobson was definitely attractive, but definitely not what he wanted in a woman. How could she be Annie?

But what if she was? What if a sweet soul resided under the brass? Should she be punished for her reputation? He wrestled up a smile. "Nice to meet you, Annie."

She laughed. "Honey, last thing I need is another man."

Another nurse stepped forward, a tall woman in a pink-flowered Hawaiian dress. She had frizzy blonde hair and buckteeth in a big grin. "Hiya, ducky. Welcome to Termini. Coming to the party, right?"

Tom smiled with genuine warmth. Her loud dress and greeting didn't mesh with what he knew of Annie, but her looks did. "It's an honor to meet you, Annie."

She guffawed and then fluffed her hair. "I got the curls, ducky, but Little Orphan Annie's got red hair. What do you think? Should I go red?"

Tom stared at her in confusion. What on earth was going on?

Rose Danilovich stepped forward. "I'm glad you're here. You're cordially invited to a beach party tonight."

Tom's gaze darted up to Clint. Rose was Clint's girl. She couldn't be Annie.

"Welcome to Termini." A curly-haired brunette grasped his arm. "I'm so excited you came."

A bombshell of a blonde patted his shoulder. "Hey, you're kind of cute. Want to be my date tonight?"

"Welcome to Termini."

"Please come to the party."

"You don't want to miss it. We have a band and everything."

Tom turned around slowly, buffeted by welcomes and invitations. One thing was certain. Annie had a sense of humor, and somewhere in this crowd she was enjoying herself. He broke out in laughter. "All right, Annie. Which one are you? Come on. Joke's over."

Mellie's presence drew him, turned him to her. She was the only one who hadn't welcomed him. Hadn't invited him. But she was too beautiful to be Annie.

She stood apart from the crowd, wide-eyed, chewing those lush lips of hers. The same expression she wore when Quincy asked if Tom wanted to dance with her. Part fear, part . . . longing.

Hope ballooned inside, and understanding flooded his mind. He tried to step closer to her, but the other women stood in his way, chatting and welcoming and inviting.

Tom fixed his gaze on her, full of his own fear and longing. "Is it you?"

Her head moved. Was it a nod? A shake of the head?

Her chin dipped, and she pointed to her heart.

Something on her dress glinted in the sun. A pin set with stones of blue and turquoise and gold and green, as exotic and unusual and beautiful as the woman he loved.

"My Annie." His voice came out thick and husky. "My Mellie."

She sucked in a loud breath, and her chest heaved as if she were going to cry. Just like a woman. His woman.

Tom whooped for joy, silencing the crowd. "It's you. Thank God, it's you!"

She stepped back, her eyes bigger than ever.

"Excuse me, ladies." Tom grinned at the women around him. "Let me through. I've got some hugging and kissing to do."

"Not yet, buster." The frizzy-haired blonde blocked his way. "We've got our orders. She gets a head start."

"A head start?" Tom peeked around the blonde.

Mellie mounted a bicycle and pedaled away.

"What? Mellie! Where are you going?" Tom called. "You can't get away from me that easily."

"She'll let you catch her," Rose said. "But she needs a head start. Trust her on this."

Okay, he'd let her have her way. Tom lifted his head. "Listen to me, Annie-Mellie Blake," he shouted. "Get your head start. But I'll catch you, and when I do, I'll kiss the breath out of you. I love you. You hear me? I love you."

47

Mellie heard him, all right. Now she had to coordinate her heart and mind with her ears.

She pedaled hard down the road that led behind the airfield's tent complex, her breath choppy. He wasn't disappointed. He was thrilled. Oh goodness, he was thrilled.

"He loves me," she whispered. "He loves *me*."

Everything went according to plan until the last minute. He looked so cute when Clint led him blindfolded to the door, his big hands groping at the air. Then his adorable confusion when he saw the women. Instead of being enticed by the beauties, he'd met Mellie's gaze and locked on to her. In fact, his reactions to Kay and Goosie and the others proved looks didn't matter to him. She loved him even more.

But when she showed him the brooch, her plan disintegrated.

She expected a strained, polite smile. She planned to lead him away to the private spot she'd chosen to talk things through over a picnic lunch.

She hadn't expected his joyful reaction, his proclamation of love as if . . .

As if she were the one he wanted all along.

"Oh goodness." Her chin quivered. She tightened her jaw muscles and pulled in a deep breath to keep from crying.

Mellie passed the last tent and set off through the olive grove on the new road Tom's battalion had built.

Bicycle chains clinked behind her. "Hey there, young lady," Tom shouted. "I need an explanation."

Looking back, Mellie ventured a mysterious smile. "Do you?"

He stood on the pedals to get more speed, and that marvelous grin lit his face. "You had me convinced you weren't pretty."

"I . . ." She faced front so she wouldn't crash into an olive tree. Kay was right. Self-pity was less attractive than a monkey mouth.

"You're beautiful. Beautiful. You're like . . . I don't know. Give me the name of an exotic flower."

"An exotic flower?" She frowned. What was he talking about? "Like an orchid?"

"Yeah." His grin widened. "You're like an orchid. The other girls are everyday flowers like daisies and roses, but you're an orchid. My orchid."

Papa called her his orchid too. Mellie's vision blinked in and out in the dappled light through the grove, and her thoughts joined the rhythm. He thought she was beautiful? But he'd rejected her, over and over.

"All this time it was you." His voice grew nearer. "I wasn't a heel after all."

"A heel?"

"Yeah. I loved Annie, but I couldn't get Mellie out of my mind. I thought I was falling for two women at once. About drove me crazy."

"You did? You were?" She turned onto the road into town and glanced at him. He gave her an exaggerated pout. She'd never even considered that. Why, that must have been difficult for him. "Oh, you poor thing."

He cut the corner, fell in beside her, and shot her a wink. "You can make it up to me with a kiss."

A laugh bubbled out, but she shook her head, both to deny him and in amazement. "I don't understand. You were falling for me? But you . . . I'm confused."

"Finally, your turn to be confused."

She drew a deep breath and navigated a slight curve in the road bordered by low whitewashed walls. How could she get things clarified without sounding pitiful? "All right. If you were falling for me, why didn't you want to dance with me?"

"Simple. I loved Annie. I knew if I held Mellie in my arms, I'd fall harder for her . . . you. I didn't want to jeopardize what I had with Annie."

So honor restrained him? Not repulsion? She turned to him, but the soft intensity in his eyes threw her. The bike wobbled. She gripped the handlebars tighter. Maybe having this conversation on the road wasn't a wise idea.

"I was right," he said. "Dancing with you was dangerous. I almost kissed you."

"You did?" She cut her gaze to him, then back to the road. So she hadn't imagined the romance of that moment. "But you—"

"I was in trouble. I avoided you, but everywhere I went— bam! There you were. Each time, I grew more and more attracted to you. But I loved Annie. All this time, the same woman. Now I see. Now it makes perfect sense."

Over the hill before her, waves crashed to the shore, and in her mind, thoughts crashed into each other. He really had avoided her, but for the opposite reason she imagined. Never before had she been so glad to be wrong. "Oh, Tom. I can't believe this. It's all so . . . wonderful." But no word could convey her full wonder.

"Wouldn't this be easier if we stopped?"

She shook her head, got hair in her eyes, and brushed it back. The bike zigzagged, and she gripped the handlebars. "You'll understand when we get there."

He gave her a mischievous grin. "What's to stop me from veering in front of you and making you stop so I can kiss you?"

The reality of his love seeped further inside and tugged up a smile. "What if one of us got injured and spent the rest of your leave in the hospital? That should stop you."

He grumbled and eased to the left around a hairpin turn. "Bossy woman."

"You already knew that."

"And I love you for it."

His voice rumbled through her, but a sharp turn to the right kept her from observing his expression.

"How long have you known?" he asked in a quieter voice. "When did you figure out I was Ernest?"

"The day we met." She took advantage of a straight leg of road to send him a soft smile. "When you told me you were an engineer in the 908th and wanted to build bridges, I suspected. Your personality fed my suspicions. Then your friend mentioned Sesame and I knew."

He fell silent as they made another tight turn. Too silent. His brows drew together, and his lips tucked in.

Had she said something wrong? "Tom?"

"When you told me you loved me, you already knew who I was. You knew my name."

Understanding and relief washed through her, followed by a wave of compassion. She guided her bike around the last turn. "Yes, darling. I've loved you—all of you—for months."

He raised his eyes to hers. In them, she saw a reflection of the devastated little boy she'd prayed for, but only a reflection, overpowered by the light of the man he now was. And the strength of him stole her breath.

Tom braked and planted his feet on the ground, his gaze intense. "We're stopping now."

Mellie laughed and pointed to a quaint medieval bridge. "But darling, we're here. Look."

The bridge won Tom's attention. His eyes brightened, his lips parted, and he pedaled forward.

An abandoned stone bridge stood to the side of the road, not connected to it. Rather the road went on a hundred feet farther and intersected a larger road with a boring modern vehicular bridge. A dry creek bed ran under both structures, old and new.

Tom drew even with Mellie, gave her a quick smile, and rode to the far side of the medieval bridge. Ahead of them lay the town of Termini Imerese with Monte San Calogero rising beyond.

"Wow. Look." Tom swung off his bike and walked it down the incline to the streambed. "A pointed arch bridge."

"I knew you'd like it." The top of the bridge formed a sharp angle, but a rounded arch carved out the hollow space. Mellie maneuvered her bike down the slope also.

Tom pulled off his garrison cap and service jacket and dropped both on top of his bike. With his gaze on the structure, he reached one hand to Mellie as if they always held hands.

Overwhelmed by the moment, she hesitated, then set her hand in his, and his rough, callused fingers closed over hers and connected them.

He walked forward. "Interesting what they did with the approaches." He pointed to two ramps that paralleled the streambed and made the bridge look like a giant stone armchair.

Tom's gaze darted around, and Mellie's heart warmed as she visualized the numbers and equations zipping through his mind. She could watch him forever.

He led her under the bridge, a cool space that smelled of vegetation and old stone, and he ran his hand up along the arch. "Nice."

"Very handsome." Mellie took in every angle of his face, relieved at the shift in attention and glad to savor his presence.

Tom led her behind the bridge into a narrow triangle of shade. Then he wheeled to her, grabbed her around the waist, and pressed her back against the bridge, grinning. "Thought you could distract me?"

She laughed in surprise, but her laugh caught on the way out. He was so near, his mouth only inches from hers. She tried to give him a playful look. "I succeeded."

"Not for long." He twirled his fingers into her hair. "I've resisted you long enough."

Unsure what to do with her hands, she wrapped them around his waist.

He drew her closer, his blue eyes liquid and warm. "I can't believe this is happening."

"Neither can I," she whispered, overcome by the love in his eyes. Did her love shine as brightly?

"We'll adjust." His voice grew husky. He trailed his fingers across her cheek, then over her mouth, tracing the upper lip, exploring the lower, playing with them like clay, accepting her, loving her.

Even a kiss couldn't feel as good as his touch, could it? Her eyes fluttered shut, but she forced them open so she wouldn't miss a moment.

"I love you, Tom." Her breath brushed over his fingers.

"I love you too." He slid his hand behind her head, leaving her lips lonely, aching for more of him.

He bent his head closer, but paused, his eyes blurring into one before her. One last question, one last doubt hovered in the slim space between them.

"Forever." She lifted her mouth to erase his doubts.

His lips caressed hers and melted into hers. She pressed him closer and slid her hands up his firm back. A soft moan escaped, but was it his or hers?

Love surrounded her, a palace built of letters and prayers, and glittering with their hopes and dreams. Music billowed in her head, and she knew she'd sing her nightingale's song for him, only for him, for the rest of her life.

His kiss meandered over her cheek to her ear. "Oh, Mellie. My Mellie."

She wanted to smile, but her lips felt tingly and thick. She pressed a kiss to the side of his neck above his collar. "I'm adjusting."

"Not me. I need a lot more of those kisses." He leaned his forehead against hers, and his content sigh warmed her.

Mellie stroked his cheek, memorizing the feel of him. As a child she'd studied this face in black-and-white, feeling for the little boy. For the last few months, she'd studied this face in living color, getting to know the man. Now she had the privilege to study this face in the flesh, loving the man.

"I can't believe—" Her voice caught. "I'm so glad I cut out that newspaper clipping all those years ago."

"And I'm glad I fetched your letter from the trash." A smile twitched in one corner of his mouth. "Did you ever imagine . . . ?"

"That we'd fall in love? Never. Did you?"

"Nope. But God did."

Mellie brushed her hand over his smooth hair. "I'm glad the Lord has a better imagination than we do."

Tom didn't speak or smile. He kissed her again, and that kiss said more than a hundred letters or a thousand smiles.

48

Tom burrowed his toes into the sand, which still retained the heat of the day. He tried to focus on the men's conversation. Hard to do when he only wanted Mellie back at his side.

"Let me get this straight, Hutch." Roger Cooper crossed his arms, then raised one hand to stroke his chin. "You've got a bachelor's degree, same as Gill and Clint here, more than me and more than these ladies, and the Army made you an enlisted man?"

"Yes, sir." Technical Sergeant John Hutchinson stood a few inches taller than Tom, with brown hair and eyes. "The Army only cares about ratings, and the position of pharmacist is rated as enlisted."

"Drop the *sir*," Clint said with a smile just visible under the darkening sky. "This is a party, and we won't report you."

"Not fair how the Army works," Tom said, but his gaze roamed over Hutch's shoulder. How long did it take ladies to change? Why did Mellie have to change at all? It was plenty warm and would be all evening. He sure wouldn't mind if she stayed in her swimsuit.

The afternoon had been perfect—a picnic under their bridge, a bike ride back to the base, and a stroll to the beach, filling in the blank spots in their history together, frolicking in the surf, holding her close, kissing her soundly, her bare wet arms around his neck.

On the other hand, maybe it was best that she changed.

"Do you think the Pharmacy Corps will be the solution?" Clint asked.

Tom zoomed his attention back to the conversation and put on a serious face.

"It's too soon to tell," Hutch said. "Roosevelt signed the legislation only a month ago, and things move slowly in the Army."

"Ain't that the truth?" Coop said.

Hutch dug his hands into the pockets of his rolled-up trousers. "Most pharmacists I know joined other services so they could get a commission. They fly planes, lead platoons, command ships. But I want to practice pharmacy."

Tom nodded. He'd serve as a private as long as he could build.

Hutch raised his chin. "We hope the Corps will change things, allow us to practice our profession as officers, same as physicians, dentists, vets, and nurses."

Speaking of nurses, feminine laughter rolled toward them, and three skirted silhouettes approached. Tom easily made out Mellie's curvy silhouette.

"It's about time," Clint said in a loud voice. "What'd you gals do? Sew whole new outfits from scratch?"

"Yes, Clint. That's exactly what we did." Rose rolled her eyes. "You men slip trousers over wet trunks, throw on your shirts, don't even do up the buttons, and you're done. We ladies take care with our appearances."

Tom laughed with the others but held his arm out for Mellie, and she slipped underneath where she belonged. He pressed a kiss to her head, her hair still damp and curly and smelling of saltwater.

"I missed you," she whispered. Her arm circled his waist, and she raised that special smile, even more beautiful than before, relaxed and lit by love.

"I missed you too." He didn't care about the audience. He lowered a kiss to her lips.

"To-om," she protested.

He winked at her and caressed her shoulder. "You didn't complain earlier."

"Oh brother," Georgie said, but with a happy gleam in her eye. "Come on, Hutch. I want to introduce you around."

Hutch gave them half a smile. "I haven't known her long, but I do know when the lady gives an order, you follow."

"You catch on quickly." Georgie led him away. "Besides, those two couples will get mushier and mushier."

"You'd be the same way," Rose called. "If Ward were here."

Mellie stiffened in Tom's embrace, and Georgie shot Rose a strange look over her shoulder. What was that all about?

"Rose," Mellie said once Georgie and Hutch had advanced down the beach. "Don't give her a hard time. She's fine."

"She's playing with fire. He's engaged, and she might as well be."

Clint jiggled Rose's shoulder. "Nothing to fear. He's enlisted. She's an officer. They couldn't date even if they wanted to."

"Yeah." Rose still looked suspicious.

"Don't worry," Mellie said. "She loves Ward, and she's the most faithful soul I know."

"What about me?" Tom ducked his chin to get her attention. "I resisted you because I loved you. How's that for faithful?"

She gave him a cute little smile with a wrinkle of her nose, an expression he wanted to see often. "You almost lost me in the process. How's that for ironic?"

The thought made him shudder although the temperature hadn't fallen below ninety. He drew her even closer to his side and fingered her damp curls. "I couldn't . . . I can't . . ." He coughed to rid his voice of the huskiness.

"Hey, they started the music," Clint said. "Come on, Rose. Let's go cut a sandy rug."

Tom didn't take his eyes off of Mellie. "Want to pretend to dance?"

"So we can hug and kiss in a socially acceptable manner?"

He clapped his hand over his heart. "Shocked. I'm shocked, I tell you. The thought never crossed my mind."

"Really? It crossed mine."

His chuckle stayed low in his throat. He led her to the area on the beach where the band played "Moonlight Serenade," but past the crowd of dancing couples, close to the water, and he pulled her into his arms.

She laid her head on his shoulder. "I wish you didn't have to go back to Milazzo. I wish we could be together."

"Me too." He rested his cheek on her head. Who knew where the war would send them next? They might be stationed close together again, but they could be sent to different continents. He rubbed her back, the blue cotton of her dress soft under his hands. "No matter what, we'll be together forever."

She raised her head, and forever shone in her eyes.

He swallowed hard. She wanted a future together as much as he did, but it was too early. "I warn you. I don't know what I'm doing here."

"Neither do I."

"That's why I'm not proposing right now."

Mellie's mouth fell open.

He squeezed his eyes shut. "That came out wrong. What I mean is we're both new to this. We're both new to genuine friendship, not to mention love. If it weren't for that, I'd propose right now."

"You would?" Her voice came out soft.

He nodded and gave her a little kiss. "I also want to make sure you know what you're getting into. You'd be saddled with my name for the rest of your life. You need to think about that."

"I already have. I love your name. It's who you are, and I love *you*."

Tom's throat thickened and cut off speech. He whirled her around to the music and gazed up to the sky, where the first stars peeked out. Someone loved him for who he was, and not just anyone—the right one.

Mellie nestled her head under his chin and sang to the music, a love song for him. Lord willing, he would savor that voice for the rest of his life.

When the song ended, he cupped her face in his hand and kissed her, long and deep and sweet, and he felt her weight against him as if her knees had given way.

"Oh, Tom," she murmured. "You're undoing me."

He gave her his best attempt at a roguish grin. "So you'll remember me after I leave."

"Oh, I will." She pulled up straighter in his arms and took his face in her hands. "Just so you know, I agree with you about waiting, but my answer is yes."

"Someday. Then we'll travel and build bridges and raise little MacGillivers and you'll sing us all to sleep every night."

Her eyes glistened, and he lowered a kiss to the orchid petals of her lips. Their future soared between them, a bridge strung together with letters, suspended by prayers, bolted by love, and paved with their shared hopes and dreams.

He smiled, and the fullness of her smile grew under his. "A fine future indeed."

Dear Reader,

Thank you for joining Tom and Mellie on this journey. If the locations in the story are unfamiliar, or you just love maps, please visit my website at www.sarahsundin.com for more detailed maps of the Algerian/Tunisian area and of Sicily with the story locations indicated.

The idea for the Wings of the Nightingale series came while researching my second novel, *A Memory Between Us*, in which the heroine becomes a flight nurse. The more I learned about the five hundred young women who pioneered medical air evacuation, the more I wanted to tell their stories. The 802nd Medical Air Evacuation Transport Squadron was one of the two original units, and on March 12, 1943, the 802nd flew the first official flight staffed by nurses.

Although all characters in this novel in the 802nd are fictional with the exception of the commanding officer, Capt. Frederick Guilford, the challenges they faced and the joys they shared are real.

Tom's unit is based as closely as possible on the actual 809th Engineer Aviation Battalion. However, the highly mobile nature of this story and my desire to place Tom and Mellie together at certain times created a plot nightmare. To save myself hours of therapy, I created the fictional 908th Engineer Aviation Battalion. The airfields and battles are real; however, the details for the incidents at Kairouan and Ponte Olivo are fictional.

Acknowledgments

Sometimes writing a novel is supreme bliss, and sometimes it's a sweaty smack-down match. I couldn't do it alone.

Above all, thanks go to the Lord God, who showed me the greatest mercy of all and teaches me daily how to live out that mercy.

On my personal home front, my husband Dave, and my children Stephen, Anna, and Matthew humble me, put up with writer weirdness, and encourage me. I love you all!

In my desperate search for a rare, out-of-print book, I had the joy and honor of talking to Dorothy White Errair, president of the World War II Flight Nurse Association and an actual World War II flight nurse. I babbled something along the lines of, "You're my hero!" Her daughter, Melinda Errair Bruckman, is dedicated to collecting and preserving these amazing women's stories. Please visit their beautiful website at www.legendsofflightnurses.org. If you have information about any of the flight nurses, they'd love to hear from you.

The Stanford Auxiliary Library had that rare, out-of-print book, and the staff went above and beyond their duties to accommodate me. Thank you.

James Burfoot, whose grandfather, Frank Stocker, served in the 809th Engineer Aviation Battalion, sent me copies of his grandfather's official documents, written narrative, photographs, and precious letters written to his young daughter. What a treasure. While story needs led me to create the fictional 908th, the details and color from these documents aided me immeasurably.

Thank you also to Warren Hower of Hower Research Associates, whose professional expertise and a whole lot of sleuthing located rare documents in the National Archives.

Thank you, thank you, thank you to my talented critique partners, Judy Gann, Bonnie Leon, Marci Seither, Ann Shorey, and Marcy Weydemuller. These lovely ladies offer great insight on writing and the friendship and prayer that sustain me.

As for prayer, I'm abundantly blessed by my vibrant church and small group. I'm convinced you guys account for 98 percent of my sales. Dave is appreciative, and you know what I mean.

Deepest thanks go to my agent, Rachel Kent of Books & Such Literary Agency, who pushed me to keep improving this book and encouraged me greatly. And I have to thank my editor, Vicki Crumpton. Not only does she keep buying my work, but she helps me improve and makes the editing process a joy. As for the team at Revell, I can only say, "Wow." Their talent, support, and hard work are unsurpassed in the industry. Plus, they're just a whole lot of fun.

And I'm so thankful for you, dear reader! Please visit my website at www.sarahsundin.com to leave a message, sign up for my quarterly newsletter, read about the history behind the story, and find tips on starting a book club. I pray you will keep growing as a new creation in Christ.

Discussion Questions

1. A long history of rejection causes people to protect themselves in various ways. Compare how Mellie, Tom, Larry, Goosie—and even Kay—protect themselves.

2. Our society can be harsh on women who don't meet its standards of physical beauty. How do you see this in Mellie's life? In the world around you? Do you find yourself subconsciously judging others on their looks?

3. Tom's story was inspired by a news article about a man facing execution who had a small son. What challenges did Tom face because of his father's notoriety? What challenges do you see for children of infamous—or even famous—people?

4. What do you think of how Tom's mother raised him? How would you have handled a similar situation?

5. Five hundred women served as flight nurses during World War II, and seventeen were killed in action. Considering

the role of women at the time, flight nurses were pioneers in many ways. What ways do you see?

6. Sesame plays an important part in Tom's life. How does Sesame help him? How has a pet helped you?

7. In the field, Tom and Mellie deal with a difficult way of life—mud, bugs, living on the go, and the constant threat of attack. How do the various characters deal with these situations? How would you?

8. How were letters vital to Tom's and Mellie's individual growth and to their relationship? Have you ever had a close correspondence with a pen pal?

9. How does Mellie handle condescension from Captain Maxwell and Sergeant Early? How have things changed since the 1940s?

10. Both Tom and Mellie were raised by the opposite-gender parent. What issues does that cause in their lives? What can single parents do to overcome these challenges?

11. Mellie comes to friendship late in life. What insights into friendship did you gain from her journey?

12. What insights into leadership do you gain from Tom's example and from those around him?

13. What does Mellie learn about mercy through this story? Is there any way you need to show greater mercy to those around you?

14. Tom struggles to bridge his inner self and his outer self. Have you ever lived a less-than-genuine life? How did you find balance?

15. The next novel in the series follows Lt. Georgie Taylor and pharmacist Sgt. John "Hutch" Hutchinson, and the third novel follows Lt. Kay Jobson and C-47 pilot Lt. Roger Cooper. From what you've seen of these characters, what might you expect?

Sarah Sundin is the author of *A Distant Melody*, *A Memory Between Us*, and *Blue Skies Tomorrow*. In 2011, *A Memory Between Us* was a finalist in the Inspirational Reader's Choice Awards and Sarah received the Writer of the Year Award at the Mount Hermon Christian Writers Conference. A graduate of UC San Francisco School of Pharmacy, she works on-call as a hospital pharmacist. During WWII, her grandfather served as a pharmacist's mate (medic) in the Navy and her great-uncle flew with the US Eighth Air Force in England. Sarah lives in California with her husband and three children.

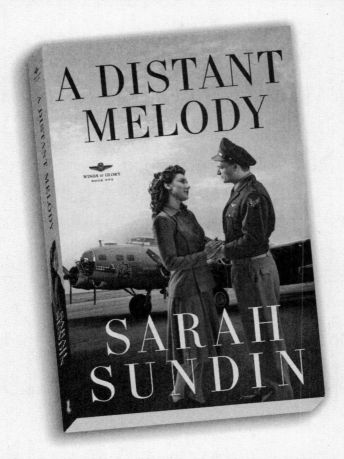

"This rich tale will delight historical romance fans."

—Suzanne Woods Fisher, author of *The Choice*

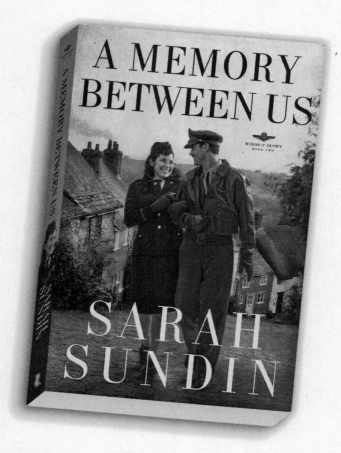

When Jack lands in the army hospital after a plane crash, he makes winning Ruth's heart a top priority mission. Can Jack break down her defenses? Or are they destined to go their separate ways?

Revell
a division of Baker Publishing Group
www.RevellBooks.com

"Sarah Sundin is a master at lyrical writing, and she has that rare talent of being able to combine humor with heart-pounding action. I couldn't stop turning the pages."

—MELANIE DOBSON, author of *Love Finds You in Liberty, Indiana* and *Refuge on Crescent Hill*

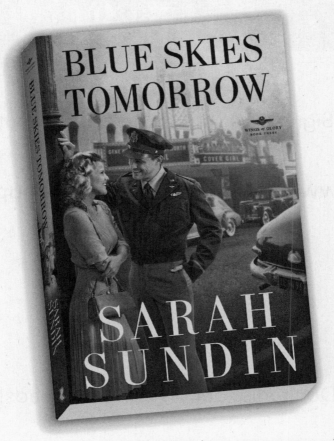

A young war widow covers her pain with the frenzy of volunteer work until the spark of her romance with a WWII pilot propels them both into peril.

 Revell

a division of Baker Publishing Group
www.RevellBooks.com